DOWNFALL OF THE CURSE

THE KYONA CHRONICLES BOOK FIVE

DEBORAH GRACE WHITE

LUMINANT PUBLICATIONS

DOWNFALL OF THE CURSE

By Deborah Grace White

For Mum and Dad.
Your gifts to me can never be quantified,
and everything good in my life is part of your legacy.
Thanks for making me who I am.

Kynton
Forest of Rune
Dragon Rea
Kerr
Montego
Pravat
GREAT RIVER
KYONA
Nerita
Argath
Alezae
MARSHLAND
NORTH L
SOUTH L
BALENOL
BASE TREE
Rebecca Evans

North Wilds
ELISA
VALORIA
DRAGONCAVE
LOCH ARINE
Arinton
Basal Headlands
Wyvern Islands
Bryford
ANDS
ANDS
Nohl
Razed's Bastion
Jeweled Peaks
Thirl
THORANIA
Logging Camp
SPICE FIELDS

CHAPTER ONE

"Lucy, you almost forgot this."

Lucy turned at the sound of her mother's voice, tearing her eyes away from the ship bobbing gently on the tranquil water.

"Almost forgot wha—oh." She felt a slight rush of panic at the sight of her mother holding out her dagger and sheath, apparently unconcerned about the multitude of witnesses.

"Mother!" Lucy hissed. "Do you have to wave that about?"

Her mother gave her an unimpressed look. "I'm not exactly slashing the air with it, am I, Luciana? How did you come to leave it behind?"

Lucy ignored the question. After only one more moment of hesitation, she snatched the dagger out of her mother's hand, stashing it in the pack slung over her shoulder. It was clear that the older woman was not going to concede the point, and giving in was the surest way to avoid drawing extra attention to the exchange.

Her mother frowned at the bag, in which the weapon was now concealed. "There's a reason it's on a belt, Lucy. You should be wearing it all the time, just in case."

"Because that will make a great first impression on all my Balenan relatives," said Lucy dryly.

Her mother's frown only increased. "Stop worrying so much about the impression you're going to make." Her voice was uncharacteristically sharp. "They can accept you or not as they choose. Don't change who you are to satisfy the insufferable idiots who populate the Balenan court."

Lucy couldn't help but raise her eyebrows at the unusual outburst from her gentle mother. Then again, if anyone knew about the personal cost of playing a part to satisfy entitled courtiers, it was the woman standing in front of her. But her mother's next words quickly gave her a new source of anxiety.

"Maybe your father is right, and this whole trip is a bad idea. It's not too late to—"

"Don't be silly!" Lucy interrupted. "I want to go! I'm not going to let them bully me, of course I'm not." She glanced at her bag, which somehow seemed to have tripled in weight since the addition of the slim, lightweight weapon. "It's just that..." She met her mother's eyes, not quite able to keep the anguish out of her voice. "Do you really want me to show up in the Balenan court carrying the weapon I used to kill my own uncle, a man who happened to be a senior member of that court?"

For a long moment her mother held her gaze, her expression serious, and far too perceptive. "No," she said at last, her voice gentle but unyielding. "I want you to show up in an unfamiliar place, on your guard for both yourself and your brother, carrying the weapon you used to defend the life of your youngest brother."

Lucy frowned slightly, her mother's words turning her mind back to their previous conversation on this topic. She wished she could see this matter the way her mother did, but she couldn't quite make herself believe it. And she had no more desire to tell her mother the full reason for her reluctance to take her weapon than she had during that earlier discussion.

"Did I just hear you saying that Lucy will be looking out for me, Mother?" The voice of the oldest of her brothers brought Lucy out of her memories. "Because that's an insult! Surely we all know I'm going along on this trip to look out for her."

Lucy rolled her eyes, a small smile playing around her lips. Matheus spoke with his usual good humor, but she knew him well enough to recognize the hint of truth in his words. His pride really was a little wounded.

Their mother smiled at her fifteen-year-old son, but there was a hint of sternness in her voice as she addressed both of them. "I hope and expect that you'll both be looking out for each other." She glanced back at Lucy. "And with that in mind, I'll be more at ease knowing that you're actually wearing the weapon I've taken great pains to train you how to use. Believe me when I tell you that Balenol is an unpredictable place."

"You're not even wearing your dagger?" Matheus demanded, looking at Lucy like she was out of her senses.

Lucy rolled her shoulders uncomfortably, glancing around to make sure none of the members of the Kyonan court who had traveled to Alezae to farewell the delegation were in earshot. The last thing she needed was for people to overhear her family talking about her weapons training like it was completely normal for a seventeen-year-old girl to be armed at all times.

"Let's not get into this now, Mother," she said quickly, ignoring her brother's words. "I'll put it on later." Her mother still looked unsatisfied, so Lucy raised an eyebrow at her. "Or did you want me to hike up my skirts and strap it on right now, in front of all these people?"

Matheus rolled his eyes, but their mother's expression twitched in amusement. "If you really do want to get on that ship, I suggest you stop talking about hiking up your skirts in public. If your father hears you saying anything like that, he'll have the trip canceled and you back home before you can say 'independence.'"

Lucy chuckled. At least there she and her mother were in complete agreement. "I hope Father can see the irony of how much he's been fussing and worrying, after giving Uncle Cal so much grief about not wanting Jocelyn to go on her big adventure to Valoria."

"I can't," her father's voice interjected unexpectedly. Lucy spun around to see him approaching, accompanied by Cody, a leader in their forest community of Raldon, and one of her parents' oldest friends. She smiled in greeting at Cody, but grimaced slightly at her father as he threw an arm around her shoulders, continuing to defend himself. "Because the situation is—"

"Totally different," finished Matheus and Lucy in unison, exchanging a long-suffering look. Their mother looked like she was trying not to laugh, and their father had clearly noticed it.

"Something you'd like to say, Scarlett?" he asked with dignity.

"Not at all," she said meekly, her eyes brimming with humor. "It's just that I can't help but notice that Cal and Elnora—" she tilted her head to the Kyonan king and queen standing nearby with their own children, "—are also farewelling a son and a daughter, and neither of them look particularly worried."

Lucy's father frowned in the direction of his oldest friend. "Well, what's Cal got to be worried about now? Jocelyn's got her husband going along with her this time. And Eamon is a different story altogether."

Lucy tried to keep her face impassive at the mention of the Kyonan crown prince, her gaze determinedly averted as her father continued to speak.

"Sending your son off isn't nearly as terrifying. Take

Matheus here," their father added, giving his son a grin. "I don't mind him going in the least. The worst he can do is get into a sword fight here and there, and where's the harm in that?" Matheus chuckled appreciatively as the older man turned back to his daughter. "But Lucy on the other hand—"

"Relax Father," Lucy interrupted. "I won't be getting into any sword fights."

"That I wouldn't mind," said her father darkly. "It's all the young fools in the Balenan court I'm worried about. The way they all fawned over your mother was nothing short of embarrassing."

"They're probably all a little old to be fawning by now," said Lucy's mother, amused.

"Maybe," said her father skeptically. "But somehow I doubt their sons will be any better."

"And you never *fawned* over Mother?" Lucy challenged, feeling that the conversation had focused on her for quite long enough.

"Of course not!" her father protested, clearly outraged at the suggestion. "Never!"

"I don't know if I'd say *never*, Jonan," said Cody reflectively, putting a brotherly arm around the shoulders of Lucy's mother, much in the manner her father still had his arm around Lucy. "I remember a few sappy looks. And you seemed mighty interested in whether she was going to marry Prince Giles."

"Nonsense," said Lucy's father, sounding put out. "Scarlett never had the smallest interest in marrying Giles."

"Sure, but you didn't know that," said Cody reasonably. "All I'm saying is you weren't totally immune to whatever mania caused them all to make fools of themselves over Scar." He looked down at the stunningly beautiful Balenan woman, a speculative light in his eye. "In fact, I seem to remember the night you found out she was secretly the rebel leader, you were falling all over yourself with awkward comments about how the dress she wore at her father's ball made her look half—"

"Yes, yes, that's quite enough reminiscing," Lucy's father interjected hastily, over the top of the protests of his two oldest children. Lucy made a mental note to drag the rest of that story out of Cody on the voyage. Good thing he was coming to Balenol with them.

"We were talking about Lucy, not Scarlett," her father continued airily. His expression became troubled as he looked at his only daughter. "Be careful who you trust, Lucy, won't you?"

"Of course I will," said Lucy, a hard edge to her voice. "I've learned the importance of being careful where I give my trust."

She didn't miss the look her parents exchanged, but she turned her gaze away, not wanting to hear their opinions. She'd heard it all before. Her eyes fell instead, inevitably, on the royal family. She hadn't realized how close they had approached, and her face burned slightly as she involuntarily met Eamon's eye.

She looked away quickly, but not quickly enough to avoid the anguish on his face. He had obviously heard her words.

"Just don't come back engaged like Jocelyn did," her father continued darkly, apparently oblivious to the proximity of the other family. "I'm sure about half the court will try to propose to you."

Lucy's eyes again darted to Eamon, against her will. If anything, he looked even more anguished than before.

"It wasn't so bad for Jocelyn to come back engaged, was it?" The cheerful voice of Kincaid, Princess Jocelyn's husband, broke in on the conversation, finally alerting Lucy's parents to the approach of the Kyonan royals.

"Of course it wasn't," said Lucy's mother with a warm smile. "And it's really a bit much for Jonan to complain about anyone coming back engaged, since thanks to him, I came back from my big adventure already married."

"She does have a point, Jo," said King Calinnae impishly, joining the conversation.

Lucy's father once again looked outraged. "That situation was—"

"Totally different," chorused Lucy and Matheus, grinning impudently.

"Well, it was," protested their father. "Your mother's father was a heartless tyrant—not to mention I'd conveniently gotten rid of him—so there was no family to get upset about it."

"I don't seem to remember Giles seeing it that way," said his wife dryly. "Not to mention Scanlon."

But this unfortunate mention of her brother cast an instant pall over the group. As much as she hated to admit it to herself, Lucy was as vividly aware of Eamon as she always had been, and it was impossible to miss his sudden discomfort as he looked at his feet.

"Are you ready Lucy, Matheus?" Jocelyn asked quickly, covering the awkward moment. "I think it's nearly time."

"More than ready!" said Matheus enthusiastically. His eyes wandered over to his two younger brothers, harassing the ship's crew with questions. "We just have to make sure Miles and Benjy haven't stowed away, and we'll be good to go."

"I suppose it is nearly time," said King Calinnae, looking worried after all. "Are you sure it's safe, Scarlett?"

Lucy's mother pulled her gaze away from her two youngest sons to smile reassuringly at the king. "At least in Balenol. I don't know anything about the current state of Thorania, so I can't speak to that."

"I wasn't talking about Thorania," said the king. "I've had extensive communication with King Abner, and I'm satisfied as to the delegation's safety while they're in Thirl." He gave the Balenan woman an apologetic look. "No offense, but it's Balenol I'm still concerned about."

"I know, and I'm not offended," said Lucy's mother. "I even brought all of Giles's letters with me in case you wanted to look back over them again. The arrangements are all in place for trade negotiations, and he guarantees the safety of the delegation while they're in Nohl."

"Hm." Uncle Cal didn't sound convinced. "I seem to remember hearing the same thing before I sent you and Jo to Balenol last time, and as I recall, Jonan was about two minutes from losing his head, and then the two of you almost got yourselves killed stopping a military coup. Are we sure we can really trust Giles's guarantee?"

"He has a point, Scar," Lucy's father muttered. His wife silenced him with a look, her eyes telling him clearly that it was not the time or place to get into his fraught relationship with her royal cousin.

"It really is different now," Lucy's mother said earnestly, her eyes passing from the king to his wife. "Giles is about to be crowned king. Last time he didn't have the power to enforce our protection. Now he does."

"We've been over this, Cal," interjected Queen Elnora patiently. "You know King Giles has made it clear he wants to restore relations between our kingdoms. We met him ourselves, when he came here. And the other princes have been three times. You know as well as I do that none of them are anything like Lord Wrendal. And don't forget just how many guards we're sending with Eamon, not to mention the Valorian guards going with Jocelyn and Kincaid." She smiled at Lucy and Matheus. "And the Kyonan guards are under instructions to consider you in their charge as well, you know. At least while you're with the delegation."

The king still didn't look entirely satisfied, but his wife laid a hand on his arm. "It will be all right, Cal," said the queen softly. "Jo and Scarlett would hardly be sending Lucy and Matheus if they weren't confident the situation was very different from how it was twenty years ago."

"Exactly," said Lucy's mother reassuringly. Her eyes wandered back to the ship, their expression suddenly wistful. "Part of me wishes I was going, to be honest. It's been a long time, and I would like to be there for Giles's coronation." She shook her head, as if flicking off the melancholy. "But things are still a little unsettled in Raldon."

Lucy's father finally let go of her shoulders to put an arm around his wife. "I know you'd like to be there, Scar. We'll go for a visit in the next year or so. Once things calm down here, and Giles is settled in as king."

She smiled up at him. "I would like that."

"But in the meantime," said Cody cheerfully, "those of us who actually want to make it in time for the coronation should probably get on the ship."

"Yes," said Lucy's mother briskly. She turned her attention to her two oldest children. "Remember, what Cody says, goes. And even though you're there on behalf of the family rather than in an official capacity, don't forget your actions reflect on your kingdom as well. While the delegation is still with you in Balenol, I want you to consider Lord and Lady Rodanthe in charge."

Lucy nodded at the mention of the most senior Kyonan courtiers on the trip. She and Matheus had met them only briefly, and knew little about them. But the king and queen must trust them, as they had assigned them to act as lead negotiators along with the royals. It was generally accepted that they were also there to keep an eye on the younger members of the group.

Lucy's mother glanced back toward the vessel. "I'd better go and retrieve Miles and Benjy. I'm assuming they've attempted to hide themselves in the hold by now."

"I'll do it," volunteered Lucy quickly. She had no desire to prolong her farewell with her parents, thus giving her mother further chance to ask uncomfortable questions about Lucy's attempt to leave her weapon behind. Plus she wanted to spend as little time as possible in such close proximity to Eamon. She said a quick goodbye to her parents, and to the king and queen.

But her father had other ideas.

"A word, Lucy," he said, following her out of earshot of the rest of the group. She looked at him inquiringly, and he glanced back toward the royals. "What your mother said about Lord and Lady Rodanthe, and what Elnora said about the guards is well and good, and I'm not disagreeing with either of them. But Cody is the one I really trust. I don't want you going anywhere without him, all right?"

"I know, Father," Lucy said, as patiently as she could. She had no desire to ditch Cody's escort, as her father surely knew.

Her father gave her a long look, then pulled her into a one-armed hug. "Come back safely," he said, the words a command. She returned the hug briefly, nodding as she turned toward the water. "And not engaged!" her father added, as she hurried in the direction of the ship.

Lucy rolled her eyes, hoping no one had overheard. It may have just been her own eagerness to be off, but it seemed as though the ship itself was bobbing impatiently in Alezae's harbor. She was hoping to make her way straight on board. But when she disclosed her errand to a crew member, he told her to wait on the quay, offering with an indulgent smile to fetch her two youngest brothers, whom he confirmed had indeed disappeared into the bowels of the royal vessel. Lucy was left hovering impatiently near the gangplank, waiting for the sailor's return.

"I can't believe the prince is going to be gone for months!"

Lucy stiffened at the simpering voice, but didn't turn around. Even without sight she had no difficulty recognizing the speaker as Sonia, one of the noble girls whom she had seen following Eamon around like a lost puppy every time she visited Kynton.

"I know. The castle will be lifeless without him. I'm desolated."

Lucy rolled her eyes. Of course wherever Sonia was, Vanessa would be also. She shouldn't be surprised that the two of them had accompanied the royal delegation to Alezae, so as not to miss a single moment of Eamon's time in Kyona. She wondered, not for the first time, how they expected their friendship to survive in the extremely unlikely event that either one of them achieved their obsessive dream of marrying Eamon and becoming Kyona's future queen.

"At least the *foreigner* is going back where she belongs." The venomous note to Sonia's words told Lucy that the girl was well aware of her proximity, and intended for her to hear every word. She kept her eyes straight ahead, refusing to give them the satisfaction of engaging with their pettiness.

"Finally," Vanessa agreed, with an angry titter. "My mother said that once she and her brother get to Balenol, they probably won't let them leave again. She said that the new king's invitation to his coronation is probably just a trick to try to lure them all over there."

Lucy frowned. She knew these girls were ridiculous, and she shouldn't take anything they said seriously. But she also couldn't help but remember her own mother's warning, that Balenol was an unpredictable place.

"Well, they're welcome to her, and her brother," scoffed Sonia. "And if they think they can lure Prince Eamon, they'll soon learn their mistake. He could fight off anybody."

Lucy barely refrained from scoffing herself. She had thought that way once, not so long ago. She had thought Eamon the picture of perfection, a noble warrior prince able to outmatch any villain.

No longer.

"No doubt she'll try to have her claws into him, batting her eyelashes like she always does. As if he'd be interested in a *Balenan*."

Lucy gritted her teeth. Her anger had nothing to do with their slight on her connection with Eamon, she told herself. Nothing at all. But she hated being called Balenan. She was Kyonan. Her father was Kyonan, and she'd lived in the kingdom her whole life.

"She won't have much chance," Sonia was saying smugly. "You remember the prince's itinerary. He's only in Balenol for the coronation, then he's going on to Thorania on *royal business*." The idiotic girl said the last two words with as much pride as if she herself had been sent on royal business, and Lucy rolled her eyes again. Lord and Lady Rodanthe would probably be doing most of the negotiating, anyway. "The foreigner won't be able to turn her wiles on him when he's in a different kingdom."

Lucy saw her brothers appear on the deck of the ship with relief. She had reached her limit with pretending not to hear. Another moment and she would have said something she might regret, like that the two girls were welcome to their fantasy prince. But it wasn't true, not really. Because no matter where she and Eamon stood, she had no desire to see either of these vapid fools as queen of Kyona.

"Why can't I go?" whined Benjy, as he was shepherded off the vessel by several crew members. They ushered him forward ruthlessly, but they all had smiles on their faces, and Lucy could understand why. Her ten-year-old brother had a way of warming people to him, and the fact that he was unaware of it was half the charm. Her mood softened at the sight of him. She couldn't really regret her violence against her uncle. Not when it had been Benjy's life in the balance. She just wished so very desperately that she hadn't been put in that position.

"You know why, Benjy," she said patiently. "Now stop trying to stow away." She extended her gaze to include Miles. "Both of you."

"But I'm almost thirteen," Miles sighed, no real conviction in the complaint. "I should be able to go if Matheus can."

Lucy didn't bother to argue with them, just made soothing promises about the gifts she would bring back from her foreign adventure as she shooed them back toward the rest of the family. Only when she had seen them safely rejoin her parents did she turn back to the ship, asking no one's permission this time before boarding. She was more than ready to be gone from Kyona for a while. If only she could so easily leave her demons behind.

CHAPTER TWO

The three week voyage felt twice as long in the confined space of the ship. She had counted on the company of her best friend as a way to avoid Eamon, but she hadn't allowed for how much time Jocelyn would spend with her new husband.

Lucy supposed she shouldn't be surprised. They had only been married a couple of months, and it was quite an undertaking for them to go on such a substantial trip so soon. But as a prince of Valoria and a princess of Kyona, the couple presented such a convenient way for both kingdoms to send representatives to attend the coronation of Balenol's new king. Eamon had been a late addition to the delegation, his parents realizing that the coronation was a convenient starting point for the prince's business in Thorania, the kingdom to Balenol's east.

Lucy had been less than thrilled when she had learned of his inclusion, but it had already been decided that she and Matheus would go, to represent their mother's family. The former Lady Scarlett Wrendal was a cousin of the new king, their mothers having been sisters. And as the Kyonan noble girls had pointed out, Eamon wouldn't be joining them in Balenol for long. Unfortunately Jocelyn and Kincaid were going on to Thorania with Eamon. It was a shame, because Lucy didn't get to see as much of her best friend as she would like, now that Jocelyn lived in Valoria's capital.

Which made it all the more annoying that Joss was too busy with her prince to make the most of the friends' time on the voyage. But unless she wanted to insert herself into their tête-à-têtes, she had little choice but to find another option. She spent most of her time with Matheus or Cody, but neither was a very satisfactory companion.

Matheus had forgiven Eamon far too readily for launching the attack against their community several months ago, supposedly while under the magical influence of their evil Balenan uncle. The oldest of her brothers had returned to his habitual hero-worship of her former sweetheart, and he was all too ready to make the most of the fact that neither Jocelyn nor Lucy was eager to seek out the Kyonan prince's company.

And Cody, although he had always been one of Lucy's favorite people, and her most trusted ally, wouldn't stop nagging her about training.

"We can't train on the ship, Cody," she sighed for what felt like the twentieth time. "There's nowhere to do it unobserved."

"But you haven't trained in weeks," he argued. "We'll be in Nohl soon, and you're out of practice. Does it really matter if anyone on this ship sees you training? Your parents aren't here, so what's the problem?"

"Matheus is still here," she reminded him dryly. "Not to mention Joss and her husband."

"Not to mention Prince In-Disgrace?" Cody retorted remorselessly. "All of those people know how deadly you are with a weapon, Luciana. There's no reason to hide from them how regularly you train. There's no reason to hide it from your parents, while we're on the topic. We both know they'd be delighted that you're actually choosing to sharpen your fighting skills beyond the sessions they forced you to do."

"Ugh, Cody," complained Lucy, loftily ignoring the jibe about Eamon. "We're not going to have this argument again. You know why I don't want to tell them about our little secret." She batted her eyelashes in mock coquettishness.

Cody just rolled his eyes. "You make it sound so sordid."

She laughed. "You know what I mean. I have my reasons. So let's not get into it."

"I'll drop it in a heartbeat if you'll train with me," said Cody pleasantly. "There's a nice big space on deck."

Lucy snorted. "Not likely."

"Come on, Luce," Cody complained. "It's been so long that I'm worried about losing my edge, too. Have you forgotten that last time I was in Balenol I was a renegade slave, at constant risk of being captured and executed? I need to be sharp, and ready for anything when we arrive."

"I don't think so, Cody," said Lucy flatly. "Guilt won't work on me. Don't even try to pretend you didn't see your years with the resistance as a grand adventure, because I've known you all my life, and I won't believe it for a moment."

The tall Kyonan man laughed. "It's true," he admitted. "Well, mostly. Let's just say that this voyage to Balenol is much nicer than my first one, but once we arrived I was only a slave for about five seconds before I made a break for it. In all honesty, the resistance was a better community than any I had growing up on the streets in Alezae. Why do you think I was the only former slave willing to brave a return to Balenol to come babysit you kids?"

Lucy opened her mouth in a furious protest, but Cody sobered before she could say a word. "But I was one of the lucky ones, Lucy. One of very few. It's not a safe place, and there's a reason your mother didn't want you to come without your weapon."

"How did you know about—hey!" Lucy realized the answer to her own question. "You're the one who ratted me out to my mother!"

"Of course I did," said Cody unrepentantly. He frowned at her. "Why would you want to leave your dagger behind, Lucy? I thought you never went anywhere without it? When did that change?"

Lucy hesitated. Truth be told, she was uncomfortable as much from the reminder that she was keeping secrets even from Cody—who had always been her closest confidante—as from the topic itself. But she was saved from replying by the approach of Jocelyn, who had apparently torn herself from her husband long enough to remember her best friend's existence.

Lucy shook her head, trying to clear the uncharitable thought. When had she become so bitter? She was happy for her friend, and she had no reason to be sour that Jocelyn was enjoying being married.

She turned to greet Joss, wishing her smile didn't feel so arti-ficial, but Cody reached out quickly to grasp her arm.

"Just tell me you're at least wearing it now," he said quietly. Lucy hesitated for a moment before giving a curt nod, and he released her arm, placated if not satisfied.

"Lucy, what will you wear for the official reception in Nohl?" Jocelyn was asking, her mind clearly far from any thoughts of weapons or training. "I'm supposed to wear ceremonial Valorian attire, but I'm concerned it will be laughably out of place in a South Lands court."

"Come and look at my dress," said Lucy, taking Jocelyn's arm and leading her friend away from the irritatingly persistent Cody. "My mother oversaw its creation herself, so depending on how much fashions have changed in the last twenty years, it's probably our best picture of what to expect." She chuckled. "My father wanted me to wear a burlap sack, of course."

Jocelyn laughed lightly, and Lucy shot her friend a sideways look. The princess was certainly more carefree these days. Lucy hadn't known about the secret her best friend had carried all her life, and she had never recognized the toll it took on Jocelyn until the burden was lifted. Lucy had never thought of the other girl as an unhappy or fearful person, but she realized that compared to the way she was now, she had been.

She felt a familiar surge of mingled guilt and resentment over her former ignorance of Jocelyn's secret. She had been struggling with the emotions for months, but she shoved them down, as she was in the habit of doing. She didn't want to have any bitterness between herself and her best friend. It just wasn't worth it.

They arrived in Nohl, the capital of Balenol, right on schedule. Lucy exchanged a wry look with Jocelyn as they stood on the deck, straining to see the welcome delegation through the thick curtain of rain that was steadily soaking them all. She knew her friend was thinking the same thing she was. It seemed they needn't have spent so much thought on their outfits for their grand arrival. Regardless of what they wore, it would all be little more than sopping rags by the time they encountered anyone important.

They were ushered off the ship with as much ceremony as the conditions allowed, Lucy hovering protectively near Matheus, whom she realized perfectly well was trying to hover protectively near her. She held back the smile that she knew would wound his young pride. They had the opportunity to take in no more than a brief impression of a stone quay stretching toward a grimy neighborhood before they were handed up into waiting carriages.

Lucy breathed a sigh of contentment the moment her face was out of the rain. It was a relief to be able to see properly. But as soon as she took in the interior of the carriage, she started, her senses once again on the alert.

She had assumed the carriage would be unoccupied, but a richly dressed woman who looked to be in her late sixties sat on one of the padded bench seats, watching Lucy's arrival with great interest. Before Lucy had figured out the most appropriate way to greet the stranger, Matheus had joined her in the carriage. No one else followed, so it seemed the young royals and the other delegates had been accommodated in one of the other conveyances. She hoped Cody had been looked after as well, and wasn't left to walk in the rain.

"You are very welcome, my dears," the woman said, and Lucy blinked in surprise at the warmth of her tone. The speaker's eyes lingered on her, and she almost looked like she was holding back tears. "You, of course, are Luciana. You look so much like your mother, as I imagine you are often told."

"Yes, ma'am," said Lucy respectfully. The woman's eyes moved to Matheus, her smile growing. "And you must be Matheus." Her eyes roamed over their faces, as if eager to take in every detail. "I'm so delighted you've both come. I was very sorry not to be able to join my sons on their visits to your family in Kyona. But Rupert," her voice hitched slightly, "was never in a position to be away from Nohl for so long."

Lucy's eyes widened slightly as she realized what the woman had probably assumed she already knew. This was their mother's Aunt Mariska, the sister of their mother's own mother, who had died when she was an infant. Lucy knew that Aunt Mariska had been more like a mother than an aunt, raising her niece as her own.

Aunt Mariska, who had married far above her common status, and had become the wife of Prince Rupert. Which meant that the king who had just died had been her husband. And that the new king, Lucy's second cousin King Giles, was this woman's son.

"It is gracious of you to receive us yourself, Your Majesty," said Lucy, trying without much success to capture in a restricted head bob the grace and respect of a full court curtsy. Carriages were not the place for royal introductions.

"Oh please, my dear," said the dowager queen quickly. "Let us not stand on ceremony. Your mother is as dear to me as my own sons, which makes you like grandchildren to me." She smiled warmly. "I would be delighted if you would call me Aunt Mariska, as she did."

Lucy and Matheus exchanged an uncertain look, and Lucy could see that her brother was having as hard a time as she was imagining referring to this stately, bejeweled royal as 'Aunt'. It was funny, because they'd been calling the Kyonan king and queen 'Uncle' and 'Aunt' all their lives, even though there was no blood relation.

Fortunately no response was required, as Queen Mariska began to ask them solicitously about their journey, and to discuss the upcoming coronation. After some minutes, Lucy managed to find a long enough break in the conversation to offer her condolences to the dowager on the recent death of her husband.

"Thank you, my dear," said the older woman after a moment. She hesitated briefly, then reached over and squeezed Lucy's hand. "Rupert was a good king, and I loved him dearly. The illness was sudden and unexpected, and I can't deny that I still miss him a great deal." She took a deep breath. "But he would have been as proud as I am to see Giles take the throne."

Lucy and Matheus said everything that was appropriate, and

the conversation mercifully moved on. Lucy quickly gave up trying to make anything out through the constant downpour. She had ascertained that they had crossed the large river that she knew ran through the city to open up into the port, so she supposed they must be nearing the castle neighborhood.

Sure enough, within minutes, they found themselves drawing up in a large courtyard. Servants appeared through the rain to usher them inside, too quickly for Lucy to get more than a glimpse of a stone castle, more forbidding and less decorative than the one in Kynton with which she was so familiar.

Thankfully they were all allowed to freshen up in their rooms before being expected to greet anyone else. Lucy was a little surprised, and even a little touched, to discover that she and Matheus were to be accommodated in lavish royal suites in the same part of the castle as the Kyonan and Valorian royal visitors. It was a far cry from what she had heard about how her father had been received on the only visit her parents had made to Nohl after their marriage. It seemed her mother had told the truth when she said things were different now Giles was actually in charge.

Still, the arrangement meant she would once again be in close proximity to Eamon, a situation that was becoming wearisome. There was only so long you could keep giving someone the cold shoulder without loss of dignity, and her repeated avoidance of him on the ship had started to feel ridiculous.

You could just forgive him.

The thought came unbidden, and Lucy mentally swatted it away, frowning as she regarded herself in the tall looking glass in her room. Eamon had betrayed her trust in more ways than one, and it wasn't something she could just shrug off. She would never forget what she had felt when she realized he had been the one to give the order for the royal guard to descend on the peaceful settlement of Raldon, with instructions to round up the children of the freedmen and brand them like slaves.

Enough. She shook the thought off. This wasn't the time to dwell on it. She needed all the poise at her command if she was going to make a good impression on the Balenan court. She wanted them to see a gracious and elegant young woman, as polished as any nobleman's daughter, not a bitter and resentful shrew, whose beautiful face hid a violent and calculating heart.

She had heard the sounds of the others gathering in the corridor, and waited for them to give up on her and head off, probably assuming she'd gone on ahead. She preferred to go alone, needing the extra time to settle her thoughts. She followed soon after, retracing the route they had taken on arrival in the castle. She wound her way down a spiral staircase, catching the occasional glimpse through a rain-soaked window. It was still pouring, and the sound of the rain against the building was pleasant. It was strange not to experience the chill that came with rain in Kyona. The air was so hot and heavy here, even in the midst of a downpour. Her parents had described the different climate, but she still hadn't been able to really understand it until she arrived. She imagined it would take some getting used to.

She was so lost in her thoughts, that it took her a moment to realize she must have taken a wrong turn. The corridor she was walking down wasn't familiar. She hesitated, turning back and forth in her indecision. Should she retrace her steps, or push on? Before she had moved, she heard voices up ahead, and turned hopefully toward them. Perhaps it was servants, who could direct her to the welcome luncheon.

"Inform my mother I will be delayed slightly. I will follow up this report before attending—"

Lucy hurried forward, frowning in confusion as the clear commanding voice was suddenly drowned out by an increase in the volume of the pounding rain. She rounded a corner up ahead in time to almost collide with a royal guard, hurrying past her with the evident purpose of carrying the message she had overheard.

As soon as her view was clear, she saw another guard standing at attention against the wall of the corridor. She also saw the reason for the additional noise from the storm. Large wooden double doors had been flung wide, evidently leading to a balcony. Lucy was a little turned around, but she thought that the balcony must look down on the royal courtyard through which they had entered the castle.

A man was standing on the balcony, apparently unconcerned by the rain soaking into his hair and saturating his costly, formal attire. Lucy paused, suddenly hesitant. If she was right in her guess of who this was, it would be a presumption to ask him for directions. The guard cleared his throat meaningfully, and she turned to see him giving her a hard look, clearly prompting her to move along.

She swiveled, ready to comply, but couldn't resist one glance back at the middle-aged man on the balcony. As she looked, something caught her eye, and she froze, frowning. Had she just imagined it, or had she seen a flicker of flame at the balcony's edge, where the elaborate railing met the stone wall? Surely that was impossible in the midst of all this rain.

But even as she thought it, she saw the fissure appear in the stone floor of the balcony. She realized with horror that the man was unaware, still leaning against the railing as he peered out at the torrent beyond.

"Look out!" she screamed, racing forward unthinkingly.

The guard sprang into action with a cry, probably intending to restrain her, just as the man on the balcony turned around, a startled look on his face. His eyes passed from Lucy to the widening crack in the stone balcony, and he lunged for the safety of the corridor without a moment's loss of time.

Lucy barely had time to register that he wasn't going to make it before the entire balcony disappeared with an ear-splitting crack.

CHAPTER THREE

She threw herself forward onto the ground with an inarticulate cry, just as the man's torso reached floor level. She had hardly been aware of her instinctive action in throwing out her arm, and she was as surprised as the man must have been when he grasped hold of it.

She yelled involuntarily in pain as her arm was wrenched by his falling weight. But she didn't lose her grip, and after a moment she could see why. He had grabbed a protruding edge of stone with one hand and her arm with the other. It was fortunate that his reflexes were so quick, because she was sure she couldn't have held his weight all on her own.

Even with the help of the stone bearing half his weight, she was struggling to hold on. Her head and shoulders were now out in the pounding rain, and the muscles in her arm screamed in protest. It was all she could do not to let his hand slip through hers, and there was no way she would have the strength to help pull him up.

Before she could panic, the guard appeared at her side with a shout. The man transferred his grip to the much stronger offered arm, and Lucy allowed herself to fall backward with relief as the guard and the near victim combined their strength to pull him back into the safety of the castle.

She leaned forward just as the man reached solid ground, peering down at the mess below. As she had guessed, the balcony stood above the royal courtyard, which she could dimly make out about three stories down. The wreckage of the collapsed structure made her draw in a sharp breath. There was nothing but rubble, and she shuddered to think what would have happened to anyone who had fallen with it. She glanced around, trying to ascertain whether anyone had been underneath it when it fell. She thought she saw a flicker of movement near the castle entrance, as though someone was hurrying inside. She squinted, frowning as she tried to see through the sheets of rain, but if someone had been there, they were gone now.

"You saved my—"

She turned to face the man who had been on the balcony, only to find him staring at her, his words cut off.

"Scarlett!" he said, sounding dazed. Lucy rubbed a wet shoulder, uncomfortable, as the man collected himself. He did so quickly, shaking his head.

"I beg your pardon, I'm afraid I was knocked around by the fall. You must be Luciana, of course. You were a small child last time I saw you, in Kyona. You look startlingly like your mother now that you are grown." He smiled, his rather severe face softening slightly. "You probably do not remember me, but I am of course your mother's cousin, Giles."

Lucy smiled awkwardly. "You are very kind, Your Majesty. I do remember your visit." It was a stretch of the truth. She only had a very hazy memory of the Balenan state visit to Kyona that had occurred when she was little. She remembered the two subsequent ones more clearly, but Prince Giles—as he then was —had not been part of those. Only his two younger brothers.

"But I am straying from the point," said the king briskly. "I must thank you for alerting me to the danger, and for offering me your hand. I would certainly have fallen without your assistance." He frowned at her arm. "I think you must have taken quite a jolt. I will have my personal physician examine you."

"It's not necessary, Your Majesty," said Lucy quickly. "I'm fine."

"We will let the physician be the judge of that," said King Giles. His tone brooked no argument, and Lucy gave up the protest.

"Thank you."

The king was looking at the gaping hole now disclosed by the gently flapping double doors, a slight frown on his face. "I cannot imagine how the entire balcony came to collapse," he mused, seeming to speak mainly to himself.

Lucy hesitated, wondering whether to mention the flame she thought she had seen. But she wasn't at all sure, and it seemed so impossible that she was reluctant to make such a fool of herself.

"Your Majesty," said the guard, who was hovering with evident alarm next to the king. "Please allow me to escort you away from the area."

"Yes," said the king briskly. "Luciana and I are both overdue at a luncheon as it is." He gave her a sharp look. "How did you come to be here, incidentally?"

Lucy swallowed. "I lost my way, to be honest, Your Majesty. I heard you speaking with your guards and was coming toward you to ask directions."

"Fortunate that you did," he said mildly. He turned to the guard. "Take a message to—no." He hesitated, his eyes resting again on the ruined balcony, their expression thoughtful. "You will accompany us to the luncheon first."

The guard nodded, his relief at not being instructed to leave his sovereign evident. They commenced a short way along the corridor before they encountered a servant. The king gave a curt command explaining the nature of the accident and instructing the servant to stand watch at the opening to ensure that no unwary wanderer fell afoul of the new hazard.

Lucy followed the king and his guard with a furrowed brow. Did the king's decision not to send his guard away mean that he suspected foul play? She thought again of the flame and frowned. Had she really seen it? What, if anything, had it been? Perhaps nothing more than firelight from one of the many torches in the corridor reflecting off the smooth wet surface of the stone.

They reached their destination quickly. Evidently King Giles felt safe once they arrived at the royal reception room, because he sent his guard off with instructions to have a squadron dispatched immediately to guard the area of the accident, and to supervise temporary repairs to board up the opening. Then he courteously ushered Lucy through the door ahead of him.

She emerged into a room that, while stately, was much smaller than she expected. She had anticipated that much of the Balenan court would be present for the welcome luncheon, but she had evidently been mistaken. Her eyes passed over the people present—the dowager queen smiling warmly at her when their gazes met—and she concluded that it was only the Balenan royal family. She recognized Prince Astor and Prince Roland from their visits to Kyona, as well as Prince Astor's family. Prince Roland also seemed to have acquired a wife and children since that time. She wasn't sure whether to be relieved at the smaller gathering, or suspicious about what it said of the feelings of the court regarding the visitors from the North Lands.

Matheus, Jocelyn, Kincaid, and Eamon were of course present, as well as Lord and Lady Rodanthe. Lucy was pleased to see that Cody had been included. He held himself with his habitual confidence, but she thought she detected wariness in his eyes as he scanned the room. For the first time, she fully comprehended the reality that he alone of their group knew what it meant to have been a slave here. How strange it must be for him to be not only back in Nohl after twenty years, but a guest at a royal reception in the castle itself. His eyes alighted on Lucy, and he gave a curt nod of reassurance, whether for himself or her she wasn't sure.

"There you are Lucy," said Jocelyn, sounding relieved as she stepped forward to meet her friend. "We wondered what had become of you! Are...are you all right?"

Lucy followed Jocelyn's eyes down her person, and she grimaced. Not only was she wet from the shoulders up, her hair once again slick and matted, but her clothes were coated in finely crumbled stone from the balcony collapse. She hadn't quite realized what a mess she was. She glanced at King Giles, and saw that he was similarly covered, although his regal bearing was undiminished.

Jocelyn's gaze also passed from Lucy to the tall man behind her, and her eyes widened slightly.

"Giles, allow me to introduce our young guests to you," said Queen Mariska, her calm voice giving no indication that she had noticed the fact that her son had arrived to the official luncheon wet through and covered in grime. She performed the necessary introductions, and everyone bowed and curtsied with appropriate respect.

"And it appears you have already met Luciana, Giles," said the dowager queen, turning to Lucy at last. "Doesn't she look like Scarlett?"

"She does," agreed King Giles, in his smooth, deep voice. "Although I believe she has her hair from her father." There was a barely discernible twitch in his face at the mention of his cousin's Kyonan husband, and Lucy stood a little taller. King or not, she hoped this man didn't think he could criticize her father in front of her.

King Giles appeared to notice her change in posture, and his lips sloped upward in the smallest of smiles. "That look of defiance is his, too, I think," he said, so quietly only Lucy could hear.

Though unexpected, the humor in his face was undeniable, and Lucy softened in spite of herself.

"Stubborn as a mule, my mother calls him," she said, her voice equally quiet, and the king let out a soft chuckle.

"Allow me to introduce you to my own family," he said, his voice back at normal volume. Lucy curtsied deeply as King Giles formally presented her to his wife, Queen Verena, and their children. His wife, who looked to be younger than the king, was elegant and gracious, if a little aloof. King Giles had not married as young as his cousin, and his oldest son and heir was only twelve.

But the crown prince and his younger sister and brother all had open, friendly faces in addition to their courteous manners. On first impression at least, Lucy thought her mother's reflections were accurate, that Balenol's future was much brighter with Giles and his line on the throne. Certainly the chances of positive relations, perhaps even an alliance, between Kyona and Balenol were better than they had ever been.

Lucy glanced at the visiting royals, the sight of Jocelyn and Kincaid making her think inevitably of the time-honored royal tradition of marriage alliances. She felt a flash of relief that Balenol's only princess was ten years old, and therefore clearly too young to be considered an alliance possibility for the eighteen-year-old Eamon, who was now Kyona's only unwed royal.

Eamon glanced up and met her eye, a questioning look in his. Lucy looked away quickly, her face flushing with embarrassment. She hadn't even realized she'd been staring at him, and she chastised herself for her thoughts. Why should she care whether there was a marriage alliance available for Eamon? His choice of a future bride was nothing to her, after all. Nothing whatsoever.

"Allow me to apologize to all our guests for my late arrival," said King Giles, in the formal tone that seemed habitual for him, "and for greeting you in such a state. The truth is I was met by an unfortunate accident only minutes ago, and Luciana came to my rescue. I do not exaggerate when I say she saved my life."

The room fell silent at once, the shock palpable. Lucy tried to tell herself that it was purely surprise and alarm that the king's life had been in danger, but she couldn't help but see the incredulity on the faces of some of the Balenan royals as they looked at her. Even Lord and Lady Rodanthe looked startled. If they found it hard to believe that she was capable of intervening in such an accident, she could only imagine what they would think if they knew the full extent of her skills. Particularly the deadly ones she'd used last time she'd saved someone's life.

The king described in curt detail the incident that had taken place, and the shock in the room turned quickly to alarm. To Lucy's embarrassment, she found herself flooded with expressions of gratitude, even the unapproachable Queen Verena thanking her earnestly. There were many outraged comments about how the advanced decay of the stonework could have gone unnoticed, and Lucy found herself frowning.

She hadn't been able to bring herself to tell King Giles about her strange observation—she certainly wasn't going to say it in front of this crowd. But the stonework hadn't looked deteriorated to her. She had witnessed the fissure appear from nowhere. But how could it have been intentionally done? How could someone set up an attack that relied on so many circumstances conveniently coming together? And fire couldn't make a stone balcony collapse, anyway. She must have imagined it.

"What is it, Lucy?"

She started in surprise at the familiar voice. She hadn't realized Cody had moved so close. He was looking at her shrewdly. Her doubts must have been more evident on her face than she had intended.

"Nothing," she said quickly, communicating with a subtle shake of the head that she didn't want to discuss it now.

Cody nodded slowly, accepting the silent command. "Thank goodness you're all right," he said, his light tone belied by the worry in his eyes. "Your parents would have killed me if you'd fallen off a balcony on your first day here."

"I'm fine," said Lucy quickly. "I wasn't in any danger." She looked up to find Eamon watching her with the same worry line between his eyes that Cody still wore. She wanted to roll her eyes. She wasn't so fragile.

With all the kerfuffle, Lucy was starving by the time she actually had the opportunity to eat the elaborate luncheon that had been prepared for them. And it was fortunate she was so hungry, or she might have struggled to do justice to the feast. The food was unfamiliar and, if she was honest, a little unpalatable. But all the guests rose to the occasion, not wanting to give offense.

The conversation ranged over many topics, and with so many people in the room, Lucy was not part of every discussion. But it seemed most of the group was listening when the dowager queen asked Lucy and Matheus about how their parents were doing.

"They're both well, thank you," said Matheus politely. "Mother especially sends her greetings. She was sorry she couldn't attend the coronation herself, but she and Father couldn't get away from Raldon at this time, not with things..." he glanced at Lucy, clearly searching for a diplomatic way to allude to the recent crisis, "...unsettled."

"No greetings from your father?" asked Prince Roland, the youngest of the king's brothers.

"Oh yes, Father sends his greetings as well, of course," said Matheus hastily.

Prince Roland nodded. "I was sad they couldn't come. I would have liked to have seen Jonan again, as well as Scarlett." He grinned. "There's never a dull moment when he's around."

"Yes, well." King Giles's voice was dry, and Lucy raised an eyebrow. "It's not that I don't want to see Jonan," he clarified. "It's been a long time, and I would be glad to meet him again. But his presence in Nohl might be more problematic than usual right now."

He cleared his throat. "Recent events in Kyona were...unfortunate, there is no denying."

Lucy barely refrained from snorting at this mild description of the devastating effects of the unsanctioned visit of her mother's brother, Lord Scanlon Wrendal.

"And I need hardly repeat that Lord Wrendal acted without the knowledge or support of the crown in his schemes against Kyona," King Giles was continuing. "But nevertheless...there was quite an uproar the previous time your father visited Nohl, not long after he had killed the former Lord Wrendal. For him to visit again now, so soon after the subsequent Lord Wrendal died, also at his hand, might create unnecessary tension between our kingdoms."

Lucy had been watching the king with a furrowed brow when he began this speech, but by the end she was looking at her feet, her cheeks flaming and her heart racing. She glanced up to see Eamon's eyes burning into her, and quickly looked down again. She could feel not only his eyes, but Matheus's, Jocelyn's, even Kincaid's, trained on her face. No one said anything, but she knew what they were all thinking. Every one of those people had been there to see what happened, and they knew perfectly well that contrary to general belief, Lucy's father had not had any hand in the death of his brother-in-law.

The conversation mercifully flowed on around her, and she took several deep calming breaths before raising her head to rejoin the discussion. Her fellow visitors were still shooting surreptitious glances at her, and although there was nothing unfriendly in their faces, she still felt tainted by the knowledge they all concealed. She shuddered to think how the Balenan court would respond if they knew what she had done. Perhaps it wouldn't even be safe for her here. She saw Cody looking between her and the others in evident confusion, but she refused to meet his eyes. He hadn't been close enough to witness the true cause of Scanlon's death.

"Did you say your town is called Raldon?" one of Prince Astor's sons, a young teenager, was asking Matheus. "I've never heard of any place with a name like that."

"Oh, um, yes." Matheus looked as awkward as Lucy felt. "Our mother named it, actually."

"How did she come up with it?" asked the boy, apparently oblivious to the discomfort of his distant cousins.

"Uh..." Matheus looked to Lucy again, but she wasn't sure what to say either, still rattled from her previous embarrassment. Cody, it appeared, had no such hesitation.

"She named it after Raldo, a person." His face was uncharacteristically hard, and he pushed on before anyone could ask for clarification. "He was one of the Kyonan nomads born and raised in the jungle here, outside Nohl." He met King Giles's eye with what Lucy thought was a reckless challenge.

"One of the resistance, I mean. He was one of our key leaders. I suppose you never even knew his name, but in fact he was one of Scar's closest friends. He was the last Kyonan to be beheaded by the crown before Jonan and Scar broke the curse, and we all sailed back across the sea. I believe if you were to look at the wall in your execution chamber, you would find his name etched there, alongside those of many other good men and women who died for our cause."

The Kyonan man paused for a moment, folding his arms across his chest. "You know, the cause of getting free from the tyrannical slavery your kingdom forced us into, for no other reason than being Kyonan."

CHAPTER FOUR

ody's prolonged speech was met by a silence so deafening that Lucy could have sworn everyone in the room could hear her swallowing convulsively. Lady Rodanthe was frowning slightly in Cody's direction, and Queen Verena shot her husband a look that contained just the tiniest hint of accusation. It made Lucy suspect there had been some debate about whether to include the untitled, unrelated former slave as part of the formalities.

Cody stood straight, his expression unyielding as his eyes passed around the group. Lucy felt torn in equal parts between pride at Cody's fearless confidence, and embarrassment that he was surely fulfilling all the less charitable predictions of the Balenan royals.

"A dark time in our history, indeed," said King Giles at last, his tone neither combative nor apologetic.

It must be a fine line this man had to walk, Lucy reflected, to avoid conflict with Kyona while still keeping his own people happy. Lucy knew that however unjust it might be, many Balenans felt cheated—even attacked—by the departure of the slaves whose unpaid labor had strengthened their economy for generations. And King Giles must be vulnerable to his courtiers' criticism on a more personal level as well, due to his close relationship to the high-ranking noblewoman who had turned out to be secretly leading the infamous slave resistance for years before her abrupt departure.

Lucy had often heard her mother comment that she didn't envy Giles any part of his role. She knew that neither her father, nor any of the former slaves, were impressed by any suggestion that either the Balenan royals, or the kingdom's population more generally, were deserving of any sympathy whatsoever. But watching the careful way King Giles chose his words, Lucy couldn't help but see her mother's point.

"I imagine I have seen this man's name on the wall of the execution chamber," the king was saying. "Although I must confess, it is not familiar to me. There are, as you say," he nodded to Cody, "many names on the wall."

"Indeed," the dowager queen interjected quickly, "we have all seen them. After Rupert became king, he initiated a program where people—commoners and nobles alike—were encouraged to visit the execution chamber, view the names on the wall, even spend time locked inside, if they chose. The idea was to help people imagine what it would be like to be in another's shoes. To encourage compassion." She looked at her eldest son with pride. "It was Giles's idea."

"Is that so, Your Majesty?" Cody's tone was thoughtful, and Lucy recognized the grudging respect hidden in his words. She was both surprised and impressed herself.

King Giles inclined his head slightly in acknowledgment of Cody's question.

"Did it work?" Lucy asked curiously. "Did it...soften people?"

The king gave a wry smile. "Its effectiveness was varied." He shook his head indulgently. "Some of the younger courtiers even went as far as to spend the night in there. It certainly seemed to have a profound impact on them."

"I was one of them," chimed in Prince Roland unexpectedly. "I was young and eager, and thought it would be an adventure." His look turned more serious. "I will certainly never forget the experience. I can't imagine what it was like to spend a night in there knowing the blade awaited you in the morning."

Cody was watching the other man with a frown, making no effort to hide his surprise. Clearly the Balenan royals were not quite what he had expected.

"Well," said Queen Verena, her tone making it clear that the conversation was closed. "We can all be thankful that neither the chamber nor the blade is in use anymore, so that we are free to turn our thoughts to more pleasant topics." She looked at her husband. "Will this accident with the balcony affect the coronation, do you think?"

"I can see no reason why it should," King Giles replied with his usual calm, neither his words nor his tone giving any acknowledgment of the abrupt change of subject. "I have already given orders to have the doorway boarded up so that no one else will be in danger of falling out." His eyes passed to Lucy, the flicker of a smile on his face. "And thanks to Luciana's intervention, I am still here to be crowned."

Lucy returned the smile awkwardly and was relieved when they were dismissed shortly afterward.

"Are you really all right, Lucy?" Jocelyn asked quietly as she walked Lucy back to her room, so that she could once again change her dress.

"Of course I am," said Lucy bracingly, seeing no need to mention the fact that her arm was still painful from nearly being torn from its socket. "*I* wasn't the one to nearly fall to my death."

Jocelyn shook her head. "It's remarkable—and very fortunate—that you happened along when you did."

"Yes," Lucy agreed. "I was lucky to be in the right place at the right time." She hesitated, debating with herself over whether she should mention the flame that she may or may not have imagined, but she decided against it. "I just hope King Giles won't make a big deal of it in front of the whole court or anything," she said anxiously. "I don't think I want that kind of attention drawn to me."

"He won't," reassured Jocelyn. "I wouldn't be surprised if he doesn't mention it to anyone else at all." Lucy looked at her friend skeptically, and Jocelyn smiled. "I know a little of how court works, remember? King Giles needs to look strong. He may seem confident, but Balenol is not like the North Lands. I think in some ways his position as monarch is more precarious than my father's, or Kincaid's father's. I don't think he would want people to know that he nearly lost his life from something as mundane as falling from a balcony in his own castle."

Lucy nodded thoughtfully, sobered by the reminder that there was so much she didn't know about how royal life worked. She had tried, at one time, to make a study of it, but there were still many things that seemed obvious to Jocelyn yet made no sense to Lucy. Perhaps she had been naive to ever think she could fulfill the role of a princess. It was probably for the best that she no longer aspired to marry Eamon, she told herself, refusing to acknowledge the sharp pain the thought seemed to send through the region of her heart.

Despite her insistence that she was fine, Lucy felt disproportionately wearied by the events of the day. Immediately after lunch, Lucy received a brief visit from the king's physician, who declared her arm in no danger of lasting harm. The rest of the afternoon was spent in a tour of the castle that felt endless, and by the time the evening meal arrived, she was exhausted.

"Does the rain ever stop?" she asked Cody wearily as the visitors made their way to the dining hall to the continued dull pounding on the outside of the stone walls.

He smiled. "Eventually. For a while. Sometimes we go months with very little rain, but at other times it can rain for days and days without stopping."

Lucy looked sideways at him, wondering if he had caught his own slip in referring to Nohl as if it was his home. "That must have been pretty miserable when you were living in the jungle," she observed.

Cody chuckled. "Not really. We weren't out in the open, mostly. But the mud was pretty awful. Still, easier to sneak around the city in a downpour. Everyone can hardly see past the end of their noses."

Their conversation was cut off as they reached their destination. Mercifully, they were once again to dine with only the Balenan royal family. From what Lucy knew of court life, she suspected it wasn't common for the royals to eat in such relative seclusion, and she could only imagine it was a courtesy for the newly arrived guests.

"I heartily approve of the fact that the official welcome gala isn't until tomorrow night," Jocelyn said to the group at large as they were ushered into the dining hall. "An informal, low pressure evening meal on the day of arrival...that's the way to welcome foreign dignitaries." She shot Kincaid an impudent look. "Valoria should take a leaf out of Balenol's book."

Kincaid grimaced in acknowledgment of some point Lucy didn't understand, but he didn't comment as he took his seat beside his wife at the long table.

It might just be an intimate family meal, but the dining hall where it was held was still elaborate and impressive. The walls were lined with tapestries, mostly depicting colorful jungle scenes. Lucy recognized the red hibiscus flower that her mother had often described to her, as well as a beautifully woven depiction of the rapids that she knew could be found not far up the river from the city.

But the real feature wasn't the tapestries. The room was long and narrow, as though it had been built especially to accommodate the enormous wooden table that extended from one end of the hall to the other. Perhaps unsurprisingly for a kingdom that chiefly traded in timber, the table itself was a beautiful piece of craftsmanship. Its surface gleamed with polish, but the many sturdy legs that held it up were left intentionally unfinished, retaining the appearance of tree trunks. Lucy could only see it once she was sitting down, but the exterior edges of the table were carved with intricate, meaningless patterns.

The whole thing was impressive, and beautiful in its way, but not exactly warm or homelike. The air was still heavy with moisture, and the room was dim, the torches along the walls doing little to dispel the gloom of the gathering night. Perhaps it was because she was sitting down to eat directly across from a tapestry vividly depicting a jaguar pouncing on a terrified monkey, but the general effect was a little intimidating.

She joined the conversation mechanically, her mind circling around the following night's gala, on the eve of the coronation. She felt apprehensive about being presented to the Balenan court, but there was also a strange stirring of excitement.

She had always thought of herself as Kyonan, and in her forest town of Raldon, no one questioned that identity. But during her many visits to the capital, Kynton, she had often come up against attitudes like those Sonia and Vanessa had obviously intended her to overhear at the port. Her mixed heritage and darker coloring would always make her a foreigner to some people, regardless of the fact that she had never set foot outside Kyona before she traveled to Valoria a few months ago for Jocelyn's wedding. And to the stuffier members of King Calinnae's court, the fact that her mother was a noblewoman by birth counted for nothing. Not only was her mother from a foreign court, she had renounced her title upon marrying Lucy's very common father, and never looked back.

The opinions of such people had never mattered much to Lucy as a child. But somehow, as she got older, she realized to her own embarrassment that she did care. She cared far too much. Perhaps it was because she wanted so much for people to see her as they saw her mother—elegant, beautiful, and educated. Or perhaps it was because she started to dream of a future life in the very heart of the court, where her success or otherwise at gaining the people's respect might very well affect the well-being of the kingdom.

Not that she had any anticipation of being Kyona's future queen now.

Of course not.

But still, it rankled that to some people, she would never be able to measure up. And although she had never liked being referred to as anything other than Kyonan, she couldn't help but wonder how it would feel to be among the Balenan court. Here, she was the daughter of a well-known noblewoman, and she looked much like the locals. Her mother might have become infamous due to her activities with the resistance, but if the royals were ready to forgive and forget, perhaps the rest of the court would be, too. And from all she had heard, her mother had been admired to the point of obsession by most of the court before the revelation of her double life.

Lucy didn't know what to expect from the court—much like the dining hall, Balenol seemed a strange mix of welcome and intimidation. They had been treated graciously on all counts, but there was an ever-present, hard-to-define tension that made Lucy wonder if danger lurked nearby. Perhaps it was an inevitable result of the unspoken history of oppression between the kingdoms. Well...unspoken until you threw Cody into the mix, Lucy thought with an internal grimace.

But in spite of all of it, she couldn't help but wonder if there was a chance she might feel at home here. Perhaps, if she could make a good enough impression, the people of Balenol might accept her in a way the people of Kyona seemed unlikely to ever fully do.

From all she knew of Balenol, she hardly knew whether to hope for that acceptance or dread it.

CHAPTER FIVE

"*There you are, Lucy! I've been looking everywhere for you. Enjoying the view from up here again? Surely you're not missing home already. You only just got here.*"

"*You've been looking for me?*" *Lucy tried not to look too delighted.* "*Is Joss trying to find me? Did she ask you to look?*"

"*Joss?*" *repeated Eamon. He joined Lucy on the ramparts, his forehead furrowing in the way she found adorable.* "*No. I think she's having a riding lesson.*"

"*Oh.*" *Lucy looked at her lap, still trying not to grin like the lovesick fool she was.* "*Why were you looking for me, then?*"

"*Because...I don't know.*" *Eamon looked awkward.* "*I wondered if you wanted to...*"

"*To what?*" *Lucy looked at him hopefully.*

"*To train with me,*" *said Eamon suddenly, sounding pleased with himself, as if he had come up with something brilliant.*

"*Ooh, yes!*" *Lucy was on her feet in a heartbeat.* "*Will you teach me that move you used yesterday, on the visiting knight?*"

"*You were watching that?*" *Was it Lucy's imagination, or were Eamon's cheeks slightly pink?*

"*Of course,*" *she said as casually as she could.* "*Jocelyn and I often watch the training." She flashed him a wicked grin. "I wanted to join in, but Jocelyn was too embarrassed."*

Eamon chuckled. "You should have. No one would have seen you coming." He smiled at her with all the superiority of a fifteen-year-old talking down to a fourteen-year-old. "Except me, of course. I could try to teach it to you, but I'm not sure your flimsy little sword could pull it off."

His grin only broadened at Lucy's gasp of outrage. "I'll make you take that back, Prince Eamon," she promised. "My sword can do anything yours can."

Eamon laughed lightly. "Talk is cheap, Luciana. Prove it!"

Lucy narrowed her eyes at him, then turned on her heel and hurried toward the steps, her feet almost flying in her eagerness to get her weapon and take him on. She heard Eamon approaching behind her and quickened her pace, grinning ahead when she heard his answering laugh.

But the next moment her breath seemed stolen from her throat when she felt his hand grasp hers as he passed her.

"Come on then," he challenged, as he pulled her along, the two of them running now through the corridors. "Time to see if you can fight as well as you talk!"

Lucy's heart thumped unevenly, and it was all she could do to keep from grinning like an idiot as they raced through the castle, disregarding the titters of servants and the scandalized disapproval of passing courtiers. Eamon had the light of adventure in his eyes, as if he was a carefree child instead of the almost-grown crown prince.

Except that he still clasped her hand in his, something he had never done before. And Lucy—her pulse racing, and her mind aflame with hopeful excitement—had never felt less like a child.

LUCY WOKE WITH A GROAN, wondering why she felt so uncomfortable. The bed was soft and warm, but her leg ached. She rolled over, and winced as she identified the culprit. How had she come to fall asleep with her dagger strapped to her leg? She frowned as she sat up, pushing her hair out of her eyes. Had she forgotten it, or had she intentionally left it on? She wasn't in the habit of wearing it while she slept, but she was still a little off balance from being in a new place.

She dressed quickly for the day, trying not to dwell on her dream about Eamon. She had woken from many similar dreams in the months since she had made it clear to him she no longer wanted a future together. She might spend her days rankling over the nightmare of Eamon's betrayal, but at night, her mind seemed determined to bombard her with bittersweet memories of the past.

She shook the thought off. She didn't have time for such things now. She wanted her mind to be focused on where she was, and on the evening's gala where she and the other visitors would be formally presented to the Balenan court.

Her brother was waiting outside their rooms, looking better rested than she felt. It took Lucy a moment to realize why the castle felt so different as she and Matheus made their way through the corridors, toward breakfast. Then, all of a sudden, it hit her—sometime during the night, the rain had finally stopped. The castle felt quiet and peaceful, as if the very walls were relieved to have respite from the downpour.

Breakfast passed uneventfully. The clearer conditions made it possible for the visitors to be shown around the city after the meal, something that had been impractical the day before. As she was led through the Balenan capital, Lucy tried to picture her mother here, walking these drab gray streets, mingling with the locals, who seemed more often than not to carry stern expressions. It was hard to imagine. The city of Nohl seemed in every way so unlike the casual forest community where Lucy had grown up.

She noted with interest that the castle courtyard, a spot she knew had been a focal point of slave punishment, was now nothing more than an empty expanse of stone. Many people hurried across it, intent on their business, and apparently they held market days there sometimes. But the whipping post where her parents had met, and the execution blade that had almost claimed her father's life, were no longer present.

Cody gave a low whistle when he observed this change.

"I guess the king was serious about trying to change people's thinking, after all." He shook his head. "The courtyard looks so strange without the blade." Cody gave a smirk. "The Overseer would turn over in his grave if he could see what the city has become."

Matheus chuckled along with Cody, apparently feeling no discomfort at the reflection on their grandfather, but Lucy remained silent. She rubbed her arm, which was still sore from the previous day's misadventure, and waited for the conversation to turn away from her mother's father. She always felt unnerved at the mention of her grandfather, and even more so since her eventful introduction to her uncle. She adored her mother, and aspired to be like her in most things, but it wasn't pleasant to think of the tainted bloodline she had come from.

Lucy tried to shake off such thoughts as she prepared for the gala that evening. She had a feeling that spurning her Balenan heritage was not the best way to endear herself to the local dignitaries.

Their tour of the city had finished before lunch, allowing plenty of time in the afternoon for the guests to get ready for the evening's event. Still, Lucy felt far from prepared as she and her brother again traveled the halls together on their way to the gala.

"What's up with you, Lucy?"

"What do you mean?" Lucy turned to her brother, the question coming out more curtly than she had intended. They were waiting outside the castle's ballroom, and Lucy's nerves were growing by the minute. Apparently they had to be announced like royalty, despite their common status.

Matheus raised his eyebrows at her tone. "You're fidgeting worse than you did the time you thought Father had found out we were the ones to steal his throwing knives."

Lucy made a shushing motion with her hand, glancing anxiously at the doors in front of them. Mercifully, they were still closed. "What is it with my family's obsession with talking about weapons at public functions?" she muttered.

"Are you talking to yourself, now?" Matheus asked incredulously.

"I'm just a little nervous," Lucy admitted. "We don't know what to expect, after all."

Matheus snorted. "They're not going to eat you, Lucy."

"We'll see," said Lucy grimly, smoothing a ruffle out of her voluminous skirts. Her dress was an elaborate creation, with layer upon layer of sheer green material.

She knew that she looked glorious in it. Lucy didn't think that she was vain—she tried not to value her appearance above its worth. But there was no point pretending she was unaware of her own beauty. It was hard to see how she possibly could be, having been complimented on it as long as she could remember.

And it would be equally foolish to pretend that she didn't want the people on the other side of that door to admire the way she looked. It was part of making a good impression, after all. But it wasn't enough by itself. She had learned that from her mother. Being admired in such a way was not the same as being respected.

Her mother was the perfect model of what it took to not only impress people, but make them warm to you. And her beauty was only one part of it—it was as much her sweet nature, her intelligence, her capability, the quiet elegance she wore unconsciously at all times and in all company. Lucy would give a great deal for people to see those same things when they looked at her.

"Luciana and Matheus of Raldon, Kyona, of the Wrendal line."

Even through the heavy door, the clear voice cut through the noise of the ballroom beyond. Lucy and Matheus had only a moment to exchange a startled look before the doors swung wide, and they found themselves confronted with a sea of curious faces, all pointed eagerly in their direction.

Lucy swallowed her nerves, raising her head proudly and reminding herself that she was representing her family and her kingdom. She refused to let herself be rattled by the unexpected introduction as a Wrendal—a name with no positive associations for her.

She swept into the room, Matheus walking beside her with all the awkwardness of a fifteen-year-old appearing for the first time at such a function. Unlike Lucy, her brothers had never been interested to attend the balls and parties that they were regularly invited to at the castle at Kynton. Lucy tried to project confidence as much for Matheus as for herself as she scanned the room.

Her first impression was the clothes. The men were dressed in somber hues, and Matheus's Kyonan garb didn't look too out of place, although its fabric was not as stiff or as heavy as the locals' clothes. But the women wore much brighter, more vibrant colors than their counterparts in Kyona. The room seemed filled with a swirling rainbow of skirts, and as Lucy had heard her mother describe, the dresses were sheer compared to those worn in the court at Kynton, most leaving the shoulders and arms bare. A glance to the side showed Matheus blinking rapidly, looking awkward, and unsure where to direct his eyes.

But Lucy was mesmerized. The dresses were beautiful, and

she suddenly wished her mother hadn't been so conservative in insisting that Lucy wear something a little more covering than the prevailing fashion in Balenol. She liked the idea of the freedom that would surely come with such a garment, and not just because of the stifling heat that still pervaded the air, even at nighttime.

From the clothes, her gaze moved to the faces. She knew a moment of anxiety, wondering if her foreign clothes would make her look ridiculous and prudish to these people. But she needn't have worried. For every face that showed thinly veiled suspicion—and there were quite a few—two others showed blatant admiration. She could see from the widened eyes of courtiers who were surely too old to be impressed by her beauty that her similarity to her mother had been noticed by more than just King Giles.

Before she could stop herself, she found her eyes doing what they had always done, at every ball she had ever attended. She could tell herself she didn't care, but it was no use. She just couldn't seem to help seeking out Eamon's lithe, golden-haired figure, looking for his reaction to her arrival.

And she wasn't disappointed. A small part of her—the part that didn't seem to have gotten the message that she didn't care —had wondered whether he would think she looked tame and unattractive next to all these local women, flaunting a scandalous amount of skin in their form-hugging dresses. But if Eamon had been gawking at the unfamiliar dresses before, it was apparently all out of his system. Because Lucy knew the moment her eyes alighted on him, as she had known at every other ball they had attended together, that he only had eyes for her.

And there was no denying that his reaction to her appearance in her gown was everything her vanity could desire. Lucy had learned from a young age to recognize the look in a man's eye when he was taken with her. She could remember, with perfect clarity, the first time Eamon had looked at her like that, when she was fifteen, and he was sixteen. It had been one of her favorite memories.

The thing was, half the men in the room were looking at her like that at this moment, and that fact was clearly not lost on Eamon, either. She turned her gaze away as his eyes swept the sea of faces, his expression now tinged with anxiety. She was here to make an impression on the Balenans, not to worry about what Eamon was thinking or feeling.

Once she had formally greeted her royal hosts, she moved toward Jocelyn and Kincaid, seeking the security of their company. She had picked Cody out of the crowd soon after her entrance. He hadn't merited a formal announcement, and she wondered if that had always been the plan, or if it was the result of his outburst during the welcome luncheon the day before.

He was looking around him as though the ballroom was a den of vipers. When his eyes rested on Lucy, they contained none of the admiration but all of the worry that Eamon's gaze had held. Lucy sent him a look that was her public equivalent of rolling her eyes, intentionally directing her steps away from him. She had a feeling that given half the chance, Cody would spend the evening glaring down any young man who tried to approach her. Which would defeat the purpose of coming on this trip *without* her father in tow.

Eamon would probably love nothing more than to do the same thing, she acknowledged to herself. But at least the reason he didn't want other men to dance with her was because he wanted to dance with her himself—something that no one could accuse Cody of wanting to do.

In any event, their suspicious expressions were enough to make Lucy avoid them both, because she had every intention of dancing and being admired, regardless of either man's opinion about it.

And in fact, she didn't even make it to Jocelyn and her husband before she was approached by an eager young local, several more following in his wake. Matheus continued past her and her new group, looking slightly disgusted at the way the men were falling all over themselves to compliment his sister.

Lucy tried not to show it, but there was undeniable tension in her shoulders as she surreptitiously watched her brother walking alone through the group of Balenan strangers. It took a supreme effort of will to suppress the instinct to rest her hand on her concealed weapon, and she didn't let herself relax until she saw Matheus join Cody.

But she knew her brother would be safe with the older Kyonan man, and she allowed her full attention to return to the men in front of her. She hoped desperately that no one had noticed her suspicion or her combative stance as she had scanned the room for threats to her brother. She pictured the way her mother held herself at such events, graceful and calm, with a smile and a kind word for everyone. Lucy tried to emulate that manner, smiling graciously and accepting the Balenans' introductions and offers of refreshments with a serene expression.

It was exhausting, but it was an act with which she was familiar. She had been playing a similar part at the court in Kynton for some time now. And the return for her efforts was satisfying. Every one of the men in front of her was clearly very impressed with what they saw. There was no denying that being admired was a welcome boost to her confidence, but as her eyes flicked involuntarily to Eamon, who looked like he was liable to shatter the wine glass in his hand as he watched the group unblinkingly, she tasted a bitter edge to her success. It was impossible not to wonder if this facade of demure elegance, made so much more convincing by her beautiful face, was what had always brought that same look of admiration to Eamon's eye.

All the more reason to be glad things were at an end between them, she told herself firmly. Her mother had been delighted to escape a formal court life here in Nohl, and Jocelyn had often chafed against the restrictions of her royal position. Perhaps Lucy had been mad to think that she would enjoy the role of princess by Eamon's side.

Before Lucy could get too caught up in these thoughts, dancing was announced, and she was mobbed by eager invitations. Her spirits lifted at the promise of activity. She had always enjoyed dancing, and she was starting to chafe at standing around. She accepted someone's hand at random, and was soon swept into motion. She was relieved to discover that her mother had been right that the dances were similar to those favored in Kyona. Still, the extra lessons her mother had given her were sure to come in useful.

Lucy's partner was not especially stimulating company, but he was a competent dancer, so Lucy was satisfied. She pasted a polite smile on her face and tuned him out, focusing on the release of swirling across the stone floor. Her eyes scanned the crowd as she moved, taking note of the location of the rest of her party. She was not surprised to see both Matheus and Cody standing out of the dancing, looking well pleased with their escape.

It seemed that the Balenan king and queen were not going to dance, both sitting in state at one end of the large room. But Lucy noted that Prince Astor, the king's brother, had taken Jocelyn's hand for the first dance. It made sense—as a princess of both Kyona and Valoria, Jocelyn held by far the highest status of any of the visiting women. And Eamon had evidently been primed on his duty before the gala, because he was dancing with Prince Astor's wife. Kincaid, who was below Eamon in status, not being a crown prince, was dancing with Prince Roland's wife. She looked much more jolly than the other Balenan princess, and the Valorian prince actually appeared to be enjoying the dance, if you could ignore the way his eyes regularly strayed to his wife.

It all reminded Lucy forcibly of the politics of who was dancing with whom at the Valorian couple's wedding, only a few months before. She had been painfully aware of Eamon's eyes watching her on that occasion. And although she had made it clear she didn't want to speak with him, it had still rankled that he hadn't even asked her to dance. Not that she had lacked partners. She hadn't sat out a single dance, and she had enjoyed herself immensely. It had all been a very welcome distraction from the distressing events at Raldon, which had been still so recent.

Lucy caught Jocelyn's eye as they passed on the dance floor, her friend's for-formal-occasions expression not lost on her. She tried not to look smug as she returned her wandering attention to her own partner. She was the only one of the group who was at least dancing with someone close to her in age. There were perks of not being titled.

Still, after three more dances with three more equally unexciting partners, Lucy had to admit that the shine was wearing off. Jocelyn and Kincaid were dancing contentedly together nearby, their duty to their royal positions apparently satisfied. Eamon seemed also to have reached the end of whatever list of dignitaries he was working through. He was at that moment in conversation with Prince Roland, the younger of the king's brothers, and he had a drink in his hand, which made Lucy more jealous than all the rest. She was parched, and wearier than she would have expected. Normally she could dance the night away at a ball, but the hot heaviness of the air here seemed to sap her energy in a way a whole night of festivities in Valoria hadn't done.

The music began to quieten, signaling the end of the dance, and Lucy's partner led her off the floor with flattering reluctance. She saw another hopeful local approaching, and she headed off his inevitable request by commenting on how thirsty she was. More than one Balenan hastened toward the refreshments, eager to supply her need, and she sank into a nearby chair. She was just wondering if she could politely decline to dance with whichever of the lingering group was surely about to ask her, when a familiar voice cut through the chatter, making her heart stand still for a fraction of a second.

"Dance with me, Luciana?"

CHAPTER SIX

For a moment Lucy just blinked up at Eamon, wondering how he had gotten across the room so quickly. His voice and expression were steady, but she could see an uncertainty in his eyes that had never been there before on the countless other occasions he had asked her to dance. He had always been sure of her answer.

Lucy's eyes narrowed slightly at the thought. He had always been so sure of everything, and look how that had turned out. She lifted her chin slightly, ready to decline his offer with the crushing politeness she had perfected in recent months.

But before she could say a word, Eamon stepped slightly closer and spoke again, his voice lowered so that only she could hear.

"Lucy, if you snub me in front of all these people, I think it will be the meanest thing you've ever done."

She blinked rapidly, her eyes captured by his frank gaze in spite of herself. She couldn't help but be disarmed, as much by his tone as by his words. The hint of anguish that had haunted his every word to her in the last few months was gone. He spoke to her not as an admirer, but as Eamon, reminding her without needing to say it that they had been friends and childhood companions long before they had entangled themselves with any thoughts of romance.

She extended her hand almost without realizing it, and he pulled her to her feet, ready to enter the throng.

"I was just going to have something to drink," she said in a last, half-hearted attempt to avoid the dance she refused to admit she wanted.

"I'll gladly get you a drink after the dance," said Eamon.

Lucy frowned at his uncompromising tone. This was the Eamon she knew, the one who was far too used to leading. There was no trace of the unexpected vulnerability that had made him seem like the boy she had grown up with rather than the commanding young man she had fallen in love with. But she would only look foolish if she tried to back out of the dance now, so she let him sweep her onto the floor.

For a moment they danced in silence, their eyes not meeting. Lucy hated herself for her own weakness, but she couldn't deny that she felt overwhelmed by the sensation of being in his arms again. They hadn't touched, not even in the smallest of ways, since that day at Raldon. And now he was holding her intimately, with hands that were just as strong as she remembered.

"Thank you," he said at last, and Lucy's eyes flew to his in surprise.

"For what?"

He gave a lopsided grin, one that had always been irresistible to Lucy. "For not humiliating me in front of all of Nohl."

She looked down again. "You were right. It would have been unnecessarily mean."

Eamon was silent for so long that she snuck a look back up at him, unable to help herself. He was looking at her with a wry expression.

"What?" she asked, unreasonably annoyed by his scrutiny.

"I'm just trying to figure out what level of meanness you consider 'necessary', according to your schedule of punishment."

She frowned, irritated by his lighthearted way of referring to the rift between them. "I hope I'm not so petty as to be 'mean' to anyone. But it wouldn't do you any harm to be turned down once in a while. It's good to be humbled, sometimes. Even for princes."

Eamon made a noise of disbelief. "If you don't think I've had any experience of being humbled lately, Lucy, then you haven't been paying attention. Believe me, I've never been so aware of my shortcomings in my life."

Lucy dropped her eyes again, confused by the way he was talking. Ever since he had started to look at her as more than a friend, Eamon had always been as focused on impressing her as she had been on impressing him. It was something entirely new for him to talk openly to her about his shortcomings.

"I'm sorry I didn't let you get a drink first," Eamon added suddenly. "You do look tired."

Lucy raised an eyebrow, trying to restrain the chuckle that wanted to escape. "Telling a lady she looks tired isn't exactly gallant."

Eamon chuckled himself. "It's not, is it?" He glanced over her shoulder, and following his gaze, she saw her gaggle of admirers watching them, looking disconsolate. "But I thought you might have had more than enough of gallantry for one evening."

"You're not wrong," Lucy admitted with a sigh. She wasn't going to say it, but it had been Eamon's appeal to their underlying friendship that had won her over, after all, not any lover-like attentions.

"In light of that," said Eamon, almost as if he could read her thoughts, "I won't tell you that you look ravishingly beautiful tonight." His voice dropped slightly, as his eyes burned into hers with a familiar intensity. "However much I might want to."

Lucy looked down to hide the smile she couldn't restrain.

"I wouldn't expect such compliments, anyway," she said, fishing for his thoughts. "Not in a room full of such...dashingly clad women."

Eamon grinned. "Scandalous, isn't it? Imagine if anyone tried to wear a dress like these Balenan ones to a ball in our castle."

Lucy was silent for a moment, a jumble of emotions cascading over her at the way he said "our castle". Her sudden confusion was dispelled, however, by the rogue thought of how delighted both Sonia and Vanessa would be to have an acceptable opportunity to show off so much of their trim figures in front of the crown prince. She snorted. "I can think of a few who would jump at the chance."

"Well, they'd miss their mark," said Eamon, with another glance around. "Exotic fashion or not, none of the women in this room can hold a candle to you in your Kyonan gown."

"I thought you weren't going to compliment me," said Lucy dryly, trying to hide just how pleased she was with this reassurance.

"So I wasn't," said Eamon quickly. "I was supposed to be apologizing for stealing you away from the refreshments." He jerked his head toward the group of young Balenans who were still watching them with disgruntled expressions. "I was just worried that I'd lose my window, like at Joss's wedding."

Lucy raised an eyebrow. "I don't know what you're talking about. You didn't even try to ask me to dance at Joss's wedding."

"That's what you think," said Eamon with feeling. "You were always so surrounded, I couldn't get close."

"Hm." Lucy knew it didn't suit her feigned disinterest to reveal how aware she'd been of Eamon's movements at that event, but she couldn't help herself when she remembered the shameless way he had flirted with Princess Lavinia, Kincaid's young sister. "You seemed well enough entertained by the partners you did manage to approach."

Eamon's incredulous laugh was the last sound she expected. She stared at him, ready to be affronted, and he looked instantly contrite.

"I'm sorry, it's just...Princess Lavinia is an absolute handful, but it seems she knows what she's doing." He shook his head. "She was as unimpressed as I was to see you dancing the night away with that Lord Henrik." Eamon scowled slightly as he named the dashing Valorian nobleman who was Kincaid's best friend. "She seemed to think flirting would make you both jealous."

"I wasn't jealous!" Lucy gasped in outrage.

"I didn't say you were," said Eamon mildly. He met her gaze with unexpected frankness. "But I was."

Lucy lowered her eyes, again feeling confused and wrong footed. It took her a moment to put her finger on why this declaration felt so different from his compliments on her appearance. But when she stole a glance up at him, and saw the uncertainty in his eyes, she realized that the vulnerability was back. He was once again admitting to weakness, to not being confident of his success. And she wasn't sure how to respond.

"Eamon..." She was glad he interrupted her, because she didn't know what she was going to say.

"I'm sure you're sick of hearing it, Lucy," he said quietly. "But I need you to know how sorry I am." She kept her eyes lowered, and he hurried on, seeming determined to make the most of the rare opportunity to talk to her alone. "I'm leaving for Thorania soon after the coronation, and I won't see you for weeks, maybe months. I don't want to leave things this way."

She remained silent, unsure of what to say. She didn't doubt the sincerity of his words, and there was a part of her—there really was—that wanted to forgive and forget. But she couldn't forget. And however genuine his apology might be, it somehow did nothing to remove the myriad emotions that swirled through her whenever she remembered his betrayal. She simply didn't know how to move past her anger over what had happened. She didn't think any number of apologies could wipe it away.

"I suppose..." Eamon hesitated, clearly disheartened by her prolonged silence. "I suppose I have no right to expect you to forgive me. Now or ever."

Lucy looked up at him at last, meeting his eyes and then immediately wishing she hadn't. The expression she saw shook her to her core. He looked lost in a way she'd never seen before. She had thought, just minutes ago, that he had always been too sure of himself. But she wasn't at all prepared for how it would feel to see him without that cloak of certainty that had always characterized him.

It made her feel uncomfortable, and strangely unanchored herself. And no more able to find words of reassurance for him. In fact, she couldn't seem to find any words at all.

"May I be so bold as to interrupt? I believe the lady was looking for refreshment?"

Lucy turned away from Eamon, blinking at the speaker, whom she didn't recognize. She hadn't even realized that the music had died away, and that she and Eamon were no longer moving.

"Thank you," she said mechanically. "I was." She reached out and took the offered glass, downing its contents convulsively. It wasn't the most ladylike of actions, but she was more rattled than she cared to admit by the interaction with Eamon.

Speaking of the prince, he was watching the newcomer with narrowed eyes, his face a mask of barely concealed frustration at the interruption to the first real conversation he and Lucy had shared in months. Lucy had the impression that with the slightest encouragement from her, he would have thrown diplomacy to the winds and refused to allow the other man to cut in.

But she didn't give any such encouragement. She had a feeling that the further this conversation continued, the more its direction would spiral out of her control. What she needed was space to think it all through, and she doubted Eamon would be capable of understanding that right now.

So when the other man offered her his arm, she didn't hesitate to take it.

"Thank you for the dance, Your Highness," she said quickly to Eamon, adding his title for the benefit of their unknown audience. She tried not to, but she couldn't help looking back at the prince as the other man led her away. It was as much the fact that he had somehow been left holding her empty glass like a serving boy as the bereft expression on his face that made her wince.

"I won't ask you to dance." The unexpected words brought her attention quickly back to her new escort. "You've been besieged since the moment you entered the room, and—if you'll forgive me for saying so—you look weary."

"Oh," said Lucy blankly. "Yes."

"I imagine you would prefer to take a turn in the cooler air." The man spoke casually as he led her toward double doors, that she could see opened onto a balcony. He was clearly confident that he had read her accurately. He had, in fact, but Lucy had a vague sense that it was presumptuous of him to be so sure of her. Still, after the unnerving lack of self-assurance in the usually confident Eamon, there was something strangely relieving about the cool authority with which this man compelled her to follow him.

She gave a quick glance around the room, noting that Cody

was watching her progress intently, and allowed herself to relax. There was no harm in letting this man lead her wherever he liked in such a public setting.

In moments they were out of the stuffy ballroom, and Lucy found herself drawing a deep, shuddering breath. She hadn't realized just how overwhelmed she had been in the packed space until she stepped out of it. She took in her new surroundings with interest. The balcony was long but shallow, and a number of other partygoers were clumped along the railing at intervals, taking advantage of the soft night breeze.

"It's not much to look at in the dark," said her companion, his voice betraying no extraordinary interest, "but I believe this balcony looks toward the city wall. You can usually see the jungle from here, or so I am told."

Lucy followed his gaze out into the blackness, but as he said, there was no view now. She shot a sideways look at the man, surprised by his apparent unfamiliarity with the place. From his dress and his air of authority, she had assumed he was someone important within the Balenan court. He was older than her, by more than a decade at her best guess, but he was quite handsome, his coloring similar to hers, and his features regular and well formed.

He looked over and caught her looking, his eyebrows lifting slightly as an attractive smile played around his lips.

"I've been remiss, haven't I?" he said pleasantly. "I haven't introduced myself. I'm a visitor here, like you, a guest of Their Majesties for tomorrow's coronation. My name is Rasad."

"A visitor to Nohl?" Lucy asked, her brow furrowing. Surely he was Balenan. His coloring didn't match anyone in the North Lands...well, anyone other than her family.

"A visitor to Balenol," he corrected, his look of amusement making her feel like he could read her thoughts. "I come from Thorania. I am here representing King Abner."

"Oh." Lucy berated herself for her foolishness in not realizing his origin immediately. Of course there would be dignitaries attending from the neighboring kingdom as well as from across the sea. "Do you live in Thirl?" she asked lamely, unable to think of anything more interesting to say.

This Rasad was courteous enough, but his casual attention was a far cry from the eager admiration of the younger men who had been fawning over her before Eamon's approach. She felt surprisingly wrong footed by her inability to read his opinion of her.

Rasad smiled, the expression undeniably attractive despite the fact that he again seemed slightly amused. "I spend a great deal of time in the capital, yes," he acknowledged. "But my holdings are further north, on the coast. It's beautiful up there, Luciana, just like you." Lucy blinked, not sure whether she was more thrown by the casual use of her name, or the unexpected compliment. "Perhaps you would like to see the northern and eastern parts of our kingdom before you leave the South Lands. It's very different from the Balenan landscape."

"By the Balenan landscape, you mean endless jungle," said Lucy lightly, unsure how to respond to his other comments.

"Indeed," agreed Rasad, with a chuckle. "The jungle does extend some way into Thorania, but there is much more to our kingdom." He gave her a candid look. "We also do not share the...historical complexities...of the relationship between Balenol and your own kingdom."

Lucy smiled wryly, taking his meaning with perfect clarity. To her knowledge, Thorania had never stepped in to assist the oppressed Kyonans in Balenol, but neither had the kingdom engaged in the slave trade itself. In fact, the latest rumor was that quite a number of Balenol's slaves had escaped over the years into the neighboring kingdom, with their descendants living in Thorania to this day. It was for that reason that Eamon and the others were going to Thorania after the coronation.

"Yes," she said mildly. "Relations between Thorania and Kyona are not as complicated, no doubt. In fact, I understand that your king has requested assistance from the Kyonan royals in addressing the plight of Kyonan descendants who remain in your kingdom, and may wish to relocate back to the North Lands."

"Yes, that's correct," said Rasad, inclining his head slightly. "It was at my suggestion that His Majesty made that request."

Lucy shot a sideways look at the Thoranian, trying not to show how startled she was by his casual declaration. Just how influential was this man? He had mentioned no title, but he said he had holdings in the north, so he must be fairly wealthy. And apparently he had the ear of his king.

"You look tense, Luciana," said Rasad, his tone mild but his eyebrows raised. "Are you afraid of heights? Perhaps it was not so courteous of me to bring you out onto a balcony."

"Oh." Lucy followed his gaze and pulled her hands from the railing quickly, sliding them into the folds of her skirts instead. She hadn't realized how tightly she had been clinging to the balustrade, but the truth was that she was a little wary of being on a balcony, after the accident that had so nearly claimed King Giles's life.

"No," she said hastily. "I'm not afraid of heights, not generally. But..." She hesitated, color rushing to her cheeks as she realized how foolish she sounded. "But it is a long way down, isn't it?"

Rasad didn't answer. He just met Lucy's eyes with a penetrating look. She found herself unable to hold his gaze, although what she had to hide she couldn't have said.

"Well," he said at last. "If you are sufficiently rested, maybe we should once again brave the crowds?"

"Yes, of course," said Lucy, taking his offered arm with relief. She found herself unusually awkward in this impressive man's presence, as if she didn't know what to do with her limbs. She couldn't remember ever having that problem before.

Rasad led her back into the ballroom, and she blinked at the brightness of the light after looking out into the blackness with him. The gala was still in full swing, but she found herself weary of it all, and wishing she could be in her bed.

She rallied enough to send an exasperated look toward Cody, who was hovering so close to the doorway onto the balcony that he had almost certainly been eavesdropping on every word of her conversation with the Thoranian man. He met her look squarely, clearly unrepentant, before letting his eyes pass to Rasad, their expression shrewd and calculating. In all honesty, Lucy didn't mind. She would be curious to hear later what Cody made of the man, because she wasn't at all sure how to assess him herself.

Her eyes quickly picked out the other Kyonans in the room. Lord and Lady Rodanthe were seated near the Balenan sovereigns, watching the dancing, although their eyes regularly flicked to the young royals. They didn't seem to have noticed Lucy's departure from the room, and she didn't blame them. Their authority over her and Matheus—and even Cody who, although older than her, was significantly younger than them— had never been well defined. They probably considered her and her brother to now be delivered into the care of their royal Balenan family.

Eamon was standing with Jocelyn and Kincaid, ostensibly speaking with Prince Astor's oldest son—the only one of their generation of the Balenan royals who was old enough to attend the event—but in reality watching her progress with Rasad. Eamon looked no more impressed than he had done when they had parted ways, and Lucy avoided locking eyes with him. She didn't want to get caught up in his angst right now.

Following Rasad's lead absently, Lucy found herself approaching a refreshment table from behind. On the other side of the table, several younger members of the Balenan court were drinking from gleaming goblets, their eyes fixed on the Kyonan and Valorian royalty whom Lucy had just been watching herself.

"What do you make of these North Landers?"

Lucy paused at the question. The speaker was a young man, and he was clearly unaware of her presence behind him, separated from his group by the heavily laden table.

"The royals in the party seem respectable enough," another man responded, his voice indifferent. "Hopefully they and the other delegates have the authority to negotiate a trade treaty, and they're not just wasting our new king's time."

"I thought they were going straight on to Thorania after the coronation," interjected another young man. "I don't think they'll have much opportunity to negotiate a treaty."

The indifferent one sighed at his companion's ignorance. "They're returning here afterward." His voice turned sour. "Although I don't know why Thorania gets first chance to negotiate with them."

Lucy wanted to roll her eyes. *Maybe because they didn't enslave our people for generations?*

"What about the dragon rumors?" asked one of the female courtiers in the group, her voice slightly breathless. "Do you think it's true that the Kyonan king promised that if we made an alliance with them, their dragon allies would give us magical protection?"

The first young man snorted. "Where did you hear that piece of nonsense?"

"Lots of people are saying it," retorted the girl, clearly offended.

Several members of the group chuckled openly at her, and Lucy barely refrained from joining them. The chance of King Calinnae making such an offer was non-existent, but the chance of the dragons agreeing to uphold it was even less. The girl who had spoken gave a defiant flick of her hair.

"Laugh if you want, but everyone knows the Kyonans have some kind of deal with the dragons. It's how they broke the magic that was keeping the slaves here." She turned her head toward the visitors, and her tone turned thoughtful. "I don't think an alliance would be such a bad thing. Even *you* said the royals seem respectable," she shot at the indifferent boy, who was clearly the critic of the group. She giggled. "The prince is quite handsome, if you ask me."

"Handsome?" protested another girl. "Stop drooling over a Kyonan—you're embarrassing yourself."

The girls started to bicker lightly, and Lucy shifted, not sure whether she was more irked by the admiration of the first girl or the derision of the second. Of course Eamon was handsome—any imbecile could see that. But these girls had no business either pointing it out or denying it.

"The Kyonan king and queen are certainly bold to send their heir here," said the critical one, cutting through the ongoing argument. "If my father had his way, the prince would be pressed into service to make a point to these Kyonan upstarts."

Lucy frowned, anger rising up in her to hear Eamon spoken of that way. But before she could get too worked up, the first speaker cut his friend off with a snort.

"Your father has always been sour. He needs to catch up with the times. His Majesty wants good relations with Kyona now, and I have to say I think he's wise. We can't go back to how things were in our parents' day. Everyone but them can see it."

"I didn't say I agree with my father," the other man said mildly. "I'm sure King Giles knows what he's doing."

"The girls are positive prudes," giggled the girl who had refused to acknowledge Eamon's appeal. "It's like they're wearing tents."

Lucy felt her face heat, none too pleased to have her earlier fears confirmed. She had momentarily forgotten about her escort, but she was suddenly burningly conscious of her hand on Rasad's arm. She found herself wishing desperately that she wasn't overhearing this conversation while in the company of the enigmatic stranger.

She chanced a glance at him, and found him cocking his head toward the group with an eyebrow raised. He looked down at her and met her eye, his expression inviting her to share the joke of the Balenans discussing her in her presence without realizing it. She gave a weak smile, trying to tell herself that it was simply entertaining, and not humiliating.

"Different fashions, I suppose," one of the young men was responding. "I don't think you could call the one who's half Balenan a prude. She's ravishing."

Lucy's face burned more brightly than ever.

"Half Balenan? I think you mean half Kyonan," responded the man whose father was apparently stuck in the past, his voice cold. "Really, I wouldn't think you'd be so easily taken in, like all those fools who've been fawning over her all evening."

The first speaker shrugged. "Who said anything about being taken in? I said she's ravishing, not that I want to marry her."

"I should hope not," shuddered one of the girls, sounding none too impressed with the man's repeated compliment to Lucy's looks. "Talk about tainting your family line."

The man shrugged. "Well, as to that, her mother was a Wrendal after all. One of our best families, in its day."

Lucy frowned, a strange feeling creeping over her at the man's use of the past tense. She had never had any love for her Wrendal heritage, but it was strange to realize that the family line was now gone completely. Thanks to her own action in killing Scanlon, the last Wrendal. She barely suppressed a shudder.

"Her mother may have been born a Wrendal, but she was little better than a harlot," said one of the girls snidely. "She didn't just marry a Kyonan, but a Kyonan *commoner*. I heard the Kyonan king wouldn't have her, so she just took the first man who would. And it looks to me like the daughter is cut from the same cloth."

Lucy felt her free hand curl into a fist, not so much at the insult to her, but at the slight to both of her parents. She knew a sudden savage desire to pull out her blade and make the girl swallow her words, but she suppressed it with horror. It was a timely reminder of what she was trying very hard not to be. She glanced self-consciously at Rasad, fighting the irrational fear that he had read her violent thoughts. But he wasn't looking at her at all, his gaze focused on the group of locals, his expression still faintly amused.

"Personally, I feel sorry for the Kyonan," said another girl, her tone of compassion unconvincing. "She seems to think all those boys are genuinely interested in her. She probably doesn't realize that they're all hoping she's as loose as her mother. I imagine she's hoping to snare one and get the title her mother threw away, but she's just going to be humiliated. They might want to entertain themselves with her, but it's not like any of them would ever consider actually allying themselves with a *Kyonan*."

"You are severe," said one of the men, a hint of amusement in his voice, and the girl shrugged her pretty, bare shoulders.

"I'm just being frank. I mean, look at the company she keeps. Do you realize that the man who's here as some kind of a guard to her and her brother is actually a former *slave*?"

Lucy bristled in defense of Cody, but the others in the girl's group seemed more inclined to be impressed than derisive.

"Is he really?" said the first speaker. "He must be brave to come back here. I'd love to get close enough to see his mark. I've never actually seen one in real life."

Lucy turned away, hoping Rasad would take the hint and move on. She had heard more than enough. The Thoranian man did seem to sense her discomfort, and he gallantly led her away, making for a different table on the other side of the room. Lucy tried to keep her face impassive as both anger and embarrassment washed over her.

She knew she shouldn't be surprised. And she even knew she was foolish to take the courtiers' words to heart—she was no stranger to the jealousies of court life. But it still stung to be reminded that she and her party were nothing but curiosities. Of course these Balenans would be derisive of her. It had been absurd to imagine for a moment that she would find more acceptance in Balenol than in Kyona, where she was at least known to the court, and familiar with the culture.

It took her a moment to realize that they had stopped walking, and a moment longer to realize that Rasad was looking down at her, his eyes shrewd but kind.

"Balenans have always been narrow minded," he said softly, his gaze not wavering from her face. "In Thorania, people are not like that. Anyone in King Abner's court would be enchanted by you, Luciana. Anyone with eyes, that is." Lucy barely realized that he was raising her hand to his lips, her mind scrambling to catch up with this latest casually dropped compliment. Rasad pressed a kiss to the back of her hand, capturing her gaze with his own as he spoke.

"Think about my invitation, Luciana. I think you would be pleased with Thorania."

And then, with an incline of his head, he was gone. Lucy was left blinking, her thoughts strangely befuddled, hoping she hadn't inadvertently agreed to something without realizing it. She really didn't know what to make of this Rasad. *Had* he issued an invitation? She remembered him talking about his kingdom, but nothing concrete.

Her confused gaze roamed across the ballroom. One pair of eyes was impossible to miss, they burned into hers with such intensity, even across the crowded space. Eamon looked like he was ready to murder someone. And for no sensible reason that she could identify, the back of Lucy's hand seemed to burn with guilt on the spot where Rasad had kissed.

CHAPTER SEVEN

"Hurry up, Matheus!" Lucy tapped her foot impatiently. "Do you want to be late for the coronation after we sailed all the way to the South Lands to be here for it?"

"Relax," Matheus yawned. "We're not going to be late."

Her brother studied her with bleary eyes as he joined her in the corridor outside his suite. "How are you looking so polished, anyway? You were up as late as I was. And who plans a morning coronation after an all-night gala the night before?"

"Oh Matheus," said Lucy indulgently. "You think that was an all-night gala? We were barely up past midnight." She ruffled her brother's hair condescendingly. "You need more practice. That was nothing."

"Get off!" scowled Matheus, pushing her hand away indignantly. "I thought you were in a hurry! Messing up my hair will just make us more late."

Lucy chuckled. "Don't worry, it was already awful. I was going to have to fix it for you anyway."

Matheus groaned, but didn't actually protest as Lucy carefully re-ordered his hair. Like her, Matheus had inherited their father's dark, thick hair. But on him it looked less elegant and more like a haystack.

"Satisfied?" Matheus grumbled when she finally stepped back, surveying him with a critical eye.

"I don't know if I'd go that far," said Lucy in her best maddening-older-sister voice. "But you'll do."

Matheus swatted her arm away as she tried to straighten his tunic. "Aren't we waiting for the others?" he asked, as Lucy led the way in the direction of the vast throne room they had been shown in their tour.

"They're probably not ready yet," she said airily. "We can meet them there."

Matheus favored her with a derisive snort. "You mean you're trying to avoid Eamon still. Now I know why you're supposedly worried about being late when the coronation doesn't start for ages."

"I don't know what you're talking about," said Lucy loftily, tossing her hair in a practiced manner.

"Of course not," said Matheus dryly. "You seriously need to let it go, Luce. You can't stay mad at him forever. You know he would never come after the freedmen on purpose. He was under some kind of enchantment—you're the only one who can't seem to accept that."

"Can we talk about something else?" Lucy said impatiently, less than impressed at being lectured by her little brother.

"Sure," said Matheus agreeably. "How about last night's gala? You certainly seemed to enjoy yourself." He shot her an accusatory look. "So much for being worried the court would eat you. Eat you up, more like."

Lucy remained silent for a moment. She wasn't proud of it, but she had lain awake for far too long the night before, stewing over the insults she had overheard. She wished she could be as unconcerned as Matheus seemed to be about how their family was perceived, but it rankled to know how scathingly the court here spoke about them. She loved her family, and she wouldn't change her heritage, not really. But it wasn't entirely comfortable to be suspended between two worlds, never fully accepted in either. To the Kyonans she was Balenan, and to the Balenans she was Kyonan. And in neither case did the foreign blood win her any favor.

Not to mention the fact that the nobility would never fully accept her as one of them, with a common father. She knew that even Jocelyn had felt the impact of prejudice within the court over her mother's common background, even though her mother had been Kyona's queen for decades. No one cared about such things in Raldon, of course. But in Kynton, there were always people like Sonia and Vanessa who were only too ready to hint constantly at her unsuitability for court life.

"I enjoyed the dancing," she answered her brother at last. She hadn't mentioned what she'd overheard to Matheus the night before, and she decided not to say anything now, either. He didn't need to share the discomfort of being insulted. "But it was so hot compared to home."

"I suppose that's why the women here wear so much...less," said Matheus reflectively. "I wonder why the men don't."

"Because no one wants to see your shoulders," teased Lucy, earning herself a brotherly shove.

"Lucy, Matheus!"

They had almost reached the throne room, and Lucy felt her heart sink at the salutation. So close.

"Joss," she said, turning around with a smile that she knew was unconvincing. As she had anticipated, Eamon was there as well, keeping stride with his twin. As was standard for the Kyonan heir, he had two Kyonan royal guards trailing behind him. Lord and Lady Rodanthe were also walking not far behind, deep in conversation with one another.

"There you are!" Jocelyn was saying. "Why didn't you two wait for us? We obviously weren't far behind you."

"*Apparently*, Lucy was concerned about being late," said Matheus, raising a challenging eyebrow in response to Lucy's glare. "What?" he muttered, as the others hurried to catch up to them. "I'm on Eamon's side."

"Thanks for the display of family loyalty," grumbled Lucy, but the others joined them a moment later, so she suspended the sibling squabble for the time being.

"Cody's not with you?" asked Kincaid, looking around as if expecting the older Kyonan man to leap from behind a suit of armor. "He won't miss the coronation, will he? Should we have made sure he was awake?"

Lucy and Matheus exchanged a look, chuckling. "Trust me," Matheus said. "He's awake."

"Cody's never slept in a day in his life," said Lucy, taking pity on Kincaid's confusion. "He's got way too much energy for that. My mother says that he's as over exuberant now as he was when he was thirteen." She shook her head. "He's probably been up for hours, and managed to fit in some sparring in the royal training yard." Her voice turned slightly bitter. "If he could find anyone willing to demean themselves to train with a Kyonan."

Jocelyn raised a questioning eyebrow, clearly aware that there was some story behind her best friend's comment. But she seemed to accept from Lucy's flick of the head that they would have to talk about it later.

"Shall we head in, Your Highnesses?" Lady Rodanthe cut in, inclining her head toward the nearby doorway into the throne room.

"Actually, Lucy," said Eamon quickly, trying to catch her eye. Lucy's heart sank. "Can I talk to you for a minute?"

"I don't want to be late," she said half-heartedly, her gaze on an unremarkable tapestry on the far wall.

"Rubbish, Lucy," said Matheus briskly. "There's plenty of time. We'll wait here for you."

Lucy glared at her brother, but he met her look with an unconvincing expression of innocence. Her eyes passed to Lady Rodanthe, and she saw that while the older woman didn't look especially impressed, she wasn't actually going to challenge the prince's request for a private conversation.

"We will locate our seats," the noblewoman said, her firm tone a reminder that they all had an important event they mustn't be late for.

"It will only take a minute," said Eamon, the pleading note in his voice weakening Lucy's defenses a little. She had spent the rest of the ball the night before avoiding him and his stormy gaze, and she didn't particularly want to talk to him right now. But she wasn't heartless. She knew it was humiliating enough for him to basically beg in front of the others, and to turn him down completely would be unkind.

"All right," she said as casually as she could.

Others had started to arrive for the coronation, a slow but building stream of people brushing past the visiting group to enter the throne room. Many shot them curious looks, huddled in the corridor as they were, and Lucy could see Eamon's guards watching the passing parade with alert and suspicious eyes.

Eamon looked around for a moment, clearly as unexcited as Lucy was about the idea of trying to have a personal conversation in the midst of the bustle. The throne room was clearly long, because even the closest other door was a bit of a walk away. Eamon gestured toward it.

"Perhaps in there?"

"All right," sighed Lucy again, without any marked enthusiasm. What was there to say that hadn't been said already?

But she followed Eamon anyway, the Kyonan guards close behind the pair. Eamon pushed his way into the room, which seemed to be some kind of medium-sized antechamber, and the guards surged past Lucy in order to satisfy themselves that the space was secure.

Eamon shut the door behind him, turning to Lucy with a serious expression.

"I know you want to get to the coronation, Lucy, so I'll be quick. I wanted to talk to you about that man last night."

Lucy raised an eyebrow. Apparently Eamon hadn't sought her out for another opportunity to apologize after all.

"What man?" she asked, her tone icy. "I danced with so many men, you'll really have to be more specific."

Eamon scowled, his expression clearly saying that he knew she was trying to be provocative.

"Well, you didn't dance with this one. I'm talking about the older man. The one who took you out onto the balcony."

"What about him?" asked Lucy. "What concern is it of yours?" Her tone was anything but encouraging, and Eamon hesitated before answering.

"I'm not trying to tell you what to do, Lucy, but everyone in our delegation is my responsibility, in a sense."

"So you're in charge of etiquette now, are you?" Lucy challenged. "Lady Rodanthe hasn't expressed any concern over my dancing last night."

Eamon sighed, frustrated. "I'm not suggesting it was breach of etiquette. I'm just saying, we all know how unpredictable Balenol can be, and we need to be careful."

One of Eamon's guards shifted slightly behind him, pulling Lucy's attention to the man. She didn't know his name, but she recognized him as one of the guards who regularly attended the crown prince. She was pretty sure he'd been at the ball last night, in fact. However, in that setting Eamon's guards had hovered against the wall, out of earshot. Unlike now.

The guard didn't meet her eye, of course, but Lucy still

flushed slightly at the reminder of their audience. It was one of the things she had liked most about Eamon visiting her at Raldon instead of her going to Kynton. His guards didn't tend to hover so close in the peaceful forest community.

Eamon followed her gaze and frowned, seeming to realize for the first time how close the guards were standing. Lucy could only suppose that he was so used to it that he barely even noticed their presence anymore. But evidently he realized their proximity bothered Lucy. After a moment's hesitation, he grabbed her arm and pulled her unceremoniously to the other side of the room. At a meaningful glare from Eamon, the guards retained their place by the door, although they both looked reluctant to do so.

"If you're quite done hauling me around," Lucy snapped, pulling her arm free from Eamon's grip. "You're not responsible for me, Eamon. I'm not part of the official delegation, as you know perfectly well. And I know as well as you do—better, probably—how dangerous Balenol can be. But it just so happens that Rasad isn't Balenan. He's from Thorania."

"*Rasad*, is it?" asked Eamon, his eyes narrowed.

Before Lucy could respond, they were both startled by the sudden opening of a door near where they were standing. It didn't lead into the corridor, like the door they had come through. Lucy's surprise quickly turned to dismay when she saw who was entering the room, flanked by guards and dressed in a ceremonial outfit of almost overwhelming magnificence.

"Your Majesty!" she said, dropping quickly into a curtsy.

She kept her head lowered for longer than necessary, as she fought the flush of embarrassment that arose at the realization that they had chosen the formal antechamber to the throne room for their cozy chat. Even when she rose from the curtsy, she couldn't bring herself to look the king in the eyes, instead focusing on the several Balenan guards who flanked him.

They had tensed at the unexpected appearance of others in the room, but seemed to have relaxed when they observed that it was only Lucy and the Kyonan crown prince. Lucy had sensed the similar alarm from Eamon's guards when the others had entered the room, but each set of guards seemed to have dismissed the other as harmless.

"King Giles," Eamon was saying, sounding embarrassed himself. "My apologies for this unintentional intrusion. We did not realize—"

It all happened so quickly, Lucy didn't know what had first alerted her. The sound of a blade being drawn was jarring in its very familiarity, because the context was all wrong. Before she had even had time to turn toward the noise, she had reached for her weapon on instinct. Her hands had already closed around the dagger, her skirts bunched to allow access, before she realized with horror that the king, and all his guards, were watching her with blank astonishment. Her hand stilled even as she turned her head to see who had drawn steel—the instinct to identify the danger was too strong to resist, but she couldn't let them see her use her weapon. She couldn't let them see what she was really capable of.

Eamon had clearly been surprised by her actions as well, but he wasted no time gawking at her disarranged skirts, instead following her gaze instantly, back toward the door through which they had entered.

Lucy had barely registered what she was seeing when Eamon's cry broke the shocked silence. Unlike her, he didn't hesitate as he threw himself at King Giles, shoving the monarch forcibly into one of his own guards with not a moment to spare.

For a horrifying moment Lucy remained frozen in place, everything seeming to slow down as the blade—thrown by one of Eamon's own guards—buried itself into Eamon's arm, now occupying the space where the Balenan king had stood seconds before.

Eamon's grunt of pain as he hit the ground seemed to unlock the rest of the room from its stupor. Lucy was dimly aware of the other Kyonan guard tackling his rogue companion, two of King Giles's guards racing to subdue the man as well. The other Balenan guards had formed up around their sovereign.

But Lucy had eyes only for Eamon. Her scream of horror was lodged in her throat as she dropped to her knees beside him, her mind reeling at the sight of the blood now pouring from his arm.

"Eamon," she gasped.

His eyes were shut, his face bunched in pain. He had fallen on his injured arm, and the blade was still protruding. Lucy blinked rapidly, trying to dispel the sick feeling in her stomach. For a moment all she could see was the sight of her uncle, dead on the ground with her blade in his heart, and his thick, red blood pooling around him. But she resolutely forced the image away, trying to return to the current crisis.

Her hand hovered over the blade, uncertain whether to pull it out or leave it in. She knew nothing about healing and injuries. Something dripped off the edge of her nose, and she realized that she was crying. She wiped the tears away with the back of her hand, impatient of the distraction.

"Eamon, talk to me," she said desperately.

"I'm all right," Eamon said, his eyes shooting open at the sound of her voice. "I'm fine. I just had the wind knocked out of me. Is the king—"

"You didn't just have the wind knocked out of you," said Lucy, angry with him for no reason she could articulate. Even so, a knot of tension had loosened in her chest at the alertness of his tone. "You have a dagger sticking out of your arm."

"I'm fine," Eamon repeated, pushing himself up with his uninjured arm. "Is King Giles safe?"

Lucy followed his gaze, belatedly remembering the real target of the astonishing attack. King Giles was back on his feet, his expression hard and calculating as his gaze flicked between the two of them and the cluster of guards at the door. The Kyonan guard who had thrown the dagger had been disarmed, and was being held roughly by two of King Giles's guards, his expression belligerent. The other Kyonan was racing across the room toward his injured prince, his face pale.

The door into the corridor burst open, causing two more of the king's guards to surge forward. Jocelyn tumbled through first, drawing up with a gasp as she was confronted with the drawn blades of the Balenans. She stumbled back a step, into Kincaid, who leaped forward, positioning his wife behind him before Lucy could blink. She saw Matheus hovering behind the couple, his mouth hanging open and his eyes wide with horror as he surveyed the scene before him.

King Giles calmly assessed the new arrivals for a moment before he spoke, his voice as steady and commanding as ever.

"Close the door behind you, Matheus."

Lucy's brother started at the unexpected instruction, but he did as he was told quickly, hurrying into the room and pulling the door shut. The guards in his vicinity lowered their weapons slightly, so that Jocelyn, Kincaid, and Matheus were no longer being held at sword point.

King Giles returned his attention to the knife still lodged in Eamon's arm. "Summon a physician," he barked to the room at large, and one of his guards hastened to obey. He had barely left the room, via the door through which the king and his group had entered, when several more Balenan guards appeared in the doorway, as if from nowhere. Two of them grouped around the king, while the others raced to join the guards still restraining the Kyonan who had thrown the blade.

The king met the visiting prince's eyes, his expression impossible to read. "It seems you saved my life, Your Highness." The words were courteous, but the tone made Lucy shiver.

Eamon shook his head, more pale than Lucy had ever seen him. "I don't know what to say, Your Majesty," he stammered, his voice much less confident than usual. "The man has been one of my personal guard for years. I cannot imagine what—that is, I can hardly believe—" He was clearly struggling for words. "I am as horrified by his actions as you are, Your Majesty. Please believe that Kyona would never participate in...would never..."

Lucy felt a cold rush go over her body as the full implication of the incident broke in on her. She looked between the hard-eyed king and the mutinous guard, her breath catching in her throat. A member of the Kyonan delegation—one of the prince's own guards—had just tried to assassinate Balenol's new king. The danger of war between the two kingdoms had never been greater.

The king was silent for a moment, his expression shrewd as he took in Eamon's inelegant stuttering, as well as the blood dripping steadily down the prince's arm.

Eamon took a deep breath. "My father is as determined as you are to heal relations between our kingdoms, Your Majesty," he said, his voice much steadier. "It is for that reason he sent me to Nohl, to witness and celebrate your coronation on behalf of Kyona. We are fully committed to a harmonious future."

Lucy found herself nodding by the end of Eamon's speech. It was all true, and he had spoken well, she thought. The king seemed to agree, because something shifted in his expression.

"You were lucky the blade struck your arm," he said, his tone thoughtful. "It is clear to me that it could just as easily have taken your life." He met Eamon's eyes, and some kind of understanding seemed to pass between them, because Eamon sagged slightly in apparent relief before the king had even spoken his next words. "I thank you for your actions. Your intervention, Your Highness, certainly lessens any suspicion that the man acted on behalf of the Kyonan crown."

Eamon nodded, his face paler than ever despite his evident relief. Lucy bit her lip anxiously. She didn't think he should be on his feet—he had lost a lot of blood, and it was still flowing freely.

"Thank you, Your Majesty," Eamon was saying, but before he could go any further, a silver-haired man with an anxious expression bustled into the room, flanked by two guards. His bag proclaimed him as the physician the king had sent for, and he wasted no time in reaching his sovereign's side.

"I am unhurt," said King Giles curtly. "You will see to Prince Eamon's injury."

The physician turned his confused gaze on the visiting prince, his eyes widening at the sight of the dagger in his arm. He bustled over to Eamon, and Lucy averted her eyes, not eager to witness the extraction.

Her mind was still reeling from the unexpected crisis, and the emotions swirling through her were too numerous and too confusing to process. For reasons she couldn't immediately identify, her shock and fear seemed to be laced with shame as she tried to comprehend how close both King Giles and Eamon had come to dying. Her legs shook as she sank into a nearby chair, relieved that no one seemed to be paying her any attention. She could only be grateful that her own peculiar behavior seemed to have been forgotten in the uproar that followed.

"Is the injury serious?" The king's voice was dispassionate as he addressed the physician.

"No, Sire," the man said, his eyes still focused on his work. "I apprehend no lasting impact."

Lucy glanced over, more of the tension leaking from her at the man's words. She was relieved to see that the knife had been removed from Eamon's arm, but she looked away again quickly at the sight of the continued flow of his blood.

"I am glad to hear it," said King Giles, apparently dismissing the matter from his mind. His gaze turned to the restrained Kyonan guard, his expression becoming hard once again. "It seems I am to be made a liar in my edict that the execution blade is no longer needed in Nohl."

CHAPTER EIGHT

"Wait, Your Majesty."

Lucy turned in astonishment at Eamon's protest. He had said this guard had been with him for years, but surely he didn't think he could save the man. Not after he had openly tried to kill Balenol's king.

King Giles raised his eyebrows, a measure of suspicion visibly returning to his face. "You would dispute my right to execute this man?"

"Of course not, Your Majesty," said Eamon quickly, lowering his head in a respectful gesture. "You are Balenol's king. I would not presume to dispute your right to do whatever you please. But this matter is of great interest to Kyona, also. I would beg your...indulgence in allowing my people to conduct our own interrogations before the matter is...finally resolved."

King Giles studied Eamon for a long moment, his gaze too penetrating for comfort. "I will consider the request," he said at last. He nodded to a senior-looking guard. "Take the man to the dungeons for the time being. And take a message to Queen Verena that the coronation must regrettably be delayed by half an hour."

The senior guard looked startled. "You intend to go ahead with the coronation as planned, Your Majesty?"

"Of course," said the king, raising one regal eyebrow. His gaze swept around the room, which seemed stiflingly full of people. "I expect the full discretion of each one of you. This matter is to be kept quiet for now."

Lucy was quick to nod her compliance, along with the rest of the room, but internally she was surprised. She remembered what Jocelyn had said about the king needing to look strong, but still...Keeping a balcony collapse a secret was one thing, but an assassination attempt? Hopefully it meant that King Giles was still as eager to avoid war as everyone on the delegation was.

Well, she reflected, as she watched the rogue Kyonan guard being led roughly from the room, not everyone on the delegation, apparently.

Once the guard had been hauled away, the king followed him through the internal door, flanked by the rest of his guards. Within moments the visitors were alone in the room, save for the physician who was still binding up Eamon's arm. The prince's remaining guard hovered anxiously nearby, his face still unnaturally pale.

The group stood in stunned silence until the physician finished his work. "Well, Your Highness," the man said at last. "You have been lucky. As I said, I don't anticipate lasting damage, but you must rest, and not just for a day or two. It will take some time to recover your full strength." He began to pack up his bag. "I suggest you return to your chambers now. I will visit you in a few hours to check the bandage."

"I will attend the coronation first," said Eamon quickly. The physician pursed his lips, but either he didn't care enough or he didn't consider himself to have the appropriate rank to challenge the visiting prince, because he didn't actually argue. His work finished, he wasted no time in leaving the room.

"Are you sure that's wise, Eamon?" Jocelyn's anxious question mirrored Lucy's own concerns.

Eamon shrugged, wincing slightly as he rolled his shoulder. "I think it's more important than ever to show our support."

"But you convinced him," Jocelyn said quickly. "I'm sure you did. He knows we weren't behind it."

Jocelyn certainly seemed to have pieced together what happened quickly. Kincaid hovered protectively near her, still scanning the room for threats, and Matheus looked utterly confused. But the princess was very much in command of herself.

"I hope so," said Eamon heavily. "But it's still a terrible thing to have happened. You know how many eyes are on all of us. Who knows what people will say if I don't appear at the coronation?" He shook his head. "It's all very well for King Giles to say he'll keep it quiet, but there were a lot of people in this room. And an assassination attempt moments before the coronation, carried out by one of my personal guards...well, who knows what the ramifications will be?"

"So that really is what happened?" Kincaid asked, looking aghast. "What could the motivation have been? And how could a traitor have made it into your personal guard? Surely the guards who came on this trip were selected with the greatest care!"

"They were," said Eamon grimly. He spoke to Kincaid, but his eyes were on his twin, her furrowed brow a reflection of his own. "And nothing would ever make me believe it of him if I hadn't seen it with my own eyes."

"And felt it with your arm," said Jocelyn dryly. The worry line between her eyebrows deepened as she looked at her brother's bandaged arm. "I don't like this, Eamon. Something isn't right."

"That's a bit of an understatement," snorted Kincaid.

"No, I mean..." Jocelyn glanced at Eamon again, seeming to struggle for words.

"You came running in here pretty quickly, Joss," said Lucy slowly, her eyes narrowing slightly as she studied her friend. "Were you waiting right outside the door or something?"

"No," said Jocelyn hesitantly. She again looked at Eamon. "I thought...I thought I felt something. Then I heard you shout, and I ran..."

"You felt it, too?" Eamon asked eagerly, seeming to forget the rest of the group for a moment as he stepped toward his sister. "I didn't imagine it, then." He glanced at Lucy for the briefest second. "Lucy was the one who realized something was amiss first, and in the chaos I didn't immediately identify it. But I felt it, I know I did. Right before he drew his weapon."

"Wait." Lucy's flat voice seemed to bring both twins back to a sense of their surroundings. "What are you saying?"

Eamon met her eye reluctantly. "You wouldn't have felt it, Lucy, but there was a surge of power. I know there was. Something was at work here, some kind of—"

"And by power you mean magic?" Lucy interrupted, her temper rising rapidly. "You think he was under some kind of magical influence?"

"I do," said Eamon eagerly, apparently not alive to her tone. Kincaid's brow was furrowed in thought, and Matheus was looking between the Kyonan twins, his mouth wide with astonishment.

"And that's why you asked for mercy," said Jocelyn softly. She looked anxious again. "I don't know if we'll be able to save him, Eamon. Not after something as serious as this. We can't risk war by pushing too hard, and no one's going to believe us when we say he wasn't acting of his own free will."

"I wonder why," said Lucy bitingly, and everyone in the room turned to stare at her. She avoided Jocelyn's eye, instead directing her anger toward Eamon. "It's just your favorite solution, isn't it? An excuse that can cover any offense."

"Lucy!" Jocelyn's voice was sharper than Lucy had ever heard it.

She turned toward her friend, but not before she saw the flush rising up Eamon's neck. Good. Let him be ashamed. She could hardly believe he was trying to apply his explanation for his behavior in Raldon to this completely unrelated incident, like he was determined to supernaturally explain away any uncomfortable reality.

"Well, it's ridiculous," she said to Jocelyn, her voice impatient.

"That doesn't mean it isn't true," Jocelyn snapped. "I've seen much stranger things, believe me. And it's not just Eamon. I felt it too. Are you calling me a liar?"

Lucy raised her hands in frustration. "No, of course not. I've heard your stories, and it's not that I don't believe them. But we're in Balenol, Joss. We're an ocean away from the Kyonan mountains and the dragons and all that magic power business. How would someone be influencing that guard to attack King Giles?"

"That's what we need to figure out," said Jocelyn shortly. "And we're not so far separated from it all as you might think, Lucy. Or have you forgotten your parents' story? The one about the curse that originated in our *far-off* mountains but was powerful enough to keep generations of Kyonans trapped right here in Balenol?" Lucy had never seen her sweet-natured friend look so fierce. "Not to mention that Scanlon came from here. Who knows what he left behind when he sailed for the North Lands, ready to make mischief? Maybe he had allies who stayed behind."

Lucy shrugged, her discomfort doubling at the mention of her deceased uncle. "I thought you said he got his power from a dying dragon. Are you saying the dragon gave its magic to more than one person? I thought it didn't work that way."

Jocelyn sighed, running a hand up her face. "I don't know how it works. There's a lot we don't know." Her eyes narrowed again. "Which is why we shouldn't discount what Eamon and I felt." The princess turned back to her brother, who had remained silent since Lucy had chastised him. "Eamon, at least tell me you'll go change. You can't attend the coronation covered in blood."

Eamon jerked out of his stupor. "Yes," he said quickly. "Of course I'll change. I'll go now."

"Eamon." Jocelyn put her hand on his uninjured arm. "You did a very good thing just now. A couple of very good things." A meaningful look passed between them, which Lucy didn't fully understand. "I'm so glad you're all right. It's very lucky you were here, and that you realized something was wrong and reacted so quickly."

"Yes," said Eamon hesitantly, glancing at Lucy.

He didn't say anything, but she didn't miss the way his eyes flicked to her leg, where her weapon was concealed. The one she had visibly reached for before stopping herself. Lucy dropped her gaze, her heart racing a little faster. It seemed not everyone had forgotten her behavior, after all.

The king and his guards might have had no idea why she started bunching up her skirts in that unladylike way, but Eamon would have instantly realized that she was reaching for a weapon. Eamon knew she had sensed the attack coming before he had. And he had very good reason to know how capable Lucy was of incapacitating the guard, even from across the room. But he had clearly also seen her hesitate in the moment of crisis, and she could read his confusion on his face.

But he didn't challenge her on it, just hurried from the room with his guard close behind him.

Guilt warred with relief within Lucy's overwrought mind. If she had acted as her instincts prompted her to, Eamon wouldn't have been injured. And he'd been lucky. He could all too easily have been killed by that blade. And whatever her current feelings were toward him, she felt absolutely sick at the idea of something serious happening to him. But if she had taken down that guard...if she had done what her hands had been itching to do...she would have been exposed, and in front of Balenol's king of all people.

She started to mechanically move toward the door with the others, ready to head into the coronation at last, but her best friend's voice drew her up short.

"Actually, Lucy, can I have a word?"

She eyed Jocelyn suspiciously. The request was uncannily like Eamon's earlier plea for a private conversation, and that hadn't turned out so well. "What is it, Joss?"

But Jocelyn waited until Kincaid and Matheus had left the room, and the two girls were alone, before speaking.

"Lucy, how could you? You were way out of line."

Lucy blinked in surprise at the direct attack. "I don't know what you're talking about!"

"Yes you do," said Jocelyn, unimpressed. "I've been keeping my opinions to myself, not wanting our friendship to get mixed up in your fight with Eamon, but enough is enough. I'm done sitting by while you treat my brother so badly."

"While I—?" Lucy sputtered for a moment, struggling to find words for her rising anger. "I hardly think I'm the one who's treated him badly, Jocelyn!"

"Well, I do think it," said Jocelyn bluntly. "I know he made a mistake, a very big one. But you can't punish him forever."

"A mistake? He used his position to send the royal guard after my friends and neighbors, Jocelyn! He ordered them to round up the children and *brand* them! You think I should just fall back into his arms the moment he says he's sorry?"

"No one said anything about falling into his arms," said Jocelyn quickly. "If you're no longer interested in him in that way, that's your own affair. But it doesn't justify you belittling him and humiliating him in front of other people."

For a moment Lucy was silent, stung by the open rebuke. She didn't want to admit it, but the bare fact of Jocelyn's accusation was as rattling as the princess's words. It was unlike her gentle friend to chastise like this. "It was just Matheus and Kincaid," she muttered at last.

"Matheus is led by you, Lucy," said Jocelyn, her tone still unnaturally stern. "And Kincaid is foreign royalty, not to mention Eamon's new brother-in-law. You don't think it matters to Eamon what both of them think of him? You think it's easy for him to be made a fool of in front of them?"

"If he came across as a fool, it's only because he was making a foolish suggestion," argued Lucy impatiently. "Surely you don't really think some kind of magic was involved in what just happened, Joss. It's natural for Eamon to be horrified that it was his own guard who turned traitor, and to want to explain it away, but not everything can be—"

"Eamon's feelings on the matter have nothing to do with what I sensed," interrupted Jocelyn shortly. "*I* felt the power, Lucy, not just Eamon. Maybe if you could open your mind to the reality that there are forces at work that you don't fully understand, you'd find it a little easier to forgive Eamon for what happened. I know you were placed in a terrible position when Eamon unleashed Scanlon on your community. And I know you're still suffering from it. But maybe you could think about what he's suffering, too. He's racked with guilt over something he can't change, and wasn't fully in control of in the first place.

You have no idea what it's like to be under the power of a magical force you can't understand."

"Don't I?" snapped Lucy, before she could stop herself.

Jocelyn's brow furrowed in confusion. "What is that supposed to mean?"

Lucy just shrugged a shoulder, regretting having let the words out.

"No," said Jocelyn, her expression growing hard. "Tell me what that meant. When have you ever been influenced by dragon magic?"

"You tell me," said Lucy, struggling to keep her varied emotions in check. "All I know is that since I was a child, I thought Eamon was the strongest, surest, most trustworthy person alive. Every word out of his mouth was wise and true and confidence inspiring. I never questioned how I felt any more than I questioned him. But that's his power, right? The power he never thought he should mention to me, even though it apparently drips from every word he says. Maybe I have more experience of being enchanted than all the rest of you."

For a moment there was a stunned silence, as Jocelyn stared at Lucy with her mouth open. "Lucy," she said at last, her voice barely more than a whisper. "Is that what you think?" She swallowed. "Lucy...what you felt for Eamon was real. You weren't... bewitched into caring about him. How could you think that?"

Lucy shrugged again, furious with herself for the tears that stung her eyes, trying to escape. "How would you even know? I thought you said that you couldn't always tell when you'd used your own power. How would you know if he'd been using his?"

"It's not the same, Lucy," said Jocelyn quickly. "Eamon was always more in control of his power than I was. And he would never use it on you to try to get you to like him. Everything between you was genuine—surely you can't really doubt that?"

"I don't know what to think anymore," said Lucy dully, a

single tear slipping down her cheek in spite of herself. "You're supposed to be my best friend, and yet all our lives you struggled with this unbelievable secret, and you never said a word to me. Can you really blame me for not being in a hurry to trust Eamon again, when clearly neither one of you ever really trusted me?"

Tears were leaking out of Jocelyn's eyes now, too. "Lucy, I'm so sorry. I should have told you. It wasn't because I didn't trust you, I swear. It was because I was so afraid of myself, of what I might accidentally do. I never even told my parents."

Lucy didn't respond. Her eyes were lowered, but she could feel Jocelyn watching her steadily.

"I can't deny that you have every reason to feel betrayed," said Jocelyn at last. "But you haven't *seemed* angry with me. Just with Eamon. Is all of this the real reason you're still angry with him?"

Lucy made a sound that was intended to be a snort, but came out more like a sob. "I don't need extra reasons. The attack at Raldon was enough." Jocelyn looked unconvinced, and Lucy pushed on hastily before her friend could probe further. "And I'm not angry with you, Joss, not really. I wish you'd told me, but what's done is done, and I don't want to fight about it. It's not worth losing my best friend over."

"But it's worth losing Eamon?" Jocelyn challenged. Lucy just shrugged, and her friend sighed. "Lucy, if I've done something that hurt you, put the blame on me. I don't want to escape your anger at the cost of it all heaping onto Eamon. I think he has more than enough to carry without adding my crimes."

She met Lucy's eye, her expression unflinching. "Lucy, you're my best friend, and I always want to be right with you. But the truth is that I have my own life now, one that's happy and full of purpose. Even if you never forgave me, as heartbroken as I would be, I would recover. It wouldn't ruin my life. So if you have to be angry with someone, be angry with me. Because from where I sit, your inability to forgive Eamon is threatening to ruin not only his life, but yours as well. And that breaks my heart even more."

And without another word, Jocelyn turned away, her quick strides taking her to the door in moments. And Lucy, her tears flowing freely at last, found herself alone.

CHAPTER NINE

Lucy had been to a few official royal functions, but King Giles's coronation was by far the most tortuous. The ceremony seemed to drag unbearably, and it may as well have been in a different language for all the sense she actually made of it.

The whole visiting delegation was subdued, each one of them sitting unnaturally stiffly in their chairs, eyes darting around the large throne room uneasily. Lord and Lady Rodanthe were sitting between Eamon and the Valorian royals, their tight lips and stiff posture communicating their stress. But Cody was the worst of them, his dismay at having once again been absent for a life-threatening incident so strong that he had to be talked down from bustling Lucy and Matheus straight back to the harbor. He sat between them, making no effort to hide his troubled expression as he scanned the crowd continuously for threats.

Lucy was little better herself. It wasn't that she felt in any danger, but she was shaken to the core by the confrontation with Jocelyn, not to mention the belated impact of the incident she had witnessed. Her relief at escaping notice was rapidly being eclipsed by her horror at how easily her hesitation could have cost either King Giles or Eamon his life.

Her distress was only amplified by the sight of the Kyonan prince sitting near her. His face was still a shade too pale, and his arm rested awkwardly in his lap. In spite of the heat, he wore a stiff formal jacket that covered his bandage, and made him look at a glance like all was normal. But the rigid set of his shoulders convinced her he was in considerable pain. She wished he had taken the physician's advice and rested in his chamber, but she didn't try to convince him.

His remaining guards were sticking so close to him, she doubted even she could get near enough to speak to him. Lucy felt for the guards. Instead of the usual shift of two at a time, each and every one of them was hovering protectively near their injured charge, their anxiety and shock at the actions of their fellow guard clear on their faces.

She was vaguely aware of Rasad sitting in state with a number of others whose slightly different garb suggested their Thoranian heritage. He caught her eye and smiled casually in greeting, but he made no attempt to talk to her. She was glad. Somehow, thanks to Eamon's unfinished warning about the man, he had become mixed up in the whole incident in her mind, and she had no desire to put on an indifferent front for him right now.

But finally, in spite of all the silent turbulence swirling through the throne room, the ceremony was complete, and King Giles was officially crowned. Lucy breathed a sigh of relief, as much that her mother's cousin had survived long enough to properly take the crown as that she could finally get away from the formalities. It hadn't escaped her notice that this second near-fatal incident made the first accident all the more suspicious.

Once the ceremony was over, the visitors withdrew to their

own part of the castle, instead of milling around like most of the attendees. Lucy supposed they would have to re-emerge soon for the formal luncheon, but a break would do them all good. She saw one of Eamon's guards hurrying to find the physician, and was glad that the stubborn prince was going to be looked at again. Perhaps the physician would be able to convince him to sit the rest of the formalities out.

Before Eamon disappeared into his chamber, Lucy gathered her courage to approach him. She still wasn't entirely sure what she thought about Jocelyn's outburst, but one omission had been troubling her throughout the whole ceremony, and she wanted to get it off her chest while she had the chance.

"Eamon?"

The prince turned to her immediately, looking surprised at her greeting. She saw, to her shame, that he also looked apprehensive. She really had been unkind to him over the last few months.

"I just wanted to say..." Her voice faltered, and she cleared her throat, trying again. "I wanted to say I'm sorry I spoke so harshly to you before. I'm glad you're all right. I'm grateful for what you did in there, and..." She swallowed hard, lowering her gaze. "And I'm sorry that I didn't...that I failed to..."

"It's all right, Lucy," said Eamon, and the softness of his voice almost brought tears to her eyes. "You don't have anything to be sorry for. No one expects you to be a bodyguard."

Lucy nodded, still not able to meet his eyes. It was kind of him to reassure her, but she knew that Eamon wasn't being entirely truthful. In that moment, back in the antechamber, he *had* expected her to act on the attack she had seen coming, and he had been confused by her hesitation.

Not wishing to prolong the discussion, she turned away, heading for her own suite. But she wasn't destined to reach the sanctuary of her chamber. She had almost reached the door when Cody pulled her up short. He had been hovering close enough that she was fairly sure he had heard every word of her interaction with Eamon, and his gaze was far too shrewd as he interrupted her progress.

"A word, Lucy?"

She barely restrained a groan. Was there anyone in the group who didn't want to pull her aside this morning? She hoped Cody wasn't going to chew her out for once again finding herself in danger, because her emotions were so close to the surface, she would probably end up either pulling a blade on him or sobbing on his chest, depending which way he prodded her.

However, she recognized the look of determination in the older man's face, and she made no effort to resist as he tugged her into an unoccupied parlor in the same wing as their guest suites.

"What really happened, Lucy?" Cody said without preamble, the moment they were alone.

"What do you mean?" Lucy asked unconvincingly. "We already told you. Eamon's guard went rogue and threw a dagger at the king. Eamon pushed him out of the way, and took the blade in his arm."

"Lucy." Cody was clearly unimpressed. "Do you really think I can't tell when you're hiding something? What was all that Prince Eamon was just saying about you not being a bodyguard?"

Lucy wrapped her arms around herself, uncomfortable. She debated trying to make something up, but Cody wasn't likely to be easily deterred. "I hesitated. I hesitated, and Eamon saw it."

"Hesitated?" Cody prompted when she didn't elaborate.

Lucy sighed. "I was the one who realized what was happening, not Eamon. I went for my weapon, and Eamon saw me do it. But I stopped myself. I couldn't bring myself to use it in front of

King Giles and his guards. Not to mention Eamon." She buried her face in her hands, her emotions suddenly getting the better of her. "And Eamon was almost killed because of it. And if he hadn't been so quick to react, the guard would have killed the king, and we would probably be at war with Balenol right now."

She didn't look up, but she could hear Cody's frown in his voice. "I don't understand, Lucy. Why didn't you want to use your weapon? When the stakes were so high, why would you hesitate?"

Lucy lowered her hands at last. "I didn't want to be exposed for what I really am," she said, her voice barely more than a whisper. "Again."

"What does that even mean?" Cody asked, clearly impatient but trying to speak gently.

"I know you don't understand, Cody," said Lucy dully. "But I don't want people to see me as a deadly fighter."

"But you are a deadly fighter," said Cody blankly. "It's one of your most impressive characteristics."

Lucy made a noise of frustration. "Impressive to you, maybe, but do you think the court in Kynton will admire me for that? Do you think the court in *Nohl* will admire me for that?"

"Who cares if they admire you?" Cody said impatiently, but Lucy cut him off.

"I do! I care! I've worked hard to get people to see me the way they see my mother, and I don't want to be shown up for the fraud I am. Not again!"

Cody stared at her for a moment, his expression confused. "What do you mean *again*?" he asked at last. "What aren't you telling me, Lucy?"

Lucy turned away slightly, a strange suffocating feeling rising up in her chest. For a moment she kept her mouth clamped firmly shut. But all at once she realized how much she wanted to tell Cody, to get it out in the open.

"My father didn't kill Scanlon," she said abruptly. "I did."

"What do you mean?"

She took a deep breath. "It was me who threw the knife that killed him. Father just stepped in front of me to make it look like he did it. But everyone who was right there saw what really happened. Eamon, Jocelyn, Kincaid, Lord Henrik. My family. They all know."

For a moment there was silence. She snuck a glance at Cody, and saw him looking at her with a strange expression.

"You saved Benjy's life."

She shrugged. "I killed someone."

"In order to save your little brother's life."

Lucy just shrugged again, trying to keep her emotions in check.

"Why would you be ashamed of that, Lucy?" Cody's voice was incredulous. "Why would you regret using your skills in that situation?"

She sighed. "I don't regret it, exactly. Of course I'm glad that Benjy didn't die. But I wish it didn't have to be me. I wish it *had* been Father, and he obviously wishes that, too."

"Why do you assume that?"

"Why else did he take the blame?" Lucy asked dryly. "If he didn't think what I did was shameful?"

Cody was silent for a moment. "I don't think that's why he took the blame," he said at last. "But I can see why you would misunderstand. I imagine he was trying to protect you. Emotionally. I'm sure he wasn't ashamed of you." He furrowed his brow as he watched her. "Why didn't you tell me before now? You must have known I wouldn't be shocked. Far from it. I'm glad all our countless hours of extra training were put to such good use!"

Lucy raised a helpless shoulder. "I don't know. It's not that I thought you'd disapprove, of course not. I just didn't want to talk about it, I guess."

Cody frowned. "You've talked about it with someone, though, surely? Your mother?"

Lucy nodded. "Yes. She insisted on having a heart to heart conversation about it." She made a face. "That just made it worse."

"What do you mean?"

"I mean that she was full of sympathy and understanding. She agreed with you that I should be proud of having saved Benjy, not ashamed of having killed someone. But she said that she understood what I was feeling perfectly. She said that she had blood on her hands way too young, and she knows far too well the impact it has. The guilt, the darkness it brings into your heart. She said she never wanted that for me."

"And why did that make it worse?" asked Cody cautiously.

"Because!" Lucy raised her arms in a gesture of frustration. "She doesn't know what I really am! Even she would be disgusted if she knew what's in my heart. I wish I *had* felt guilty and horrified by what I'd done when I killed Scanlon. She told me about the first time she took someone's life, and how it ripped her apart. She seemed to think it must have been the hardest thing I'd ever done. And in some ways it was. But in another way it was easy. Way too easy. And I wasn't horrified because I felt guilty for killing him. I was horrified because I felt exposed! Because everyone saw how deadly I really am."

She paused, breathing hard, but Cody said nothing. He was watching her with confusion, clearly trying to make sense of her rambling thoughts.

"You don't understand, Cody," Lucy said wearily. "My mother thinks I'm like her—everyone does. And I've tried hard to live up to that. I look like her on the outside, and I want to be like her on the inside, too, I really do. She's strong and capable as well as beautiful. She knows how to defend herself, but she's not deadly like I am. I admire her for being willing to start the resistance, even when no one else in Nohl cared about the slaves. But she's a gentle spirit inside, you know she is. She's told me, lots of times, how much she hated the fighting, the bloodshed, the violence. She hated being put in the position of having to fight."

Lucy turned appealing eyes on Cody. "I'm not like that, Cody, not truly. Well, you know that better than anyone. Why do you think I want to keep our training secret from even my family? I don't want them to know what's really in my heart. I don't want them to know how much I *love* fighting. I love the feeling of power that comes with being deadly with a weapon, being stronger and faster than other people." She spread her arms wide. "What does that say about me? All my life I've wanted to be like my mother, but I'm not!" She shuddered. "From everything I've heard, I think I'm more like her father. More like her brother."

Cody listened to her tirade with a furrowed brow. When he spoke, he did so in his usual matter-of-fact way, no heat to his words.

"You haven't got the slightest clue what you're talking about."

Lucy raised an eyebrow. "Excuse me?"

"It was already obvious to me that you're at war with yourself over your particular abilities," said Cody, as if she hadn't spoken. "I mean, it was nothing but self-conscious foolishness to insist we keep our extra training secret. But I didn't see any harm in it. I figured you'd grow out of being embarrassed, and I thought it was more important to hone your natural talent than to argue with you about the strange form your vanity was taking. But I had no idea how deep the problem went." He sighed. "You're being ridiculous, but I suppose it won't fix anything for me to say so." His eyes narrowed thoughtfully. "I'll have to show you."

"What does that mean?" Lucy asked shortly. From anyone

else, she would have been offended at such an unflattering dismissal of her deepest, darkest insecurities. But from Cody it was strangely reassuring. He had always had a way of making every catastrophe seem manageable.

"It means we're training tomorrow, and I'm not taking no for an answer," he said simply. "Meet me in the castle courtyard just after dawn." He ran his eyes up and down her slim form, his expression clearly disapproving as he took in her immaculately fitted gown. "And don't come dressed like that."

"But Cody—"

He cut her off with a raised hand. "Just after dawn, Lucy. Don't be late."

And without giving her a chance to respond, he strode briskly from the room.

CHAPTER TEN

Lucy tapped her fingernails against the hilt of her dagger impatiently. The shadows blanketing the courtyard were only just beginning to soften with the gray light of dawn. She had given in to what she knew Cody wanted and had dressed in the leggings and tunic that were often worn by women in the forest community of Raldon. It was absurd to train in a gown, and she had a feeling Cody wouldn't go easy on her today. But she wasn't exactly eager for any of her new Balenan admirers—or critics—to see her dressed this way, and she was anxious to be gone from this very public meeting place.

"*Don't be late, Lucy,*" she muttered in a disgruntled way.

She took a deep breath, trying to dispel her grouchiness before Cody joined her. It wasn't really his fault she was so on edge. In all honesty, she was grateful to him for pushing her so hard. The truth was that it had been years since she had gone this long without training, and she was itching for the release of a good sparring session.

But she hadn't slept well, and her patience was consequently low. She had dreamed about Eamon again. This time her mind hadn't been assaulting her with happy memories of the past—she only wished it had. Instead the dream had been a tangled mess of memory and fiction. She had again watched the dagger plunge into the prince, only to realize with horror—and an even more horrifying twinge of vengeful satisfaction—that it had been her own hand that had thrown it.

The sight of him lying on the ground, blood pooling around a fatal wound, was nothing but the fabrication of an over-wrought mind. But the look in his eyes, the regret, the betrayal, the heartbreak, had been straight out of her memory. She had seen that look on his face a dozen times, most potently on the day he ordered the attack on Raldon.

"Ready to go?"

The soft voice made her jump, but she supposed she shouldn't be surprised. Cody had always been known for his ability to sneak around undetected. It had been his most valu-able skill in his rebel days, and was one of the many areas he had trained her in.

"I've been ready since dawn, as instructed," she said waspishly. "What took you so long, old man?"

Cody just grinned, heaving something further up his shoul-der. Lucy raised her eyebrows as she took in his burden.

"Bow and arrows? And did you bring me a sword?"

"We're going to cover a few bases today," Cody said placidly. "I assume you brought your dagger?"

"Would I be wearing this scandalous get up if I wasn't armed?" Lucy asked with a long-suffering sigh.

Cody snorted. "It covers much more of you than the Bale-nans' dresses."

"Ah yes, but it's not just about how much skin you can see," said Lucy sagely. "It's about the power of suggestion."

"Whatever," said Cody, starting across the courtyard. "That's more your area, so I'll take your word for it."

"Ah!" Lucy teased, as she followed close behind him. "So the master admits he needs training from the apprentice."

"I didn't admit any such thing. I'm interested in learning *useful* things."

"One day, Cody," said Lucy severely, "you'll meet a woman who you want to impress. And then you'll wish you'd paid more attention to these *useless* skills."

"Maybe," shrugged Cody, unconcerned. "But if I haven't been caught by now, it seems like I probably never will be. And," he added, his voice provocatively superior, "if I did meet someone I liked, I wouldn't come to a child like you for advice."

Lucy ignored the insult, well aware he was trying to rile her. It was actually quite a novelty for Cody to engage with her at all on such a frivolous topic. He wasn't wrong that this was more her area. Yet another way in which she couldn't measure up to her mother. The older woman's legendary beauty had turned her off anything that felt like flattery, making her disgusted by all the vanity and shallowness of court life. It was a well-known joke in the family that she hated being told she was beautiful.

But if Lucy was honest, she loved being complimented in such a way, just as she loved the excitement of appearing at a ball in a beautiful gown, knowing she would be almost universally admired. And she had been quite enticed by the idea of a position in court, the type of position her mother had been born to but had rejected. It wasn't that she had learned nothing from her warm-hearted mother—she had always made an effort not to play with anyone's heart. But that hadn't been difficult to resist, really. Not when she had been in love with one, and only one, admirer since she was about fourteen.

And she was back at Eamon. She redirected her thoughts resolutely to the conversation with Cody. She couldn't help but be amused by the total lack of emotion on the older man's face as he spoke about romance.

"If you haven't been 'caught'?" Lucy giggled, nudging Cody with an elbow as they walked. "You make it sound like slavery."

He grunted. "I know it isn't always like that," he acknowledged. "It's worked out well for your parents, for example. But Jonan did better than most, to land a wife like your mother. Someone who's more interested in adventure than in the cut of her dress. I mean, half the resistance were in love with her, after all." He grimaced. "Half the court were as well, but for all the wrong reasons."

Lucy gave Cody a long sideways look, a hint of anxiety surfacing in her mind as she surveyed his impassive countenance.

"Were *you* ever in love with my mother, Cody?" she asked, trying to make the question sound casual. She had wondered before now, but never had the nerve to ask.

Cody shot her a look of unaffected astonishment. "Me? In love with Scar?" He made an incredulous noise in his throat. "Of course not. I was still a child when she was running the resistance. Looking back now, I realize just how young and vulnerable she was, but to me she seemed like the most capable of adults. She was a legend to us—almost invincible. And in any event, by the time I was old enough to think about such things, she and Jonan were well and truly married." He grinned at her. "With a troublesome little nuisance on the way, probably."

Lucy nodded, satisfied. She looked around her at the waking city, realizing they had left the castle neighborhood behind some time before. "Where are you taking me, anyway?"

Cody's grin grew. "To see my world." He met her eyes, his look suddenly more serious. "Your mother's world."

Lucy quickened her step to match his, intrigued. "Do you mean the jungle?" She felt a thrill of excitement. The green canopy she could see over the city wall had been calling to her since she arrived. Would it feel similar to her beloved forest home?

Cody shook his head with a smile. "Not just the jungle." He stopped abruptly, and Lucy careened into his back before steadying herself. Cody gestured back toward the castle, still visible rising above the other buildings.

"All of that back there—the fancy titles, the luxury, the exalted company—that's all you've seen of Nohl so far. And I know that the royals are your mother's family, but we in the resistance knew her in a way they never did. That whole world... that wasn't her life, not really. You say you want to be like your mother, and that you have to curb your fighting instincts to achieve that. But you've got this picture in your head of a well-behaved noblewoman, forced by circumstances to get her hands dirty occasionally in helping a bunch of renegade slaves, but shying away from fighting whenever she could." He shook his head again. "But that's not the Scar I knew. That life was her mask, not her real self." His expression became stern. "And you're hiding yourself away almost as much as she did, but with nowhere near as good a reason."

Lucy was silent, unsure what to think as she followed his gaze back toward the castle, and the opulent life she had been immersed in since her arrival in Balenol.

"Come on, Luce," said Cody, and she could hear that the grin was back in his voice. "Let me show you the real Nohl."

And before she knew what he was about, he had taken off, sprinting through the grim gray streets. Lucy felt her heart lift at the release as she raced after him, trying to emulate the smooth and silent way he moved from shadow to disappearing shadow. It was easy to picture him as a young boy, slipping unseen through these same streets, nimble and catlike.

They reached the river in no time, turning south to follow along its banks until they reached the city wall. The huge wooden gate was closed, suspended over the rushing torrent, the water beating against its lower edge. Lucy gave a low whistle as she took in the ferocious speed of the current.

"My father really swam under that?"

"Well, I didn't see it myself," said Cody cheerfully. "But so he claims."

As they watched, the gate began to swing wide, indicating that the city of Nohl was open for business. In a few moments, Lucy could see the jungle crowding against the road beyond the gate. No one was waiting on the other side to come in—she could only suppose people avoided traveling through the jungle at night.

As soon as the way was clear, Cody strode forward confidently, heading for the smaller gate set into the stone wall next to the river. Clearly the path they were on continued on the other side of the wall.

"Halt, there. Who are you?" The guard's surprise was evident in both tone and expression as he took in Cody's obviously Kyonan form. Lucy wondered when the man had last seen a Kyonan. Not since the slave era, probably.

Cody raised an eyebrow. "I thought interrogation was usually for people coming into the city, not going out of it."

"We're members of the Kyonan delegation here for His Majesty's coronation," cut in Lucy quickly. Diplomacy wasn't Cody's strongest area, and she had no desire to spend the morning in the dungeons waiting for rescue by someone official.

The guard's eyes flicked to her, widening visibly as he took in her unusual garb. She resisted the urge to tug on her tunic.

"But you're not Kyonan," he said bluntly.

Lucy sighed. "I am, actually." She tried to keep the irritation out of her voice at the maddeningly familiar comment. "But my mother is Balenan. I'm related to the royal family." With any luck, that would be enough to get him to leave them alone.

The guard paused, clearly piecing together who she was. But he was still suspicious, his eyes lingering on the weapons still slung across Cody's back.

"What's your business outside the city?"

"Hunting," said Cody impassively.

The man narrowed his eyes for a moment, but didn't seem able to think of a reason to actually detain them. He waved them through, his eyes following them as they walked quickly down the path. Lucy barely noticed his scrutiny, she was so intrigued by the thick jungle rising up right alongside them. It was a still day, and no breeze stirred the palm fronds dangling over the path. She felt as though her hand should be able to slice through the air, it was so thick. The hum of insects, and the throaty trill of unfamiliar birdsong reached out from the trees, as though drawing her in.

"That's what we get for taking the gate like honest citizens," grumbled Cody, clearly still disgruntled about the guard's interference. "We should've gone under the wall." His tone turned musing. "I wonder if the tunnel is still intact?"

"The tunnel?" repeated Lucy, distracted from her contemplation of the foliage. "There's a tunnel?"

"Of course there's a tunnel." Cody flashed her a grin. "Do you think we could just stroll through the gate like that in our resistance days? We had all the trappings of a secret rebel band." He chuckled. "We couldn't all get away with swimming under the barrier like reckless idiots."

Lucy grinned back, not offended by this comment on her father. He would be the first to acknowledge his tendency toward recklessness.

"Well, if you had all the trappings, I hope that means you're taking me to a secret rebel lair deep in the jungle."

"Not that deep," said Cody cheerfully. "Scar had to be able to get back and forth easily within a night, so that her dear old father wouldn't find out she'd been gone. We should get there within half an hour, if you don't slow me down too much."

Lucy gasped. "Really? You're going to take me to—"

But Cody didn't wait to hear the rest of her question. A glance behind had revealed that they were now out of sight of the city wall, thanks to a bend in the road, and he dove off the path without preamble.

"Only if you can keep up!" he called back over his shoulder.

Lucy plunged after him, her eyes glinting with excitement at the prospect of visiting an abandoned rebel base. But first, she intended to make Cody eat his words about her slowing him down. She had grown up in a forest, after all, and she wasn't hampered by skirts right now. How hard could it be to keep pace with him?

She soon discovered her error. This jungle was nothing like her well-known Forest of Rune. She hadn't thought it possible, but the air was even hotter and thicker under the canopy, and sweat was soon trickling down her face. The strange cries and endless buzzing sounds were unnerving, coming at her from all sides.

But none of this was what made it so hard to keep up with Cody. The undergrowth in the jungle made the forest brush back home seem like a few harmless twigs. Lucy could barely see the ground here—ground which was squelchy and thick, despite the couple of days since the last rain—and the under-growth was often as high as her hips. It was more like wading through a swamp than running through a forest. She tried not to think about the critters that might be concealed in the foliage, and was glad her legs were fully covered in her leggings, rather than exposed under skirts.

She soon realized that Cody was playing with her, going just slowly enough that she could generally keep him in sight, but never allowing her to fully catch her breath. The challenge was invigorating though—she pushed herself harder, relishing the freedom of not wearing skirts, of not being under scrutiny.

She had just forced her way through a particularly stubborn patch of undergrowth when she realized that she hadn't seen Cody in a minute or so. She looked up, scanning the area suspiciously.

"Cody?" she called.

There was no answer. She moved more warily, sacrificing speed for finesse as she picked her way forward. So he wanted to play that game, did he? After another careful look around her, she bent low, trying to apply the tracking skills she had learned in her own forest to the quagmire that was this jungle.

Just as she thought she'd found his tracks, she leaped back in alarm at a whizzing sound near her ear. Her blade was already in her hand as she heard the inevitable thud. She stared for a moment at the arrow buried in a mossy tree trunk less than a foot from her. Recreating the whizzing sound in her mind, she sent her gaze along what she thought the arrow's trajectory must have been. Sure enough, Cody was sitting comfortably halfway up a nearby tree, making no effort at concealment as he watched her.

"What was that for?" she asked, exasperated.

Cody ignored the question. "I saw your mother do that once," he said calmly. "Except she hit her mark. Took the soldier right through the chest. He was dead by the time he hit the ground."

The casual declaration was met by a prolonged silence. Lucy had no idea what to say as she struggled to picture it.

"He was guarding a group of slaves from the logging camp, who were supposed to be foraging in the jungle. We attempted to liberate them cleanly, but it went wrong. We got two of the three, but one was left behind with the soldier. We knew perfectly well that their orders were to kill the slaves before allowing them to be liberated, so at that point it was the soldier or the slave. Scar didn't hesitate. She lured them—the slave and the soldier—into a boggy area. The moment the man pulled his weapon on his captive, she took him out."

Lucy looked again at the arrow still embedded in the tree trunk. She had seen her mother spar, lots of times, but it had always been for training. It had seemed like a game, somehow. Even in the attack on Raldon several months before, she had fought only defensively, inflicting nothing more than minor injuries. It was hard to picture her actually killing someone.

"That sounds..." she trailed off, her thoughts in a jumble.

"Ruthless?" Cody finished for her.

She nodded.

"She was ruthless," he said calmly. "She had to be. We were in a war, and she was one of our main commanders. You think she just led information-gathering patrols, or handed out blankets to rescued slaves? You should know her better than to think she'd hesitate to risk her own safety, or that she'd hide behind others when the task was unpleasant. Whatever the resistance was doing, you could be sure she'd be in the thick of it."

His eyes took on a reminiscent gleam as he gazed unseeingly into the forest canopy. "Poor Raldo lived in a constant state of stress as a result. He didn't say it, but we all knew he was terrified she'd get herself killed."

Lucy remained silent. She had heard many stories of Raldo, the well-respected resistance leader who had been executed after sacrificing himself to save both of her parents. She had an affection for him, even, as the namesake of her beloved forest settlement. But like her mother's rebel past, he had always seemed more legend than fact. Somehow, here in the jungle where the whole story had unfolded, quite a lot of things were feeling much more real than they ever had before.

"Come on," said Cody, swinging himself down from the tree

to land with a soft thump. "If you want me to take you to the base tree, you have to lift your game. No way I'm leading you there with you leaving tracks like that behind you." He gestured back the way they'd come, indicating the clearly visible trail left by Lucy's blundering progress through the undergrowth.

Lucy looked at Cody in some amusement. "No one's following us, Cody. There are no enemies trying to find the base, not anymore."

Cody met her eyes, his own expression serious. "You don't know that for certain. I didn't survive by taking risks based on assumptions. Whenever you don't have all the information—which is always—the best approach is caution."

Lucy thought of the two near-fatal incidents that had befallen King Giles in the lead up to his coronation, and she realized Cody was right. She couldn't be certain there was no enemy at work in Nohl.

She lowered her gaze, chastised. "I don't know how to move stealthily in this terrain," she admitted with unusual humility.

"I know," said Cody, his voice more gentle. "I'll teach you."

She nodded, determined to be a good student. They began to move again, much more slowly this time, Cody making no attempt to outdistance her. Cody was as patient a teacher as he had always been, and Lucy paid close attention to everything he told her.

It was well over the estimated half an hour that she followed Cody carefully through the jungle. But at last he pulled up in front of her, his little intake of breath betraying that even her usually stoic mentor was overcome by the significance of the moment.

"What is it?" Lucy asked eagerly, looking up. All she could see in front of her was a massive tree, one of many, but notice-ably larger than its immediate neighbors. Its branches formed a canopy above them, and a tangled mess of vines covered its trunk. It was an impressive specimen, now she looked at it, but she wouldn't have marked it as anything unusual if Cody hadn't stopped right in front of it.

"We're here," said Cody, sounding almost emotional. "This is it. The base tree."

CHAPTER ELEVEN

Lucy gazed with renewed interest at the enormous tree. Another legend becoming reality in front of her. She turned to Cody, and he smiled at the excitement in her eyes.

"Come on. Let's see what's left."

She followed him eagerly as he started toward the tree. She couldn't see an opening, but Cody seemed sure of his direction. Lucy watched in fascination as he pulled out a blade, quickly hacking his way through a section of vine growing up the tree's trunk.

But once the vine was gone, Lucy still found herself staring in confusion at the bark of the tree underneath. She opened her mouth to ask if Cody was sure it was the right tree, when he pressed right up to the trunk and stepped sideways. Lucy gasped in spite of herself as he disappeared into a fissure that had not been visible from her angle, even without the clinging vines.

She hurried after him, pausing only for a moment before sliding herself into the long vertical slit in his wake. She shuddered as she felt spiderwebs brushing against her face, but it didn't slow her down. Within moments she emerged into what felt like a large, open space. It was too dim inside for her to make anything out clearly, but she could hear Cody moving around nearby.

She stood still near the opening, waiting patiently for her eyes to adjust to the lower light. Sunlight filtered through the way they had come, and from other slits elsewhere in the space. Before long, she was able to make out the proportions of the tree's hollowed-out interior. It was a large space, but not as large as she had expected. It was certainly cunningly hidden by nature, but Lucy could think of several problems sure to arise from any attempt to hide a significant number of people inside for any length of time.

As her vision improved, she could see Cody several feet ahead of her, kneeling on the packed earth, and sweeping his hand through the carpet of rotting leaves and detritus that covered the space. Lucy moved toward him cautiously, swiping her hand in front of her face as she went, pushing aside the spiderwebs that seemed to crisscross the whole area.

"Here we go," said Cody cheerfully, his voice strangely muffled in the enclosed space.

Kneeling beside him, Lucy realized that he had uncovered a square wooden trapdoor. There was no handle that she could see.

"How did you lift it up?" she asked curiously.

"We did it from inside," Cody explained, using a small blade to dig around the edges of the door as he spoke. "It was designed to be difficult to find, and difficult to open from outside even if you did find it." Having cleared the cracks around the door, he started wedging the blade in firmly, to use it as a lever. "The resistance used this base, but it was here before we existed. It was a hideout of the jungle nomads. Survivors from the first resistance, a couple hundred years ago."

Lucy nodded, well familiar with the story. "The one led by

Alben the Liberator. The one that died out when they all tried to escape back across the sea and the ships all sank. That was when they found out about the curse keeping slaves from returning to Kyona."

"That's right," said Cody, grunting as he wiggled the blade back and forth. "Alben's resistance might have died out, but the people didn't all die out. There were a bunch of survivors, and some of them ended up escaping into the jungle and somehow surviving out here. That's who Raldo was descended from, actually."

"Yes," said Lucy absently, her eyes on Cody's progress. The trapdoor was starting to budge. "I remember Mother telling me that he was never actually a slave. Just his ancestors were."

"Got it!" Cody cried triumphantly as the wooden square lifted. His little bounce of excitement made him seem more like a boy than a grown man, and Lucy restrained a smile.

Cody flung the door wide, but his enthusiasm took a sudden check as he looked down into the blackness of the hole beneath.

"What is it?" Lucy asked anxiously, drawing slightly back from the edge. If something was making Cody nervous, she wanted to be far away from it.

"Nothing," said Cody, an unreadable look on his face. "It's just so strange. I've never seen it dark like this before. There was always light—there were always people. We used to tap out a rhythm on the door, and whoever was on duty would open it. And Raldo would be in there, or Scar, or Stan...someone ready to receive a report, or give us a mission. There was always food—nothing to write home about, of course, but still. There was always a welcome."

Lucy remained silent, trying to respect the significance of the moment for her companion. It wasn't like Cody to wax nostalgic, but she could imagine how surreal this experience must be for him. He had seemed so casual in agreeing to her parents' request that he accompany Lucy and Matheus on the delegation, that it was easy to forget that he was the only one of the whole group who was not coming to Balenol for the first time. He was returning to his childhood home, one which had all manner of mixed memories. And Lucy was well aware that her own presence beside him did little to change the reality that he was returning alone to the place of his community.

"Well, come on," said Cody, after another moment's contemplation. "Lights aren't going to spring on if we wait here long enough." Without further hesitation, he lowered himself confidently into the blackness of the hole. A soft thud told Lucy that his feet had hit some kind of wooden surface.

"Ha!" he shouted a moment later, his tone triumphant. "There's still a torch here. Maybe I can..." His voice trailed off as he rummaged in his supplies, and soon Lucy could hear the sound of a flint striking. After several attempts, Cody succeeded in lighting the torch.

Lucy closed her eyes momentarily against the sudden blaze of light. But when she opened them again, she felt her excitement building at the sight of the underground base stretching before her. She hastened to follow Cody down onto the wooden platform, trying to stay close to him and the sole light as she followed him down a set of rickety wooden stairs onto the wide surface below.

Cody moved confidently through the dim space, and in a short time, a number of other torches had blazed to life, illuminating the abandoned chamber. Lucy gazed around her in silent amazement. It was a surreal sight. The dust and decay of two decades lay on every surface, but she could still get a sense of what the room had been. And it clearly hadn't been touched since the departure of its former inhabitants.

"You left in a hurry," she said softly, running a hand over a wooden table, noting the bowls still scattered across it.

"We did," said Cody, a touch of humor in his voice. "Once we felt the curse break, it was all Stan and the others could do to keep people from running straight to the harbor. It was weeks between then and when we actually left, and no one wanted to prolong our departure when the opportunity finally came."

He wandered over to a corner of the space, sweeping a layer of dust from the surface of a carved bench with a casual hand. "This was where your mother and the other leaders used to sit, when exchanging reports and giving instructions. This is where they planned their attacks, too." He smiled reminiscently. "I was always trying to hover close enough to overhear their plans, hoping they'd decide I was finally old enough to fight as well as scout." His expression turned rueful. "They never did."

Lucy followed him across the room, trying to picture her mother as a young Cody had known her—no older than Lucy herself, but leading a large and effective slave resistance right from the heart of the court.

"Tell me more," she said suddenly. "About what my mother was really like back then."

Cody smiled, clearly pleased with her interest. "She was unstoppable. She was lethal with a weapon, but more compassionate than anyone I'd ever met." He turned, looking Lucy in the eye. "Honestly, Lucy, she was a lot like you are. You see her sweetness, and I'm glad. But she can be calculating and hard headed, too. I know you don't like to think of yourself as deadly, but you are. And you get that from her."

He smiled grimly. "And yes, on some level I think that wily side of her came from her father. But for you to say that you're like the Overseer at heart because you like the rush that comes from being a skilled fighter..." He shrugged. "Well, I shouldn't be surprised, I suppose. I guess that's just the kind of idiotic thing I would expect from you in one of your moments of identity crisis. But it bears no connection to reality."

Lucy frowned, but not because she was offended by his uncomplimentary characterization of her opinions. She could never really take offense at Cody—he was always blunt, but he never spoke in malice. She frowned because she was deep in thought, trying to reconcile his comments with her own perceptions.

"Sure, the Overseer also liked the feeling of power," Cody was continuing. "And he used to beat children as a way to reinforce that power. Plus beheading unwary victims for fabricated acts of 'insubordination' was a regular form of entertainment for him."

Cody shook his head. "He was a rotten apple, Lucy. The only reason you imagine for a moment you're like him at heart is because your life has been sheltered and happy. The truth is you can't even begin to comprehend the darkness that was in his heart."

Lucy was silent for a moment, mulling it all over. "Do you really think that's true?" she asked seriously. "That I'm nothing like he was? That my...lethal instincts are a good thing?"

For a second Cody looked exasperated, but he didn't speak. His expression gave no warning of his intention, but Lucy's instincts—honed by Cody's extensive training—kicked in the moment Cody's hand moved. By the time his blade was up, her own was in position, blocking him.

Cody grinned. "Do you really think that instinct is a bad thing? Why would anyone not want to be good at defending themselves?" His expression turned serious. "Not to mention defending others." He raised a challenging eyebrow. "Others like Benjy."

"Of course being able to defend people is a good thing," Lucy admitted, disengaging her blade from Cody's with a practiced flick of her wrist. She stepped back, but Cody immediately followed, and she was forced to once again intercept his attack. "But that's not the same as enjoying the fight. My mother is good at defending herself and others. But nothing you say will convince me that she likes fighting."

She was panting by the end of her speech, Cody pressing her hard enough to make her persist in her focus, but not enough to really challenge her.

"True," Cody acknowledged. "But maybe she doesn't get quite the same thrill because she's not actually as good a fighter as you are."

Lucy grinned in spite of herself, waiting for Cody to relax his posture in response before she dropped into a sudden roll. The motion took her under his outstretched arm. She sprung to her feet behind him, her blade pressed against the back of his neck before he'd had time to turn.

"Maybe."

Cody chuckled, still not facing her. "Not bad for the belle of the court, but you wouldn't survive a day in the resistance at that speed. I could see that move coming a mile off."

Lucy snorted, pulling her blade away from his neck but keeping it raised in a fighting stance. "Is that why you hadn't turned in time to block me?"

"I was taking pity on you," said Cody outrageously, turning around at last. "Trying to give your bruised ego a little boost."

"That would be a first," said Lucy dryly.

Cody chuckled again, before he lunged forward. Lucy met his attack with enthusiasm, determined to best him again and make him admit her prowess. The thud of their feet on the packed earth of the floor and the metallic clash of their weapons were muffled strangely, absorbed by the enclosing walls of their unusual training ground.

For several minutes they sparred, blades flashing in the firelight, Cody's familiar chuckle sounding every time Lucy pulled off a move that particularly pleased him. Lucy felt her own spirits soar with the release. The weeks since her last training session with Cody felt more like years, and in the moment she couldn't imagine why she had been so reluctant to spar during that time. It was the most invigorating feeling.

"Enough," Cody said abruptly, pulling back and wiping a hand across his brow.

Lucy stepped back as well, panting and trying to wipe the sweat off her own face in a surreptitious way. She had been so caught up in the fight she had forgotten to complain internally about the stiflingly moist air, but it was certainly making her tire more quickly than an equivalent training session would have back home.

"You're excellent with a blade, Lucy," said Cody fairly. "I don't deny it. But that's really only effective if someone comes at you with a knife."

He picked up the extra sword he had brought along and tossed it through the air. Caught off guard, Lucy recovered her focus only just in time to catch the larger blade by the hilt and avoid injuring herself.

"It's at least as likely that an opponent would be armed with a sword," Cody continued. "And let's be honest—your swordplay could use some work."

Lucy grimaced in acknowledgment of the observation. She sheathed her familiar dagger in a swift motion, bringing the sword up in front of her without loss of time. She knew how Cody trained, and she had long ago learned not to expect fair warning.

Sure enough, Cody was on her before she could blink, and it took her full focus just to hold off his blade. She threw herself into the familiar activity, once again forgetting about the heat, her inner conflict, everything. There was only the moment, the clang of metal, the scuffling of feet, the thrill that came with a well-executed parry. She could almost have laughed aloud. When she wasn't in the heat of a fight, she might wish she didn't enjoy it so much. But when she was sparring, none of that mattered.

Cody kept her training for what felt like hours, never letting her rest long enough between bouts, never failing to take advantage of any time she lowered her guard. He was the better swordsman, and he was clearly holding back for the sake of her learning. But he was pushing her hard enough to keep her constantly on her toes.

"All right," he said at last, lowering his blade. "That's enough with the swords for today." Lucy kept hers raised for another wary moment, in case it was a trick of some kind. Cody loved trying to catch her off guard. As much as she complained to him about it, it was part of what made him such an effective teacher.

But when Cody actually sheathed his sword, Lucy copied the motion, breathing a sigh of relief. "I'll never be able to match you with a sword, Cody," she said, craning her neck from side to side in an attempt to relieve the tension. "You're just too much taller and too much stronger."

"True," said Cody matter-of-factly, no hint of gloating in his tone. "But you're good, Lucy. And you can always improve. If you reached your full potential, you'd be able to hold your own against most people."

Lucy didn't respond, looking again around the dimly lit space. "It's strange," she said softly. "Being here, seeing it in real life. It's not like I imagined."

"Well, this isn't exactly what it used to look like," said Cody fairly. "This is just a ghost of the base it used to be."

Lucy wandered toward the far side of the room, still drawing in deep breaths as her heart rate slowed to a more normal pace. "It must have been pretty claustrophobic, especially with lots of people inside."

"I guess so," said Cody with a shrug. "You get used to it. And the slave barracks were worse." His eyes followed her progress across the space, noting that she was examining a hollow area carved into one wall. Cushions were still visible, although years of decay had eroded their original shape. "That was Raldo's place," Cody explained, his voice holding no particular emotion.

Lucy looked up, surprised. "Raldo actually lived here?"

"More or less. He did go back and forth to other nomad settlements, but he was here most of the time. He preferred to stay close to Nohl. Mainly to keep an eye on Scar, I think." Cody nodded toward the cushions. "He used to sleep there a lot."

Lucy stared down at the cramped little living space, a wave of sadness washing over her at the hardships of the life so many of her countrymen had been forced to lead. One of the cushions was starting to fall apart, and she frowned as she glimpsed something underneath it. Reaching down, she unearthed a small leather journal.

"What's that?" asked Cody curiously, his voice suddenly right behind her. Lucy had to fight not to jump.

"I don't know," she said. "It was under one of the cushions." She turned the volume over in her hands. "It looks like a journal. Maybe it was his."

Cody frowned. "It's hard to imagine Raldo keeping a journal, somehow." He gestured with his head. "Have a look inside and find out."

"It's not..." Lucy hesitated. "It's not invading his privacy or something?"

Cody snorted. "He's been dead for twenty years, Lucy. I don't think he'll mind."

With a shrug, Lucy flipped open the journal, moving toward one of the torches Cody had lit. "It's a journal," she confirmed. "But I don't think it was Raldo's." She squinted at the page. "I can't see his name anywhere."

"Is there a date?"

"Uhh…" Lucy thumbed through the pages, back to the front. "Yes." She showed the first entry to Cody, and he leaned in for a better look.

"Much too early to be Raldo's," he said thoughtfully. He tilted his head to the side as he calculated. "That's more like Alben's era. A bit after, perhaps." He waved a hand. "What does it say?"

Lucy cleared her throat, still feeling strange to be reading someone else's journal. But she read the first entry obediently.

I have returned to Balenol, and my heart is too heavy to carry everything inside it. I think I will write it all down, to see if this little book will take some of the burden for me. Although at the moment, it just makes it worse. The journal was a gift from her, after all, and she was the one who taught me to read and write.

I'm in the jungle. I should be grateful. Considering how long I was away, I've been lucky to meet up with some of the other survivors of the terrible shipwreck disaster.

Lucy looked up with a gasp of understanding. "This was written by one of the slaves who was part of Alben's resistance! One of the ones who survived when the ships all sank because the curse was preventing the slaves from sailing back across the sea, to Kyona!"

"Yes, thank you Lucy," said Cody dryly. "I'd figured that much out."

Lucy rolled her eyes, returning her gaze to the words on the page.

WE MAY NOT HAVE BEEN SWALLOWED by the sea, but if we survive like this, stranded in this jungle, it will be more than I bargain for. Perhaps these pathetic scribblings will be all that's left of me in a month.

The others in our little group have confirmed what I feared. Alben was captured when the ships went down, and executed immediately. They say he saved a great many from the water first, some of whom are here, having escaped into the jungle.

But that's small comfort. The resistance is dead. It's over.

I don't know if others escaped into Thorania like we did. There must have been more, but we didn't come across any. Some of the others here can't believe that having made it into Thorania, I turned around and came back to Balenol by choice. But I couldn't stay—I couldn't bear to watch what was happening.

The problem isn't that I returned to Balenol. It's that I returned without Isidore. I don't know how to recover from that. But it's too close—I don't wish to write about it. My heart will have to carry that burden by itself for a bit longer.

"IT'S SIGNED 'HAYDN,'" said Lucy, reaching the end of the entry.

Cody frowned. "Never heard of him. Bit of a downer, wasn't he?"

Lucy didn't answer. Something about the despair of this long-gone rebel touched her heart, and she felt unexpectedly moved. She was also intrigued by the mention of slaves escaping into Thorania. That was what Eamon and Jocelyn were going to the neighboring kingdom to investigate, after all. Maybe they would be interested in any information this journal might offer.

"Come on," said Cody, turning away from Raldo's former

space. "I didn't bring this bow for decoration. Let's get back up to the surface and work on your archery."

"All right," said Lucy absently, waiting to make sure Cody wasn't watching before slipping the leather book into a pocket of her leggings. The older man's curiosity might not be roused, but Lucy wanted to know more of this Haydn.

CHAPTER TWELVE

The afternoon was well advanced before they slipped back through the gate into Nohl. The guard on duty was different, but it was clear to Lucy that he had been looking out for them. He didn't challenge their entry, but he watched their approach closely, and before they were within earshot he muttered instructions to a nearby boy who took off in the direction of the castle. Lucy's heart sank as any hope of remaining inconspicuous in her training gear disappeared.

But in fact their trip through the bustling city was uneventful. People stared at Lucy as she passed in her strange getup, but she didn't see any faces she recognized. On their way back through the jungle, Cody had glimpsed a jungle pig through the foliage and had very sensibly brought it down with an arrow, to support his story that he had taken Lucy to the jungle for the purpose of hunting. The royals would surely think it was strange that the Kyonan had taken it upon himself to provide meat for the well-stocked castle, but they probably thought all the Kyonans were strange anyway.

When they entered the castle courtyard, Lucy picked up the pace, eager to reach the sanctuary of her own chamber. She had been deeply impacted by what Cody had shown her and told her about her mother's former life, and there was a lot to think about. But that didn't mean she was ready to publicly embrace an identity as a fighter, and she wanted to change back into a gown before seeing anyone she knew.

She parted ways with Cody in the entranceway, hurrying up the broad steps and wincing as she caught a few startled looks from well-dressed locals. She had almost reached her room when she heard a door open nearby and was hailed by a familiar voice.

"Lucy! There you are. Come in for a moment."

Lucy changed direction with a sigh, hurrying into Jocelyn's suite instead of her own. At least it was still out of sight of curious servants and critical courtiers. She barely restrained a groan when she entered the room. She should have realized that Kincaid would likely be there, but she hadn't expected both Eamon and Matheus to also be present, as well as Lord and Lady Rodanthe. She was suddenly acutely aware that she needed to wash after her extensive training session.

Kincaid looked surprised by her attire, and Lady Rodanthe pursed her lips slightly, but Jocelyn, Eamon, and Matheus all greeted her without comment, clearly too distracted by other matters to note that her clothes were out of place. It was a testament to how normal it was for women in Raldon to dress in such a fashion.

"Where have you been all day, Lucy?" asked Jocelyn. "Lady Rodanthe said Cody told her he was taking you out of the city early this morning, but I thought you'd be back hours ago."

"As did I," chimed in Lady Rodanthe, her gaze shrewd as it rested on Lucy.

"That's right, I was with Cody," said Lucy, not elaborating. She thought she saw Eamon's brows draw together slightly, but she ignored him.

"Anyway," Jocelyn hurried on, "we're just talking about what we're going to do about our...situation."

"By situation do you mean the assassination attempt?" Lucy asked.

"Yes," sighed Jocelyn. "There's no denying that the whole fiasco has put us in a difficult position. Eamon and I are trying to figure out whether we should delay our departure for Thorania. We're supposed to be leaving in a couple of days, and traveling with the Thoranian delegation on their trip back to Thirl."

"It is difficult," said Lord Rodanthe heavily, his eyes troubled as they rested on Eamon's injury. "I will not deny that I am extremely alarmed by this incident. Honestly, I wonder if we should simply return to Kyona immediately."

"Absolutely not," said Eamon flatly. "We came here to treat with the Thoranians, and we're going to do just that. Besides," he added, his voice dry, "if the whole delegation flees the kingdom immediately after my guard attacked King Giles..."

"It makes Kyona appear guilty of an attempted assassination, yes," Lord Rodanthe acknowledged. Lucy had to feel for the man. He looked more stressed than she had ever seen him as he visibly weighed the risk of further injury to Eamon or another of his charges against the risk of war between Kyona and Balenol. "Nevertheless, I am not eager to linger in Balenol," the nobleman said at last. "As we have been saying, our safest and least suspicious course is probably to continue on to Thorania as scheduled."

"The trouble is," Jocelyn explained to Lucy, "we don't like to leave while the guard's fate is...unresolved. But we're also especially eager not to overstay our welcome, given...well, everything."

Kincaid cleared his throat. "Do you think it's worth trying to...you know, persuade the king not to execute the guard until we return from our visit to Thorania?" His eyes flicked to the Kyonan courtiers before returning to his wife.

"It's all right," she said quietly. "You can speak freely."

"In that case," Kincaid said, looking meaningfully between Jocelyn and Eamon, "surely either one of you could convince the king if you tried."

Lucy raised an eyebrow. "If you mean what I think you mean, isn't that a bit dishonorable?"

Kincaid shrugged. "I don't see why. Joss and Eamon's power isn't a bad thing. Not if they're using it for a good cause. It's an extremely useful asset, actually. And we shouldn't waste it."

Lucy frowned, surprised by the thoughtful rather than confused looks on Lord and Lady Rodanthe's faces. The Kyonan king and queen must trust the noble couple more than she realized. But in all honesty, Lucy was equally surprised by the Valorian prince's casual reference to his wife's unnatural magic ability. She would have thought it would unnerve him a little more, but he spoke as placidly as if he was commenting on Jocelyn's hair color.

She glanced at Eamon, and she thought he looked uncomfortable. It must be strange for him to have his power, for most of his life such a closely guarded secret, discussed so openly.

But Jocelyn showed no such discomfort—presumably she was used to Kincaid's perspective on her abilities. The princess sighed.

"I'm not against the idea of using my power to save the poor man from execution—at least until we figure out for sure whether he was acting of his own free will. But it's a diplomatic quagmire to use our magic on a foreign monarch."

"Just what I was thinking, Your Highness," Lord Rodanthe said approvingly, looking relieved at Jocelyn's words.

"Except King Giles doesn't know about your power, does he?" Kincaid argued. "No one here does. He certainly didn't seem to notice yesterday when Eamon used his power to convince him that Kyona was not behind the attack."

Jocelyn quirked an amused eyebrow at her husband. "You caught that, did you? You're getting better at detecting it."

Kincaid grinned. "My mountain blood does come in handy every once in a while."

Lucy frowned as she thought back over the conversation in the antechamber. She remembered how convincing, how infallible Eamon had suddenly seemed when reassuring the king. That had all been magic?

A strange chill passed over her. It was maddening—and alarming—that she had been unable to detect it. But why would she? She had no mountain people in her ancestry, and none of the blood of Kyona's royal house of Dragonfriend ran in her veins, either. Her heritage was nothing but a murky mix of enemy kingdoms. Her frown deepened into a scowl.

"Well, I think it's unconscionable," she said curtly.

There was a moment of silence, as everyone searched for a response to her unnecessarily sharp comment. Lady Rodanthe's eyebrows were furrowed as she looked at Lucy, as though she was torn between disapproving of her tone, and wondering if she was actually right.

"Well," said Jocelyn at last, clearly deciding to take a diplomatic approach. "Maybe it won't be necessary."

Lucy didn't miss the look that passed between the twins, the one that said they would discuss the matter further in privacy. She drew in a breath, trying to rein in her disproportionate reaction. If she wasn't careful, her outbursts would achieve nothing but having the royals shut her out of their strategic discussions next time.

Lord Rodanthe took over the conversation then, discussing practicalities of the visit to Thorania.

"Where did Cody take you?" Matheus asked her curiously, letting the conversation flow around them.

"To the jungle," she replied, her eyes gleaming as she remembered all she had seen. "It was incredible."

She suddenly felt guilty that they hadn't invited Matheus. He had just as much right to learn about their mother's past as she did, and she knew Cody had only excluded him because of her insistence that they do their training in private.

"We have to go together next time," she said, promising silently to repair the omission. "He showed me the rebel base."

"Really?" Matheus said, eagerness in his voice. "You have to take me there, too! Was it amazing?"

"It was," she said, pausing. "But also unsettling." She shook her head. "And hot. I need to wash before dinner."

Matheus looked like he wanted to question her more about what she had seen, but she made good her escape without giving him the chance. She was still trying to decide what she thought about it all, and didn't want to unpack her reflections for her brother.

By the time dinner was served, Lucy was clean and composed and once again dressed in a gown, one of her least conspicuous ones. But it was evident from the moment she entered the dining hall that she was the focus of a great deal of attention, and not the kind she liked.

It took all of her carefully cultivated grace to keep the flush from her cheeks as whispers and stares followed her all the way up to her seat. She didn't stop to talk to anyone, sliding straight into a chair next to Cody. But if anything, the muttering increased. It only quietened when King Giles stood, formally welcoming the visitors once again and opening the meal. This was no private royal family dinner. Much of the court was in attendance, and the dining hall felt almost as crowded as the ballroom had done at the gala.

"What's going on?" Lucy asked Cody quietly, as servers began to bring food around.

The Kyonan man looked at her in surprise. "What do you mean?"

"I mean everyone is staring and muttering!"

"Are they?" Cody glanced around, clearly not concerned. "Maybe they're jealous of your gown or something."

"No, that's definitely not—" Lucy cut herself off with a sigh. There was absolutely no point trying to have this conversation with Cody.

She glanced over to where Jocelyn was sitting, and caught her friend watching her. Jocelyn smiled in greeting, but not quickly enough to hide the anxious look that had been on her face a moment before.

Lucy felt her stomach drop uncomfortably. Jocelyn knew something she didn't. Although as she scanned the room, noting the many eyes still scrutinizing her, she wondered if perhaps she did know. Her heart sank. If only she could have slipped into the castle by a back entrance that afternoon.

The meal crawled by. The moment people began to move about, Lucy slipped away from her seat, taking a chair next to Jocelyn. She had noticed Lady Rodanthe's eyes on her fairly often, but she would much rather hear whatever it was from Jocelyn.

"Tell me, Joss," she said flatly.

Jocelyn sighed, and Lucy couldn't help but notice that Kincaid, sitting on his wife's other side, hurriedly engaged his neighbor in conversation, looking uncomfortable.

"I've caused some kind of a scandal by wearing my forest clothes earlier, haven't I?"

Jocelyn sighed again. "It wasn't just the clothes, although I think that was enough to set some of the loose tongues wagging." She rolled her eyes. "Ridiculous, isn't it? Considering what they wear here."

"I knew it was a bad idea to go out in public in—" Lucy cut off her bitter thoughts, apprehension rising within her as she ran through Jocelyn's words in her mind. "What do you mean it wasn't just that, though?"

Jocelyn glanced over Lucy's shoulder, and with a supreme effort of will Lucy stopped herself from following her friend's gaze. She had no desire to meet any of the judgmental eyes fixed on her.

"Apparently word spread that you spent the day out in the jungle with Cody."

Jocelyn waited for a response. When Lucy's face remained blank, the princess grimaced apologetically before adding, "With just Cody."

"Oh." Mortification battled in Lucy's mind with an absurd desire to laugh. It was Cody, after all.

"Yes," said Jocelyn, sounding like she found it as stupid as Lucy did. "And dressed...well, scandalously according to local custom."

Lucy groaned. "Surely people can't think—" But again she cut herself off. She knew exactly what people could think if they were so inclined. If only they *had* invited Matheus. It hadn't even occurred to her to take a chaperone—such considerations had been the last thing on her mind. Honestly, she had been surprised even to learn that Cody had told Lady Rodanthe of their intended trip. She was certain he had been thinking only of issues of security when he had done so. But Lucy should have foreseen something like this.

"It's stupid, I know," said Jocelyn soothingly. "And I know it's uncomfortable to be talked about by malicious gossipers. Believe me, I know. But what does it really matter in the end? Anyone who was looking for something to criticize was always going to find it, no matter what we did. The king wants good relations with Kyona and Valoria, and that's what we really came to ensure."

Lucy was silent for a moment. That might have been why Jocelyn and Eamon came. But she and Matheus had come for more personal reasons. They had come to represent their family, and to visit the royals who were their cousins. And, in Lucy's case, to discover if the Balenan court could fulfill her childish desire to be accepted. A desire the Kyonan court was all too often reluctant to satisfy.

"It's ridiculous, is what it is," she said, her irritation rising.

"It's not that ridiculous, really."

Lucy turned her head so fast at the unexpected interjection that something clicked uncomfortably in her neck. Eamon had materialized behind her chair. She wondered darkly how long he'd been standing there.

"Excuse me?"

"Of course people are foolish to be so narrow minded about clothing and such," said Eamon fairly. "But it's not so ridiculous for people to ask questions when you disappear for a whole day with a man and no other companion."

Jocelyn was skewering her twin with a look that suggested no high opinion of his intelligence. Lucy felt like rolling her eyes herself.

"But it's Cody!" she protested, spreading her hands in a gesture of appeal.

Eamon shrugged. "Cody is a man."

"An old man," retorted Lucy.

Eamon made a noise in his throat that was somewhere between amused and impatient. "He's not old, Lucy."

"He's my parents' age!" said Lucy. "Or not much younger." She looked to Jocelyn for support. "Cody's been bossing me around like a second father since the day I was born. He couldn't be more like an uncle to me if he was my actual flesh and blood. The idea of a…" she struggled to even say the word, "*romantic* connection between us is as disgusting as it is absurd."

"We know that, Lucy," said Jocelyn quickly. "Of course we do." Her eyes flicked to Eamon, a silent message in them.

"Yes, we know," the prince chipped in belatedly. The faint hint of relief in his tone might have been Lucy's imagination. "But we're not the ones criticizing."

"Aren't you?" asked Lucy tartly. She pushed herself from her chair in a fluid motion, tossing her hair over her shoulder. "I'm going to my suite."

Jocelyn put a hand on Lucy's arm. "Don't worry about it, Lucy." Her cheerful tone sounded a little forced. "It will be fine."

Lucy just nodded, not trusting herself to respond. She was putting on an indifferent front, but inside she was mortified by the whole situation. The fact that Eamon followed her as she started across the room did nothing to decrease her embarrassment.

"What *were* you and Cody doing all day?" he asked, apparently unable to help himself.

"That's none of your business," said Lucy haughtily.

Eamon raised an eyebrow. "Oh yes, that answer will definitely make everyone less suspicious."

Lucy stopped walking, turning to glare at him. "I thought you weren't the one criticizing."

He sighed. "I'm sorry, it's just…I don't like to hear people talking about you as if you're something I know you're not. It makes me angry."

"Well, how do you think it makes me feel?" Lucy shot back. Glancing around, she saw an unsettling number of eyes fixed on them. "You're probably damaging your reputation just talking to me," she said acidly. "So how about you let me be?"

Eamon followed her gaze, a look of pure scorn passing over

his handsome features. "Don't be ridiculous. I don't care about the opinion of these narrow-minded people."

Lucy stared up at him for a moment, the truth of his words washing over her with surprising force. He meant what he said, and it wasn't just the sincerity on his face that told her that. It was years of watching him grow and thrive in the Kyonan court. Eamon had always been confident and poised. It was one of the things that had always so impressed Lucy about him, because she herself had never been as secure as he was. On the contrary, she always felt like she was watching every step, every word whenever she was in Kynton.

Of course, Eamon had been born to his position. But so had Jocelyn, and Lucy knew that she had always struggled with the pressure of court life. Not Eamon. He had never been rattled by the opinions of those members of court who were relentlessly negative. So many times Lucy had witnessed him shrugging off a malicious comment, or a condescending manner. And never, not even for a moment, had he paid the smallest heed to anyone who expressed reservations about his connection with the half-Balenan family in the forest.

He didn't care what the overly critical faction of the court in Kynton thought. Of course he wouldn't care about the opinions of the Balenan equivalents. He wasn't self-conscious like she was.

But he cared what she thought. And her sustained rejection was slowly crushing him. Thinking back to his uncharacteristic hesitation and uncertainty at the ball, she could suddenly see that with blinding clarity.

She turned away, wishing she knew how to care less, like he did. Wishing things weren't such a mess between them. Wishing she had skipped dinner altogether to avoid this room full of dozens of judgmental strangers and one far too familiar prince.

"Lucy?" Eamon's voice was hesitant. He seemed to have

noticed her sudden struggle with her unruly emotions. "What did I say?"

"Nothing," she said hastily. "I just need some time."

"Can..." Eamon's hopeful expression was heartbreaking. "Can I walk you to your room?"

Lucy looked down, not ready to sift through the varied emotions of the evening. "I don't think that's a good idea," she said, trying to keep her tone light. "Thank you for the offer, but I'll be fine."

With a supreme effort, she resisted looking up at him as she bobbed a quick curtsy for form's sake, then turned and swept from the room.

CHAPTER THIRTEEN

"It's time. Are you ready?"

Lucy's heart pattered wildly as she nodded at her best friend. Jocelyn looked like she might be ill, but Lucy was so excited that she could barely spare a thought for nerves. She felt like she'd been waiting her whole life for this moment, and it couldn't come fast enough.

"Thank you for coming," said Jocelyn, for probably the twentieth time. "I could never have faced my first ball without you."

"Thank you for being a nervous wreck!" teased Lucy as she followed her friend out of the princess's lavish royal suite. "If you hadn't begged my mother to take pity on you, there's no way she would have let me attend a ball at the castle." Lucy wrinkled her nose in disapproval. "She thinks fifteen is too young to attend balls."

Jocelyn laughed. "To tell you the truth, I was half hoping my parents would think I was still too young at sixteen." She sighed. "But apparently the opening night of the tournament is an important enough occasion that we're all supposed to attend."

"Is Eamon dreading his first ball as much as you are?" asked Lucy, trying to sound nonchalant as she looked down at her gorgeous lavender gown, officiously smoothing an imaginary wrinkle.

If Jocelyn noticed the slight flush on Lucy's cheeks, she didn't comment. "I don't know. I don't think he's spared much thought for the ball at all, to be honest. He's absolutely sick over the fact that he's not allowed to compete in the tournament." Jocelyn shook her head indulgently. "He's pleaded and pleaded with Father, but tradition is that competitors must be seventeen or older, and Father refuses to bend the rules just because Eamon's the prince."

Lucy sighed. "That's too bad. He must be disappointed." She refrained from adding that she was disappointed. It would definitely have increased her interest in the tournament if she could have watched Eamon pitting his strength against all the visiting knights and nobles.

They had just about reached the ballroom, and Jocelyn slowed, putting a hand on Lucy's arm. "Tell me I can do this, Lucy."

"Of course you can!" said Lucy firmly. "You're graceful, and you're poised, and you look absolutely stunning in that gown." It was all true, and she wished Jocelyn would believe it for once. "You were born to this role, Joss. You just need to have a little more faith in yourself."

"Thanks Lucy," said Jocelyn, still looking anxious. "You're much better at this than I am. You would make a good princess if only we could switch lives. I think I'd quite like to be a forest-dweller."

Lucy knew from Jocelyn's light tone that she was only joking—mostly. But she couldn't help the flush that rose to her face. She had been indulging in girlish dreams of being a princess lately. But they had nothing to do with swapping roles with Jocelyn. They were centered on quite a different route to the title. And the title was not in the least what captured her interest.

They entered the ballroom to great fanfare. If Lucy knew her friend at all, Jocelyn was wishing she could slink in undetected. But Lucy couldn't deny to herself that she took great delight in the dramatic entrance. She hovered respectfully a step behind Jocelyn, not wanting to steal the princess's moment, but her eyes darted eagerly around the large space.

The room was decked out beautifully, the swirling skirts and copious amounts of flowers creating a dazzling rainbow. It was all she could do not to bounce on the balls of her feet. She followed sedately behind Jocelyn, greeting the king and queen with a sweeping curtsy that she had practiced to perfection. When she rose to her feet, she saw King Calinnae smiling down at her in good-natured welcome.

Queen Elnora also smiled, but there was something in her expression that told Lucy that the woman who had been like family since the day of Lucy's birth would be watching her closely throughout the evening, and would make a full report to Lucy's own mother. The thought didn't trouble Lucy. She had no intention of doing anything scandalous.

Jocelyn moved off to endure a series of dull formal introductions, leaving Lucy to drift toward a refreshments table. As she scanned the crowd for a familiar face, Lucy began to realize how much attention she was attracting. She felt her cheeks grow warm, but it was as much from pleasure as embarrassment. This was her big debut as well as Jocelyn's, and although she had no official role or responsibilities, of course she had hoped to make a good impression.

It seemed she had succeeded.

An astonishing number of eyes were turned toward her, and there was no mistaking the admiration in their gaze. There were a few unfriendly expressions, but they seemed to all be worn by young women. Lucy ignored them, still searching through the crowd in the hope of seeing...

Eamon.

There he was. He was caught up in the formalities that had claimed Jocelyn's attention, and he wasn't looking at her. But as she watched him, admiring how princely and confident he looked in his ceremonial attire, he seemed to feel her gaze. He looked up suddenly, and their eyes locked. His initial warm smile of greeting was almost instantly swept away by a thunderstruck expression as his eyes trav-

eled over her figure. Even from across the room, Lucy had no difficulty recognizing the fire behind his eyes.

She looked down quickly, trying to remain graceful while on the inside she wanted to dance and squeal with triumph. That was the big impression she had been hoping to make.

Before she could even raise her eyes, an unfamiliar young man appeared before her, and she found herself receiving her first ever invitation to dance. She accepted it readily, unable to help glancing at Eamon as the man swept her onto the floor. The prince was clearly struggling to keep his attention on whatever introduction he was supposed to be taking part in.

From that point on, Lucy barely had time to draw breath. She danced constantly, never turning down an offer, determined to make the most of her first ball. Some of the men she danced with were respectful and courteous in their admiration, but others were more eager, paying her overblown—and at times not entirely appropriate—compliments.

It was all overwhelming. She couldn't deny that she enjoyed the admiration, but the scale of it was more than she had bargained for. She tried not to get carried away by it all, her mother's voice constantly in her head. The older woman had indeed been reluctant to let her daughter attend this event, and she had subjected Lucy to a very candid conversation before agreeing to it. Lucy had thought her mother's concerns exaggerated, but clearly she had known much better what to expect.

She had favored Lucy with some startling insights from her own experiences, and given her some confronting advice. It was the first time she had ever directly commented on the striking beauty for which Lucy was so often complimented, and which was widely recognized to be inherited completely from her mother.

Bearing her mother's warnings in mind, Lucy tried very hard not to flirt. And it wasn't just because she knew she was being watched, and wanted to be allowed to attend more balls in future. It was also *because she wanted to prove to herself that she was worthy of her mother's trust. Lucy was determined that any concerns about it all going to her head would prove unfounded.*

She thought she was doing pretty well, on the whole, until a familiar voice brought her heart rate back up to frantic.

"May I cut in?"

Her current partner didn't look too happy about the request, but he could hardly say no to the prince. He relinquished Lucy's hand with a stiff bow and melted into the crowd.

"Do you want to dance with me, Lucy?" Eamon asked, his eyes burning into hers with an unfamiliar intensity.

She suddenly couldn't find her voice, so she just nodded. Eamon placed his hand in hers, his touch not awkward or overeager like the other men close to him in age, but confident and steady. He had always been that way. And she had always been powerless to resist him, if he only knew it.

Her chances of keeping her head tonight suddenly seemed nonexistent.

"You look beautiful," Eamon said after a moment of silence.

Lucy dropped her gaze, blushing furiously. "Thank you."

"It was nice of you to come and keep Joss company. She's been so nervous about tonight."

Lucy laughed. "It wasn't exactly a big sacrifice for me, being invited to a royal ball." She grimaced. "And I haven't been much help to her. I've barely seen her all evening." She looked around the room, searching for her friend. "How's she doing?"

"Brilliantly, of course," said Eamon, his voice warm as he spoke of his twin. "She's so much more capable than she thinks. She just needs to have a little more confidence in herself."

"That's what I told her!" said Lucy. "She's the only one who can't see how wonderful she is."

Eamon smiled down at her, his gaze infused with the same warmth, and with something more.

"I didn't know you could dance so well, Lucy."

Lucy barely restrained a snort. "I think you knew exactly how well I can dance. We took dancing lessons together, remember?"

"Oh, yeah," he said, sounding surprised. "I'd forgotten." His eyes burned into hers, their intensity making her heart stutter erratically. "It was different, somehow."

"Yes." Lucy couldn't agree more.

The dance was over all too quickly, and Eamon was occupied for the rest of the evening. After another hour, Lucy was starting to flag. She was relieved when Jocelyn sought her out to say that they were free to retire. They had almost made it to the door, Jocelyn apologizing ruefully for having abandoned her friend for most of the ball, when they heard quick steps behind them.

"Leaving already?"

"Oh, it's you, Eamon," said Jocelyn absently, glancing at her twin in surprise. "I wondered who was chasing us from the room."

"Sorry, Joss," he said apologetically. "Mother said there's one more person you need to meet."

Jocelyn groaned, quietly enough that only the two of them heard her. She turned to her friend. "Sorry, Lucy, I thought I was done. Do you mind waiting a minute?"

"No need for her to wait," said Eamon, much too airily. "I can walk her to your room."

Jocelyn stared at him like he had lost his mind. "Walk her to my room? What, are you worried that she'll get abducted while she strolls through the castle?"

"Happened to Mother once," said Eamon quickly, and Jocelyn rolled her eyes.

"It's fine, Joss," said Lucy quickly. "I'll meet you back at the room."

"Thanks Lucy. I won't be long. I hope." Jocelyn turned toward her parents on the far side of the room.

Lucy looked up at Eamon. There was a twinkle in his eye as he offered her his arm, and she couldn't help but grin back at him as she *took it. He led her through the familiar halls of the castle, chatting about nothing in particular as they made their way to Jocelyn's suite, where Lucy was staying. Much too soon, they found themselves outside the door.*

Lucy turned to say goodnight, but the words died on her lips when she saw the way Eamon was looking at her.

"Did I tell you that you look beautiful?" he asked quietly.

She cast down her eyes, not quite able to hide the smile curving her lips. "Yes, you did."

"Oh. It's just..." Eamon stepped slightly closer. "I've always thought you were the sweetest girl in the world, Lucy. It seems a bit excessive for you to be the prettiest, too."

Lucy felt her cheeks flame, her smile growing wider. She chanced a glance up, and saw that Eamon was fidgeting, for once looking as awkward and uncertain as a sixteen-year-old should.

Then, all of a sudden, he leaned forward and kissed her cheek, so quickly she almost wasn't sure it had happened. Before she could blink, he was disappearing down the corridor, his lean figure bouncing with the same nervous energy that was coursing through her.

Lucy pressed her hands to her burning cheeks, barely able to hold in a squeal. The night had gone better than she could possibly have dreamed. All the exaggerated compliments and superficial admiration faded instantly from her mind, irrelevant and unimpressive next to Eamon's words and actions.

She could hardly believe it was real, and she couldn't imagine how she would ever sleep that night. The future stretched before her, rosy and full of promise, as she dared to hope that all of her dearest wishes would come true.

LUCY LAY UNMOVING for several minutes after she woke. A chill seemed to be spreading through her, in spite of the heavy warmth already filling the air. She could really do without these dreams, but apparently her mind was as determined to reproach her as Jocelyn was. And Cody. And even Matheus.

And even more uncomfortably, Lady Rodanthe. The noblewoman had followed Lucy to her suite the night before. The ensuing conversation had been so awkward Lucy cringed to remember it. The older woman was clearly as uncertain as Lucy as to the nature of her authority over the unofficial subgroup of the delegation. She hadn't seemed altogether sure whether to chastise Lucy for her unintentional indiscretion, or whether to take responsibility herself for not giving Cody stricter parameters when he told her about the intended outing.

Lucy groaned, sitting up in a fluid motion. She suddenly wished she could return to the dream after all. She'd been happy then, and innocent enough to believe it would last forever.

She dressed mechanically, wondering just how much of a mess she had created with her poorly thought-out disappearance the day before. Was the royal family angry with her? Had she embarrassed them with her behavior? She was here at their invitation, after all. She chose a modest gown, one that she hoped wouldn't attract attention. Her desire to make an impression had evaporated.

As she studied herself anxiously in the looking glass, her eyes were caught by something behind her. She turned around, her gaze falling on the small leather journal she had taken from Raldo's belongings the day before. In all the mortification of what followed, she hadn't taken the time to have another look.

She picked it up, only too glad to have some excuse to delay emerging from the sanctuary of her chamber. Her eyes scanned the first entry again, wondering about the identity of this Haydn, and the Isidore he spoke of with such heartbroken longing. Then she flicked over to the next entry.

. . .

W*ELL*, *here I am a month later, and my gloomy predictions have proved unfounded. The group of survivors I was fortunate enough to stumble upon are better organized and more resilient than I realized. It is no accident that they have survived this long. It is a well-organized community, in spite of the challenging conditions we're living in.*

We have a rotation system, some hunting while others take patrol duty, and others prepare food. There are no children among us, but one of the women is with child. If I'm honest, I fear for that infant, and for the rest of us. Will we be able to remain undetected with a small child among us? And what a way to grow up, stranded here in the jungle. But the mother-to-be is delighted. She says that her child will not be born a slave, and that however hard this life may be, at least the baby will be allowed to live or die in the company of his parents, instead of being taken away to be raised by an uncaring master.

There is something in that, I suppose.

We had a scare a few weeks ago, not long after I joined the group, and decided to relocate deeper into the jungle, away from Nohl. We have made our way to one of Alben's lesser-used bases, and turned it into a home of sorts. There are many dangers so deep in the jungle, but I think it is worth the risk. We rarely come across patrols of soldiers now. They probably believe that any survivors from the ship disaster would not have lasted this long in the unforgiving jungle.

They underestimate us.

I think about Isidore, every day. I wonder if she's happy, if she's all right. So many times in those first couple of weeks I made up my mind to return to Thorania, to find her, to forget everything else and just choose to be with her.

But I couldn't do it. And I know I never will. She had made her choices, and I can see no reason why she would listen to me now when she wouldn't before. She stayed by choice, and I think she will be safe, away up in the north. I know in my heart that we will never meet again, and that thought is more bitter than everything else.

I try to keep busy with my new community, not to dwell on the past. We must look to the future, however grim it might be.

But I can't help remembering how things used to be. I wish I had known Isidore before she was taken, back in Kyona. She must have been the light of her family's life. Given everything, she did amazingly well to adapt and survive here. She is the only instance I know of where the slavers took the child of a noble family. How heartbreaking to think that her family probably never even knew what became of her. And what an adjustment for her to find herself a slave. It was bad enough for the rest of us, but to go from such privilege and comfort to the life we were forced into...

Well, it's no wonder she was bitter. Weren't we all? I am glad at least that her time as a slave was short, before we liberated her. I was so reckless and eager back then, still intoxicated by the delight of being liberated by Alben myself, far too confident in my ability to free others without getting caught.

And I knew the moment I laid eyes on her that we couldn't leave her behind. She had to be free. She was not made for such a life as she was living.

I wish I could believe she will find happiness in the life she has chosen now. But it is a long time since I saw happiness in her.

Thinking of the past is painful, but it's easier than dwelling on the future that we lost when the ships went down. All our dreams, all our plans. How impossibly big they were. All the things we were going to do once we returned to Kyona. And now I will never see my home again, just as I will never see Isidore again. All I will ever see is this jungle, for however long I can survive here.

Perhaps it is for the best as far as Isidore and I are concerned. Her family would no doubt have been beyond delighted to receive her back again, seemingly from the dead. Whether they would have been happy to find her promised to a street urchin who spent half his childhood as a slave in a foreign land, is much less certain. Perhaps we never really had a future, and we were always just dreaming impos-sible dreams.

At least I, like most of us here, have no family to mourn me back home. This is my family now. And we are surviving together—more than surviving. We are a community. I am glad that I found them.

LUCY SHUT the book with a snap. She had no desire to read further. Haydn's life was hardly a pleasant escape from her own troubles.

She once again studied her reflection, trying to find anything that needed fixing. But she was stalling, and she knew it. With a sigh, she moved to the door, ready to seek out the others. She had to stop avoiding them—better to face the group, Eamon included, than to wander around alone, attracting the stares of every judgmental Balenan courtier who happened to cross her path.

To her horror, she found Cody lingering right outside her door, a bow again slung across his shoulder.

CHAPTER FOURTEEN

"Cody!" she hissed. "What are you doing here?"

He took in her attire with surprise. "Waiting for you. What are you wearing, Lucy? How will you train in that?"

"You can't seriously think we're training again this morning!" Lucy protested. "Don't you realize what a mess we've made?"

Cody stared at her blankly. "What are you talking about?"

Lucy sighed, willing herself to be patient.

"Cody, there's a huge scandal over what we did yesterday. Surely you noticed how the whole room was staring at us at dinner!"

Cody still looked confused. "You said something about that, didn't you? But I can't say I noticed anything. Do you mean people found out we were doing weapons training, and they disapprove?"

"Not exactly," said Lucy, suddenly uncomfortable. It was bad enough talking about the gossip with Jocelyn and Eamon. Having to explain it to an oblivious Cody was infinitely worse. "We were...indiscreet to have disappeared for so long just the two of us. People got the wrong impression. They think we were up to something...clandestine."

Cody just stared. "Why would they think that? This sounds like another one of your over-sensitive reactions, Lucy. We go off all the time in Raldon, and no one thinks anything of it."

Lucy sighed again. She had to remind herself that her parents had sent Cody along for his ability to protect her and Matheus in a fight, not for any skills in navigating court etiquette. It wasn't his fault Lucy has made this misstep, any more than it was Lady Rodanthe's. Lucy realized, with a rush of shame, that her mother had trusted Lucy to know how to handle herself without close guidance on such matters. She had been haunting the court at Kynton for years, after all.

"We're not in Raldon, Cody," she said, trying to speak patiently. "We're guests in a royal court, and the same rules don't apply. It's my fault. I should definitely have predicted this. I just wasn't thinking. I never would have pulled such a stunt in Kynton, so I should have known I couldn't get away with it here."

"It all sounds like a big fuss over nothing," said Cody dismissively. "You're not seriously going to let such nonsense stop you from training today, are you?"

Lucy sighed. Cody just didn't understand how these things worked. "I'm sorry, Cody, but I can't. It's not something I've made up—it's a real problem." She chewed her lip anxiously. "I just hope I haven't alienated the royal family."

Cody made an impatient noise, but Lucy cut him off with a wave of her hand.

"You just have to trust me on this one, Cody. Take Matheus instead. He's dying to see the base tree." Lucy didn't add it aloud, but she also hoped that if Cody spent the day with Matheus in the jungle, it might help convince people that there had been nothing untoward in her own outing.

Cody didn't look impressed, but Lucy gave him no opportunity to argue. She hurried off down the corridor, eager to put some distance between them before anyone—especially Lady Rodanthe—saw them meeting together outside her room.

She had hoped to catch the rest of the group, but it seemed they had grown used to her preference for arriving alone, and no one was waiting for her. She made her way toward the dining hall, feeling dispirited. At the last moment, she decided she couldn't face a crowd of strangers. She veered off in the direction of a pleasure garden that the visitors had been shown during their tour of the castle. It was in an internal courtyard not far from the dining hall. She would walk there for a while, try to clear her head. She wasn't all that hungry anyway.

At first the lush foliage of the garden—so different from the equivalent features in the palace at Kynton—did little to soothe her agitation. It was too similar to the jungle, too reminiscent of her embarrassing misstep the day before.

But as she strolled through the maze of palm fronds and moss-covered trees, she felt herself begin to relax. The greenery was bursting out of its bounds, drooping over the stone paths, making it seem like she was a world away from the castle. It was easy to imagine she was alone.

"Did you notice that the Kyonan girl didn't show her face at breakfast today?"

The snide voice broke into Lucy's thoughts, shattering the illusion of solitude.

"I'm not surprised," a second girl replied with a snicker. "After being caught like that yesterday."

"Scandalous, isn't it?" the first speaker responded, with obvious relish. "They say her mother was just the same, sneaking off to the jungle at all hours with a string of slaves."

The voices were getting closer, and Lucy turned away quickly. She had heard more than enough, and she had no desire to encounter the gossiping locals. She hurried into the next walkway, feeling more weary than upset. The overheard conversation was no surprise—it was exactly what she had known the spiteful members of the court would be saying.

She turned the corner and drew up short, barely able to restrain a gasp of dismay at sight of the man standing there, looking calm and commanding.

"Good morning, Luciana," said Rasad, his words courteous but his gaze still holding that faint hint of amusement. He inclined his head. "You look as lovely as ever."

"Thank you." Lucy bobbed a slight curtsy, still unsure of the Thoranian's rank.

His eyes flickered back the way she had come. "These Balenans seem determined to prove me right in my criticism of their narrow-mindedness, don't they?"

Lucy felt her face growing red. The embarrassment that she had been too weary to feel before flared into life now that she knew there had been another witness to her humiliation. Rasad seemed to have a knack for being on hand to overhear when she was insulted.

"I..." she struggled for words, but Rasad came to her rescue.

"No need to say anything, my dear Luciana. I know better than anyone how foolish my neighbors can be." He offered her his arm.

Part of Lucy wanted to make a quick escape, but there was something compelling about the Thoranian man, just as the first time they had met. She found herself accepting the offered escort, following his lead as he guided her through the winding paths of the garden.

"I am sorry that you have not had an entirely pleasant visit to Nohl so far," said Rasad, after a moment. "But selfishly, I hope it will make you more inclined to accept my invitation."

Lucy frowned, in no mood for cryptic comments. "What invitation is that?"

"The invitation to accompany me and the rest of the Thoranian delegation when we return to Thirl tomorrow. You would be welcome to stay as guests in the palace, as the Kyonan prince and the Valorian prince and princess intend to do."

Lucy looked up at him in surprise. "You're inviting me to go to Thorania?"

He inclined his head. "And your brother, of course."

"But...why?"

Rasad looked faintly surprised. "I thought I told you the other night. I think you would like my kingdom."

Lucy didn't miss the territorial edge to his tone as he said "my kingdom", and she wondered again who this man was that he could issue an invitation for foreign visitors to stay in the palace.

Rasad was still speaking, his lip curling in scorn as he glanced in the direction of the gossiping voices, which had long since faded. "I know you have Balenan blood in you, but I think you might feel more at home in Thorania than here. We are not so insular. We have long been used to the presence of Kyonans, and those of mixed heritage. I have Kyonan blood in my own ancestry, in fact."

"You do?" Lucy looked at the self-assured Thoranian, appraising him with new eyes.

"Certainly," he said calmly. "As I said, it's not uncommon in Thorania."

"You said it was your idea to invite the Kyonan royals to visit," said Lucy slowly. "And I understand that the purpose of their visit is to address the matter of Kyonan descendants who may wish to relocate to Kyona now that the passage is clear. Are you one of the ones who wants to live in Kyona?"

Rasad didn't immediately answer, and Lucy thought something flickered behind his eyes. But the next moment, his expression was as unruffled as usual. "No," he said smoothly. "I have no wish to leave Thorania. I think, if you grace us with a visit, you will understand why."

Lucy was silent, trying to process the unexpected invitation. Rasad had succeeded in making her curious about Thorania, and she couldn't deny that she was flattered by his obvious desire for her approval. But she couldn't help but wonder whether she fully understood the nature of what he was offering.

"I imagine you'll want some time to think about it," said Rasad courteously. "I'm sorry that time is so short, with us leaving tomorrow. But I hope you will consider the matter."

"I will," she assured him seriously. "Thank you for your generous invitation."

He gave a slight bow, leading her gently but inexorably toward the edge of the garden. He engaged her in light-hearted conversation as they walked, saying nothing of significance, and offering her no overblown compliments. It was clear from his speech that he was a person of high privilege and education, and used to a position of command. The more time she spent with him, the more flattered Lucy felt by the personal invitation.

It wasn't until they had entered the corridors of the castle that he raised her hand in a more intimate gesture.

"Think about my offer, Luciana," he said, his voice and eyes suddenly intense. "Thorania would be honored by your visit, as would I." He pressed his lips to the back of her hand, then turned and strode away with a confident step, leaving Lucy dazed and reeling. He was the most confusing person she had ever met, but she couldn't deny that there was something magnetic about him.

She suddenly became aware of someone's eyes on her. She turned quickly, thinking of the malicious girls from the garden. Her alarm drained away when she saw that it was only Eamon, but the expression on his face quickly chased away any feeling of relief. His eyes were so fiery as they rested on her that she felt a flush rising to her cheeks, before she remembered that she had nothing to be ashamed of. She lifted her chin slightly.

"Eamon. What brings you here?"

"I was looking for you," he said, his voice steely. "I was concerned that you missed breakfast."

"I wasn't hungry," said Lucy colorlessly.

There was a moment of silence as Eamon apparently tried to think of a diplomatic way to express his thoughts. He failed.

"What did that man want? That was Rasad, wasn't it?"

Lucy raised an eyebrow. "I don't see how that's any business of yours."

Eamon scowled in the direction Rasad had left. "I don't trust him."

"Aren't you supposed to be strengthening ties with Thorania?" Lucy snapped. "You should be trying to get in Rasad's good books, not alienating him. He's very influential in the Thoranian court."

It was Eamon's turn to raise an eyebrow. "Yes, I heard he's some kind of advisor. But Lord Rodanthe didn't seem to know much about him. What is his rank, incidentally?"

Lucy felt herself flush slightly. "I don't know," she admitted. "But he has the ear of the king. It was his idea to invite you to visit Thirl, to discuss the Kyonan descendants living in the kingdom."

"His idea, was it?" asked Eamon flatly, his handsome face showing scorn. "Who told you that, him?"

"As a matter of fact, he did." Lucy glared at the prince. "And if you're implying that he was making it up to impress me, that's ridiculous. He hardly seems like the type of person to show off."

"Ridiculous, is it?" said Eamon cuttingly. "If he's the one who wanted us to come, isn't it strange that he hasn't identified himself to Lord Rodanthe in any of the discussions regarding our visit? Since you're such an expert on him, tell me this. If he's so senior in diplomatic matters within Thorania, why is he taking such an interest in you?"

"Thank you," snapped Lucy. "Very complimentary."

She turned, ready to march off in a huff, but Eamon reached out with lightning speed, stopping her with a hand on her arm.

"You know what I mean, Lucy," he said impatiently. "I'm not trying to insult you. I'm just saying you don't have a formal role on this delegation. You're here as a relative of the Balenan royal family, so what interest would Thorania have in you? If this Rasad is so interested in relations between his kingdom and Kyona, why hasn't he made any effort to speak with me, or even with Jocelyn?"

Lucy shrugged. "Maybe because you've been glaring daggers at him since the moment you first saw him." She lifted her chin in the air. "Maybe I'm giving a better impression of Kyona than you are. That's probably why he's issued me a formal invitation to join the delegation and stay at the palace in Thirl."

"He has?" Eamon let go of her arm in his surprise.

Lucy nodded. "He wants me to leave with the group tomorrow."

"And are you going to?"

Lucy didn't immediately answer. The truth was that she wasn't sure, but she didn't think Eamon had earned any right to hear her reservations. Of course, she was only going to be allowed to go if Cody could be brought to agree, but she didn't want to admit that either. If she was honest with herself, she had been flattered by Rasad's assumption that she was free to make the decision herself.

"I don't like the idea of you going as his guest," said Eamon, frowning to himself.

"Why not?" asked Lucy, firing up at once.

Eamon's expression was once again fiery. "I thought you

were upset about all the gossip from yesterday," he challenged. "I don't see how it helps for you to be having clandestine meetings with another man, and accepting invitations to stay with him."

"How dare you?" Lucy gasped. "Clandestine meetings? In the castle gardens in the middle of the morning? I haven't done anything inappropriate, and you're the last person I have to answer to for my actions! How dare you turn Rasad's invitation into something sordid? You're behaving like a child, and I refuse to listen to you."

She turned with a flounce, striding away before Eamon could stop her again. Whatever doubts she had harbored about Rasad's offer before were swept away in the tide of her anger. Whether she would have accepted the invitation without the prince's intervention she would never know. But she certainly intended to accept it now.

CHAPTER FIFTEEN

If she had any second thoughts the next day, she was far too proud to show it in front of the others. Eamon still seemed unconvinced as they waited for the Thoranian delegation in the castle courtyard, but as Lucy was pointedly not speaking to him, he had no opportunity to say so. Jocelyn was delighted that her friend was to join them after all on their onward journey, and her cheerfulness helped soothe Lucy's uncertainty.

The dowager queen had seemed disappointed that her great-niece and great-nephew were departing so far ahead of schedule. Lucy felt a little guilty at the older woman's sadness, but they would pass back through Nohl on their way home, so it wasn't a final goodbye. Plus, she felt reinforced in the wisdom of her decision by the combination of another dinner punctuated by whispers and stares, and the open relief on Queen Verena's face when Lucy suggested that she and Matheus accompany the Thoranian delegation.

Clearly she had caused the royal family some embarrassment, although King Giles was too well mannered to say so. Lucy wondered whether it was the rumors of indiscretion that made things uncomfortable for her mother's cousins, or the fact that her behavior must have inevitably reminded people of her mother's treasonous activities.

Either way, she had no desire to overstay her welcome.

Matheus had little choice but to accompany her, given that Cody had agreed. The older Kyonan had admitted to some curiosity about Thorania. What he hadn't admitted, but Lucy suspected, was that in light of the two near-fatal incidents Lucy had witnessed, he had some doubts about his ability to ensure Lucy and Matheus's safety in Balenol once the delegation and their guards had left.

At any rate, Cody had made it very clear that either both of them went or neither of them went. He had been tasked with keeping them safe, and he couldn't do that effectively if they weren't in the same place.

Not that Matheus seemed to mind. Lucy wasn't sure whether it was because he had also become curious about the kingdom of Thorania, or because he wanted to continue traveling with Eamon, whom he admired far too much for Lucy's liking.

Lucy knew her mother had said to consider Lord and Lady Rodanthe in charge, but she couldn't bring herself to seek their permission, not after the excruciating embarrassment of her last conversation with the noblewoman. She knew it was possible they wouldn't be thrilled to have the company of the three additional members of the party as they traveled onward—their responsibility for the little group, such as it was, had only been intended to apply until the delegation left for Thorania. But Lucy comforted herself with the reflection that even if she had asked them, they would hardly have said it was either unsafe or improper for Lucy and her brother to go to Thorania, since they and their own charges were doing exactly that.

In any event, she was pleased to learn that Cody had taken up her suggestion and had shown Matheus the base tree the day before. It was only fair that her brother should share in the experiences that had so impacted her in the jungle. She was pretty jealous when she discovered that Cody had even taken Matheus through the tunnel, but it was too late to insist he show her, too. Perhaps on their way home.

The Thoranian delegation was significantly late in joining them, but Rasad, at its head, looked unhurried as he trotted his mount toward the waiting Kyonans and Valorians. Lucy didn't miss the scowl Eamon sent in the older man's direction, but no one commented on how long they had been waiting.

The Thoranian greeted the royals formally, his eyes sweeping over the assembled party before coming to rest on Lucy. He sent her the smallest of smiles as he exchanged courtesies with Eamon. There was something conspiratorial, almost intimate, in the expression. Lucy felt a strange fluttering in her stomach as she took in once again how handsome the older man really was. She wasn't sure whether she was more confused or flattered by Rasad's attention, but the slight scowl on Eamon's face as he struggled to speak politely to the Thoranian was enough to make her determined to keep her expression level.

"I have to say, I never imagined I'd actually go to Thorania." Cody's cheerful voice cut into her thoughts. Clearly he was oblivious to the subtle interactions going on around him. "Of course," he continued, "I never expected to be back in the South Lands at all."

"You never thought about going over the border when you lived in the jungle?" Matheus asked curiously.

"Nope," said Cody. "I had more than enough to occupy me here, with the rebels. There were slaves who got away over the border on occasion." He nodded toward Lucy. "Like the ones in that book, actually, all those generations ago. I guess it's not surprising."

"What book?" asked Matheus, but Lucy hurried to talk over

him, not wanting to tell him about the journal for some reason. Illogically, she felt that it was hers, and she didn't want to share it. Plus she wasn't sure she wanted Cody to know she'd taken it from the base tree.

"How long does it take to get to the border, Cody? Do you know?"

"We will be there not long after nightfall." Rasad's smooth voice made Lucy turn quickly, cursing the slight flush that rose to her cheeks. "Luciana." The Thoranian took her offered hand, raising it to his lips in a polite salute. "Let me say again how delighted I am that you have decided to join us." His gaze passed over her two companions, and he inclined his head. "And my warmest welcome to both of you as well."

Matheus mumbled something that passed for a polite greeting, but Lucy couldn't help but notice that one of Cody's eyebrows was slightly raised. He showed none of the anger that Eamon seemed to feel every time he laid eyes on Rasad, but he clearly shared the prince's mistrust to some extent. Truth be told, even Lucy wasn't sure whether she could trust Rasad.

"I hope you'll ride with me?" This time Rasad undeniably spoke specifically to Lucy, and although it sounded like a question, something in his manner made it clear that the matter was already arranged. Lucy found her horse drawing alongside the Thoranian's before she was even conscious of having directed it there.

"I was pleased to learn that you all intended to ride," Rasad said conversationally as they drew out of the courtyard, heading south. "I had expected that I would need to provide a carriage, and that would certainly have slowed our progress."

"We've all been riding since we were children," said Lucy. "Well," she glanced back over her shoulder at the other two, riding in a pair not far behind, "all but Cody. And he's competent enough." She returned her gaze to the front, her eyes picking out the golden heads of Eamon and Jocelyn, alongside Kincaid's auburn one. "The royals are obviously very well trained in horsemanship, but Matheus and I aren't too far behind them."

"I can see that you have an excellent seat," Rasad agreed admiringly. "I'm glad, because it will increase your enjoyment of Thorania, I think."

"What do you mean?" asked Lucy, looking up at him. She couldn't help but notice that he handled his own horse masterfully.

But Rasad just smiled. "You'll see."

Lucy was intrigued, but she didn't press him. She snuck a sideways look at his face. His smile was open and genuine, and she had no doubt whatever he was thinking about brought him genuine enjoyment. The expression made him look younger and more approachable—and if she was honest, more handsome—than she had seen him before.

"So," she said, casting around for something to say. "We'll reach the border today?"

"This evening," corrected Rasad. "We'll camp on this side of the river, and cross in the morning. It's not far from the river to the capital."

Lucy looked sideways again, noting that the easy smile was still there. "You look happy," she ventured.

"I'm glad to be going home," Rasad said simply. He met her look, amusement back in his eyes. "You're going to like Thorania, trust me."

They had almost reached the city wall, their route leading them alongside the river. Lucy glanced back the way they had come, at the harsh gray walls of the castle rising above the other buildings.

"I'm starting to think you're right," she said lightly, remembering the look on Queen Verena's face when Lucy had spoken of the early departure.

The cavalcade left Nohl by the same road Lucy and Cody had taken a couple days before. The giant wooden gates stood wide, and Lucy was fascinated to see the traffic coming down the river. Huge wooden pylons floated through the gap in the wall, lashed together into rafts. The men riding on them deftly kept their makeshift vessels in the center of the stream with long poles.

"Timber is Balenol's main export, but I suppose you already know that," said Rasad, noticing her interest. He gave her another conspiratorial smile. "These days, the Balenans have to fell the trees themselves."

Lucy gave a small smirk, unable to stop the surge of vindictive satisfaction as she thought of the drop in Balenol's prosperity since they lost their slave labor.

When she had traveled through the city in the previous few days, she had felt the stab of discomfort as she took in the evidence of poverty that was all around. Nohl was certainly a less prosperous city than Kynton, and it was clear that many of its citizens were struggling. But even though the same signs were there as she rode through the streets of Nohl at Rasad's side, her sympathy seemed to have decreased.

She had wanted to like Balenol—a small part of her had even wondered if she would like it better than Kyona. But other than the kindness shown by a couple of the royals, the kingdom had so far given her little reason to warm to it. The superficial admiration of those who had complimented her at the welcome gala counted for nothing. She recognized it for the shallow facade it was—certainly none of those people had been in a rush to approach her over the last couple of days, once she had fallen into disgrace.

Her eyes were once again drawn forward to the three royals

who were just passing through the gate ahead of her. Eamon's hair glinted so brightly in the morning sunshine that he hardly needed a crown to signify his status. She couldn't help but remember what he'd said about how little he cared about the opinion of those vapid nobles who admired her one day and shunned her the next. He had much more reason than they did to avoid her, but he hadn't shown any inclination to do so yet.

"The Kyonan prince didn't seem entirely happy about your decision to accompany us," Rasad said suddenly, apparently noticing the direction of her gaze. "Do you know why that would be? Does he share that sentiment we've observed in others about mixed heritage?"

"What?" Lucy said, startled. "No, of course not. Nothing like that. My family has been close with Kyona's royals all my life."

"Really?" Rasad spoke politely, but there was just the faintest hint of disbelief in his voice.

Lucy couldn't help the flush that rose to her cheeks. She wasn't sure how to explain to the Thoranian that the distance he had observed between her and the rest of the party had been at her own instigation, not theirs. And, she realized with a flash of shame, at times she had even included Matheus in her isolation, maneuvering ways for the two of them to avoid the royals.

"Ea—the prince did have his reservations about us joining the delegation to Thirl," she admitted. "But it wasn't for any reason of...of...it was just that..."

"It's quite all right, Luciana," Rasad rescued her smoothly. "I am not owed any explanation."

Lucy subsided, her face more flushed than ever. She and Rasad were passing through the gate by this time. Their passage mercifully required them to travel in single file for a short distance, allowing her to pull ahead where the older man couldn't observe her embarrassment. Her eyes narrowed as they rested again on Eamon, irritated with him for making his disapproval so obvious and thereby putting her in such an uncomfortable position.

They followed the road south for a while before it swung east, cutting into the jungle as it headed toward the border with Thorania. As the road turned, Lucy's eyes strayed to the jungle on the western side of the path, remembering her glimpse into the rebels' world with Cody. The consequences of that day on her standing in the Balenan court had been unfortunate, but she couldn't regret the experience.

Even as she looked ahead toward Thorania she could feel the weight of the little journal that she had tucked into a pocket of her gown. The long-dead Haydn had ventured into the neighboring kingdom, along with his Isidore, whoever she was.

Presumably Haydn had carved out some kind of life for himself in the jungle community, if his journal had survived long enough to be handed down and kept by subsequent generations of jungle nomads. Lucy found herself wondering whether Isidore had been equally fortunate in Thorania. It was unlikely that the answer would be found in the volume now pressing against her leg as she rode. Most likely Haydn himself never found out what became of his former companion. Certainly Lucy never would.

Lucy was ready to make camp long before they actually did. The day began hot and humid, and became even more so with every passing hour. The scenery was nothing to get excited about either—endless jungle on both sides of the road. She had no doubt that there were plenty of fascinating features to discover within the foliage. But they were not visible from the cleared track the group continued to plod down for league after league. They stopped infrequently for rest and food. No one complained, but Lucy could see on the faces of her fellow visitors that everyone was as weary of the trek as she had become.

When the cool of evening finally came, Lucy would have been very happy to stop and sleep right where they were. But Rasad, showing no sign either of heat or fatigue, pushed the group calmly on. Visibility was poor on the road once the sun had gone down, the overhanging trees blocking the light of the moon. Their pace slowed considerably, but still they pushed on. Not long after, Lucy heard the sound of water ahead, growing steadily louder as they moved toward it. Finally, they emerged from the jungle into a cleared area on the bank of a large river. Only then did Rasad call a halt.

Lucy fell from the saddle gratefully, wishing she had the privacy to rub her sore backside. She hadn't been making idle boasts to Rasad—she genuinely was a good horsewoman. But a whole day in the saddle was much more than she was used to, and she knew she would be aching unbearably the next day. She hoped that Rasad had been telling the truth when he said that Thirl wasn't far across the river.

Rasad issued a few curt instructions, and there was a flurry of activity around the travelers. A host of servants had accompanied the delegation, serving food at their rest stops. In a remarkably short space of time, they set up a series of canvas tents and ushered the Kyonans and Valorians into them.

Lucy was surprised by how pleasant they had managed to make the makeshift accommodation. It was more than sufficient. She was not generally used to the level of luxury she had been enjoying at the Balenan castle, and she was certain that after the demands of the day, she would sleep like the dead in any set up.

The group shared a quick meal, everyone too tired for conversation. Lucy retreated into her tent as soon as she could politely do so, and was asleep within minutes.

She fell immediately into a dream, so seamlessly it felt

unnatural. The scene felt too real, too detailed, but it wasn't any haunting memory assaulting her unconscious mind. It was something altogether unfamiliar.

She found herself in the mountains of Kyona. How she knew with such certainty where she was, she couldn't have said, given it was a place she had never visited. She had heard Jocelyn talk about the mountains, from the unusual people of the mountain capital of Montego, to the rugged terrain the princess had traversed in her unplanned detour toward Valoria's north. But Lucy found herself in neither of those places.

She was standing on a broad rocky plateau. A cave loomed behind her, and in front of her, the ground dropped away off a steep cliff. It was daylight in her vision, but the narrow bridge spanning the chasm disappeared almost immediately into gloom.

Not that Lucy paid much attention to either the cliff or the bridge. She was a little distracted by what was on the plateau.

Sitting serenely in front of her, his monstrous tail dangling off the edge of the cliff, was a dragon.

An enormous dragon.

Dragons were another thing Lucy had heard Jocelyn describe but had never seen herself. Still, she was sure Jocelyn had never described this one. She couldn't have forgotten a mention of a coal black beast so gargantuan he almost looked like another mountain in the range. Surely this creature must be larger than Elddreki, the dragon Jocelyn had traveled with and had told Lucy about in some detail.

"Greetings, young human," the dragon said, pulling Lucy from her trance-like contemplation of him.

"Is this...is this real?" The words felt foolish as they came out, but Lucy was so shaken by the sheer impressiveness of the beast that she couldn't gather her thoughts.

She knew she was dreaming—which was strange in itself—

but she couldn't shake the certainty that what she was seeing was no creation of her own mind. The dragon before her was intricate in detail, from the bearded ridge along each temple to the terrifyingly long and lethal talons on the ends of his scaled feet.

"Certainly," the dragon answered calmly. "I have summoned your mind while you sleep."

"But...why?" Lucy asked stupidly. She blinked rapidly, trying to clear her mind. She should probably show more respect, but she had no training on the etiquette for conversing with a monstrous reptile.

"Because I wished to speak with you." The dragon regarded her silently for a moment, his snake-like orbs unsettling in their intensity. "Do you know who I am, young human?"

Lucy swallowed, stopping herself just in time from saying, "A dragon". Instead she shook her head mutely.

"I am Qadir," the creature said, his voice as deep and dark as an underground lake. "I am the ruler of the dragon colony at Vasilisa. You have heard that name, I think?"

"Yes," Lucy confirmed, her voice coming out as a squeak.

She had certainly heard of Vasilisa, the heart of the Dragon Realm hidden in Kyona's mountains. Her father had even been there, or very close to it, when he was her age.

She wondered suddenly if she was standing in Vasilisa right now. The thought made her uneasy, even if she was only there in vision form. Even Jocelyn and Kincaid—who had traveled extensively with the dragon Elddreki—had never actually been to Vasilisa. She felt sure she shouldn't be there, dream or not.

"And you have heard of me?" Qadir prompted.

Again Lucy nodded. Her father had actually met the ancient dragon-ruler when he had visited the Dragon Realm, although he had spoken mainly about the younger—and more approachable—Elddreki. But she knew enough to be aware that Qadir had a centuries-old friendship with the Kyonan royal house. The house to which King Calinnae belonged, that was now known as the house of Dragonfriend. Eamon's house.

What the dragon-ruler would want with her, she couldn't imagine. But it wasn't as though he had accidentally stopped at the wrong tent. He said he had summoned her mind while she slept. She hadn't known dragon magic could do that, but she supposed it shouldn't surprise her after the stories she had heard about the beasts of legend.

"What...what did you want to speak to me about?" she tried tentatively.

"I wished to thank you," said Qadir evenly. "Not only on my own behalf, but on behalf of dragonkind. It seems you have done us a service, and we are in your debt."

By the end of this speech, Lucy's mouth was hanging open in a very unladylike way. For a prolonged moment she could only stare at the dragon.

"I've done you a service?" she managed at last. "What service could I possibly have—"

"You destroyed the abomination that we had failed even to identify, let alone eliminate," Qadir interrupted her. "We of Vasilisa were not even aware of the existence of the dragon colony located in the place the humans call Wyvern Islands. We certainly did not know that one of their number had forfeited his magic to a human, thereby warping the receiver."

Lucy shut her mouth with a snap as his words fell into place. The "abomination" in question was her uncle, Scanlon. The one she had killed in order to save Benjy's life. Jocelyn, after swearing her to secrecy, had explained it all to her. Although she hadn't wanted to acknowledge that her friend was telling the truth—and therefore that Eamon wasn't entirely culpable for his actions—she had taken in every detail of the story.

Dragons who had chosen immortality couldn't die except in

one way—by forfeiting their magic to another creature in an act of suicide that twisted the recipient as surely as it destroyed the giver. Scanlon had somehow managed to find the one dragon desperate enough to do just that, and convinced him to pass over his magic. The result was that Scanlon had gained a subtle but powerful magic that caused people to trust him implicitly.

"I do not know if you have been made familiar with our history," Qadir continued, unruffled by Lucy's evident consternation. "I am aware that Elddreki told things to his human companions that perhaps...Suffice it to say, there was a time when many dragons engaged in this appalling act. The creatures that resulted could not be allowed to survive. We hunted them down and destroyed them all."

Lucy kept her mouth shut. She wasn't sure whether she would get herself, or Jocelyn, or even Elddreki in trouble if she admitted that Joss had told her all of this. She had hardly known whether to believe that so many creatures of legend—unicorns, werewolves, even mermaids—had been the result of dragons forfeiting their power to regular animals.

"We were sure we had eradicated them," Qadir said. "We believed that no dragon would again be lost enough to undertake such an act. We certainly never imagined that any of our kind would be so foolish as to give their magic to a human." Qadir's tail twitched ever so slightly. "But there was much we didn't see," he went on, his tone as calm as ever. "It seems our farsight is more limited than we imagined."

He looked down at her, his gaze burning in its strength in spite of the distance created by his immense size.

"We became aware of events only after they had transpired. I was led to believe that your father had rendered us a service in removing the human who had been tainted by the stolen magic. But I recently visited his mind to express my gratitude, and to his credit he did not attempt to maintain the deception." The dragon leaned his head down slightly as he studied Lucy with discomfiting focus. "Although he did not seem eager to reveal that you had in fact been the one to right the wrong in question."

"No." Lucy found her voice at last. "I can imagine." And she certainly could imagine her father's reluctance to turn the attention of this terrifying beast toward his daughter. She had never felt so grateful for his protectiveness, although she had to agree that he would not have been wise to attempt to lie to Qadir about what had actually happened.

"Well," said Qadir, as if closing the matter. "Whatever his hesitations, the fact remains. You did us a service, and as I said, I am grateful. I will keep my eye on you."

"Keep your eye on me?" Lucy repeated, bewildered and a little intimidated. "How would you do that?"

"Not all dragons can exercise their farsight across such a distance, it is true," Qadir said, apparently acknowledging a point Lucy hadn't realized she'd made. "But I can. It has not been my custom to watch the activities of other kingdoms beyond Kyona. And I do not mean to suggest that I will watch you constantly." He made an alarming guttural noise that seemed to be a chuckle. "Far from it. But I have an interest in you now, and your line. I will follow the journey of your life loosely with my farsight."

Lucy just blinked, unsure what to make of any of it. It was a relief that he wouldn't be watching her all the time, since apparently that was something dragons could do. His talk of her line, and the journey of her life, made her think it might be another decade before he thought to check in on her. Which was fine with her.

"Thank you?" she said at last, the words coming out like a question.

Qadir inclined his head in a stately gesture. Lucy dipped her own head, feeling that a curtsy would be out of place, and when she raised it, the dragon was somehow just gone. In fact, so were the mountains. She looked around in confusion, the gloom pressing against her eyes more every second until she couldn't see a thing. Then, all at once, she found herself awake in her makeshift accommodation on the edge of the jungle, taking great unsteady gulps of air as she tried to return to reality.

CHAPTER SIXTEEN

Lucy woke to sounds of bustle. At first she thought it was still the middle of the night, as it had been when she had woken from her astonishing vision of Qadir. But despite it still being dark outside, there was no mistaking the sounds of the camp being packed up.

She hastily readied herself, trying to remember if Rasad had said anything the day before about leaving before sunrise. Perhaps he had mentioned it after she had retired for the night.

She pushed out of her tent to find the other North Landers already assembled, looking as groggy as she felt. Rasad's men, however, were already in full swing. Lucy had to admire their efficiency as they reduced her night's accommodation to a bundle of poles and canvas within minutes.

"How was your night?" Jocelyn asked, stifling a yawn as they watched the approach of the servant who was bringing their horses over.

"Not very restful," Lucy responded.

"Couldn't sleep?"

"No, it wasn't that," said Lucy slowly, not meeting her friend's eye. She wasn't sure how much to tell. "I had...a dream."

"A dream?" Jocelyn repeated. Lucy's tone had clearly caught her interest. "What kind of a dream?"

Lucy glanced at the others, standing in a clump nearby. No one seemed to be listening in, but she lowered her voice anyway. "Actually, it was more like a vision. I mean, it was *real*. I spoke to the dragon-ruler. He sort of…called me somehow. To the mountains." The words came out in a rush, and the relief of having them out was immediate. It helped that although Jocelyn's eyes were wide and her mouth was hanging open, she didn't question Lucy's sanity.

"The dragon-ruler called you in your dream? But…why?"

"He wanted to thank me, apparently," said Lucy dryly.

"Thank you for what?" Jocelyn still looked stunned, and her whisper was growing a little too loud for Lucy's liking.

"Shh," she hissed, glancing around. It was one thing for the others to overhear, but the last thing she wanted was for Rasad to find out what she'd done. "He wanted to thank me for…you know…getting rid of Scanlon."

She said the name so quietly that Jocelyn probably couldn't hear, but she would know what Lucy meant anyway. For a long moment the princess was silent, her expression thoughtful.

"Of course," she said at last. "The dragons feel strongly about eliminating any creatures who've received forfeited dragon magic." Her tone turned rueful. "One almost fried me once, thinking that my," her voice dropped to a mere breath as she also glanced around to make sure no one was nearby, "my power was the result of a dragon killing itself." She grimaced. "They call such creatures abominations."

"Yes, Qadir said that," Lucy said quickly.

The horses had arrived, and Kincaid started toward them with an offer to help boost his wife and her friend into their saddles. Jocelyn waved him away impatiently, leaning closer to hear Lucy's words. Kincaid retreated without complaint, but with a curious glance that convinced Lucy he would be interrogating his wife for details later. She supposed Jocelyn would tell him all about it. There was no real reason why she shouldn't, but the thought still made Lucy uncomfortable.

"Anyway," she said hastily, relieving a helpful servant of her horse's reins and waiting until he had retreated to continue. "I don't know anything about forfeited dragon magic, but I have no problem calling Scanlon an abomination. He earned that title the moment he held a knife to my ten-year-old brother's throat."

"Can I assist you?"

Rasad's smooth voice made Lucy jump, her heart racing more erratically than it had during her encounter with the dragon-ruler. She turned, noting with dismay that he was standing much closer than she had realized, unnoticed in the darkness. How much had he heard?

If he had caught her mention of dragons, or magic, or her dead uncle, he gave no indication of it. Lucy accepted his offer of assistance in getting into the saddle without comment, too mortified to find words. Why was he always nearby at inconvenient moments?

It helped restore her poise when she noticed, once settled in the saddle, that Eamon was glowering at the Thoranian man who had dared to give Lucy his help. She made no effort to hide it as she rolled her eyes. Eamon never failed to make a fool of himself when Rasad was around, but that wasn't Lucy's problem.

"I hope you will permit me to ride beside you again, Luciana," said Rasad, mounting quickly into the saddle of his own horse. "I would dearly love to see your reaction when we reach Thirl."

"Of course," said Lucy, a little shyly. "I would be honored." And she *was* honored by the ongoing attention.

She sent Jocelyn a glance, trying to communicate without words that they would have to finish their conversation later. For some reason the princess looked troubled, but gave a curt nod before turning toward her husband, who had once again approached her.

Lucy watched them for a moment, trying not to feel jealous. It must be nice to be in their position. They were happy together, and their relationship was uncomplicated. Both families—both kingdoms—had been equally pleased with the marriage and the alliance it represented. It was hard for Jocelyn to leave her home kingdom, of course, but it was surely worth it to be so happy, and to have someone beside her who looked at her the way Kincaid did.

Lucy pulled her gaze forward with an effort. Her eyes slid over Eamon, who was still frowning in an unfriendly way, and landed on Rasad. He was watching her with a faint smile, the admiration clear on his face.

"You look altogether too lovely to have only just woken," he said softly, the abrupt compliment taking her by surprise.

She felt her cheeks heat slightly, but she didn't know if he'd be able to tell in the low light. "You flatter me," she said awkwardly.

He smiled. "Not at all." But he seemed to read her discomfort, and he deftly turned the conversation to lighter topics as they set off, this time leading the cavalcade.

They crossed the river by way of a broad bridge, constructed from timber that no doubt came from the jungle around them. The first hints of light began to streak across the sky as they reached the other side. Despite the Thoranian man's casual conversation, Lucy felt strange to be leading the group by his side.

But as the landscape lightened, she quickly became distracted by her surroundings. On the other side of the river, the jungle fell away, stretching out to the north and south, but leaving a clear path due east. Lucy could see that this ground had not been cleared by human hands. It was a natural end to the trees, and she felt herself breathing more freely, in spite of the continued humidity.

In the distance, she could see some kind of mountain range, the peaks silhouetted against the growing light. They hadn't been riding long, and the sun still hadn't fully risen, when she realized that the dark mass immediately in front of her was not a lone mountain standing apart from the others, as she had supposed. It was a city.

For a moment she was bewildered, wondering why they hadn't just pushed on the night before if they really were so very close to the capital. But then the sun crested the distant peaks, and all other thoughts fled from her mind.

Rasad reached over and stopped her horse with a hand on the bridle, but Lucy hardly noticed. She gasped audibly at the sight before her as the rising sun appeared as if by design above the glittering towers of Thirl.

A quick glance at Rasad, who wore a very satisfied expression, suggested that the timing of their approach was indeed by design. But her eyes quickly turned back to the city in front of them.

She had assumed that Thirl would be similar to Balenol's capital in design and feel. But she had been mistaken. It wasn't made of dour stone like Nohl, or even the neat, pleasant cobblestones of Kyona's capital city. It was constructed of a pale, golden substance, with a reddish hue brought out by the rays of the climbing sun.

"It's sandstone," Rasad said helpfully, as though reading her thoughts. "Quarried from our own eastern regions."

Lucy just nodded, her attention still riveted on the panorama coming into focus, colorless silhouettes painted gradually in golden and red as the light of the new day washed over the kingdom.

The buildings were square and flat-roofed, but here and there lattice work could be seen rising from some of the grander dwellings, the sun glowing through the carving. And the sunlight did more than glow. The more elaborate structures sparkled, their edges and corners glinting like stars that had disobeyed the order to fade with the advent of the sun. Catches of brighter color even shot out here and there, purple and blue and red. Nowhere more impressively than on the palace, which rose majestically above the rest of the city, occupying what seemed to be a slight natural rise at the center of the capital.

"We quarry more than just sandstone in the east." Rasad's quiet voice broke in on her amazement. Despite the fact that they were still on horseback, he seemed impossibly close. "Have you heard of the Jeweled Peaks?"

Lucy shook her head mutely.

"One day I will take you there," Rasad promised, and the certainty in his voice made Lucy's stomach flop strangely. "Thorania is rich in natural beauty, and natural wealth. We mine many precious gems here, and not all of them get exported across the sea." He smiled in satisfaction. "Some of them grace our capital."

"I can see why you wanted to wait until sunrise to approach Thirl," said Lucy at last. "It's one of the most beautiful things I've ever seen." It was true. The vista was dazzling in its brilliance.

"It would certainly be a waste for your first glimpse of our city to be in the dead of night," agreed Rasad with a smile. "I'm glad you like it."

"I'm sure anyone would," said Lucy politely, glancing behind her as she spoke to test her words. The others did look impressed, their eyes as wide as Lucy's had been. But while Jocelyn, Kincaid, and Miles were all staring unblinkingly at Thirl, she noticed that both Eamon and Cody were watching her instead.

There was a slight crease between Cody's eyebrows that told her he was concerned, although she wasn't sure about what. Her eyes slid involuntarily to Eamon, and their gazes locked for a moment. She looked away quickly, flushing slightly. There was something unsettling about his expression, and she couldn't immediately identify what it was.

"Come," said Rasad, the invitation laced with the tiniest hint of command. Lucy had the impression that he was so used to giving directions that he wouldn't know how to stop if he wanted to.

She urged her horse forward obediently, following the Thoranian toward the broad wooden gate that was just being opened in readiness for the new day. It was only as they drew close to the gate that her eyes were drawn to another feature of the landscape, away to the south.

Not far from the capital, a large tent city appeared, bustling with activity in the early morning. Lucy squinted at it in the growing light. The men moving purposefully through it looked like soldiers.

There was no time to do more than take note of the encampment before they reached the gates. The guards sprang to attention as they passed through, saluting Rasad as though he was royalty. He acknowledged the gesture with a dip of his head that was every bit as regal as the self-assured grace with which King Giles carried himself. She noticed that Rasad was sitting straighter in his saddle, his indefinable quality of confidence stronger than ever now that he was back in his own kingdom.

The thought of Rasad's influence made Lucy uneasy for reasons she couldn't articulate. The sensation made her think again of Eamon's expression as he had watched her take in the beautiful city of Thirl. Suddenly it hit her what had seemed strange about the look. She had become used to seeing him scowl every time he looked at Rasad, but in that moment he hadn't been glowering at the older man at all. He had been looking at Lucy, and there had been no anger or resentment on his face. Just the same concern that etched Cody's brow.

She found herself frowning, and she pushed the thought from her mind. She wanted to focus on this incredible new place, not worry about what—or who—was behind her.

They rode through the streets of Thirl with all the air of a parade. The city was still waking, but small crowds gathered to gawk at their progress. A lot of eyes were directed to Lucy, riding alongside Rasad, and she felt more conspicuous than ever. People bobbed their heads to the Thoranian man, and took in the rest of the group furtively. It was easy to see that it was a much more prosperous city than Nohl, but there was also an edge of caution to the crowd's behavior that Lucy couldn't help but notice.

Still, it was hard to find fault when surrounded by such new and beautiful sights. The first flush of dawn had passed, but even in the steadier light, the buildings glowed and sparkled enchantingly.

Markets were starting to operate, and a barrage of smells assaulted Lucy's nose. She turned her head in the direction of one of these groups of stalls, trying to identify the unfamiliar scents.

"Thorania is also famous for its spices," Rasad offered, smiling as he watched her drink it all in. "We have vast spice fields in the southeast."

"That I did know," she said with a smile. "We use Thoranian spices in Kyona. But obviously not all of them, because I'm smelling some I'm sure I've never come across before."

"Very likely," Rasad agreed. "Some of our delicacies are an acquired taste."

They rode on in silence, Lucy's attention fully captivated by the sights and sounds around her. The morning bustle was in full swing now, and it was fascinating to witness. The people were similar in appearance to the Balenans—to Lucy herself—but their manner was different, more open, less suspicious. Perhaps because it was more rich in natural resources, Thorania seemed to have built its prosperity without resorting to slave labor, and therefore had suffered no decline when Kyona was restored to its own position of power.

People darted out of the way of their group, the wary glances they threw toward the travelers seeming out of place when contrasted with the general cheerfulness of the crowds. Perhaps they were suspicious of outsiders.

But they didn't seem like a closed culture in the way Balenol did. Everywhere she looked, Lucy could see the truth of Rasad's words, as she noted the greater variety in the people's coloring. Some were almost as pale as Eamon, others darker than Lucy's mother. Even their fashion was more diverse. At the start of their ride, the garments were simpler. But as they drew closer to the palace in the center of the city, the districts seemed to become more affluent, and Lucy took greater interest in the clothing.

Some people wore clothes similar to those she had seen in Balenol. She even saw some gowns reminiscent of those packed in her own trunk, the style popular in the North Lands.

But most wore clothes of an unfamiliar fashion, the colors as bright as the Balenans' clothes, but the fabric more sheer. The women's clothes were more covering than the equivalent in Nohl, but the fabric was still light. And the men weren't confined in the stiff unyielding clothes that Balenan men wore. Many of them—men and women—wore loosely fitted pants that floated around their legs in bright cascades. The garments looked both comfortable and practical, and Lucy found herself wanting to try one herself.

Among all the different outfits, Lucy took note of how many uniformed men seemed to wander the streets, some appearing to be on duty, but many just moving about the city like all the other pedestrians.

She turned to Rasad with a frown. "Are all these soldiers from the camp outside the city? Are there always so many troops garrisoned in Thirl?"

"Your eyes are sharp," said Rasad approvingly. "There are a great many soldiers here in the capital at present, and no, that's not usually the case. They've been here for some weeks, and they will be here a few weeks more. The muster occurs annually, and it's a chance for the king to inspect his troops, and for large scale training drills to occur." His face relaxed into a smile. "It's also a chance for the men to enjoy themselves. We often hold festivals while so many are gathered."

"I'm sure they appreciate it," said Lucy politely.

They had almost reached their destination, and she turned her eyes forward. Unlike in Nohl, the palace at the center of Thirl didn't open directly onto the city's streets. It was surrounded by a stone wall, with large gates currently standing wide. Even the wall itself was only a partial visual shield, the stone intricately carved with lattices, so that those outside could see glimpses of the palace gardens beyond.

As at the entrance to the city, the guards at the palace's gates sprang to attention at Rasad's approach, and the group passed through into the grounds without check. Lucy barely took in the elaborate gardens, complete with enormous fountains and beautifully manicured walkways, before her attention was captured by the palace itself. Rising up before them, it was breathtaking in its intricacy, its jeweled surfaces sparkling in the morning sun. It seemed like the opposite of the castle at Nohl, which had clearly been designed for functionality, with hardly any thought for beauty. The Thoranian royal palace, on the other hand, overflowed with unnecessary but delightful embell-ishments. A sign of wealth, Lucy supposed.

They rode almost to the doors of the palace before servants appeared to take their mounts. They were then ushered up the broad carved staircase by more servants. Lucy would have liked to have fallen back a bit and walked beside Jocelyn, but somehow she found herself remaining at Rasad's side.

Despite the short morning ride, she felt travel worn and weary from the day before, and she was alarmed to realize that they were being led straight to the throne room. She hardly had time to catch her breath before she found herself entering a long hall, lined with beautifully carved pillars rising in two rows from the smooth stone floor. At the end was a raised dais in the same sandstone as much of the city, with a gilded throne perched on top of it.

The group was obviously expected, because the throne was occupied. King Abner of Thorania was middle-aged, considerably older than both King Calinnae and King Giles. Somewhat to Lucy's surprise, he wasn't decked with jewels or finery. He wore the unfamiliar Thoranian fashion Lucy had observed during their ride through Thirl, but other than the simple circlet on his head, he looked more or less like an ordinary person.

He smiled in greeting as they approached, making Lucy feel more at ease despite her conspicuous position at the head of the group. But even the king's apparent approachability wasn't enough to prevent Lucy from feeling bewildered and overwhelmed by Rasad's presentation.

"Your Majesty," the Thoranian said, executing a flawless bow. "Allow me the honor of presenting to you Luciana and Matheus of Kyona. And also their companion, Cody, who has accompanied them in the role of protector."

"Ah yes, I received your express regarding the addition to our guests, Rasad," said the king placidly. He once again directed his smile to Lucy and Matheus. "You are very welcome. I understand you are related to Balenol's new king?"

"Yes, Your Majesty," said Lucy, sweeping into her best curtsy. "Our mother is first cousin to King Giles."

"Good, good," said the king. "And I trust your cousin's coronation went smoothly?"

The image of the balcony disappearing beneath King Giles's feet sprang unbidden to Lucy's mind, followed swiftly by the silver flash of the Kyonan guard's dagger slicing through the air on its trajectory toward the monarch's heart.

"Yes, Your Majesty," she said, after only the slightest of pauses.

"I'm pleased to hear it." With a nod, the king dismissed her, turning his attention to the others. With all due ceremony Rasad proceeded to introduce the royals and Lord and Lady Rodanthe.

Lucy stepped back beside Matheus and Cody, trying to melt into the background. And trying to avoid locking eyes with Lady Rodanthe, whose eyebrow was ever so slightly raised. It was a mercifully brief interaction with the king before the guests were shown out of the throne room. Rasad followed them to the door, bowing over Lucy's hand as he bid them farewell.

"I must give King Abner a report on the delegation's time in Nohl," he explained. "But my people will show you to your rooms, and I will speak with you again soon."

"Thank you," said Lucy awkwardly, hurrying gratefully from the room in the wake of the others.

"Well," said Jocelyn mildly as they followed their guides down a light stone corridor. "The king was very welcoming."

"Yes," said Lucy tonelessly.

Jocelyn might be too polite to say it, but Lucy knew everyone was well aware of how unusual—and pointed—it had been for Rasad to introduce the untitled add-ons to the party before Kyona's crown prince and a prince and princess of Valoria. She knew she was unfamiliar with Thoranian customs, but it was hard to believe that such behavior was normal here when it would be considered extremely inappropriate in every other court Lucy had visited or heard of.

It soon became clear that once again Lucy, Matheus, and even Cody were being accommodated in the same elegant wing of the palace as the royal and noble visitors. The same consideration had made Lucy feel touched and grateful in Nohl, but somehow in Thirl it made her feel embarrassed.

Nevertheless, she was grateful for the chance to settle in. Her room was beautiful, the decor simple but in excellent taste. The floor was a smooth polished stone, and the bed was hung with the same kind of gauzy material she had seen the wealthier Thirlians wearing. Double doors opened onto a lovely interior courtyard, the portal hung with the same sheer and colorful fabric. The air was still moist, but without the canopy of trees, it wasn't as suffocating, somehow.

They weren't expected to be available for anything formal for some time. As glad as she was to rest, Lucy was hardly going to sleep so early in the day. She wandered idly to the canopied bed, stretching across it comfortably. She drew the slim journal from her pocket and flicked through it, skimming over Haydn's descriptions of life in the jungle, the arrival of the community's first baby, Haydn's pride in his first success at shooting down a monkey, and other such adventures. She was feeling disenchanted with Balenol, and not especially interested in learning more about the place. She wanted to know about Thorania.

She tossed the journal aside with a sigh. If she wanted to know more about this new kingdom, she would find it on the other side of those doors, not in the pages of an ancient Balenan journal.

She changed quickly into a fresh gown, pushing aside the fleeting wish that she could don one of the comfortable-looking outfits the local women wore. She had taken note of which room was Jocelyn and Kincaid's, but she hesitated before going out into the hallway. Perhaps they wouldn't want to be disturbed. Lucy wanted to finish telling her friend about her unnerving dream, and find out what Jocelyn made of the dragon-ruler's unexpected offer. But she didn't especially want to discuss it in front of Kincaid. It was easy to forget that the princess wasn't exactly free to go carousing around with her friend anymore.

She supposed Cody would expect her to alert him if she wanted to explore the city, but she had no desire to repeat her misstep from Balenol the moment she arrived in Thorania. She opened the door of her suite absently, still debating whether to get Matheus to go with her or to try to slip out of the palace alone.

But she had only taken half a step out into the corridor when she stopped short. It seemed the decision was made for her.

CHAPTER SEVENTEEN

"Rasad," said Lucy, unable to hide her surprise. "What are you doing here?"

The Thoranian raised an eyebrow. "I came to see how you had settled in, Luciana. Is there some reason I shouldn't be here?"

"Of course not," said Lucy quickly, trying to cover her confusion. "I just didn't expect you."

Rasad ignored her comment, taking in her change of outfit with his eyebrow still raised. "You appear to be preparing to go somewhere. I hope you're not displeased with your accommodations?"

"Not at all, they're beautiful!" said Lucy sincerely. "I just..." She hesitated, but Rasad was still waiting expectantly, and she found her words tumbling out in a rush. "The truth is I'm not tired, and the glimpse of the city we saw on our way in fascinated me. I was hoping to explore a little."

Rasad brightened, looking genuinely pleased by her answer. "I'm glad you liked what you saw. I would be honored to show you around the city."

Lucy hesitated again. Rasad's escort was not what she'd

bargained for. She wanted to wander, not get a formal tour. But as the silence stretched out, she realized that her reluctance wasn't exactly polite.

"That's very kind of you," she said at last. "I don't want to put you to any trouble."

"No trouble," said Rasad, that open and attractive smile back again. "I would love to show you my city. I'll have horses readied for us." He gave a barely perceptible nod, and a servant whom Lucy hadn't even noticed hovering against the wall gave a small bow and disappeared down the corridor.

"Well, if it really is no trouble," Lucy said lamely. It seemed there was little else to say. Her eyes traveled involuntarily to the door of the double suite Cody was sharing with Matheus. It wasn't entirely clear to her whether she was still supposed to be alerting Lord and Lady Rodanthe to her movements, but she knew without doubt how Cody would feel about her taking off without telling him.

"Do you need to alert your minder?" asked Rasad, amusement clear in his voice as he followed the trajectory of her gaze.

"Of course not," said Lucy, lifting her chin slightly. "I'm free to come and go as I please."

"I should hope so," agreed Rasad politely. But he still sounded amused, and it irked Lucy. Not least because she hadn't been entirely truthful. She remembered her father's words to her before she left Kyona, and she knew Cody wouldn't be thrilled about her leaving the palace without him. But if she asked him, and he said no, it would be more humiliating than she could handle right now.

"Shall we?" she asked majestically, turning from Rasad and sweeping down the corridor in what she hoped was the right direction. She hadn't made it far when her progress was interrupted by the sound of a door opening.

"Lucy! I thought I heard your voice. I was just coming

looking for you. You never told me what—oh." Jocelyn's stream of words was cut off as she noticed the man behind Lucy. She bobbed her head politely, but her eyes returned quickly to Lucy, and there was a question in them.

"I didn't feel like resting," said Lucy. "Rasad has kindly offered to show me around the city a little."

At Jocelyn's appearance, Lucy had felt instantly contrite for doubting her friend's interest, and her willingness to ditch her husband in order to finish their interrupted conversation. But still, she met Jocelyn's look with a hint of defiance, sure she could read disapproval there. If Joss was thinking that Eamon wouldn't like Lucy going exploring with Rasad, the princess would do well to remember that there was no reason in the world why Lucy should answer to him. The fact that Cody wouldn't like it either was none of Jocelyn's concern.

"I see," said Jocelyn politely. "How kind of him. Perhaps we could join you."

The words didn't sound much like a request, and Lucy sent her friend a dry look. Jocelyn smiled back blandly.

"Of course, Your Highness," said Rasad, his smooth voice giving no hint of disappointment at the interruption to the intended tête-à-tête. "You would be most welcome."

"Excellent," said Jocelyn brightly. She turned her head, calling back into the suite. "Kincaid! We've been invited to explore the city a little with Lucy and our host."

"What?" Kincaid's voice sounded muffled, and when he appeared in the doorway a moment later, he looked slightly groggy, as if he had been resting. Lucy barely suppressed a grimace. It was abundantly clear that the Valorian had no desire to join a tour of the city at that moment, but she doubted his wife was going to give him a choice.

"We'll meet you at the entrance to the palace in a few minutes," Jocelyn said brightly, apparently oblivious to the admonishing look Lucy was directing toward her. It wasn't that she didn't want Jocelyn to come—quite the opposite—but she wished it didn't have to be so painfully obvious that Jocelyn was inserting herself because she thought it was inappropriate for Lucy to go alone.

It was considerably more than a few minutes before the couple appeared in the gardens. The only reason Lucy wasn't mortified by then was that Rasad kept her occupied with a smooth stream of casual conversation, leaving her no time to dwell on the awkwardness of Jocelyn forcing herself in as a chaperone. Lucy was at least relieved to see that none of the others in their traveling party had managed to tag along uninvited.

The four of them proceeded out of the palace gates, accompanied only by one servant, and the Valorian couple's few personal guards. They made their way down a busy, well-kept street, pedestrians stepping respectfully aside when they saw the identity of the man leading the little group. The riders had naturally fallen into two pairs, Lucy riding alongside Rasad, with Jocelyn and Kincaid behind. Any attempt to speak with the Valorians would be impractical. Lucy could see she would need to confine her conversation to her host.

"You travel without guards, usually?" Lucy asked him curiously.

"One of the advantages of not being royal," he said conspiratorially, with a glance back at the Valorian couple and their shadows.

Lucy smiled. She couldn't help but agree, remembering all the times she'd wished Eamon's guards would give them a moment of privacy. It was certainly nice to speak freely, with no other listening ears.

"I noticed there were a number of Thoranian guards on the journey to Thirl," she prompted.

"Sometimes I travel with guards," Rasad agreed comfortably. "Certainly when I'm leaving the kingdom, and usually when traveling to my home in the north. But not within Thirl. At least," he smiled, "not in any part of the city I would take you to see."

Lucy returned his smile, but inside she felt a little disappointed. It seemed they were to stick to the wealthier, more ordered districts, close to the palace. But it was the bustling chaos of the ordinary people that fascinated her. She had explored just about every corner of Kynton with Jocelyn and Eamon over the years. Always with guards in tow, of course. But Kyona's king and queen encouraged their children not to completely distance themselves from everyday people. Probably because of their own less than royal upbringing, they wanted the prince and princess to have at least a small understanding of the realities of life for peasants.

"So you gave your report to the king?" she asked, turning the subject. "It doesn't seem to have taken long."

"I did," Rasad confirmed. "There wasn't much to report. He was pleased to hear that the coronation was a success, and that the relations between the Balenan royals and their visitors from the North Lands were positive." He glanced sideways at her. "At least for the most part."

Lucy sighed, tired of dancing around unpleasant truths with polite words. "If you're referring to my experiences," she said frankly, "they're completely irrelevant. I came because of the family connection between the new king and my mother. I have no part in any negotiations or formal relationship between the Kyonan crown and the Balenan one."

"You underrate your own importance, Luciana," said Rasad. To Lucy's irritation, he looked amused. "I assure you, my king did not consider you irrelevant. In fact, you and your brother hold a unique position. Few others could claim to have such a strong connection to and understanding of both Kyona and Balenol. Thorania is delighted to welcome you here, and you are every bit as honored a guest as the princes and princess."

Lucy frowned, struggling to understand what interest Thorania's king could have in her mixed heritage. Especially since it generally seemed to do her no favors in either of the kingdoms to which she could actually claim kinship.

"Do you mean the fact that I have both Kyonan and Balenan blood?"

Rasad raised an eyebrow. "Your situation is far more unique than that, Luciana. You are closely related to the Balenan monarch, and you have a longstanding personal connection with the Kyonan royal family as well. Who else—beyond your family—could make such a claim?"

For a moment Lucy was silent, taken aback by this summary. It didn't escape her notice that Rasad seemed to be better informed about her family's relationship with Kyona's monarchs than he had previously implied.

"Is that why you introduced me first?" she asked bluntly. "Before the royal visitors, I mean. It seemed a little...pointed."

Rasad raised an eyebrow. "Were they offended?"

"No," said Lucy slowly. "I don't think they were. But they're very relaxed for royalty, all three of them. And as you are evidently aware, they know Matheus and me extremely well. Still, I imagine they thought it was strange. Truthfully, *I* thought it was strange. Whatever you say about my situation, you know that I have no title. Elevating me and my brother seemed...out of place."

Rasad chuckled. "Rank isn't everything, Luciana, at least not here in Thorania. I have no noble title, but I don't think my influence suffers for it. You'll find that I'm fairly well respected." He spoke mildly, but something in his tone told Lucy that his words were an extreme understatement.

"What is your position?" she asked, no longer caring if she was being too forthright. She should have done more to find out who Rasad really was before accepting his invitation, but it was better to do so now than not at all.

"I'm His Majesty's primary advisor," said Rasad smoothly, no hint of arrogance in his voice. "His chief consultant, you could say."

"Is that an official role?" Lucy asked, impressed in spite of herself.

"It is."

"But you have no noble blood?"

Rasad smiled. "None at all." He glanced over at her. "I come from a well-respected family, one which has held a position of influence for generations, but there is no title attached to my estate."

Just excessive wealth, Lucy guessed. But of course she kept the thought to herself as she studied her companion curiously. Rasad seemed perfectly comfortable as he spoke about his role and his family's standing. If he secretly wished for a court title, there was no sign of it. But it wasn't so difficult to understand, after all. From Lucy's observation, wealth could be just as powerful a tool as rank. And for all his talk of no titles, Rasad had gained the formal role of primary advisor to the king, and at quite a young age. No wonder he hadn't hesitated to extend an invitation to Lucy and Matheus to join the delegation.

She had been so engrossed in their conversation, Lucy had barely taken in her surroundings as they rode. The sun was climbing higher in the cloudless sky, and Lucy felt uncomfortably hot. She couldn't help but glance enviously at the more climate-appropriate garments of the local women who sauntered past, looking relaxed and far more fresh than should be possible in such heat.

The street they were riding down opened ahead of them,

and Lucy caught a glimpse of a beautiful square, with a fountain rising from its center. It took her a moment to recognize it as a market, because the clamor of the marketplaces they had ridden past on their way into Thirl was entirely absent. They weren't far from the palace, and everywhere she looked there was evidence of wealth. Everyone seemed to be well dressed and at ease, not a single beggar to be seen.

"Is this an exclusive market?" she asked Rasad. "Just for the nobility or something?"

He chuckled. "Not formally. But I know what you mean. It doesn't quite have the flavor of some of the more general markets. It's not that the less wealthy are kept out by design, merely by circumstance. Only precious gems are sold in this particular square. Most of the city's inhabitants have little interest in these stalls."

"I see," said Lucy. She suspected that it was not their lack of interest that kept them away so much as their lack of resources. She supposed that Rasad was just trying to say the same thing, only more diplomatically.

"Shall we have a look?" Rasad spread his hand out invitingly, and Lucy nodded.

She couldn't politely decline, but she wasn't especially interested. It wasn't that the people wandering through the market were unhappy, but the whole scene was muted and cultivated. She couldn't help but think longingly of the vibrant chaos of the other markets she'd glimpsed, or even of the marketplaces in Kynton. She had always loved wandering amidst the hubbub, watching people haggle and argue. It was one of the things she found most exciting about leaving her peaceful forest community to visit the bustling capital.

Jocelyn and Kincaid dismounted behind them, leaving their horses in the care of the servant who had accompanied them. Lucy explained the nature of the market to them as they began to wander between the stalls. Being royals, they were well trained in how to show polite interest in everything they saw, but Lucy couldn't detect any real enthusiasm in either of them. She could only imagine that Kincaid especially was wondering why in the kingdom he had been dragged from his rest for such a mundane outing.

"Beautiful lady!" called a merchant winningly, his eyes unmistakably fixed on Lucy. "Such beauty requires no embellishment, to be sure, but should you want to add that subtle hint of elegance..." He trailed off, tilting his head suggestively toward his wares.

"No thank you," said Lucy quickly, eager to move on before the man drew attention to her.

"But my dear, it would honor me if you would take a look. These amethysts would grace your lovely self to perfection."

Lucy took a step closer in spite of herself. She had no real interest in buying jewelry—not to mention she didn't have the funds—but she couldn't resist getting a better look at the necklace he was displaying. There was no denying that it was beautiful, the purple stones sparkling flawlessly in their intricately crafted settings, suspended from a slender silver chain. There was also a bracelet to match, delicate leaves of pressed silver curling around the stones, and a pair of simple but elegant earrings.

"They're lovely," she said, stepping back quickly so that she was once again alongside Jocelyn. "But I'm not buying today."

"My dear," protested the salesman, his voice as smooth as glass. "It would be a crime to let this set—my best, you know—go to a buyer who wouldn't do it justice the way your exquisite coloring would. For the pleasure of seeing it go to such an appropriate recipient, I would let it go for an excellent price."

Lucy opened her mouth to protest, but a soft voice cut her off before she could speak.

"He's right, you know. Those amethysts truly would suit you to perfection."

"Thank you for the compliment," said Lucy, in what she hoped was a tone of finality. "But I'm not looking to buy today."

"I would be delighted to give them to you," said Rasad, as if it was a small matter. "Such a gift would be a small repayment for you accepting my invitation to join me here in Thorania."

"You're very kind," said Lucy, feeling a hint of real panic as Rasad waved a casual hand in some silent instruction to the merchant. She was painfully aware of Jocelyn shifting beside her, as if she was struggling to keep her thoughts to herself. "But I couldn't possibly accept such a gift."

"My dear Luciana, it's no great—"

"I couldn't possibly accept," Lucy repeated, more firmly. She hoped he couldn't tell how quickly her heart was racing. The idea of being given such a token by this man she barely knew— and in such a public setting—was horrifying.

"As you wish," said Rasad with his usual calm. "I wouldn't want to make you uncomfortable."

The merchant opened his mouth, clearly ready to protest, but at a look from Rasad he subsided, disappointed.

Lucy turned away from the stall, her heart still racing uncomfortably quickly. The fact that they had clearly attracted some attention after all did nothing to help. She linked arms with Jocelyn, trying to put some visual distance between herself and their host.

"Let's look over there," she said loudly, drawing Jocelyn away from the others. The princess made no objection, allowing herself to be pulled along. One of the Valorian guards broke off from the group to trail behind them. He looked only minimally watchful. It was such a controlled setting—Lucy imagined he would be much more on edge if they had ventured into the parts of the city she had actually wanted to see.

"I'm glad you said no," said Jocelyn abruptly, pulling Lucy from her thoughts. "I would have been uncomfortable if he'd given you jewelry."

"Not as uncomfortable as I would have been," said Lucy tartly. "Of course I said no. Do you really think I'd even consider accepting such a gift?"

"No," said Jocelyn. "Of course not." But the assurance was unconvincing, and Lucy felt rattled. She thought her friend knew her better than that. But apparently Lucy couldn't count on anything being as she knew it anymore.

"That's a lovely fountain," she said with an effort. She pulled her arm out of Jocelyn's on the pretext of moving closer to examine the elaborate water feature.

"Luce..." said Jocelyn, clearly not fooled by Lucy's nonchalance.

"It's fine," said Lucy quickly, unwilling to enter into a more personal discussion with the Valorian guard hovering so close.

She cast her eyes around, finding nothing of great interest amongst the ordered jewelry stalls. Her eyes were drawn to a walkway leading off one side of the square. The path itself was narrow and dark, high buildings on either side blocking out the harsh sunlight. But at the other end, she thought she could see catches of color, reminding her of the gauzy fabric that seemed to be widely used in Thirl for decoration and clothing alike. Once she focused her attention in that direction, she heard the faint sounds of a crowd. Perhaps the more interesting marketplaces of the city weren't so far away after all.

"I wonder what's down there," she said, inclining her head toward the start of the walkway. "Want to have a look?"

"Sure," said Jocelyn, but she cast an uncertain look back toward her husband. Following her gaze, Lucy saw that although Kincaid was talking to Rasad, his eyes were on the two girls.

Lucy barely refrained from rolling her eyes. "Will he really be so worried if you leave his sight for five minutes?"

Jocelyn grimaced. "I know it's silly, but he's been jumpy ever since the attack on King Giles. It bothers him that we still don't have a clue as to the guard's motives, or whether he was working alone."

"Yes, well." Lucy gave a mirthless laugh. "I suppose that's not totally unreasonable."

"But it's fine," said Jocelyn quickly. "I have a guard with me, he has no reason to—"

"No, no." Lucy cut her off with a wave of her hand. "Kincaid's just about the only one in our whole group who isn't mad at me for some reason or another. I don't want to get on his bad side, too. Go see if he wants to come."

"He will," said Jocelyn with the ghost of a grin. She checked that Rasad was out of earshot before continuing in a lowered voice. "If we're both bored out of our minds with this least interesting of all marketplaces, imagine how much he's hating it."

Lucy chuckled, but couldn't resist giving her friend a pointed look. "Especially since the poor man was on the point of taking a nap when you dragged him out here totally unnecessarily."

Jocelyn made no attempt to deny it. "Well, someone had to keep an eye on you and your elderly admirer," she said airily, traipsing off before her spluttering friend could protest.

Robbed of the opportunity to point out either that Rasad was far from elderly or that she wasn't interested in his admiration—she couldn't decide which point was more offensive— Lucy rolled her eyes at her friend's retreating back.

She didn't wait for Jocelyn to return, heading straight for the walkway and its promise of respite from the heat. The relief was instantaneous as soon as she stepped into the shadow of the high walls. Kyona was warm enough in the summer, but she wasn't used to this fierce sun.

Lucy glanced back toward the jewelry market. There was no sign of the others yet, but she thought she might as well wander on while waiting for them to catch up. The Valorian guard had naturally followed the princess, but Lucy wasn't in the least nervous about wandering around alone. She had her weapon on her, of course, but she couldn't imagine needing it in such a prosperous and orderly corner of the city.

The thought had barely crossed her mind when she heard a swift footstep behind her. She had only half turned, expecting to see Jocelyn hurrying to join her, when she felt the sudden pressure of a strong arm around her middle, trapping her arms in place and yanking her whole body backward until she was crushed against someone's chest. She had barely taken all this in when she felt herself being dragged backward toward an alleyway she hadn't even noticed before. Her gasp of surprise was lost as a hand covered her mouth, and a smooth voice spoke quietly right beside her ear.

"You'll be coming along with me now."

CHAPTER EIGHTEEN

Lucy's first thought was shock at the unexpected attack. The next, following swiftly after, was relief that Cody had pushed her to get back into her training. She wasn't conscious of any fear as instinct kicked in.

She went still for the briefest moment, letting the man pull her along without resistance. Then she executed a sudden twist. It wasn't enough to break the assailant's hold, but it was enough to get one of her arms free.

One arm was all she needed.

In a smooth movement, she plunged her elbow into the man's stomach, retrieving her dagger before the grunt of pain had left his lips. She spun out of his slackened grip, her weapon raised in front of her as she got her first look at her attacker.

He was not at all what she had expected, but she didn't allow her surprise to distract her. She slashed her dagger toward him, not aiming to do any real harm, just wanting to show that she was serious.

But he didn't allow himself to be distracted either. He had a blade of his own up before she could blink, and he threw her thrust off with such force that it took all her strength to keep her arm from being flung back completely. Undeterred, Lucy dropped into a fighting stance, sparing the briefest moment to curse her inconvenient skirts. At least she'd worn a simple dress.

The man advanced toward her, his eyes narrowed as they flicked from her blade to her determined expression. She gave him no opening. Lunging forward, she spun her dagger around, aiming to incapacitate the arm holding his knife.

The man brought his blade up only just in time, but Lucy didn't let up. She continued to press him, the clang of metal on metal seeming to echo off the high stone walls on either side of them. He met her each time, but it was clearly taking his whole attention to defend. It wasn't long before his breath was coming in pants.

Lucy's breath was short as well, but she barely noticed. She was filled with the same elation that had taken over when she was dueling with Cody, but so much more potent now, in a real fight. She tried to keep her focus on each twist and lunge, but it was impossible not to feel a thrill of satisfaction at the realization that she was more skilled than her opponent. Probably lucky for her he wasn't carrying a sword.

The man's eyes were growing rounder with every passing moment, and Lucy couldn't help but feel smug at the knowledge of how much she had surprised him. All of a sudden he fumbled, and it was all the opening Lucy needed. With a final surge, she engaged his blade one last time, sending it spinning with an expert flick.

She pressed her advantage, placing her blade instantly against his throat, forcing him to retreat until his back was against a stone wall.

"What do you want?" she demanded curtly, her breath coming in gasps.

"I wasn't trying to hurt you," he panted.

Lucy raised an eyebrow, directing a pointed look toward the man's weapon, lying on the ground nearby.

"You pulled your blade first!" he protested, sounding less menacing and more sulky by the second.

Lucy snorted. "After you grabbed me and tried to forcibly pull me down a dark alley."

"It's not dar—"

"Don't make me laugh," Lucy spat, although she didn't feel much like laughing. "Now answer my question. What do you want with me?"

"I just wanted to talk to you," he grumbled. "Find out what you know."

Lucy blinked, more confused than ever. "What makes you think I know anything of interest to you?"

It was her captive's turn to snort, although he followed it with a wince as it caused his throat to tighten against Lucy's blade.

"Well you're with Rasad, aren't you?" he said rudely.

Lucy bristled. "I don't know what you mean by 'with'. But either way, I don't see how it's any of your business."

"Who are you?" the man said suddenly. "You weren't supposed to be part of the delegation. Is it true that you're half-Balenan and half-Kyonan?"

"What's it to you?" Lucy demanded. "You're the one who owes me answers." Her eyes skimmed over his person, taking note of the affluence clearly displayed in his clothes and general air. He was older than her, but not by as much as she had at first supposed. Her gaze returned to his face, and she tightened her blade arm menacingly. "What do you care if I'm traveling with Rasad? Why did you attack me?"

He hesitated for a moment, looking suddenly even younger. "There were rumors," he said at last. "About the coronation in Nohl. That it almost didn't happen. I thought—" He cut himself off, his eyes narrowing as he searched her face. "You do know something!"

Lucy hastily raised her slackened arm again, chastising herself internally for her lapse. She had been unable to hide her surprise at his words. But she was saved the necessity of replying by the voice issuing faintly from the direction of the side street where the unknown man had grabbed her.

"Lucy?"

"Over here," she called to Jocelyn, keeping her eyes fixed on her prisoner. "I've made a new friend."

"Please, just let me go," the man pleaded, looking suddenly alarmed. "I didn't do you any harm in the end."

Lucy snorted. "Not likely." She glanced down the alley. She could hear footsteps, but Jocelyn wasn't yet in sight. "Now what rumors did you hear?"

But the man clamped his mouth shut, a defiant look coming into his eyes. Lucy sighed, but before she could press the point, Jocelyn rounded the corner, freezing in astonishment at the sight before her. Kincaid, close at her side, also came to an abrupt halt, his hand flying instinctively to the hilt of his sword.

"Lucy?" the princess asked, starting forward again. "Are you all right?"

"Absolutely," said Lucy calmly. "As you see, I'm just having a chat with my new friend..." She turned expectantly to her prisoner, but his mouth was still set in a mulish line, and he clearly wasn't going to identify himself.

"Yosef," said a grim voice. "His name is Lord Yosef."

Lucy whipped her head around, but not quickly enough to miss the fear that flitted across the face of her prisoner—Yosef—at the sound of Rasad's voice. She felt a sinking in her own stomach at the sight of the Thoranian striding purposefully toward them, a martial light in his eye as he brushed past the Valorian couple. Kincaid accompanying Jocelyn was one thing, but Lucy hadn't thought about the fact that their host would likely follow them as well.

She stepped quickly back from the young man, lowering her blade out of habit. But of course it was pointless to return it to its concealed sheath. Rasad had surely seen her wielding the weapon.

"What is this?" Rasad demanded, his eyes passing between Lucy and Lord Yosef. His voice was filled with concern as he turned to her. "Are you all right, Luciana?"

"I'm fine," she said quickly, uncomfortable with how closely the newcomer was watching her interaction with Rasad.

The advisor followed her gaze, and his expression hardened. "What mischief have you been up to, My Lord?"

"Nothing," said Lord Yosef belligerently.

"Is that what you call it when you grab strangers from behind and try to abduct them?" Lucy demanded.

But she instantly regretted her indignant outburst. Rasad rounded on the young man, and there was something about the way her former attacker flinched that made Lucy uneasy. Had she imagined the glint of triumph in the eyes of the primary advisor?

"You did what?! This is an outrage, My Lord. This time you have gone too far, and you will answer for it." He turned to Kincaid. "Your Highness, perhaps you would be so gracious as to spare one of your guards to take charge of this man for the moment. I will send my servant to the palace to summon an escort to see Lord Yosef to the dungeons, and I will speak to His Majesty immediately regarding—"

"Wait," said Lucy, stepping forward.

Rasad turned to look at her, an eyebrow raised in polite confusion. "What is it, Luciana? If you are concerned that the dungeons are too light a punishment, rest assured that it is only an intermediate step."

"No, I meant I don't want you to throw him in the dungeons." Her gaze flicked to Lord Yosef, who was staring at her with as much surprise as his persecutor. "He didn't actually harm me, after all."

There was a moment's silence. "And for that I am more grateful than I can say," said Rasad at last, looking like he was keeping his tone gentle with an effort. "You are very gracious not to press for retribution. But you are my guest here, and the guest of King Abner. Such an unprovoked attack against you cannot go unaddressed, regardless of this man's rank." He lowered his voice as he gestured toward Lord Yosef. "As I told you, my dear Luciana, title is not everything in this kingdom."

Lucy frowned at the endearment, well aware that Lord Yosef was taking in every detail.

"Maybe it was a misunderstanding," she said shortly. "I wouldn't wish to overreact."

Rasad was silent for a moment longer, his jaw working slightly. "Very well," he said at last, with a stiff half-bow. "We will take him straight before the king." His eyes narrowed as they fell once again on Lord Yosef. "But he must answer for his behavior."

"Of course," said Lucy smoothly. "I don't wish to interfere in your authority."

Rasad turned to the Valorians again, his tone stiff and formal. "Your Highnesses, would you be so kind...?"

"Of course," said Kincaid quickly, directing his guards to assist with the prisoner.

Lucy glanced over at Lord Yosef, standing motionless against the wall, right where she had left him. He offered no thanks for her intervention on his behalf, which irked her a little.

"She's going to kill me," he muttered.

"Who is?" Lucy demanded.

His head shot up, his expression supporting her suspicion that he had been talking to himself. He met her eyes, his own gaze guarded, but after a moment he sighed, his shoulders slumping in resignation.

"My sister."

Lucy raised an eyebrow, but there was no time to ask for clarification. The Valorian guards appeared on either side of Lord Yosef, and the young nobleman accompanied them without protest. Lucy replaced her weapon at last before following slowly, her brow furrowed as she tried to make sense of the bizarre turn the morning had taken.

"I'm more sorry than I can say that you were attacked, Luciana." Rasad's voice was regretful, but his eyes were still fixed on the nobleman walking in front of them.

"Please don't worry about it," said Lucy quickly. "There really was no harm done."

"You are as gracious as ever," said Rasad, inclining his head. "But I can assure you, such occurrences are not normal here in Thirl."

"At least not in this part of town," amended Lucy, unable to help herself. They had just emerged back into the jewelry market. Although the procession was attracting some interested looks, the general tone of the square remained placid.

Rasad's expression turned rueful. "Indeed. I truly didn't imagine that there was any danger to our party in this area. It was perhaps unfortunate that you wandered away on your own, but that is no excuse for Lord Yosef's behavior. He has long been something of a troublemaker, but I didn't imagine he would go to such lengths to do me a mischief."

"So he's an enemy of yours?" Lucy pressed quickly.

Rasad was silent for a moment. "Enemy is a strong word. But he is one of a few—truly a few—members of the court who have not welcomed my appointment as King Abner's primary advisor." He exchanged a meaningful look with her. "I told the truth when I said that rank isn't everything in Thorania, but of course there will always be those who resent such open-mindedness."

Lucy frowned, thinking his words over. It was certainly a believable reason for a nobleman to be no friend of Rasad's. But it didn't fit with the interaction she'd had with Lord Yosef, somehow. He hadn't seemed resentful of Rasad. He'd seemed suspicious. She didn't say as much, of course. But she was more determined than ever to discover the nature of Lord Yosef's objection to the man who had invited her into his circle for reasons she still didn't fully understand.

"I must say, I'm impressed that you were able to defend yourself so successfully," said Rasad, turning the topic with his usual tact.

Lucy looked up quickly, self-conscious about her skill being on display. But Rasad looked genuinely impressed.

"Lord Yosef may be a fool, but he is trained to wield a weapon," he said. "If you bested him, you must have trained hard yourself."

Lucy hesitated for a moment, but she saw nothing but admiration in Rasad's eyes. "Yes," she admitted. "It was very important to my parents that my brothers and I learn to defend ourselves. I've been receiving basic weapons training since I was young."

Rasad gave her a long look that was a little too shrewd for her liking. "More than basic, I would imagine." She looked down quickly, and he seemed to sense her embarrassment. His voice was soft as he continued. "It's a strength, Luciana. An admirable and worthwhile skill. You'll find that we appreciate hard work and talent in Thorania. In our women as well as our men."

Lucy met his eyes, her own expression guarded. It was both relieving and unnerving that he had read her so accurately. But she couldn't help but feel gratified by his words.

"Thank you," she said softly.

He nodded, but said no more. They had reached their horses, and after assisting her into the saddle, he moved off to oversee the transport of Lord Yosef to the palace. Jocelyn took the opportunity to draw her horse close to her friend's as they rode back toward the palace at a leisurely pace.

"Are you really all right, Lucy?"

"Of course I am," said Lucy reassuringly. She grimaced. "I'm mainly worried that Cody is going to kill me himself when he finds out I once again managed to get into a dangerous situation when he wasn't on hand."

Her own words made her think of Lord Yosef's comment, and she glanced thoughtfully at the young Thoranian. She was very curious to see the sister who was apparently going to be furious with him. But Jocelyn's next words pulled her back to their conversation.

"And Eamon's going to be annoyed with me for somehow not stopping it. Or for not telling him we were going in the first place." Her long-suffering sigh invited sympathy, but Lucy glared at her friend instead.

"What does any of this have to do with Eamon?"

Jocelyn rolled her eyes. "Don't start, Lucy. You may have decided that he's nothing to you, but you know as well as I do that he's even more concerned about what happens to you than Cody is. He's been worried sick since you agreed to come to Thorania with Rasad."

Lucy snorted. "You mean he's been jealous. He's disliked Rasad since the moment he met him."

"Does he have reason to be jealous?" Jocelyn asked, raising an eyebrow.

Lucy lifted her chin slightly. "Eamon has no reason to be jealous of anyone, not as far as I'm concerned. It's no business of his what I do."

"That's not quite what I was asking," said Jocelyn dryly. But when Lucy remained silent, she dropped it with a sigh. "I'm not saying you're wrong about Eamon's motivations. But it's not just jealousy. He is genuinely worried. We all are." She gave her friend a sideways look. "There's something going on in the South Lands that we don't understand. The attack on King Giles makes no sense whatsoever. And whether you believe it or not, I know that I felt magic when it happened. Not to mention that even though the attack wasn't successful, I honestly think that it was only Eamon's use of his..." she glanced around, "...persuasiveness that prevented a diplomatic disaster or worse between Kyona and Balenol."

Lucy listened in silence, her forehead creased. "No, I agree," she said after a moment. "Something is definitely strange." She thought of King Giles's accident on the balcony. She still hadn't confided to anyone about the impossible flame she thought she'd seen. "In fact, Lord Yosef said..." She trailed off, not sure whether to repeat the nobleman's comment about having heard rumors of the attack against King Giles.

"Said what?" Jocelyn prompted as the silence drew out.

"Nothing," said Lucy quickly. "Never mind."

They were almost back at the palace, and she pulled ahead slightly. She wasn't entirely sure what stopped her from confiding in her friend. It wasn't that she didn't trust Jocelyn, but...trust felt a lot more complicated than it had six months ago.

She dismounted quickly, hurrying up the steps to join the procession now entering the palace. She didn't know whether Rasad planned to include her in the audience with the king, but she had no intention of being left out. She wanted to find out exactly what was going on, and she didn't trust either Rasad or Lord Yosef to tell her the whole truth.

She came up behind Rasad just as he was issuing curt

instructions to a member of the royal guard stationed outside the throne room. The man hurried away to carry the advisor's message, and a minute later others arrived to relieve the Valorian guards of their charge. Lucy couldn't help but feel sorry for Lord Yosef, despite his attack on her. He was looking more anxious by the second, a sheen of sweat appearing on his forehead.

Lucy cleared her throat meaningfully as Rasad directed that Lord Yosef be led into an antechamber to await the king's arrival. The Thoranian turned to her with an expression of surprise. Lucy kept her own face impassive, but she found it hard to believe that he hadn't realized she was there. Evidently he *had* been hoping to keep her out of the proceedings.

"Are you sure you're all right, Luciana?" Rasad asked smoothly. "I would be only too glad to send a physician to your rooms to conduct an assessment."

"There's no need for a physician," said Lucy shortly. "I'm absolutely fine. And I wouldn't want to miss my attacker's appearance before the king, would I?"

"Certainly not," chipped in Kincaid unexpectedly from behind her. "I know that when hearing similar matters in Valoria, my father would want to hear the testimony of as many witnesses as possible. I can only imagine that it's the same here."

The prince spoke mildly, but it was as clear to Lucy as it must have been to Rasad that the Valorians had no more intention of being excluded than Lucy had.

Rasad cast a measuring glance at the trio before stepping back to politely usher them into the antechamber as well.

CHAPTER NINETEEN

Rasad didn't join them in the antechamber, instead striding off down the corridor. For a few minutes, no one spoke. Lord Yosef looked too nervous to speak, and the rest of them were hampered from discussing the incident freely by the presence of the prisoner and his guards.

"What do you think King Abner will make of this?" Kincaid asked suddenly.

"I don't know," said Jocelyn thoughtfully. She lowered her voice. "Did you think Rasad seemed genuinely surprised by the attack?"

Kincaid frowned for a moment, clearly thinking over what had happened. "Yes," he said at last. "I did."

Jocelyn nodded slowly, turning to her friend. "What do you think, Lucy?"

Lucy shrugged, keeping her voice low as well, but painfully conscious that the others in the room could surely hear every word. "Honestly, I don't know Rasad well enough to read him."

She glanced involuntarily toward Lord Yosef as she spoke. She saw to her irritation that he was watching her closely, one eyebrow raised in a slightly incredulous look. She pulled her gaze away, trying to appear unconcerned.

Rasad entered the room a moment later, indicating to the guards with a jerk of the head that they should take the nobleman in before the king. Lucy was surprised at how quickly the monarch had responded. She wondered if it was a quiet day or if Rasad's influence was really so great.

King Abner was once again seated on his throne, looking perplexed more than anything. He inclined his head in greeting to Lucy, Jocelyn, and Kincaid, but his eyes returned quickly to the young nobleman.

"Lord Yosef," he said, his voice mild. "What is this I've been hearing? I could hardly believe it when Rasad told me you had made an unprovoked attack on one of our guests."

"Unfortunately, Your Majesty, it is too true," said Rasad smoothly from his position at the king's side.

"I don't doubt you, Rasad," said King Abner. He regarded Lord Yosef steadily. "I expect you to explain yourself, My Lord."

"Your Majesty," Lord Yosef stammered, executing a nervous bow. "I'm afraid there has been a misunderstanding. I never had any desire to harm the young lady."

Lucy raised an eyebrow, but kept her peace.

"Was I misinformed, then," the king pressed, "when I was told that you seized our guest and attempted to abduct her from a public market?"

"Well, I...Your Majesty, I...it was a matter of..."

There was some satisfaction in watching her attacker flounder, but Lucy couldn't help but find the nobleman's hopeless attempts to explain himself a little painful. King Abner waited, his expression expectant, as the stammering drew out.

"Your Majesty!"

Every head in the room turned at the new voice. Lord Yosef's words cut off abruptly as a tall, well-dressed woman strode purposefully into the throne room.

"Lady Yasmin," King Abner acknowledged the newcomer calmly. "I imagined we might expect your presence during this audience."

"With all due respect, Your Majesty," Rasad cut in, his tone tinged with polite regret, "Lady Yasmin did not witness the event in question. She cannot have any relevant information to add to this audience."

"I imagine you would think so, Advisor," the noblewoman said. There was a glint of fire in her eyes as they rested on Rasad. "But *I* would think that any hearing relating to my brother has great relevance to me."

"Certainly you will wish to be made aware of events," King Abner said, as unruffled as ever.

"Your Majesty," Rasad objected smoothly. "Allow me to remind you that Lord Yosef's conduct is of an incredibly serious nature. His unprovoked violence is a substantial escalation of the unrest he has been attempting to create in recent months."

Lady Yasmin stepped forward furiously, but Rasad continued over the top of her wordless protest.

"This is not a situation where his sister can talk him out of trouble, as she would no doubt like to do."

"How convenient for you," Lady Yasmin began, her voice scathing, "to find an excuse to exclude me from—"

The king raised his hand, and instantly she fell silent.

"As Rasad has pointed out, Lady Yasmin and I have something in common," King Abner said. "Neither one of us witnessed Lord Yosef's actions today." The king turned his eyes on Lucy, his gaze more shrewd than his languid tone suggested. "I would like to hear from the young lady bringing the complaint."

Lucy curtsied quickly, her quick frown hidden as she

dropped her head. "Your Majesty," she said, straightening up. "It wasn't my intention to bring a complaint before you. I just…"

"Yes?" the king prompted, as she hesitated. "What did you intend to do?"

"Merely to defend myself," Lucy said helplessly.

"Defend yourself from what?" King Abner asked patiently.

"An unprovoked attack by Lord Yosef," Rasad cut in from where he still stood by the king's side. "It is admirable that Luciana was able to defend herself, but unacceptable that it was necessary for her to do so."

"You are right, of course, Rasad," said the king calmly. "But I would like to hear the account from Luciana herself." His steady gaze was still fixed on Lucy's face. "My dear, it would be helpful if you could describe what occurred."

Lucy's eyes flicked between Lord Yosef, who was watching her with a sulky expression, and Lady Yasmin, who was glaring at her brother. But before Lucy could say another word, the door once again opened, and a Thoranian royal guard strode down the length of the throne room, bowing low to his king.

"Your Majesty," he said, when the king indicated he could speak. "His Highness Prince Eamon of Kyona has requested to be included in this audience."

Lucy barely restrained a groan. The last thing they needed was Eamon getting worked up over what had happened.

"Yes, all right," said King Abner, sounding like his patience was at last starting to wear thin.

The guard bowed again and withdrew. Lucy looked at Rasad, trying to tell how he felt about the intrusion, but as always he was difficult to read. Personally, she was torn between irritation and dread at the idea of Eamon insisting on being present. Like Jocelyn had said, he was going to be at least as angry about the incident as Cody was, and probably far less rational.

The thought had barely crossed her mind when she heard

more than one set of firm footsteps approaching down the polished stone floor. She let out a long breath at the sight of not only Eamon, but Cody, Matheus, and Lord Rodanthe hurrying toward the group gathered around the dais.

"Prince Eamon," King Abner said graciously, inclining his head toward the others as well.

"Thank you for allowing us to intrude, Your Majesty," said Eamon. "We were all alarmed to hear what had happened." His eyes flicked to Lucy, and she could see that he genuinely was alarmed.

She gave him a long-suffering look intended to reassure him that she was fine as much as to chastise him for pushing himself in. And it seemed to work, because he relaxed slightly. But from her face, his eyes passed on to Lord Yosef—still flanked by guards—and his expression hardened instantly.

"If you have heard what happened," King Abner said with a touch of asperity, "you have achieved more than I have." He turned back to Lucy. "Go on with your tale. Is it true you were attacked?"

"Well, Your Majesty," started Lucy, then hesitated. She was more reluctant than ever to make an accusation against Lord Yosef now that the audience had grown. She glanced at Cody and Matheus.

Her brother looked even more anxious than Eamon had, his wide eyes passing back and forth between her and the young Thoranian nobleman. But he wasn't as used to court as she was, and she could see that he wasn't going to speak up in front of King Abner. He would save his questions and reproaches for later.

Cody didn't look as though it was the exalted company that was keeping him quiet. It was more likely that he knew no words were needed to convey his exact thoughts. She sent him a quick grimace. As she had predicted, he was clearly angry with her.

And his annoyance at her sneaking off without him didn't appear to be tempered by any anxiety for her well-being, like Eamon's had been. No doubt Cody had ascertained at a glance that she was unharmed, and therefore felt free to just be irritated.

All of this was clear to her within a few moments as she tried to decide how to describe the incident to the king. Probably best to keep it simple, she decided, swallowing nervously as she turned back toward the throne.

"In a manner of speaking, Your Majesty, yes," she said, answering the question at last. "I had wandered away from the rest of the group, who were in the jewelry market. Someone— Lord Yosef, I know now—came up behind me and seized me."

Eamon shifted slightly, but Lucy ignored him, keeping her eyes on King Abner. He was looking from her to Lord Yosef, his eyebrows raised.

"That is certainly unusual behavior," he said. "I was under the impression there was more of a fight. Did Lord Yosef produce a weapon?"

"Well...yes," said Lucy, following Lord Yosef's gaze to see Lady Yasmin, looking ready to murder her brother herself. "But only after I had done so. You see," she hurried on, feeling the need to justify herself, "he said he was going to force me to come with him, and I didn't know what he intended to do, so—"

"You're in the habit of carrying a weapon on you, then?" King Abner pressed.

Lucy forced herself to meet his gaze steadily. "Yes, Your Majesty."

King Abner nodded, his expression thoughtful. "A sensible practice."

Lucy exchanged a glance with Jocelyn. The princess was clearly as surprised as her friend at the king's reaction, or lack of it. She looked toward the only other woman in the room. Lady

Yasmin was watching Lucy closely, looking as thoughtful as the king.

"And you clearly succeeded in defending yourself," King Abner continued, "without inflicting any serious injury on Lord Yosef."

"Yes, Your Majesty."

The king nodded. "You did well."

Unsure how to respond, Lucy shifted her gaze to Rasad at the king's side. He gave her a small smile, as if to remind her of what he had told her about Thorania. She had to admit she was impressed.

"So," the king said, his tone businesslike. "You wish to bring a complaint against Lord Yosef."

Lucy could feel the tension in the room increase, both Lord Yosef and Lady Yasmin holding themselves suddenly more stiffly. Rasad leaned forward ever so slightly, giving her an encouraging nod. The silence stretched out for a painful moment before Lucy spoke.

"No, Your Majesty."

In her peripheral vision she could see Lady Yasmin's start of surprise. But her eyes were on Rasad, and she saw the expression that flitted across his face before he managed to smooth out his features again. It wasn't surprise. It was irritation.

"Luciana," he said, his voice clearly intended to be soothing. Lucy just found it condescending. "You are perfectly within your rights to pursue your complaint. You will not be criticized for wanting Lord Yosef to answer for his outrageous conduct toward you."

"I'm not concerned about being criticized," said Lucy crisply. She looked around to see that everyone in the room was watching her questioningly. "Lord Yosef was wrong to attack me as he did," she said evenly. "But he didn't harm me in the end, did he?" Her gaze flicked toward the young nobleman, a hint of defiance in the set of her mouth. "And I think the incident may have arisen from a…misunderstanding, anyway."

"Is that so?" asked King Abner, looking shrewdly between Lucy and Lord Yosef. He addressed the nobleman. "What was your reason for accosting this young woman?"

"Yes, I think we'd all like to know that," interjected Lady Yasmin tartly, narrowing her eyes at her brother.

"It was…" Lord Yosef looked even more nervous under his sister's glare than under the king's questioning. "Like she said, it was just a misunderstanding."

"I believe," said Rasad dryly, "the fact that Luciana was traveling through the city under my escort was reason enough for Lord Yosef. It is not the first time he has tried to do me a mischief, after all."

"Unless you intend to back that allegation with evidence, Rasad," started Lady Yasmin scathingly, but Rasad cut her off.

"Of course not," he said, the slightest of sneers behind his courteous tone. "We've agreed to forgive and forget past… disagreements, have we not?"

Lady Yasmin's eyes were so narrow now that Lucy wondered how she could see out of them. But the noblewoman held her peace.

"Please forgive my interruption, Your Majesty," interjected Eamon unexpectedly, bowing his head to the Thoranian sovereign. "But I would like more of an explanation as to why this man," he gestured toward Lord Yosef, "apparently thought it was a good idea to abduct Lucy from a public market."

"Yes, so would I," said Cody, frowning at Lord Yosef with more confusion than anger. "Even if he and Rasad are enemies for reasons I don't understand—or care about—it makes no sense at all. Surely Prince Kincaid and Princess Jocelyn were also exploring the city with Rasad as their guide. Why didn't he grab them?"

Lord Yosef made a noise in his throat that might have been a scoff. Lucy glared at him, and he met her eye defiantly. "What?" he muttered. "He was buying you jewelry."

Lucy felt her face go red and forced herself not to meet anyone's eye. She could see in her peripheral vision that Eamon's head had whipped around so quickly that he'd probably injured something.

"That's enough, Yosef," said Lady Yasmin sharply, and her brother fell silent at once.

"Reason enough, as I said," Rasad retorted. There was amusement in his voice, and Lucy couldn't help looking over at him. He gave her the conspiratorial smile that he seemed to reserve just for her, as if inviting her to laugh with him at Lord Yosef's absurdity. But Lucy was anything but amused.

Rasad returned his gaze to the king. "Your Majesty, I'm sure it hasn't escaped your notice that Lord Yosef didn't answer the question. He has given no explanation for his conduct, and the suggestion that it was simply a misunderstanding is—"

The king again raised his hand, and Rasad fell silent as abruptly as Lady Yasmin had done earlier.

"I understand your concern, Rasad," King Abner said calmly. "But since there was no actual harm done, I think it is up to the young lady whether she wishes to pursue the matter. If she holds to her intention to drop the complaint..." He looked questioningly at Lucy, who nodded.

"I do, Your Majesty."

King Abner acknowledged her words with a nod of his own. "That is your own affair, and I will not interfere. It seems there is nothing more to be said on the matter, except that I trust Lord Yosef will take more care in future."

The king's glance in the nobleman's direction held enough ice to make that unfortunate young man quake slightly as he executed a bow, but it was nothing to the fury on Rasad's face at the lenience shown to the offender. He seemed to accept that the audience was over, however, and he made no further protest.

The group moved quickly toward the door, ushered by members of the royal guard. Lucy wondered again what King Abner had been pulled away from in order to attend so promptly to this relatively unimportant matter. If the sovereign resented Rasad's interruption to his schedule, he gave no sign of it.

The moment the door closed behind them, Lady Yasmin turned to Lucy. "Thank you for your understanding," she said curtly, her eyes flicking to Rasad, and their expression hardening for the briefest moment. Then she grabbed her brother's arm in an iron grip, inclining her head to the group at large before hauling him down the corridor.

Lucy opened her mouth to protest, but closed it again. Whatever she'd said in the formal audience, she was determined to get more of an explanation than Lord Yosef had given so far. But she didn't want to press for it in front of Rasad any more than she had in front of the king. She would have to figure out how to track down the brother and sister in the near future, without an audience.

"Please believe me that the manners of Lady Yasmin and Lord Yosef are not standard in King Abner's court," said Rasad, frowning after the pair.

"There's some enmity between you, it seems," said Eamon, his voice as dry as it usually was when speaking to or about the advisor.

Rasad waved a dismissive hand. "Nothing of substance, Your Highness. Their father's estate is located near my home, in the north of the kingdom. The two properties were part of the same estate once, many generations ago. Their ancestor sold land to mine during hard times, and some of his descendants seem to still resent the loss to their estate. The current lord and his wife

—Lady Yasmin and Lord Yosef's parents—do not seem especially troubled by the matter. They are on their estate at present, as is generally the case. Their offspring, however," he gave a small sigh, "seem to prefer to spend most of their time here in Thirl."

Causing mischief was the clear if unspoken conclusion to his explanation.

"And you think this generations-old dispute would be enough to make Lord Yosef target Lucy simply because she was wandering around the city in your company?" Eamon pressed skeptically.

"It is a foolish reason for such a strong dislike, I agree," Rasad said, shrugging. "But Lord Yosef is a foolish young man." He met Lucy's eyes, one eyebrow slightly raised.

She had the sense he was trying to silently remind her of the reason he had previously given her for Lord Yosef's dislike, and she frowned. She still wasn't convinced that the nobleman had acted from any prejudice against those with common blood. And the land dispute didn't really explain it either. What did that have to do with her? Or with the rumors that Lord Yosef had apparently heard about King Giles's coronation?

"In any event," Rasad continued, his eyes still on Lucy, "I deeply regret that you had such an unpleasant experience on your first day in my city, Luciana." He gave a sudden smile. "But I think you've made an excellent impression on King Abner, for what it's worth. He was right when he said that you did very well to defend yourself so successfully." His eyes flicked to the rest of the group, so quickly it was barely perceptible. "Your talents will earn you nothing but respect here."

"Thank you," said Lucy shortly. She made no effort to prolong the conversation as Rasad took his leave of the group, and in a few moments the travelers were mercifully alone.

CHAPTER TWENTY

For a moment they stood in silence, no one eager to initiate conversation while standing in a thoroughfare. In unspoken agreement, they began to walk, making their way back to their own wing of the palace.

They all congregated outside Jocelyn and Kincaid's door, and the Valorian couple ushered the group inside without ceremony. The guards, after a quick search of the suite, returned to their positions in the corridor. Lord Rodanthe hovered outside for a moment, apparently wishing to discuss the matter with the guards, but the rest of them filed inside.

As soon as the door to Kincaid and Jocelyn's receiving room closed, the whole group turned to Lucy, matching expressions of expectation on every face.

"Well," she said after a prolonged silence. "That was eventful. I think I'll go to my room and...rest."

"Is that what you think?" Cody's voice was flat. "Because *I* think you're going to stay right here and explain what in the kingdom is going on."

"Agreed," cut in Matheus, frowning at his sister.

"Well I can't do that," said Lucy tartly, glaring at both of them. "Because I haven't got the faintest idea. All I know is that I was walking through the market, minding my own business, and some Thoranian idiot came up behind me and tried to drag me down an alley."

"I can still hardly believe it," Jocelyn cut in, shaking her head. "I'd only left you alone for a couple of minutes."

"You shouldn't have left her alone at all," said Eamon, frowning at his sister, but Lucy held up a hand, forestalling any further argument.

"Don't even start, Eamon." She narrowed her eyes at him. "Joss isn't responsible for me. And I can look after myself, as it turns out."

"Yes," agreed Eamon, his expression softening slightly as he looked at her. "I know you can. You're a better fighter than half the noblemen our age in Kynton. I've trained with you enough times to know you wouldn't need help to take care of one lone fool like that Lord Yosef."

He looked toward the closed door, as if the nobleman and his sister were hiding in the corridor, and his frown returned. "But you shouldn't have had to defend yourself while strolling through a market. And what if there had been more than one attacker?" He shook his head. "I just don't like not knowing what we're dealing with. The whole thing makes as little sense as my own guard turning on King Giles."

Lucy was silent, distracted from the question at hand by Eamon's unexpectedly casual reference to her fighting skills. It was true that they had trained together a great deal, but that had been when she was younger, before...well, before she had started trying to show a different side to the court, and to the prince. She had thought she was successful in keeping that part of herself hidden once people started to see her as a young woman instead of a girl. But apparently Eamon had not only remembered, but hadn't even realized she was trying to make people forget. She wasn't sure what threw her more—the fact that he still thought of her as a fighter, or the fact that it didn't seem to bother him.

Lord Rodanthe slipped inside the room as she thought it over, his brow furrowed as he moved to stand beside Eamon. Lucy wondered what account the Valorian guards had given him.

"Do you really think there's a connection between the two attacks?" Cody asked, frowning thoughtfully at the Kyonan prince. "Do you think the same people might be behind it? What would be the link? Lucy's Balenan blood?"

Eamon shook his head slowly. "I don't know. We just don't have enough information." He turned to Lucy, pulling her out of her abstraction. "What do you think, Lucy? You're the only one of us who was there for both incidents."

Lucy hesitated before answering. It probably wouldn't have occurred to her to put the different attacks together if it wasn't for Lord Yosef's comment about the Balenan king. But his words had raised questions, ones she was determined to see answered.

"I don't know if they're connected," she said at last. "But I don't think Lord Yosef, or whoever he's working with, was behind the attack in Balenol." Her tone turned dry. "And I don't think he was after me because Rasad's ancestor swindled land from his ancestor."

"Nor do I," interjected Lord Rodanthe grimly.

"No, that sounded like an excuse to me," agreed Kincaid, throwing himself onto a settle. His casual posture reminded Lucy that they were intruding on his rooms.

"I really do think I'll go rest," she said hastily, turning toward the door. "Without more information, there's not much point in discussing it further."

"Not so fast," said Cody darkly, grasping her arm with a restraining hand. "You still have some explaining to do."

"What for?" Lucy protested. "It's not my fault I was targeted by some discontented—"

"Don't act all innocent, Lucy," Matheus interrupted impatiently. "Why did you sneak off without us?"

"I didn't sneak off," Lucy contradicted, tugging uncomfortably at her sleeve. "I wanted to explore the city a little, and I thought everyone was resting. Then I ran into Rasad, and..." She trailed off, taking in the unimpressed looks on Cody's and Matheus's faces. "Jocelyn and Kincaid came with me!"

"Only because Joss insisted we force ourselves in," muttered Kincaid. He fell silent under the combined glares of his wife and her best friend.

"I have to agree," said Lord Rodanthe, his eyes passing from Lucy to Jocelyn. "We did receive your message alerting us to the outing, but next time, Lady Rodanthe and I would prefer you to speak to us personally, to give us the opportunity to accompany you if you intend to leave the palace."

"I understand," said Jocelyn, sending him an apologetic look. "None of us meant to cause any trouble."

"Of course not," said Lord Rodanthe, inclining his head in acknowledgment. "I would like to discuss this matter further, of course, but if you'll excuse me for the moment, I will go and make Lady Rodanthe aware of all that has transpired."

With a gracious nod to the group, he departed.

Cody wasn't so polite in his admonishment. "Don't do it again, Lucy," he said the moment the nobleman was gone, his voice stern. "If you're leaving the palace, I want to be there."

"And so do I," chimed in Matheus. "Quite apart from the whole people-trying-to-abduct-you thing, I don't like the idea that this Rasad is sniffing around my sister so much, inviting you to wander around with him when I don't even know you've left your room."

"Matheus," snapped Lucy, quelling her brother with a glare.

The fifteen-year-old's protective posturing would have been entertaining if it wasn't so mortifying in front of their particular audience. Matheus fell silent, but his expression was mutinous. It didn't help Lucy's credibility that Eamon was giving the younger boy an approving nod.

Lucy eyed the two of them, debating whether to give them both a piece of her mind, when Jocelyn chuckled.

"What?" Lucy demanded, rounding on her friend.

"Sorry, it's just..." Jocelyn didn't quite manage to hold back a smile. "The two of you," she gestured to Lucy and Matheus, "are exactly like they were in the throne room."

"Who?" Lucy asked, nonplussed.

"Lady Yasmin and Lord Yosef."

Kincaid grinned. "You're right. Lady Yasmin gave her brother exactly that look when he spoke without her permission."

Lucy scowled, but Matheus was the one to actually protest.

"Hey! You're comparing me to some idiot who attacks strangers in dark alleys?"

"It wasn't dark," Lucy corrected, suddenly seeing the humor of it all as she remembered Lord Yosef's attempt to defend his conduct after she disarmed him.

"That's not the point," Matheus shot at her.

"I wasn't comparing you to him generally, Matheus," said Jocelyn soothingly. "Just the way you and Lucy were interacting." She grinned at her husband. "Does Lavinia ever try to boss you and Ormond around like that?"

"Frequently," said Kincaid easily, still stretched on the settle. "But it doesn't really work out for her, considering she's so much younger. Seven years younger than me, and twelve years younger than Ormond...she never had a chance, poor thing."

Lucy barely refrained from rolling her eyes. From what Jocelyn had told her, and what she had herself witnessed when they were both attendants at Jocelyn and Kincaid's wedding,

Princess Lavinia was no one's idea of a "poor thing". The fifteen-year-old had no difficulty standing up for herself, and was much more in the habit of setting the whole castle by the ears than being bossed around by her older brothers.

"What about you?" Kincaid asked, giving his wife a pointed look. "Can you subdue your brother with a single glance?"

Jocelyn gave a very unladylike snort. "Hardly."

"Well," said Eamon with maddening superiority, "probably because we're twins, it's a little different."

"Yes," said Jocelyn dryly. "I'm sure it has everything to do with us being twins, and nothing to do with you being the most over-confident person I've ever met, to the point that you were born with the magical ability to inspire confidence in people."

"My power doesn't work on you," protested Eamon. "You can't blame that for you not being as successful in bossing me around as Lucy is with—"

"Hey!" Lucy protested. She had been slightly taken aback by their banter, still unused to hearing them openly talk about their magic. But Eamon's accusation pulled her right back in. "When you have three younger brothers, all of whom have thought that they were grown up and ready to take on the world from the age of ten, you have to be a little bossy sometimes to keep everyone in one piece."

"I don't know, Matheus seems pretty level-headed to me," said Eamon mildly.

"Thank you Eamon," said the fifteen-year-old with a dignity that couldn't fail to make even Lucy's lips twitch, irate as she was.

"If you kids are all done squabbling," said Cody vaguely, looking like he had been paying only cursory attention to their conversation, "let's get back to the point. What are we going to do about this Lord Yosef and his attack?" He turned his gaze on Lucy. "You must have had a reason for not wanting to see him punished."

Lucy sighed. "I guess I just figured I'd rather have answers than retribution." *And,* she added silently, *I have no idea who to trust, and I don't want to be used.* But she didn't especially want to discuss trust with present company.

"We'd all like answers," said Cody, his forehead creased in thought. "But we have to be careful about looking for them." He gave Lucy a long look before letting his breath out in a big exhale. "Well, at least we got one good day of training in since we've been in the South Lands, so you weren't so rusty." He gave her an approving smile. "You did well, Lucy. And I'm glad the Thoranian court knows we're not helpless."

Lucy acknowledged the compliment with a nod, eager to bring the conversation to a close. She could see Eamon looking between her and Cody, realization growing behind his eyes.

"I really do want to go rest before the meal," she said to the room at large. "It's been a bit of a strange morning."

"Yes," said Jocelyn briskly, giving her head a little shake. "And we're supposed to be meeting with our trade delegate before the formal negotiations open this afternoon, Kincaid."

Her husband let out a sigh that said all anyone needed to know about how he felt about his official duties on the trip, but he didn't actually protest.

"The Kyonan delegates wanted to meet before this afternoon as well," said Eamon quickly, as Lucy edged toward the door. "I'd better go and find them."

Lucy had the distinct impression that Eamon was making an excuse to leave at the same time as her, and she wasn't surprised when he followed her all the way to her door.

"Training," he said without preamble. "That's what you and Cody were doing in the jungle all day."

Lucy sighed. "Yes."

Eamon was silent for a moment, the confusion clear on his face. "Why couldn't you have trained at the castle? Don't you remember the training courtyard they showed us during our tour? It looked just as good as our one at home."

Lucy shrugged uncomfortably. "It was Cody's idea. He wanted to train in the jungle. And he wanted to show me some of the places from his childhood. From my parents' time in Nohl."

"Then why didn't you just say that's what you were doing?" Eamon pressed. "Instead of being mysterious, and making everyone think..."

Lucy raised an eyebrow. "Think what?"

Eamon grimaced. "You know what I'm trying to say, Lucy. You acted so secretively, it was as though..." His eyes widened slightly, as if having a revelation. "I'm being stupid, aren't I? You didn't want to advertise what you were doing because you didn't want to remind everyone of your mother's activities, and how she was—"

"Technically guilty of treason?" Lucy finished dryly. "That was in my mind, yes."

"Of course it was," said Eamon. "It should have been obvious."

Lucy squirmed slightly, too embarrassed to admit that the obvious reason had only been a secondary motivation. She had been much more concerned about everyone in Nohl finding out about her unladylike skills. She peeked up at Eamon to find him frowning slightly at her.

"You could still have told me, though, and Jocelyn."

"I don't have to answer to you, Eamon," Lucy reminded him. "I'm not strictly part of your delegation, and even if I was, Lady Rodanthe knew I was with Cody." She gave him a long look, realizing that underneath his confusion, he was genuinely relieved at the explanation. "You didn't really think that Cody and I were...I don't know...sweethearts, did you?" she asked, lowering her voice.

"Of course not," said Eamon quickly. "I just...I just couldn't understand why you would be secretive about spending time with him, and I..." He dropped his gaze. "I guess I didn't like being reminded that I have no right to ask about who you've been spending time with."

"But it's the truth," said Lucy, speaking more gently than she had to Eamon in months.

He let out a big breath. "I know." He met her eyes again, a pained half smile on his face. "It's not the first time I've teased you about meeting secret sweethearts, is it? You didn't seem to mind before." His gaze was suddenly unsettlingly, familiarly intense. "Do you remember that day? In the meadow near—"

"Don't you have a meeting to prepare for, Eamon?" Lucy interrupted abruptly. It was her turn to lower her eyes, unable to meet that blazing look for another second.

There was a moment of silence as Eamon seemed to debate whether to drop the matter. "Of course," he said, his tone brisk. "And I'm keeping you from your rest."

Without another word, he turned and strode down the corridor. Lucy didn't stay to watch his progress, slipping into her own room before he'd taken five steps. She rested her back against the closed door of her suite, pressing the heels of her hands into her eyes so hard that she began to see stars.

Did she remember that day? As if she could ever forget.

There was too much uncertainty in her current situation. The last thing she needed was to dwell on complications from her past. But Eamon—frustrating, unreliable, magnetic nuisance that he was—had forced her to do just that. There was no point trying not to relive it, she told herself. She couldn't help it now.

After a brief struggle, she gave up her fruitless attempts to convince herself that she didn't want to think about it, and let herself sink into the memory of that day. She could almost see the dappled sunshine of her achingly familiar forest home, could almost smell the summer wildflowers. She surrendered herself to the indulgence of once again being that younger, happier version of herself, the one who had no doubts, whose life was uncomplicated.

"Eamon!"

Lucy's heart fluttered at the way Eamon's whole face lit up when he heard her greeting. He turned his horse away from the rest of the group, heading in her direction.

She didn't get up from where she was seated among the wildflowers of the little meadow, just smoothed her skirts surreptitiously around her. She was doubly glad that she had stood fast against Cody's attempts to get her to train like normal this morning. Her calculations had suggested that Eamon and his group would return today from seeing Jocelyn off to the edge of the forest, and she had been right.

The timing of her walk to collect blooms from the clearing was simply a lucky coincidence. But she was more than happy to have intercepted the prince before he reached Raldon and was mobbed by her over-eager brothers.

"Don't you make a pretty picture, surrounded by wildflowers?" Eamon teased, swinging down from the saddle as his horse slowed to a stop beside her. "Not here to meet a secret sweetheart, are you?"

Lucy looked up at him through her lashes, her eyes sparkling with mischief. "I don't know. Am I?"

For a moment Eamon just stared down at her, the intensity of his expression filling her with a mixture of exhilaration and nerves.

Then he laughed lightly and dropped to the grass, settling himself in a less than regal posture, his lean and muscled frame supported on one elbow with his long legs stretched out in front of him.

"Sounds like I'd better hang around to make sure," he said.

Lucy smiled to herself. She had no objection.

A slight movement nearby called the prince's attention to the two guards who had broken off from the rest of the group to follow him over. They were dismounting nearby. Eamon gave them a long-suffering look that almost made Lucy giggle. The guards' faces remained impassive, but when Eamon followed up with a glare and a meaningful tilt of the head, they relented and retreated to a more discreet distance.

"We can head back to Raldon, if you like," said Lucy, watching Eamon for his reaction. "They don't stick so close to you there."

"True, but we'd be surrounded by your family, then," said Eamon, twirling a leaf idly between his fingers.

Lucy grimaced. "My brothers can be a little overwhelming."

Eamon laughed. "I don't find them overwhelming." He met her eye, a smile curving up one side of his mouth. "I just don't want to have to share you. What's the point of coming back without Jocelyn if we're so besieged by your family that I can't get a moment alone with you?"

Lucy's heartbeat sped up, but she tried to keep her expression serene. It wasn't an easy feat when she wanted to grin with delight at his answer.

"So you saw Jocelyn off all right?" she asked, trying to sound nonchalant.

"Yes," said Eamon, his brows drawing together slightly. "She's on her way to Montego."

"What is it?" Lucy asked, sitting up straighter at the shift in his mood. "Are you worried about her?"

"A little," Eamon admitted. "I'm not at all sure about this whole trip, you know." He gave Lucy a sideways glance. "You know that the Valorian royals are trying to set her up with their crown prince, right?"

Lucy nodded. "I think everyone knows, to be honest. But Jocelyn said that there was no obligation."

"Yes," Eamon agreed, but he sounded unconvinced. For a moment he was silent, his eyes fixed on the distance. Then he sighed. "The trouble is that Jocelyn has a way of creating obligations in her head even when no one else expects them of her."

Lucy grimaced. She wished she could disagree, but she knew Jocelyn too well. "Surely your parents won't let her be bullied into a political marriage if she doesn't want it," she said reassuringly.

Eamon smiled. "That's an understatement. My father is ready to declare war at the very idea that anyone over there might try to push Joss into it." He paused, then cast a glance toward his guards on the other side of the clearing. "That was a joke, obviously."

Lucy laughed. "I know."

"But you know how my father feels about political marriages. He certainly won't be prodding Jocelyn in that direction. Or me, for that matter."

Lucy suddenly felt Eamon's eyes on her, and she kept her gaze on her lap, her cheeks growing warm. She therefore had no warning before she felt Eamon's hand brush her cheek, his fingers warm as he tucked a stray strand of hair back behind her ear.

"And as it happens," the prince continued casually, "I have my own reasons for being extremely grateful for that."

She looked up then, unable to resist any longer. He had a crooked smile on his face, as impossibly confident and engaging as he always was. But in spite of his light tone, his eyes gave him away—they burned into hers with too much intensity.

"Is—is that so?" she stuttered, wishing she had half his self-possession.

His smile softened, losing none of its charm but becoming somehow more intimate. "Yes, it is. I happen to be very eager to have the chance to choose my own bride when the time comes."

"How nice for you," said Lucy conversationally. "Being a prince and all, you can just choose whoever you like, I suppose."

Eamon laughed ruefully, acknowledging the hit. "Not quite," he admitted. "I would still have to win the lady over, of course. Convince her to choose me, too."

"And how would you do that?" Lucy asked, cursing her breathlessness. Her every nerve was on fire with the exhilaration of their banter. They had been flirting unashamedly ever since her first ball, but this conversation was bringing them closer than ever before to genuinely serious territory.

"Well, that depends," said Eamon, giving her a speculative look. "Would most girls like a man with a bit of adventure in him, do you think? A rebellious streak, even?"

"Most girls," Lucy assented, barely restraining a smile.

"Come on then," said Eamon, speaking a little too loudly as he stood and offered her his hand. He gave her the ghost of a wink as he pulled her to her feet. "I suppose we should head into town."

Lucy followed him, perplexed, as he walked over to where the guards were standing, keeping an eye on his horse as well as their own.

Eamon received the bridle of his own mount with a grateful nod. He turned to Lucy, and her heart fluttered wildly as he grasped her by the waist, lifting her into the saddle with surprising strength. Then he swung himself up behind her in a fluid and graceful movement.

She was sure he must be able to hear the frantic beating of her heart as he leaned close, whispering into her ear, "Hold on."

Then he yanked on the reins, urging his horse toward the two guards' horses, grazing peacefully nearby. He had almost reached them when he pulled back sharply, causing his poor mount to rear up in confusion. The two other horses, still riderless, shied away from their fellow. Lucy clung on tightly, her stomach dropping as the horse's hooves flailed, but she felt surprisingly secure with Eamon's arms clamped firmly around her. When the horse regained its footing, Eamon again urged it forward much too quickly, and the two other creatures scattered.

With a shout, the guards sprang after their mounts. Lucy once again found herself gripping the horse's mane for dear life as Eamon pushed his horse into a canter, moving in the opposite direction from the guards.

He wasn't heading toward Raldon, but he didn't go far before he pulled the horse to a stop, slipping from the saddle before Lucy could blink. He reached up, and she slid toward him, allowing him to pull her off the horse's back as well.

"How was that?" he asked, his eyes sparkling and his breath coming quickly as if he, and not the horse, had just dashed through the forest.

Lucy couldn't help laughing at the boyish excitement on his face. "That, Prince Eamon, was outrageous!"

"Oh dear," Eamon said, a shade of uncertainty behind his grin. "I'm sorry you thought so."

Lucy raised an eyebrow. "And why is that?"

"Because," said Eamon, swallowing visibly, "if you thought that was outrageous, I can only imagine what you'll think of what I was planning to do next."

"Which was...?"

Eamon took a step forward, and Lucy suddenly found herself with her back against a tree. She leaned into it, raising her eyes to Eamon's from underneath her lashes, in a look she undeniably knew men found irresistible.

"This," said Eamon breathlessly, taking a final step forward to close the distance between them.

Then his hand was on her cheek and his lips were on hers, and Lucy could have sworn her feet left the ground. It was a sweet kiss, chaste, just what a girl might expect her first kiss to be, coming from a seventeen-year-old boy whom she was fairly sure had never kissed anyone before either.

She had heard plenty of gossip from some of the more flirtatious girls in the court, and she suspected they would have thought it tame and unexciting.

But to Lucy, it was perfect. Her heart soared, and she leaned up toward him, her hand shyly reaching up to cover his on her cheek.

Eamon pulled back suddenly, and before she could become too confused, Lucy heard the approaching hoof beats, too. The guards had clearly mastered their mounts.

"Would that help win her over, do you think?" Eamon asked, his voice not as steady as usual. It took Lucy a moment to understand his reference to their earlier joking conversation.

"It definitely wouldn't hurt," she said, her own voice coming out breathless.

There was no time for more. Eamon turned toward the approaching guards, stepping slightly in front of Lucy. The change on their expressions as they thundered into view—from anxiety to relief to irritation—was almost comical.

"Your Highness," said the older of the two guards explosively. He swung down from his mount the moment he reached them, looking like he was restraining himself with difficulty from grabbing hold of the prince's shoulder.

"I know," said Eamon penitently, the sparkle in his eyes giving him away. "It's so embarrassing to have lost control of my mount like that. And in front of Lucy, too!" He shot her a glance that was full of mischief. "But I got hold of him before he'd bolted far, and you'll be relieved to know that Lucy wasn't harmed."

The guard was glowering as he looked from the prince to Lucy, who was barely holding in a giggle. "Indeed," he said stiffly, inclining his head toward her. "I am pleased to hear it. And now, Your Highness," he returned his glare to Eamon, "I suggest that we rejoin the rest of the group, in the town."

"Of course," said Eamon amicably, turning to help Lucy into the saddle. He unleashed a smile on her that made her knees strangely weak as he again took hold of her waist and hoisted her up. "I'm so sorry to have delayed you, Lucy."

She just shook her head ruefully, her thoughts in too much of a whirl to find any witty banter for the outrageous prince. As he again reached his arms around her to grasp the reins, it was all she could do not to lean back into him. Even so, his nearness was intoxicating, her mind alight with the memory of his kiss. She didn't think life could get any better than this.

CHAPTER TWENTY-ONE

Lucy started awake in the darkness. It took her a moment to remember where she was, but her confusion didn't slow her reflexes as her hand flew to the weapon hidden under her pillow.

In one smooth movement she retrieved the blade and sat up, bringing the dagger in front of her. Her breath caught in her throat as the blade met another weapon with a metallic clang.

"Nice reaction time," came a soft voice from the darkness, sounding impressed and far too casual for the situation. "I could have sworn you were fast asleep."

"I was fast asleep," Lucy retorted. Moonlight filtered in through the glass doors leading toward the interior courtyard, and she lowered her weapon slightly as her eyes adjusted enough to recognize the intruder. "And *I* could have sworn I was in my own private suite."

"Yes, it is fairly rude of me to drop in unannounced like this," Lady Yasmin said lightly, settling herself into a more comfortable position on Lucy's bed. "But I thought it was the safest way to speak to you without being overheard."

"Yes," Lucy agreed pleasantly, eyeing the lethal-looking

dagger that Lady Yasmin was laying down on the covers beside her. "Nothing makes me think 'safe' like an intruder coming into my bedroom at night and drawing a blade on me while I sleep."

Lady Yasmin chuckled. "I meant safe from interference," she clarified. "But I didn't draw my weapon on you while you were sleeping, you know. I only pulled it out on instinct once you brought yours out."

"I am deeply reassured," said Lucy, her tone dry. She gave Lady Yasmin a long look. "When you say interference, you're talking about Rasad, aren't you? You don't think he would want you talking to me."

"Straight to the point," said Lady Yasmin approvingly. "I like that. Yes, I'm talking about Rasad, and no, I don't think he would want me speaking with you. Do you?"

Lucy regarded her silently for a moment, her gaze passing pointedly between the door to the courtyard—through which she assumed her visitor had entered—and the weapon still resting on the bed. "No, I don't think he would. Maybe he has reason."

"I have no doubt he has his reasons," said Lady Yasmin dryly. "I'm just not convinced they're the reasons he wants people to think."

"I thought you said you liked to get straight to the point," said Lucy.

Lady Yasmin sat back, sighing. "You're right. First, let me thank you again for not pursuing your complaint against my most idiotic of brothers, as you were undoubtedly within your rights to do."

Lucy couldn't help but be amused by the older woman's tone, although she kept her face impassive. "I didn't do it as a favor to you."

The noblewoman regarded her shrewdly. "No, I'm sure you didn't. Why did you do it? Why show lenience?"

Lucy shrugged. "I have younger brothers of my own, you know. Three of them, so bear that in mind next time you're inclined to feel sorry for yourself."

Lady Yasmin permitted herself a brief smile. "I'm all sympathy, believe me. But that's not a real answer."

"Somehow I don't feel that I'm the one who needs to give you answers," said Lucy, calmly smoothing the bedclothes around her legs.

Lady Yasmin sighed again. "You're right, of course. But I don't know if I can trust you."

Lucy raised an eyebrow. "I don't know if you can trust me, either."

Both women were distracted from their conversation by the sound of the door leading from Lucy's receiving room to the main corridor swinging suddenly, violently, open. Lucy hadn't even freed her legs from the bedclothes when a figure came barreling into her bedchamber, weapon raised.

She relaxed immediately, leaning back against the bedhead with a sigh.

"Cody. So nice of you to join us."

"What's going on here?" Cody scowled from Lady Yasmin to Lucy, as if the women were equally at fault for the situation he found them in.

"No idea," said Lucy, tipping her head toward Lady Yasmin. "Ask her."

The Thoranian woman had sprung to her feet at Cody's entrance, her blade held at her side and her expression wary. But before either she or Cody could say a word, they both swung around, adopting identical defensive stances at the sound of the exterior door once again opening. Lucy, on the other hand, didn't even bother to move this time.

"Lucy," sighed the newest arrival. "Can you seriously not go even a few hours without getting attacked?"

Lucy raised her arms in a silent gesture of protest. "Why is it my fault when random people come after me out of nowhere?"

"Matheus," said Cody, his voice sharp. "What are you doing here?"

"Following you," said Matheus, settling himself on the other side of Lucy's bed from where Lady Yasmin and Cody were still standing. "Did you forget that we're sharing a suite? Did you really think I wouldn't notice when you went barging out of the room in the middle of the night?" He gave Cody a stern look that was entirely out of place on his teenage face. "Come to think of it, I should be the one asking you what you're doing, coming into my sister's room in the dead of night." He glanced at Lady Yasmin, looking suddenly self-conscious. "Lady Yasmin will get the wrong impression." He adopted a serious expression. "My sister isn't loose or anything, My Lady, Cody's just a little over-protective. He's like an uncle to us."

"No need to explain to me," said Lady Yasmin with the hint of a smile. She had fully lowered her weapon by this time, and she glanced over at Lucy. "One of the brothers you mentioned, I gather."

"Yes, he is," said Lucy shortly. "And you're right that we have no need to explain anything to you. If you hadn't broken into my room at this hour, you wouldn't be getting the wrong impression about anything."

"I'm not getting the wrong impression now," said Lady Yasmin, definitely amused by this time. "I know how to recognize family when I see it." She laid her weapon down again, proceeding to light some candles on the bed stand, clearly quite at home.

"Family or not," Lucy grumbled, "I'm not really in the habit of letting people congregate in my bedroom when I'm trying to sleep."

"Well, no one's sleeping now," said Cody briskly. "So how about we get some explanations?"

"Sure," said Lucy, starting to get irritated. "Let's start with you explaining how and why you came racing in here."

"You were attacked by a stranger in a public market today, Lucy," said Cody impatiently. "You don't think I'm going to be keeping a close eye on you after that? What kind of a guardian would I be if I didn't notice someone sneaking into your room in the middle of the night?"

"How did you know she was in here, though?" Lucy asked curiously.

"Never mind that," said Cody, a hint of smugness in his voice. "I have my ways."

Lucy rolled her eyes, directing her next words to Lady Yasmin. "Ignore the air of mystery. People tend to be impressed when they discover he was part of the infamous resistance during Nohl's slave days. But he was actually just a kid, and they didn't even let him do any fighting."

Cody scowled briefly at Lucy, while Lady Yasmin studied him with interest. "You were part of the resistance, were you?" She sounded impressed.

Cody turned his attention to the Thoranian noblewoman. "Never mind my life story," he said shortly. "What are you doing threatening Lucy in her bed while she's sleeping? Last I checked she did you and your stupid brother a big favor."

Lady Yasmin sighed, running a hand through her long, dark hair. She was unusually tall for a woman, Lucy noticed. "She did do me and my stupid brother a big favor, and I've already thanked her for that."

"So we'll just call it bygones," said Lucy amicably. "Forget the whole thing."

"That's not what I meant," said Lady Yasmin. She fixed Lucy with a serious look. "I said I'd get straight to the point, and I will.

I want to know who you are, and I don't think I'll get the answers I need with our delightful primary advisor around. What is Rasad to you?"

Cody shifted slightly, the scowl returning to his face. Lucy ignored him, a dangerous note entering her voice as she met the noblewoman's look. "Excuse me?"

Lady Yasmin held her gaze for a long moment before letting out a breath. "All right then," she said, apparently deciding not to pursue the question. "What do you know about whatever is going on in Balenol?"

Lucy threw off her covers, pushing herself to her feet as the last of her patience fled. "First of all, I think we've already established that I don't owe you any answers. Secondly, who says there's anything going on in Balenol, and even if there was, what would it have to do with me?"

"Maybe nothing," said Lady Yasmin evenly. "And if Yosef hadn't forced my hand, I obviously wouldn't be breaking into your room to question you like this. But I think the ship has sailed on surreptitious observation." She grimaced. "You probably won't believe this, but even though he's always been impulsive and foolish, he does actually mean well."

"Yes, he seemed lovely," said Lucy conversationally. "I'm never one for the formalities, and there's something nice about someone who doesn't wait for a proper introduction before seizing you from behind and dragging you off to his lair."

Lady Yasmin sighed again. "You're justified in your opinion," she acknowledged. "Although he didn't drag you anywhere in the end, did he?" She gave a sudden smile. "I'm glad you bested him, and not just because his plan for finding out what you know was...poorly thought out. You being able to beat him in a fight has done him more good than all the rest."

"Well, naturally we're all pleased that Lucy could help your brother grow as a person," interjected Cody impassively. "But the question remains—why in the kingdom did he try to abduct her in the first place? Rasad told us some unconvincing tale about a land dispute generations ago. Has that really made you two hate Rasad so much that you try to take it out on anyone who seems to be under his protection?"

"I'm not under Rasad's protection," Lucy snapped, at the same time as Lady Yasmin protested.

"Of course that's not it. I couldn't care less about whether Rasad's ancestor bought his land fairly." The Thoranian frowned. "The only relevance of that ancient history is that our homes are close to one another's, and we've known Rasad all our lives. It's true we don't have any love for him, but it's nothing to do with a land dispute." She turned to Lucy. "And disliking Rasad isn't why Yosef wanted to speak with you."

"Then why did he?" asked Matheus.

Lucy glanced at her brother, reflecting that he had been very quiet since his arrival. She saw with a hint of amusement that his eyes were resting on Lady Yasmin with something akin to awe.

And studying the Thoranian woman more closely, Lucy had to admit that she was impressive. She exuded confidence and capability, even in this bizarre setting. The diaphanous material of her local garment glinted in the candlelight, the gentle folds suiting her tall, commanding figure well. Lucy knew a stab of jealousy at the thought of how convenient the loosely falling pants—like skirts in appearance but like leggings in practicality —would be for training.

Lady Yasmin was an attractive woman, Lucy realized. She was too tall to be considered beautiful by exacting standards, but she had pleasant features. She was at least a decade older than Lucy, probably around thirty, but she certainly didn't seem old. Lucy wondered why she was unmarried—probably too busy keeping her little brother out of trouble. *Or perhaps*, a contrary voice in Lucy's head whispered, *all Rasad's talk about Thorania's open-minded culture is just that, talk. Perhaps no one wants to marry Lady Yasmin. Perhaps being strong and capable and a fighter, as she clearly is, intimidates people here just as much as it would in Kynton.*

The room was still silent in response to Matheus's question, and it took Lucy a moment to realize that Lady Yasmin was looking at her thoughtfully. She was clearly unsure how much to say.

"Your brother mentioned something about the coronation of King Giles," Lucy prompted. She saw Cody's gaze shift to her, a frown creasing his forehead at this new information. "He seemed to think there had been some...incident that almost prevented it from happening."

"We have heard a rumor to that effect, yes," said Lady Yasmin carefully.

"Did you have spies in Rasad's delegation?" Cody asked bluntly.

Lady Yasmin sent him a shrewd look. "Spies is a dramatic description. Not all sources of information in and out of Thirl are controlled by Rasad, I'm happy to say."

Cody met the Thoranian's look squarely, and Lucy could see the grudging respect in his eyes.

"You speak of Rasad as though he has an iron grip on the city," said Lucy, raising an eyebrow. "Isn't he King Abner's trusted advisor? Isn't his exercise of authority legitimate?"

"It is," Lady Yasmin acknowledged.

"Then isn't your opposition of him treasonous?" Cody challenged.

"Of course not!" Lady Yasmin protested, looking shocked. "My family is loyal to the crown. We care for Thorania's interests, always. Just not..." She hesitated. "Just not to the exclusion of all other considerations."

"What does that mean?" Lucy asked, frowning.

"Never mind that," said Lady Yasmin quickly. "Let's say that just because Rasad's authority is legitimate, it doesn't mean his motivations or intentions are always honest."

Lucy's frown deepened. "Why are you telling us this? If you think I'm somehow connected to Rasad, why would you be telling me your suspicions about him?"

Lady Yasmin met her look seriously. "I don't know what your connection is to Rasad. But I do know that Yosef's terrible lapse in judgment today was exactly the opportunity Rasad has been waiting for to deal with us and our pesky opposition to his increasing power. You may not realize it, but you thwarted him drastically by refusing to push the complaint. Your determination not to pursue the matter told me that whatever you are or aren't, you're not his puppet."

"I'm not anyone's puppet," said Lucy indignantly.

"I'm not taking such a risk by coming here," Lady Yasmin pushed on, ignoring the interjection. "It's true that I would be in trouble if you decided to report my visit. But I'm taking the gamble that you won't, since you didn't seem to want to punish Yosef. And as for my suspicions regarding Rasad," she smiled grimly, "I haven't told you anything he doesn't know. In fact, I haven't told you anything I haven't said to his face, and in front of others." Her smile disappeared, a look of frustration taking its place. "But no one else seems to see the danger."

Lucy was silent for a moment, thinking Lady Yasmin's words over.

"What is the danger?" Cody asked. "In your opinion?"

Lady Yasmin redirected her attention to him. "Rasad is an ambitious man," she said simply. "That much no one doubts. He is, after all, very young to be appointed to the position of primary advisor. But I'm not sure any of us, not even those of us who've known him all our lives, fully understand the nature of his ambition. All I know is that since his appointment, he has put a great deal of effort into building his power and influence in the court. And with enormous success. He has the ear of the king, more so than anyone else I believe. And I wish I could shake the feeling that he has plans for how to use that influence. Plans that no one else is aware of."

She looked back at Lucy. "Like I said, he's been our neighbor all our lives, and there are certain...patterns that we've seen, both before and after his appointment. There have been incidents. Convenient coincidences that have always been to his advantage."

"Sounds solid," said Lucy dryly. "Really convincing evidence that he's up to something. I can't imagine why the rest of the court doesn't believe you."

Lady Yasmin gave a humorless laugh. "I could be more specific, but forgive me if I choose not to tell you everything I know the first time I speak with you."

"Oh, does that mean there will be more of these lovely visits?" Lucy asked, with a hint of humor. "Should I start leaving my door unlocked, to make it easier for you?"

"I've worn out my welcome," said Lady Yasmin with a hint of a smile. "I don't blame you. But let me ask directly what my brother foolishly tried to find out through brute force. Was there an attack on King Giles before his coronation?"

Lucy frowned. "I acknowledge that you don't have any real reason to trust me with your secrets. Why would you expect me to trust you? How can I possibly know whether I can?"

"You can't know," admitted Lady Yasmin bluntly. "You just have to go with your instinct."

Lucy ran a hand over her face. "That's a great theory," she muttered. "But I no longer have any faith in my instinct for who to trust."

Lady Yasmin gave her a questioning look, but Lucy ignored

it. The last thing she intended to do was go into her recent disillusionments with this stranger.

"There was an attack," she said curtly. "Someone tried to prevent King Giles from being crowned. But it had nothing to do with Rasad, believe me. I was there."

Lady Yasmin was silent for a moment, drumming her fingernails on the hilt of her dagger.

"Who was behind it?" she asked at last.

Lucy set her lips firmly. There was no way she was compromising Kyona's relationship with either South Lands kingdom by revealing that it had been one of the crown prince's own guards who had been behind the assassination attempt.

Lady Yasmin let out a small sigh, but accepted Lucy's refusal to answer without comment. "Let me guess," she said. "The identity of the attacker doesn't really make sense. Someone acted out of character, and those involved are still trying to put the pieces together, without success."

The three Kyonans exchanged a look, the unease clear on every face. None of them said a word, but they didn't need to.

Lady Yasmin gave a curt nod, acknowledging the accuracy of her guess. "Convenient coincidences," she muttered.

Lucy frowned, thinking not only of the unexplained attack by Eamon's guard, but of the bizarre balcony collapse that had come before it. Her unease grew.

"I just wish I could be sure that the timing of your arrival, during the annual military muster, was simply a coincidence," the Thoranian was continuing, still talking half to herself. She shook her head slightly, her tone returning abruptly to normal. "I'll go now." She gave a slight smile. "Thank you all for not calling down the guards on me. I would be very grateful if you would keep our little discussion to yourselves." Her eyes softened as they rested on Lucy. "And thank you again for coming to my brother's rescue. I was worried that this time he'd gotten himself into a scrape I couldn't pull him out of, and I'm more grateful than I can say that you chose not to be vindictive. I really am sorry that he attacked you. It was inexcusable, and believe me when I tell you that I'm going to punish him in my own way for the next decade or so."

Lucy shrugged. "Like I said, I have three younger brothers myself." She thought she saw Matheus roll his eyes in her peripheral vision.

"Yes, well." Lady Yasmin's eyes flicked to Matheus as well, looking like she was trying not to smile. "Like I said, I know there's no excuse. But please believe me that Yosef wouldn't have done something so drastic if it was a matter of disliking Rasad, or being generally uneasy about his influence. Incidents within Thorania are one thing, but the rumors about certain goings on in Balenol..." Lady Yasmin looked up, encompassing all of them in her glance. "It has been centuries since Thorania saw war, and we have no desire to see that change."

For a moment there was silence, as her words hung heavily in the air. Lucy didn't know what to make of the dramatic declaration. But Lady Yasmin didn't wait for a response, turning to Lucy with another smile.

"From what Yosef told me, you fight well. I usually train in the mornings, in the palace training grounds. I'd love you to join me sometime." Her smile grew to a grin. "It will be worth your while—I'm a more formidable opponent than my brother. He's not bad with a sword, and he's actually quite skilled with a bow. But the dagger isn't his weapon."

"Lucy's no pushover herself," interjected Cody defensively, the pride of a trainer clear in his voice.

Lady Yasmin didn't miss it. "Taught her to fight, did you?" she asked, looking him over appraisingly. "I'm glad to hear that women are allowed to train with men in Kyona. It's frowned upon in Balenol, I believe, but here we're more relaxed." She raised an eyebrow at the Kyonan man. "You might find me a worthwhile opponent yourself. Don't let the title fool you."

"I'm not impressed by either titles or words," responded Cody coolly, his arms crossed over his chest.

Lady Yasmin smirked, already edging toward the door to the internal courtyard, pulling something from a fold of her garments as she went. "Well I guess you know where to find me if you want to put my words to the test."

And with that she slipped out the door, barely a ripple in the colorful hangings betraying her passage. In the silence that followed her departure, Lucy heard a faint metallic scraping sound. She crossed the room curiously and tried the handle of the door. It was locked.

She glanced back at Cody. His arms were still crossed, and he was staring at the spot where the Thoranian visitor had disappeared.

"A noblewoman who can pick locks," he said, sounding impressed. "That's something you don't see every day."

Lucy sent him a long-suffering look. "Some guardian you are. You've already forgiven her for breaking into my room with a weapon in the dead of night, haven't you?"

Cody flashed her a sudden grin. "That depends on how well her actions live up to her words. It's been far too long since I've had a decent sparring session."

"Thank you for the compliment," said Lucy dryly, thinking of their own day of training in the jungle, which she at least had found grueling.

"She's certainly not like any noblewoman I've ever seen in Kynton," said Matheus, still looking slightly awestruck.

"Yes, well." Lucy couldn't keep the disgruntled tone from her voice. "I think Thorania is quite a different kingdom from Kyona."

"You should definitely take her up on the offer to train,

Lucy," said Cody briskly. "Even if she's telling the truth that her brother meant you no harm, the attack is a reminder that we don't know what we're dealing with here. It's more important than ever to be sharp."

"Mmhmm," said Lucy absently, her mind turning over all Lady Yasmin's revelations. She looked up. "So, we'll keep this to ourselves for now, right?"

"You mean keep it from the royals?" Cody asked, frowning. "You don't want to tell Jocelyn and Eamon?"

Lucy shrugged. "She asked us not to, didn't she?"

"Not specifically," said Cody. He gave her a shrewd look. "Why don't you want to tell them?"

Matheus rolled his eyes. "She's still punishing Eamon."

"It's not that," said Lucy quickly. "I just want some time to think it all over. And Eamon at least is already prejudiced against Rasad. I want more evidence before announcing that Lady Yasmin basically just accused him of plotting against Balenol. It's one thing for Lady Yasmin to speak to us about it, since none of us have titles or official roles here. It's another thing to announce her suspicions to the royalty of Kyona and Valoria. She's trying to avoid a diplomatic incident between the kingdoms, not start one."

Cody frowned at her. He didn't look entirely convinced by her argument, but he didn't protest. His gaze flicked briefly to Matheus. "You should go back to bed, Matheus. I'll meet you in our suite in a minute."

"No, I'll wait with you," said Matheus with unusual firmness.

Cody raised an eyebrow, looking slightly amused. "Are you telling me what to do now, Matheus?"

"No, I'm looking out for Lucy," Matheus retorted, his cheeks slightly pink but his expression determined.

Cody frowned. "What's that supposed to mean?"

"You might not care," said Matheus in the same tone of

determination. "But Lucy was upset over what happened in Nohl. About the rumors. If we were unlucky, and a servant or someone saw you coming and going from Lucy's room in the middle of the night, I want to be sure that they see that I'm with you. No one's going to think anything suspicious if they know her brother was with her the whole time."

Cody stared at the younger boy. "Not you, too. Who cares about all this rumor and reputation rubbish when people keep pulling weapons on Lucy as soon as I'm not looking?"

"Lucy cares," repeated Matheus firmly. "Just because it's not important to you, doesn't mean it's not important." He gave his sister a curt nod, as if to reassure her that he had her back.

Lucy stared back at him, touched. As embarrassing as it was to realize just how aware her little brother had been of the damage to her reputation in Nohl, she was amazed at how quickly he had grasped the implications. He had had almost as little exposure to court as Cody had. But while it was clearly still a mystery to the older man why he should care about such matters, Matheus had picked up on the dynamics much more quickly.

"Thanks Matheus," she said quietly. "I'm glad you're here." He returned her smile with a mixture of self-consciousness and pride, and she wondered when he had done so much growing up. She turned back to Cody. "You can talk freely in front of Matheus anyway. There's no need to send him away."

"Fine," Cody sighed. He still looked perplexed, but happy to drop the subject. "There's no great secret. I was just going to ask you—if I hadn't been watching your room, and hadn't come in here and found Lady Yasmin, would you have told me about her visit?"

Lucy sent him a cheeky grin. "Who knows? It would probably depend on how nice you were to me the next day."

Cody scowled. "You have to keep me in the loop, Lucy," he said sternly. "You can't shut me out on one of your whims."

"All right, all right," said Lucy, stifling a yawn as she waved him away. "Now get out of my room before I call the guards on you."

"What guards?" asked Cody with asperity. "Last I checked, your non-royalness, you don't have any guards. I'm it."

"And you're doing such an excellent job," said Lucy. "But I want to sleep."

Cody shook his head, turning to Matheus. "Come on then, Matheus. You'd better chaperone me back to my room."

Lucy waited until she heard the outer door of her suite close before sinking back onto her pillows. Whatever she'd said to Cody, she didn't think she'd ever been further from sleep.

CHAPTER TWENTY-TWO

Lucy walked briskly through the corridors of the palace, trying to monitor people's reactions without looking like she was doing it. To her relief, although her training clothes were attracting some curious looks, she couldn't see any sign of the judgment she'd unleashed in Nohl.

It was still an hour before she was expected at breakfast, but she had a feeling that Lady Yasmin was an early riser. Lucy hadn't needed Cody's prompt to decide to meet the noblewoman at the training hall. It wasn't only that she wanted to spar with the Thoranian, although she did. It also wasn't lost on her that Lady Yasmin had gone to some effort the night before to speak with Lucy in private, and Cody and Matheus had prevented her from doing so. If there were things the older woman wanted to say to her without an audience, she wanted to hear them.

Before she reached the training hall, the clang of metal confirmed that someone at least liked to train first thing in the morning. She entered the large open space cautiously, still not entirely sure she was supposed to be there.

It was an impressive room. Lucy had been struck by it on the tour the previous afternoon. In the castles of both Kynton and

Nohl, the training grounds were outside. But here in Thirl, the palace itself boasted a large open hall for the purpose. Perhaps it was to protect those training from the unforgiving sun.

The floor was the same polished stone as the rest of the palace, and tall paneled windows, stretching from floor to ceiling, covered the eastern wall. The rising sun hadn't yet crested the mountain range to the east of Thirl, but Lucy could imagine that it wouldn't be long before the space was flooded with light.

The walls were of smooth white stone, and polished pillars ran around all four edges of the space. The walls were lined with weapons, and the room was split into different sections. A few pairs could be seen sparring with swords in one corner, and a man on the far side of the room was wielding a long wooden staff, spinning it skillfully as he struck a cushioned target.

Lucy's eyes were drawn to one of the duos of swordsmen fighting near the eastern wall. For a moment she frowned, wondering why the figures looked familiar, silhouetted against the growing light. Then she sighed, rolling her shoulders in irritation. She should have known that Cody would be too quick to let her steal a march on him. He had clearly been suspicious the night before about how much she intended to inform him of her doings.

She moved to an empty space between two of the pillars, hoping not to attract too much notice as she started warming up. Cody and Lady Yasmin were still sparring when she finished her stretches and began some solo exercises with her blade. But the sound of a particularly violent clang followed by Cody's low chuckle pulled her from her warm up.

She looked up just as Cody glanced over and noticed her.

"Lucy," he said calmly, as if he'd been expecting her. "There you are."

Lucy didn't immediately answer, regarding her mentor with surprise. Cody was panting as he wiped an arm across his forehead. Apparently Lady Yasmin had fought well enough to give him a challenge. Lucy wasn't surprised.

What was strange was the sparkle in Cody's eye, which Lucy couldn't remember ever seeing before. It made his well-known face seem almost unfamiliar. She knew Cody enjoyed sparring, but he didn't usually show it—he said it was a distraction from the fight, and he was always lecturing Lucy about getting carried away by the thrill of combat. And now here he was, looking like he'd been having the time of his life.

"I see you beat me to it in challenging Lady Yasmin to a bout," she said at last. She kept her tone light, but her eyes passed furtively between the two of them as she spoke. Lady Yasmin was also breathing heavily, looking as collected and commanding as ever, in spite of the sweat lining her brow.

"He did, but there's enough of me to go around," the Thoranian said with an amused smile. She also seemed to be in an excellent mood.

"I'm not complaining," said Lucy lightly. "It can only work in my favor if Cody tired you out a bit for me."

Lady Yasmin chuckled. "Not so hasty. I've got plenty of energy left in me."

"Enough talk," said Cody admonishingly, as Lucy opened her mouth to reply. "You've warmed up, Lucy, let's go."

Lucy grimaced at Lady Yasmin. "Always the trainer."

Lady Yasmin just smiled. "Swords or daggers?"

"Daggers," said Lucy quickly. She had seen enough of Lady Yasmin's fight with Cody to know she would disgrace herself if she tried to cross swords with the older woman.

Lady Yasmin placed her sword carefully on a nearby bench and pulled out the same dagger she had produced in Lucy's room the night before.

Without a word, Lucy removed her own weapon from its sheath and adopted a fighting stance. She was vaguely aware of

Cody, watching her critically from the sidelines, his arms crossed over his chest in a characteristic gesture. But her attention was focused on her opponent, sizing up the taller, stronger woman as they began to circle.

Lucy attacked first, slashing out swiftly toward Lady Yasmin's blade arm. The Thoranian countered the swipe easily, taking a step backward as she blocked Lucy's blade. Recognizing it as a feint, Lucy stepped back as well, raising her blade to intercept the subsequent lunge from her opponent.

"Nice," said Lady Yasmin, flashing an appreciative smile before once again adopting an expression of great focus.

Lucy didn't respond, determined not to become distracted. Her eyes skimmed over Lady Yasmin, looking for an opening, then her blade flashed out again. Steel locked on steel, the older woman's superior strength coming into play as they pushed against each other. In a sudden motion, Lady Yasmin disengaged her blade.

Lucy didn't hesitate, raising her other arm and letting her metal arm guard take the force of her opponent's attack. Despite the fact that they were using real blades, Lady Yasmin wasn't holding back. Lucy took it as a compliment.

With a grunt, she brought her arm down, throwing off the other knife as she moved her feet in a semi-circle. Cody was now in her line of sight, but she didn't take her eyes from Lady Yasmin.

With lightning speed, she stabbed her blade toward the other woman's torso, trusting in her opponent's obvious skill to prevent an injury.

Her instinct didn't fail. Lady Yasmin countered the attack, and almost before she knew what was happening, Lucy found herself being driven backward. Her dagger flashed frantically, staving off the older woman's repeated attacks, but she knew her opponent had the advantage.

Lucy didn't stop to think, shifting her weight to one leg as she dropped into a crouch, and thrusting the other leg out in front of her. She had her foot between Lady Yasmin's feet before the other woman knew what was happening. Sweeping her leg out she succeeded in throwing the older woman off balance, although it wasn't enough to bring her down.

Lucy sprang to her feet, ready to pursue her attack, but Lady Yasmin recovered quickly enough to counter the lunge. Lucy disengaged her blade neatly, but could see no opening to renew her assault.

"That was good, Lucy," said Cody unexpectedly, stepping forward. "But you left yourself vulnerable here."

The two women lowered their blades, both of them breathing hard as Cody critiqued Lucy's performance.

"That was a neat trick with your foot," said Lady Yasmin when Cody was finished. "I haven't seen that one before."

"In that case, I'm impressed you stayed on your feet," said Lucy ruefully. "I can't count the number of times I ended up on my backside when Cody decided to teach me that one."

Cody chuckled. "It was good for you to be humbled. You'd just entered that unbearable phase of youth when you thought you knew everything."

Lucy gave Lady Yasmin a long-suffering look. "It's awful having a trainer who's known you since infancy."

"Yes, your lot is very hard," said Cody dryly. "Now swords."

Lucy groaned internally, but she knew better than to protest. Lady Yasmin had much more reason to complain about Cody bossing her around, but she didn't seem to mind, retrieving her sword readily enough.

Lucy took the sword Cody offered her, one she had frequently trained with. He obviously had been expecting her this morning, or he wouldn't have brought the blade. It was far too petite a weapon for him to fight with.

She raised the sword in front of her, running over the footwork in her mind. Her dagger always felt like an extension of her arm, something she could control and manipulate with ease. But swords were harder, clumsier.

Lady Yasmin made no move to raise her weapon, eyeing Lucy's thoughtfully. "Would you like to try one like mine?" she asked. "I think you'll find it easier to manipulate."

Lucy lowered her weapon, regarding her opponent's sword with interest. She hadn't immediately noticed, but Lady Yasmin's blade was not like hers. Not only did it look lighter, but it was curved, forming a slim crescent.

"Is that what most Thoranian swords look like?" she asked curiously.

Lady Yasmin shrugged one shoulder, inclining her head to Lucy's weapon. "We train to fight with that type of blade as well." She tossed her weapon lightly from one hand to the other. "But this is a more popular choice. You should try it."

She retrieved another weapon from the wall, similar in size and shape to hers. Lucy took it eagerly, noting with pleasure that it was as light as it looked.

Lady Yasmin wasted no time, instructing Lucy on the differences in this type of sword fight. She was a capable teacher, and in no time at all she and Lucy were attempting a practice bout, watched critically by Cody.

They fought in silence for a couple of minutes, sweat standing out on both their brows. Lucy very quickly warmed to the new weapon. Lady Yasmin was as capable a teacher as Cody, and her instructions soon had Lucy getting a feel for the blade. She felt the familiar rush of pleasure that came from success in training. She could become good with this weapon, she was sure of it.

But proficiency was still many hours of practice away. The bout required Lucy's full attention, and it took a moment for her to notice that Cody had moved away, challenged to spar with some Thoranian man whom Lucy hadn't met.

She tried not to become distracted, but she couldn't help feeling relieved that Cody wasn't going to be criticizing her fighting later. She returned her attention to Lady Yasmin, losing herself in the familiar rhythm of thrust, deflect, retreat. In spite of her exhaustion, she could feel the energy coursing through her limbs, that buzz that only a truly challenging fight could bring. And it certainly was a challenging fight. Even with her full focus, and the delightful lightness of the weapon in her hands, it was only a matter of minutes before the older woman succeeded in disarming her.

Lucy smiled as she conceded the match. "I like this blade," she said, turning it over in her hand to examine it more closely. She sighed. "But even so, I don't think the sword will ever be my strongest weapon. It's a shame, because it's so common. I don't know about here, but in Kyona, most men wear swords as a matter of course. I mean the wealthy ones, obviously," she clarified, still breathing heavily as she stretched out her stiff arms.

"It's the same here," acknowledged Lady Yasmin. "Although archery is also favored by many." She watched Lucy for a moment, a small smile on her face. "You're better than you think you are, you know. You hold yourself up against an unfair example. Cody is an extremely good fighter." She glanced at the man in question, now fully engaged in his own bout on the other side of the room. "You'll probably never be as skilled with a sword as he is, but by general standards, you're a very good fighter. And you picked up the subtleties of that new blade incredibly quickly."

"Thank you," said Lucy, looking at Cody as well. "Cody's been pushing me hard for years, so it's nice to think it's paid off."

The noblewoman smiled. "You're fortunate to have such a dedicated teacher. I never had that advantage. Thoranians aren't as uptight in their expectations as Balenans, but it's still uncommon for women to spend as much time learning to fight as I have. It's taken a fair bit of determination for me to reach this level."

"I can see you have gone to great efforts," said Lucy, eyeing the other woman with respect.

Lady Yasmin acknowledged it as she replaced her weapon. "Your training gear is interesting, by the way," she added. "Greater mobility than mine, but you'll get hot fighting in that material in our climate."

"I already am," said Lucy ruefully, trying to surreptitiously sponge sweat off her neck. "I'm not used to the heat here, or in Balenol. The air is so heavy." She eyed the other woman's outfit jealously. It was more closely fitted than the clothes Lucy had previously seen her in, but still not as tight as Lucy's own training clothes. Although the fabric was a bit heavier than general Thoranian garb—presumably for modesty on such form-fitting garments—it was still light compared to Kyonan clothing.

Lady Yasmin chuckled. "The humidity does take some getting used to. My home, in the north, is much more arid than here, where we're so close to the jungle." She sighed wistfully. "You can really breathe out there, close to the sea."

Lucy looked at her curiously. "Why do you spend so much time here in Thirl if you miss it so much?"

Lady Yasmin's expression became serious at once, and she cast a glance around them before responding. "Because there's trouble brewing here, and no one else seems to be doing anything to prevent it. Lucy..." She hesitated, and Lucy nodded encouragingly.

"It's all right. Why do you think I'm here? There's no audience now, you can speak freely."

Lady Yasmin regarded her shrewdly. "Your mind is as sharp

as your blade, Luciana," she said. "I did want to speak to you alone. I know you didn't like me asking about the nature of your connection with Rasad." Lucy opened her mouth, but the other woman held up a hand, forestalling her.

"And I'm not going to ask you about it now. I'm not going to ask you to tell me anything. I'll talk, and you can make of it what you like." She took a deep breath. "Rasad is up to something, I'm certain of it. But I don't know the extent of it, and I'm never going to find out through direct means. He knows we're suspicious of him, and he's a careful man. But he's taken you under his protection, in some form or another. You might have a chance to discover things that we can't."

Lucy frowned. "Are you asking me to spy on Rasad and report back to you?"

"I didn't say that," said Lady Yasmin quickly. "I just said that you might have opportunities we don't have." She looked troubled as she again glanced around to make sure they weren't being overheard. "I'm not asking you to tell me anything. I'm just...encouraging you to be smart about who you trust, and not to waste any chances you might have to gain information. What you do with any information you learn is entirely up to you."

Lucy was silent, thinking over the noblewoman's words. "Look," she said at last. "I think you overestimate my position with Rasad. I doubt I'm going to be able to—"

"Good morning ladies. I see my idea of a quick training session before breakfast wasn't exactly original."

CHAPTER TWENTY-THREE

The familiar voice made Lucy jump, and she turned with some consternation to see Eamon emerging from behind one of the smooth stone pillars. She relaxed as she took in his open posture and friendly smile as he looked at the two women. Nothing could more surely convince her that he hadn't overheard that they were speaking about Rasad, and Lucy's level of relationship to the Thoranian advisor.

"Your Highness," said Lady Yasmin, dipping into a curtsy. Eamon inclined his head to the noblewoman, but his eyes were on Lucy. She dipped into a small curtsy as well, partly for appearances, but mainly to hide the flush on her face. Eamon had been in official meetings all the previous afternoon. The last time she had spoken with him, she had ended up daydreaming about their kiss in the forest. It was hard to look him in the eye.

"Early morning is a popular time to train here," Lady Yasmin pushed on, coming to Lucy's rescue. "Before the heat of the day sets in."

"Very sensible," said Eamon pleasantly. "Although I admit I wasn't thinking about that. I just thought this might be my only opportunity to get some exercise in, since I'll be in meetings most of the day."

"Yes, I heard that trade negotiations started yesterday," said Lady Yasmin politely. "How was the afternoon's meeting?"

"It was more of an opportunity to meet one another than an actual negotiation," said Eamon. He gave a sudden chuckle. "Some of the advisors showed more interest in Valoria than in Kyona. I would be alarmed if I wasn't pretty sure I know the reason."

Lady Yasmin gave him an inquiring look, and he chuckled again.

"They asked Prince Kincaid and Princess Jocelyn a lot of questions that were only very loosely connected to matters of trade. I'm fairly certain they were trying to find out how much truth there is to the stories that Kincaid and Joss went traveling across the kingdom with a dragon."

Lucy hid a smile as she remembered the hopeful speculation of the Balenan noble girl who thought that the Kyonans had come to offer some kind of dragon alliance to their southern neighbors. It seemed a similar rumor was circulating in Thorania.

Eamon's voice turned thoughtful. "Dragons are pretty widely recognized in the North Lands now. But I guess here in the South Lands, where no one has actually seen one, the rumors might feel removed enough for people to doubt if they're true."

"Yes," said Lady Yasmin, curiosity burning in her eyes. "Not everyone believes the stories."

"Well they're true," said Lucy emphatically, thinking of her unnerving dream encounter with the dragon-ruler. "And," she turned to Eamon a little indignantly, "while Joss and Kincaid may have been the ones to most recently travel with one, Valoria can't lay claim to the dragons. It was your parents and my father who first rediscovered them, and it's Kyona that has a centuries-long connection to the dragon colony."

"True," agreed Eamon, seeming pleased at her possessive way of speaking of their kingdom. "But I didn't like to bring that up, since I'm still trying to figure out whether that will make Thorania more or less eager to increase diplomatic relations with us."

Lady Yasmin looked a little awed by the conversation, but she smiled at the prince's light-hearted tone. "I suppose that depends how friendly the dragons are."

"They mostly keep to themselves if the truth be told," said Eamon absently, his eyes on the weapon still in Lucy's hand. "That's an interesting sword." He raised his eyebrows at her. "But I thought you preferred your dagger, Lucy."

Lucy smiled in spite of herself. "You have a good memory. But I can be versatile."

"I know it," said Eamon, returning her smile. "And it has been a while, hasn't it? When we were talking about training together yesterday, it made me realize just how long it is since we did." He frowned slightly. "Months, maybe more."

"A couple of years, actually," said Lucy dryly. He really hadn't noticed. And she thought she'd been so successful in rewriting her reputation at court.

"As long as that?" Eamon said, startled.

"No time like the present," prompted Lady Yasmin, who had been watching their interaction with a measuring expression. "Luciana and I were just finishing up, anyway."

"No, it's fine, Lady Yasmin," said Lucy quickly, her face more flushed than ever. "There's no need to—"

"Come on, Lucy," said Eamon, a wicked glint in his eyes. "Don't be scared. We can spar with daggers instead of swords, if you like, so that you won't be completely crushed by me."

Lucy gave a gasp of outrage, unable to help rising to the bait.

"How generous of you, *Your Highness*. With such an offer, I'll just have to overcome my fear."

"Excellent," said Eamon, shedding the light jacket he was wearing. Any jacket was ridiculous in this heat, but it was probably part of his ceremonial garb. His non-sword arm was still neatly bandaged—reminding Lucy of the knife wound she had almost forgotten about, given how smoothly he seemed to be recovering from it. She knew him better than to suggest he shouldn't be sparring because of the injury. And it must have been shallower than it had appeared at first, because it didn't seem to be limiting his movements much.

Lucy didn't give him time to warm up. With the jacket off, the strong lines of his chest could be seen all too clearly through his training tunic. She hadn't seen him in such casual clothing since they were much younger, and she figured a quick offense was the best way to avoid getting distracted by how much more muscled he seemed to have become.

She discarded the borrowed sword and produced her dagger in a flash, advancing on him before his own weapon was out of its sheath.

"I see you don't plan to fight fair," Eamon said, a grin on his face as his blade appeared in his hand as if by magic. The clang of metal bounced off the stone walls as he deflected her thrust.

"Never," Lucy said, grinning back in spite of herself as she retreated a couple of paces. Out of the corner of her eye she saw Lady Yasmin move away, joining Cody who had just finished his bout. Returning her attention to her own fight, Lucy hid a smile. She suspected the older woman had intercepted Cody intentionally, as a favor to Lucy, and she was grateful.

The two combatants circled each other carefully, measuring with their eyes. There was a reason Lucy didn't want Cody, or anyone else, watching their match. Fighting Eamon wasn't like fighting anyone else. It was genuinely difficult not to become distracted, both by the necessity of letting her eyes rove over every inch of him looking for an opening, and by the awareness that he was examining her whole figure in just such a way. Lucy had once been good at tuning out her emotions in order to fight smart when sparring with the prince, but it had been far too long, and she was out of practice.

And somehow, in those intervening years, he had gone from the romanticized focus of her girlish fancies to a man, fully grown and undeniably captivating, even when she was annoyed with him.

He lunged forward with lightning speed, and she pushed her wildly swirling thoughts down ruthlessly, letting instinct take over as she defended against the attempt on her fighting arm.

She twisted her blade in a complicated flick she had perfected through hours of practice with Cody. To her own surprise, she succeeded in making a shallow slash across Eamon's blade hand, the prince not drawing back quickly enough.

She held back her gasp with an effort, trying to keep her focus as a few drops of blood ran down Eamon's hand.

The prince let out a small laugh, clearly as surprised as she was. "You're sneaky, Lucy," he said, retreating a few paces and wiping the blood off on his leggings. "And you've learned some new tricks."

Lucy permitted herself a grim smile. "Just because I haven't been sparring with you doesn't mean I've been wasting my time."

"Clearly," said Eamon, and the admiration was obvious in his voice. Lucy tried not to feel smug, but a moment later her internal gloating was cut short as Eamon advanced without warning.

She ducked and weaved rapidly as she defended, recognizing that if it came to brute strength, she had no hope of holding him off. But she was agile, and she had Eamon chasing her around their small circle as she pivoted and twisted.

Seeing an opening, she flipped her dagger outward, re-positioning her grip mid gesture in a move that had cost her hand many slices when she was learning it. She slashed below Eamon's guard, toward his stomach. He brought his arm down swiftly, but he didn't engage his blade in time, instead having to deflect her attack with the steel arm guard he wore, similar to Lucy's.

Lucy's breath was coming in pants, but it was all she could do not to grin broadly. The normal elation of a good bout was nothing to the thrill of pitting her skill against Eamon's. Every nerve tingled with the energy of his closeness, and the light in his eyes when he admired her in a ballgown was nothing to the focused determination on his face now. Not only did she find him most handsome when he wore that studied, intent expression, but it said more clearly than words that he was taking her, and their fight, seriously.

As the minutes wore on, Lucy's waning energy began to betray her. Eamon had come to the fight fresh, whereas Lucy had fought Lady Yasmin first, with not much time to catch her breath between. She held out as long as she could, but Eamon never failed to take advantage of any lapse or fumble. He was relentless in his attack, and far from resenting that he wasn't going easy on her, she admired him for it. His eyes glowed with the same exhilaration she always got from a fight, the flashes of bright blue like twin magnets that she knew would draw her irresistibly in if she let herself meet his gaze for too long. If she was honest with herself, she had never found him more attractive.

As she deflected another attack on her blade arm, she wondered fleetingly whether she would have persisted in her rejection after his misstep if he had pursued their relationship with the same intense persistence that he showed in a fight. Instead he had lost confidence and become so mired in regret that he could hardly look her in the eye anymore.

Her own thoughts confused her—it wasn't lost on her that not long ago she had been condemning his tendency to overconfidence. But her distraction cost her. As caught up as she was in her tangled emotions regarding her opponent, she inevitably lost focus, and Eamon wasted no time in pressing his advantage. She fell for his feint, lunging wildly, and his spare hand flashed out, catching her wrist in an iron grip.

He stepped close, trapping her arm in position as he squeezed, not hard enough to really hurt, but strategically enough to force her hand open. Her weapon clattered to the floor just as he laid his own against her throat, the blade flat and cold on her flushed skin.

"My victory," he said, grinning boyishly.

Lucy stared up at him, unable to find any words as her breath caught in her throat.

Eamon's expression underwent a rapid change as he took in the look on her face. He lowered his blade to his side, but maintained his hold with his other hand.

His cocky smile disappeared, his eyes becoming intense. It reminded Lucy inexplicably of the look he had given her on Jocelyn's wedding day, when the groom was finally told to kiss his bride. Lucy remembered thinking that if only Eamon could figure out how to say with his words what his eyes were saying in that moment, everything could be fixed between them.

She barely noticed how out of breath she still was from their fight. Her eyes were locked on Eamon's as her thoughts flew erratically from the moment when Kincaid had kissed Jocelyn at their wedding to the moment when Eamon had first kissed her in the forest, during their brief escape from his guards. It hadn't really been so long ago, but the Lucy in her memory seemed barely more than a child.

She didn't feel like a child now.

"Lucy." Eamon's voice was soft as his gaze dropped from her eyes to her lips. Lucy swallowed, lowering her own gaze in an attempt to break the enchantment that seemed to still tie her to him, in spite of everything. She could feel Eamon's eyes searching her face, but she didn't look up, too confused to know what she wanted.

"You fight well," he said, his voice still soft, but not as intense. "You're much better even than I remember."

She chanced a peek up at him. It was clear that he was genuinely impressed, and it softened her defeat.

"And you're even stronger than I remember," she said, her own voice soft.

For a moment Eamon's expression remained serious, as he studied her face searchingly. Then he smiled, not the cocky grin of before, but a more intimate expression that she hadn't seen on his face in a long time. He released her wrist at last, lowering his arm but making no move to place any distance between them.

"Has it really been so long since we trained together?" he asked. "We used to do it so often."

Lucy shook her head slightly. "You really hadn't noticed?"

"Very unobservant of me," said Eamon lightly. "I guess because we still saw each other so much, and because I was still training so frequently, I never put it together that both things weren't happening at the same time. I suppose when you came to visit, we were too busy, you know..."

"Flirting," supplied Lucy, her heart beating a little more quickly at her boldness in opening a topic she had so firmly kept closed for months.

Eamon's grin was instantaneous. "Exactly. Although now

that I think about it, I'm not at all sure why we couldn't have done both at once."

Lowering her gaze to Eamon's chest, which was still far too close for any other setting, Lucy had to agree. In hindsight, it was hard to think of a more effective way to get away with flirting with the prince in public. But she didn't say as much.

"So you never thought I'd stopped training?" she asked instead, looking up surreptitiously through her lashes in an attempt to read Eamon's expression.

"Stopped training?" He looked genuinely astonished. "Why would you ever do that? You're so good at it. And you love it so much."

Lucy looked up fully, startled. "How do you know that?"

Eamon gave an incredulous laugh. "What do you mean, how do I know? Weren't we just talking about how much we used to train together? You think I couldn't tell all those times that you enjoyed it just as much as I did? You come alive when you fight, and I understand why completely. I'm the same way. It's exhilarating to get lost in a good bout." He flashed a grin. "Especially when you're more skilled than your opponent."

But Lucy didn't respond to the sally. She was too astonished by how well Eamon apparently knew her. She couldn't decide whether to be irritated or impressed that her attempts to hide her true feelings from him had been such a waste of time. So much so that he hadn't even noticed the attempt. She almost rolled her eyes. How could he be so perceptive and so oblivious at the same time?

"But..." She hesitated. "We were so young back then. I'm grown up now. I'm...you know..."

"A woman?" Eamon supplied. His eyes passed briefly over her figure, as if he couldn't quite stop them. "Yes, it hadn't escaped my notice, actually. What's your point?"

"Well, just that..." Lucy struggled to pull her thoughts

together. "I have different priorities now. You don't think it makes sense that I stopped sparring with you and the knights when I started attending balls and all of that?"

Eamon frowned. "I can imagine that it makes sense to a lot of people, but it doesn't make sense to me. And it's hard for me to believe it makes sense to you." He gave her a shrewd look. "Don't try to tell me your priorities have changed that much, Lucy. Believe me, I know that you like dressing up for a ball, and being admired by every man between 15 and 70." He lowered his voice to a mutter. "I know better than anyone."

Lucy raised an eyebrow, and he hurried on.

"Not that I blame you for enjoying any of that. But I don't believe for a second that enjoying a ball makes you enjoy fighting any less." He gestured toward her discarded weapon. "Even if you could hide the fact that you got as much of a thrill from that fight as I did, you certainly can't hide the fact that you've been training often and hard in order to maintain that level of skill."

Lucy opened her mouth then closed it again. "So," she tried at last. "So when you saw me kill my own uncle in front of you, that didn't make me seem less like a...I don't know, a lady? I mean," she hastened to add, "I know I'm not a lady in terms of a title, I just meant—"

"Lucy." Eamon's tone more than his words cut Lucy off mid-flow. His eyes searched her face, their expression distressed. "Has that been worrying you?" He put a hand on her shoulder, the contact sending a spark through her. "I've never admired you more than in that moment, especially since I knew perfectly well that Scanlon's mischief was my fault. If Benjy had died because I was such a fool..."

He trailed off, closing his eyes and taking a deep breath. Lucy knew her little brother was like family to Eamon too. She realized for the first time just how much it must have tortured the prince to think that he'd almost had a hand in the death of the boisterous ten-year-old.

"Lucy, no one whose opinion you should care about would think less of you for using your hard-earned skills to stop someone from murdering your little brother." His voice softened. "And titles be hanged. You've always been more than a lady to me." He gave a crooked smile. "More like a princess."

Lucy felt a flush rising up her cheeks, but she couldn't quite meet his eye, still trying to process everything he'd said.

"What did Rasad mean yesterday?" Eamon asked suddenly. "When he said that your talents would earn you respect in Thorania, he looked right at me. It was like he was saying they wouldn't in Kyona. But what does he know about our ways? Have you said something to him?"

Lucy looked up, thrown by the abrupt change of topic. "I'm sure a man like Rasad has plenty of ways of finding out anything he wants to know about Kyona," she said evasively. "And I don't think he was just thinking of Kyona. He witnessed some of my less popular moments in Nohl. Besides," she raised her eyebrows, forcing Eamon to meet her gaze, "would he be wrong?"

She gestured toward Lady Yasmin, who was deep in conversation with Cody, twirling a dagger absent-mindedly in one hand. "Jocelyn got enough grief for doing basic weapons training. How do you think people would respond in Kynton if a noblewoman behaved like Lady Yasmin does?"

Eamon's frown deepened. "I know court isn't always the kindest place for women who want to learn to defend themselves. But my mother has been fighting this battle for decades, Lucy, not to mention Jocelyn in the last few years. We're not perfect in Kyona, but we've come a long way."

He looked down, seeming to struggle to meet her eyes. "Do you...are you saying you like it better here than in Kyona?"

Lucy studied his face, surprised by the question. She had been jealous of Eamon at times, with all her wrestling over her mixed heritage. He had no such problem. He was the epitome of Kyonan, accepted from birth merely by virtue of his position. But it hadn't occurred to her before now how personal that made the issue for him. In some ways, Eamon was Kyona, or at least Kyona's future. The kingdom's standing in the eyes of other countries, and of those he cared about, wasn't just a matter of pride. It was a matter of heart.

"I didn't say that," she answered carefully. "Kyona has always been my home, and I've only been in Thorania for a day. But there are some things about this place that I really like."

"And some people," said Eamon, so quietly she could barely hear him. He looked up, his expression vulnerable. "Was he really buying you jewelry?"

Lucy let her breath out in a exasperated huff. "You really can't help yourself, can you?"

Eamon's expression changed instantly from vulnerable to defensive.

"I don't trust him," he said, his voice dark.

"Well, that's news," said Lucy sarcastically. She stepped back, finally putting some space between them. She wasn't sure what irritated her more—that Eamon had probably been right from the start about Rasad's untrustworthiness, or that with all the very real and substantial reasons to doubt Rasad, Eamon still chose not to trust him because of his interest in Lucy.

"You need to be careful, Lucy," said Eamon stubbornly.

Lucy looked away in annoyance, and her eyes widened slightly as her gaze fell on the room behind the prince. "Eamon."

"I'm serious, Lucy."

"Eamon!"

"Just listen," Eamon persisted. "If someone wanted to attack you just because you were with him, doesn't that tell you something about—"

"Eamon, stop talking and look behind you!" Lucy hissed.

"Wha—" Eamon had only half turned when a smooth voice cut in on their argument.

"So many early risers this morning."

Lucy tried to look natural as she greeted Rasad. She couldn't help but feel annoyed with Eamon—his discomposure made it all too clear that he had been speaking of the advisor before the man himself interrupted. But the prince recovered quickly, greeting Rasad with stiff politeness.

"I'm glad to see you putting our facilities to good use, Your Highness, Luciana," said Rasad. There was a note of pride in his voice as he glanced around the impressive training hall, now brilliantly lit by the rising sun. Lucy didn't miss the way his eyes lingered on Lady Yasmin and Cody, still talking animatedly on the other side of the space.

"Are you here to train, then?" Eamon asked Rasad, a slightly combative look on his face. Lucy could only imagine how delighted Eamon would be to have the chance to let out his frustration in a physical fight with the older man.

"No, Your Highness," said Rasad, with a hint of laughter. "I'm afraid I'm no soldier." His gaze passed to Lucy. "I was looking for you, actually, Luciana."

"Oh?" Lucy asked, trying to keep her expression neutral as Eamon's brow once again darkened in a scowl.

"Yes, I have some unfortunate news. Unfortunate for me, that is. I've received a message from my steward, and I need to leave the capital to visit my home, at least for a while."

"Oh," said Lucy again, unsure how to respond. She hoped Rasad hadn't noticed the visible brightening in Eamon's demeanor. She didn't know whether to be pleased or not. Some space to think things through might be good, but if she decided to see what she could discover, as Lady Yasmin had asked, it would be difficult to do it if Rasad was far away.

"Of course the timing isn't ideal, so soon after the delegation's arrival," Rasad said, nodding at Eamon before returning his attention to Lucy. "But I did promise to show you some of the wonders of our kingdom. Perhaps my business in the north might be an opportunity in disguise."

Lucy opened her mouth, confused, but it was Eamon who spoke.

"Are you suggesting Lucy should go with you?" he asked, his disapproval clear. "To your home?"

Rasad kept his eyes on Lucy. "I would be delighted if you would consider being my guest," he said, as if Eamon hadn't spoken. "It is a beautiful part of the country, and I would love to show you."

"I..." Lucy stammered, trying to pull her thoughts together. Eamon's silent but eloquent glare didn't help. "I don't think Cody would agree to me leaving Thirl."

"Naturally he and your brother are included in the invitation," said Rasad. He gave a half-bow to Eamon. "I know the others in your party have obligations here, with negotiations underway, but you and your companions are free to go where you please, surely. I was under the impression you weren't part of the official delegation. You didn't originally intend even to come to Thorania, did you?"

"Don't *you* have obligations regarding the negotiations?" Eamon asked bluntly. "You're primary advisor to the king, aren't you? And I thought our whole visit was your idea, to help anyone with Kyonan blood relocate to Kyona if they wished to."

"You flatter me, Your Highness," said Rasad, the hint of a sneer in his smile. "I am honored that the king values my advice, but I am far from necessary to all negotiations. His other advisors will have no difficulty managing without me for a week or two."

"Will your trip be as short as that?" Lucy asked, ignoring the way Eamon was shifting his weight from foot to foot.

"I hope so," Rasad said. He flashed that attractive smile, but it looked less appealing and more studied than Lucy remembered. "We would pass the Jeweled Peaks on our journey. They truly are a sight to behold. Will you consider my invitation?"

"I'll definitely consider it," Lucy said. "And I'll speak to my brother and Cody about it. When do you leave?"

"Almost immediately, I'm afraid," said Rasad, looking regretful. "It's a three day journey, and my business is urgent, so I leave at first light tomorrow."

"All right," Lucy said. "I should prepare for the meal now, but I'll think about it. Thank you for the invitation."

Rasad took her hand and pressed a light kiss to the back of it, before giving Eamon a half-bow. The prince barely waited for the Thoranian to be out of earshot before rounding on Lucy.

"Lucy, surely you can't seriously be considering accepting?"

"That's my own affair," said Lucy shortly, out of patience with his posturing.

"Lord and Lady Rodanthe will never agree to let you all leave with that slimy worm," Eamon blustered. "Surely you can see he's not trustworthy."

"Let's not dive into the issue of trust, Eamon," said Lucy bitingly, looking around for Cody. She didn't want to waste time arguing with the prince—she needed to think.

Eamon took a deep breath. "Lucy, if you accept an invitation to stay with him at his home, you may as well announce your engagement. That's what everyone will assume."

"I thought I shouldn't care what people think," said Lucy, tilting up her head in an effort to hide her flush at the remark.

The element of truth in Eamon's words was what stung most.

If she decided to go with Rasad, it would be because she wanted to see what she could discover, like Lady Yasmin had advised her to do. But that decision would come with a cost in terms of public opinion, there was no doubt.

"You laughed at the idea that you and Cody could be romantically involved," Eamon said, changing tack. "You said it was disgusting because he's your parents' age. So why doesn't it bother you for people to think the same thing about you and Rasad?"

"Rasad is younger than Cody," evaded Lucy, refusing to acknowledge that it did bother her.

Eamon snorted. "By what, five years? If that?"

Lucy took a deep breath, forcing herself to keep her temper. "Rasad's age is irrelevant, Eamon. The point is that it isn't your business. Like Rasad said, I'm not part of your delegation. Even Lord and Lady Rodanthe's authority over Matheus and me was only supposed to stretch until we reached our relations in Balenol."

"But your relations aren't here," argued Eamon quickly. "You were never supposed to be in Thorania on your own."

"I'm not on my own," said Lucy, trying to speak patiently. "And I'm not going to run off by myself. You might be under the direction of Lord Rodanthe, but my instructions are not to go anywhere without Cody. If I go to the north with Rasad, it will be because Cody and Matheus and I have talked it over, and we've all agreed that it's a good idea. Thank you for the bout, but I need to go get ready for the day."

"Lucy—" Eamon protested, but Lucy ignored him, retrieving her weapons and striding for the door. She needed to think before she made any decisions, and Eamon was the last one to help her consider the matter objectively.

But as she crossed the room her eyes fell on Lady Yasmin and Cody, both watching her with identical expressions of concern, and she knew what her decision would be, provided Cody could be convinced.

She turned toward the door, leaving explanations for Cody until later. Lady Yasmin had an openness about her that Rasad lacked, but Lucy didn't intend to blindly trust either of them. Whatever else happened, she was determined not to be used by anyone. To be sure of that, she needed more information.

And she had a feeling that when it came to Thorania, the place to find out what was really going on was wherever Rasad could be found.

CHAPTER TWENTY-FOUR

"It's pretty impressive." Matheus spoke in the tone of one making a great concession, although his eyes were wide with amazement. "It almost makes it worth being dragged away from Thirl the moment we arrived."

Lucy rolled her eyes. "Will you stop complaining?" She gestured at the sight before them. "You wouldn't be seeing this if we'd stayed in Thirl."

"It is pretty impressive," Matheus admitted again.

Lucy ignored the understatement, returning her attention to the incredible phenomenon of the Jeweled Peaks. They were unlike anything she'd ever seen. The mountain range stretched as far as she could see to the south, and for some distance northward as well. But the mountains weren't made of the gray stone of Kyona's mountain range.

The terrain had become steadily more arid as they traveled east from Thirl, and now only the occasional small, stubby vegetation could be seen protruding from behind outcrops of sand-colored rock.

But the peaks in front of them weren't just sand dunes. The

slopes rose up as high as any mountain range, their shadows shortening as the sun climbed further in the sky.

The Jeweled Peaks hadn't gotten their name from their height, though. The sediment truly did seem to sparkle like jewels in the morning sun, the slopes painted in stripes of red, purple, and yellow. Lucy had been pleased to learn that they would be riding alongside the range for the rest of the day. She felt as though she could look on the sight for a week without getting sick of it.

"Have you ever seen anything like it, Cody?" she asked.

"No," said Cody in his usual calm way. "It's quite a spectacle."

Lucy winced at his impassive expression. Cody hadn't complained like Matheus, but she had a feeling that he regretted their hasty departure from Thirl more. And she was pretty sure she knew why.

She'd been feeling guilty about it all morning, even though it wasn't really justified. She had been the one to receive the invitation, but it wasn't as though the decision had been hers. If Cody had said no, she wouldn't have been able to go. Even if Matheus had been adamantly against it, she suspected Cody would have refused the change in plan rather than force him to come just so they could stay together. In actual fact, they had talked it over, and all three of them had agreed they should take the opportunity to learn more about Rasad and what he might be up to.

Cody had even discussed the matter with Lord and Lady Rodanthe, despite Lucy's bold words to Eamon about not being answerable to them. According to him, the Kyonan courtiers had been hesitant about the group splitting up, but had made no attempt to forbid it. Most likely they were remembering that the three of them weren't strictly part of the delegation to Thorania.

But somehow it still felt like she was the one dragging Cody away from somewhere—or someone—he didn't want to leave.

"What do you think?" Rasad pulled his horse alongside hers. "Did I oversell them?"

"Not at all," said Lucy, smiling at him. "I've never seen anything like it. They're amazing. What makes them so colorful? Is this really where you mine the jewels?"

Rasad chuckled. "The mines are on the other side of the mountains. The color you can see isn't actually from jewels—the name is just poetic. It's minerals in the sediment that create that effect. No one fully understands why, but it's a phenomenon that doesn't appear anywhere else. At least not in the South Lands."

The pride was clear on Rasad's face as Lucy nodded.

"Not in the North Lands, either."

"The Jeweled Peaks are one of Thorania's greatest treasures," said Rasad. "In more ways than one." He smiled at Lucy. "Some people are more interested in the value to be found in the mines, but I thought you would appreciate their beauty for its own sake."

Lucy returned the smile. "You were right."

"Come," said Rasad, wheeling his horse around. "If we want to reach the end of the range by nightfall, we'd better get going."

He pushed his mount toward the front of the group, but Lucy was prevented from following by a firm hand on her reins.

"Keep your head, Lucy." Cody waited until Rasad was out of earshot before speaking, his voice serious. "Don't forget why we're here. He's up to something, and we're trying to find out what."

"I think you mean we're trying to find out *if* he's up to something," Lucy corrected with a slight frown. "Let's not assume he's guilty without any proof. And no one's losing their head. Have some faith in me."

"I do have faith in you, Lucy," said Cody calmly. "But as much as I know you don't like hearing it, you're still very young. Rasad is an intelligent and experienced man, and he's used to power. Don't try to tell me that you aren't a little fascinated by him."

Lucy didn't answer, troubled by the truth in his words. She *had* found Rasad magnetic from the start. But the fact that Cody was fully convinced of Lady Yasmin's trustworthiness wasn't proof of anything. If Lucy could be misled by Rasad's appeal, who was to say Cody wasn't vulnerable to the same blindness? Either of them could be using the Kyonans for unknown ends.

When Lucy remained silent, Cody released her reins, urging his own horse forward. Lucy followed slowly, still deep in thought.

"You didn't tell him, did you? You didn't tell either of them."

"What?" Lucy looked at her brother in confusion. "What are you talking about, Matheus?"

The fifteen-year-old looked unimpressed. "You didn't tell Eamon and Joss that Lady Yasmin asked you to keep an eye on Rasad, or that you agreed to stay with him because you want to see if he's up to something. You let them think it's because you just can't stay away from him."

Lucy rolled her eyes. "If either of them thinks that, they're being incredibly stupid."

"You didn't answer my question," said Matheus dryly.

Lucy shifted her hands on the reins. "Don't lecture me, Matheus. I told them about the invitation, and that we'd all talked it over and decided to accept, to find out more about Rasad, and about Thorania. I don't have to tell them everything I'm thinking. Lady Yasmin asked us not to say anything, remember?"

"And you're going to do what a stranger asked instead of trusting our friends, who we've known all our lives?" Matheus challenged. "Don't think I missed how heartbroken Eamon was last night. He thinks you're in love with Rasad, doesn't he?"

"How should I know what he thinks?" Lucy answered uncomfortably.

She didn't want to have this conversation with her little brother of all people. She took no pleasure from the reminder of the gala they had all attended the evening before. Even the widespread admiration she had received from the local men no longer held much appeal for her. She was all too familiar with it by now—the compliments were as predictable as they were shallow.

She had barely spoken with Eamon, not trusting herself after the tension of their bout that morning. But in spite of having been in meetings all day, he had somehow heard about her decision to accompany Rasad. His agitation was written on his face for everyone to see, and it just made her more irritated with him. She hadn't felt that she owed him a personal explanation for her decision, and she had made no attempt to give one.

Of course, his discomfort might have been as much from her attire as from her impending departure. Jocelyn was in Thorania as a representative of Valoria, and she had to wear a traditional Valorian dress, even though it didn't match the climate. But Lucy had no official role. When she retired to her room to prepare for the gala and found an unexpected gift awaiting her, she had decided to be bold.

If the present had been from Rasad, she wouldn't have accepted it. But it was from Lady Yasmin, and Lucy saw no reason to deny the curiosity she'd been feeling since arriving in Thorania. The sheer fabric felt as incredible as it looked. It fell softly around her, as light as feathers on her skin. She liked the mobility of the pants, but the way they billowed made them as elegant as a ballgown. She never wanted to wear anything else.

At least, until she arrived at the gala. The garment was quite covering, but she hadn't fully realized until she entered the brightly lit room just how transparent the fabric could be. It wasn't as though she was making a stir—the rest of the women in the room were dressed similarly. But she felt exposed all the same. And she wasn't sure what made her more uncomfortable —Rasad's obvious delight at seeing her in the traditional garb of Thorania, or Eamon's distress at how fully she was embracing their host kingdom.

Lucy pulled her thoughts back to the present, cutting off any reply Matheus might want to make by urging her horse into a trot. The Jeweled Peaks were still there on her right, as magnificent as they'd been when she first saw them. But somehow their splendor was dulled. She tried to tell herself that Eamon was nothing to her, and therefore she shouldn't care if Matheus was right that the prince thought she was in love with Rasad.

But somehow she didn't quite believe it.

THEY MADE steady progress all that day. As Rasad had promised, they camped in the evening at the northern end of the Jeweled Peaks. The next day was much the same, the horses moving at a constant rate, clearly well accustomed to the dry, hot terrain.

And it was dry. Gone was the moist air of the jungle. They had reached the northern part of the kingdom that Rasad had spoken of so often, and the landscape was more arid than any Lucy had seen before.

When they passed around the northern end of the mountain range they had an excellent view of the desert stretching to the east of the peaks. They couldn't see the coast from where they were, but Rasad told them that the sand stretched all the way to the ocean.

Lucy had never seen so much empty space, but somehow there was a beauty to the blank vista. The landscape felt wild and free, the opposite of the heavy clinging air and the overgrown foliage that made the Balenan terrain feel so suffocating.

Perhaps that was why the culture of Thorania seemed to be more relaxed and open.

The most interesting thing they saw that day was a herd of wild horses in the distance. Lucy couldn't help but exclaim with delight at the beautiful sight. The magnificent animals seemed like an embodiment of the spirit of freedom that characterized this kingdom. Rasad told her that there were many herds of wild horses in the eastern part of the country.

"You've only seen us in the city," he said. "So you haven't had a chance to see us show off our horsemanship. But we are at our best when working with our equine brethren. Do you know how to ride without a saddle?"

"No," said Lucy. "But I would love to learn."

Rasad smiled. "And I would love to teach you. Perhaps we'll find time while we're in the north."

"Perhaps," said Lucy, her eyes still on the horses galloping into the desert. Even from a distance, she could see the great sprays of sand being thrown in every direction by their hooves.

They weren't traveling at an uncomfortable speed, but the pace was steady. By the end of the second day, they had reached the edge of an enormous ravine that ran from west to east across the northern part of the kingdom. Rasad told them that they had made good time. They would reach his home on the other side of the ravine the next morning.

The final day of their journey dawned clear and mild, although Lucy had spent long enough in the South Lands now to know that it would be unbearably hot within a few short hours. Lucy was up early, but as usual not as early as Cody. She emerged from her tent to see the older Kyonan standing at the edge of the ravine.

"Good morning," she said, joining him. She peered down into the gully. "Wow, it's a long way down, isn't it? I didn't get a good look last night."

"It is," Cody agreed. "I could hear the water when I was trying to sleep, but the river is bigger than I expected."

Lucy glanced westward, toward the end of the ravine. "Water must flow down from the jungle to form that river," she guessed. "It is quite a torrent, isn't it?" She followed the waterway at the bottom of the ravine with her eyes, trying to picture where it must empty into the ocean, away to the east.

"So what's your plan, Lucy?" Cody asked suddenly. "When we get to Rasad's home?"

Lucy shrugged uncomfortably. "I don't know. I'll just look around, I guess. Try to get a feel for the place, and what Rasad's life is like." She raised an eyebrow. "What about you? Do you have some grand plan?"

"I wouldn't go that far," said Cody calmly. "But you can be sure I'll do more than just look around vaguely."

"Be careful, Cody," said Lucy, suddenly anxious. She glanced around, keeping her voice low. "If Lady Yasmin is right, and Rasad is up to something he shouldn't be, he won't react well to finding you poking around his business."

Cody smiled. "I'm good at being inconspicuous, Lucy. Don't worry about me." He glanced over at her, perhaps seeing that she was still concerned. "I've always been good at avoiding notice, you know. Did I ever tell you that I was never liberated by the resistance?"

Lucy frowned. "What do you mean? I thought you said they recruited you soon after you arrived in Balenol."

"They recruited me, yes," Cody acknowledged. "But they didn't liberate me. I escaped on my own, within a week of arriving in Nohl. I got a good feel for the intake camp, then I found an opportunity to slip away." His eyes took on a distant gleam, caught in the memory. "I'd been used to living on the street, in Alezae. I figured I could survive on the streets in Nohl without too much trouble." He shook his head. "I learned pretty quickly that Nohl wasn't like Alezae, at least not for a Kyonan kid. I wouldn't have lasted long if Raldo hadn't found me."

He looked back at Lucy, pulling his thoughts from the distant past. "Anyway, it was very rare for anyone to escape without outside help. It's easy to assume that I learned all my skills in stealth from the resistance. But while they helped me improve, especially in jungle tracking, I was actually already good at that stuff." He smiled. "So don't worry about me. Worry about yourself. If Rasad thinks you're sniffing around, and realizes you're suspicious, who knows how he'll respond?"

Lucy nodded vaguely. "I'm not planning to do anything dangerous, Cody."

He sighed. "You never are, but if it's not a balcony collapsing, it's a knife attack, or an abduction attempt. I didn't realize what I was signing up for when I agreed to come on this trip."

Lucy grinned, not fooled by his long-suffering tone. "You were spoiling for an adventure, don't deny it."

Cody just grunted, but there was no time for more anyway. The rest of the camp was rising, and it wasn't long before the group was underway again.

They crossed the ravine by way of a long wooden bridge suspended across the fissure by ropes. The crossing took a long time, as they needed to move in single file. The whole structure was sturdy and well-maintained, but it still made Lucy nervous to be so high above the ravine for so long. She couldn't help glancing down often at the river far below, and the rocky sides of the slopes.

"Are we on your lands now?" Lucy asked, as soon as the whole party had reached the other side safely.

"Not yet," said Rasad comfortably. "This stretch is part of the estate belonging to Lady Yasmin and Lord Yosef's family."

Lucy noticed how his eyes flicked briefly to Cody when he said the noblewoman's name, and she hid a frown. The

Thoranian didn't miss much. She could only hope he didn't know about Lady Yasmin's midnight visit to her suite.

"My land consists of a small peninsula to the northeast of here," Rasad was continuing. "It's not far. We'll be able to see the Bastion soon."

"The Bastion?"

Rasad smiled. "It is a bit pretentious to give my home a name, isn't it? But I'm very fond of the place."

Lucy just smiled, locking away the information that it had been Rasad, and not his ancestors, who had chosen such a fortress-like name. The approach to Rasad's Bastion was an easy ride, the ground becoming flatter, with tufts of dry, brittle grass interrupting the endless sand. It wasn't long before the Bastion itself came into view. Lucy was a little surprised to see that it had walls around it, almost like the palace in Thirl, although much less decorative.

In fact, the whole place was less decorative. It was still built of the same sandstone, and still an interesting design by Kyonan standards. But it seemed built more for function than appeal. It did indeed look like a fortress that could be easily defended against attack. It didn't say much for Rasad's relationship with his neighbors, but after her interactions with Lady Yasmin, that wasn't exactly news to Lucy.

It was still morning when they entered through the heavy front gates of Rasad's Bastion. The visitors were welcomed with every attention to their comfort, and Lucy was glad to be ushered into a pleasant suite in the same corridor as her brother and their guardian.

It didn't take her long to freshen up and unpack her belongings. In the process, she was distracted by Haydn's journal. She had brought all her things from Thirl, including the slim leather book. She flicked through, looking for more references to Thorania. Toward the back of the volume, she saw the name of the kingdom, and stopped to read the whole entry.

Today has brought a very unexpected arrival. Another former slave has joined us. Like me, he crossed back over after escaping into Thorania following the disaster with the ships. But he waited much longer than I did before returning to Balenol.

Lucy paused to check the date of the entry, flicking back through the pages to compare it to the first time Haydn had written in the journal. She was surprised to see that almost two years had passed. He obviously hadn't written very frequently for the journal to span so much time. She read on.

He was once part of the resistance, like me, or he would never have found us. It is fortunate for him that we have taken up permanent residence here, at the furthest south of Alben's old bases. He had tried a few of the other former strongholds first, and was weak and vulnerable by the time he reached us.

I must confess I was suspicious at first, afraid he was some kind of spy. Why would he return after such a long time? But some of the others knew him in the resistance days, and they vouch for him. If I can't trust my own community, I have nothing.

He brings interesting news of Thorania. He has passed the majority of recent years in the capital of Thirl, eking out a living as best he can on the streets. His experience has been much the same as mine was, when I first reached Thorania with Isidore. No one was offering help, but neither was anyone looking to capture him, or return him to Balenol. The Thoranians are still determined to remain isolated from the issue, it seems.

The most astonishing thing about his tale is that he brings news of Isidore. I never thought I would hear more of her fate, but apparently she is well known in Thorania now. She married him, as I knew she would, and they are making a stir together. I have no doubt she will achieve whatever she sets out to. She was always determined.

In a way, she is the reason our newest member stayed so long in Thorania. He was amazed to see a Kyonan—a former slave, even— achieving such prominence in Thoranian society. He assumed that she would use her influence to attempt to get the Thoranians to take a stand, to help those of our countrymen still in slavery here.

I could have set him straight. If that had been Isidore's motivation, I would never have left Thorania. It would have broken my heart to stay and watch her attach herself to him, of course. But it would have been worth it if there had been some hope of helping our brothers and sisters.

But there was never any hope of that. Not in her plans.

It seems today's arrival finally realized that, and so he returned. He isn't like most of us, just wanting to survive. He's as determined as Isidore herself, although with an entirely different purpose. He wants to revive the resistance. He thinks we can carry on what Alben started, even without any help from Thorania.

We're all unsettled since his arrival, but I wonder if he's right. I've been thinking, as we all have, that there's no point in liberating the rest when we can't cross back to Kyona. But that's because I didn't believe we could really survive out here. I never could have imagined that we would do as well as we have. Our first jungle baby will turn two in a few months, and more have come since. We're thinking of spreading to a second community, using another of the undiscovered hideouts as an additional base.

What if we started using the hideouts close to Nohl? Would it really be so impossible to launch rescues from there? Would it really be so pointless to try to liberate others, even if all they could do is join us here? This life is hard, but at least we're free.

I will talk with our new arrival more tomorrow. I think many in the community will be hard to convince, but I want to hear more of his thoughts.

It's strange, after all this time, to be reminded of Isidore. Not that I've ever forgotten her, of course. But the heartbreak I felt when I first arrived here feels like a distant memory. I wish I could have seen more clearly when we were together, but I was too blinded by everything she was to me. It's only after we parted that I've come to accept what I think I knew all along.

From what we've heard today, it seems she is satisfied, or as satisfied as she is capable of being. I wish I could be glad of it. But I can't be happy about the path she's taken, and I don't believe she's happy herself. Not truly.

I barely even felt a pang when I learned that she was married, as I suspected she would be by now. It's strange how the heart heals. I was so dazzled by Isidore, by her intelligence, her beauty, her noble blood. Tara is unlike Isidore in every way. She doesn't dazzle me, but I admire her character as I can no longer admire Isidore's.

Tara softens me. She works alongside me. She is sweet and gentle, and she has helped me heal. I smile to remember that we got to know each other when she came to me for teaching. She was the quickest in the group to learn to read and write. But in the end, she has taught me much more than I ever taught her.

She has been incredibly patient with me. I didn't realize I was waiting for it, but I think this news is the push I needed to see that the past no longer holds me captive.

I will ask Tara tomorrow. We won't be the first to do our own jungle version of a wedding ceremony, and I trust we won't be the last. I would never have believed it was possible when the ship sank from underneath me, but somehow here I am. Not only alive, but excited about the future. The future we'll build together.

. . .

LUCY PUT THE JOURNAL DOWN, her thoughts captured by this latest insight into Haydn's journey. She remembered how his grief and despair had touched her when she read his first entry, grieving over Isidore, and full of doubt for the future.

In only two years he had not only forged a life for himself in the jungle, but his heart had so overcome its grief that he was eager to start a future with someone new.

Lucy put her hand on the leather, trying to draw confidence from its pages. After months, she still felt mired in confusion and heartbreak. But if Haydn could overcome it, surely she could as well. Time must be the key. She didn't have to push her way through her emotions regarding Eamon. She just had to wait long enough for them to fade.

Somehow, the thought brought her little comfort.

CHAPTER TWENTY-FIVE

Lucy drew a deep breath, reveling in the freshness of the air as much as the incredible vista of ocean before her.

"You can really breathe out here," she said, flicking her braid over her shoulder.

"Yes," Rasad agreed with a chuckle. "The heaviness of the air in Nohl, and even in Thirl, does take some getting used to."

Lucy looked out over the water, crashing on the rocks far below the cliff. "It's beautiful, isn't it? I suppose we're looking due north, aren't we? Toward Valoria. I wish I'd spent more time by the sea, but my home is in Kyona's north, a long way from the coast."

"Well, as you see, in our kingdom, the north is the coast," said Rasad. "You are welcome to spend as much time here as you choose. You must try sea bathing while you're here as well. It's a sheer drop in this spot, but further along the coast there are some excellent swimming beaches."

Lucy didn't respond, instead leaning down to pat the neck of the horse she was riding. It was a spirited little mare Rasad had selected from his own stable.

"You want a gallop, don't you?" she said to the horse. "Am I heavy and uncomfortable with this big saddle?"

Rasad grinned. "She's used to the saddle as well as to bareback riding." He gave Lucy his most charming smile. "And I don't think any saddle could make you heavy."

Lucy smiled absently. She was starting to understand her mother's feelings. Compliments to her physical appearance were becoming less and less meaningful to her.

"Do you know how to wield a bow?" Rasad asked suddenly.

"Yes," said Lucy. "I've received basic training in archery. Why do you ask?"

Rasad's eyes sparkled. "Did you know that Thorania is famous in the South Lands for our archery? The Balenans think they're good archers, because it takes some skill to hunt in the jungle. But they're not good horsemen. They don't have the open space to let their poor mounts stretch their legs. In Thorania, we combine the two. It's a shame you weren't here a couple of months ago. Our annual horseback archery tournament is quite a sight to witness. People come from all over the South Lands to watch and to compete."

"Sounds fascinating," said Lucy. "And difficult! I've never tried to shoot a bow from a horse, let alone a moving one."

"It takes a great deal of practice," Rasad acknowledged. "And a certain amount of natural talent." He tilted his head. "I could probably teach you the basics."

"That's a kind offer," said Lucy slowly. It occurred to her that it would take a lifetime to teach her and show her all the things Rasad had offered. And the attention he had been giving her since her arrival at his home a week before was making her suspect that he was hoping he might have a lifetime to do it.

It had started with the gift of a garment like the one she'd worn to the gala, "because that one had suited her so well", and continued from there. Lucy hadn't wanted to accept any of it. But it was somehow much more difficult to say no while she was a guest in his home. There was an unspoken but undeniable increase in his authority, and it was becoming clear to Lucy that Cody had not erred when he said Rasad was used to power.

For example, it hadn't been her intention to spend time alone with the Thoranian, without her brother and Cody. And yet somehow—she wasn't entirely sure how it had happened—she was spending the morning riding with him, while they were back at the Bastion.

The trouble was, if she could ignore the feeling of discomfort in her stomach, it was all extremely pleasant. The gifts were tasteful, the attention was flattering, and the lifestyle was appealing. Rasad lived in luxury, there was no doubt about it. And he encouraged her every interest. If she did stay here, embrace this life, she would never have to choose between honing her fighting skills and making a favorable impression at court.

She would have the means and the leisure to become skilled in any area where she had aptitude. She had already spent hours since arriving at Rasad's Bastion training with a curved sword like the one Lady Yasmin had lent her. She was getting quite good with the weapon, and she knew she could get much better with more practice. She would be able to spend her days doing more or less whatever she liked. She could escape the heat by swimming in the ocean, she could learn to ride bareback, perhaps she could even learn to shoot a bow from a moving horse if she applied herself. She could travel the kingdom, see the mines where the precious jewels were found, see the spice fields in the south.

And she would be able to attend as many galas as she liked. She could spend time in the captivating city of Thirl whenever the mood took her. She would have plenty of resources for beautiful clothing, and she would have a position of respect within the court without even trying. In so many ways, her life would be indescribably easy.

Of course, there was the issue of whether she could trust Rasad. But if trust could be shattered even by people she'd known and relied on all her life, could it ever be certain?

Lucy shook her head slightly, unnerved that such thoughts were even entering it. She looked up at the sky. "Should we head back? I suppose it will be time for the midday meal soon. And I'm sure you're expected."

"Yes, of course," said Rasad lightly, turning his horse toward home. "My steward is expecting me this afternoon."

Lucy nodded, keeping her thoughts to herself. Another thing that wasn't lost on her was that there had been little sign of the apparently urgent business that had called Rasad away from Thirl in such a hurry. He had been so focused on the entertainment of his guests, that she couldn't imagine he had spent any significant time on anything else.

The uneasy feeling in her stomach grew, making her ashamed of her glittering thoughts about the luxury of Rasad's life. She remembered how Rasad had appeared with his unexpected invitation while she had been sparring with Eamon, just after her bouts with Lady Yasmin.

Was it possible he fabricated the summons to pull her away from Thirl for no other reason than that he'd heard a report that she was speaking with the Thoranian noblewoman? Lady Yasmin had said that Rasad wouldn't want Lucy talking to her. And his instinct wasn't wrong—the noblewoman had wasted no time in sharing her suspicions about Rasad with Lucy. But it was surely a big gamble to take. If Lucy had declined the invitation, Rasad would have had to leave without her, giving Lady Yasmin open access in his absence.

Unless he was so sure of her already that he had never

doubted her answer. Lucy's face burned as she followed Rasad along the top of the cliff.

It was with relief that she saw Cody and Matheus waiting for them as soon as they entered the Bastion.

"Pleasant ride?" Cody asked, a hint of menace in his voice.

Lucy sighed. It hadn't been her idea to leave her guardian behind, but she couldn't exactly say so in front of Rasad.

"Very pleasant," she said. "Let's go together soon. It's an incredible view of the sea."

Cody's eyes searched her face, but he said no more. When they all reconvened for the meal, he made a point of sitting next to her. Lucy wanted to be exasperated by the protective gesture, but the truth was she felt grateful. Even with her doubts, Rasad's presence was as magnetic as it had always been, and she felt overwhelmed by the constancy of his attention.

"How did you spend your morning?" Rasad asked Cody and Matheus, as the food was served. A serving boy brought a steaming dish for Rasad's inspection. The advisor flicked his hand impatiently, and the boy scurried back out of the room, bearing the dish with him.

"Your steward gave us quite an extensive tour of the Bastion," said Cody, his face expressionless as he ripped a piece of some type of flat bread that had been placed on his plate. "I must say, you have an impressive armory for a private residence."

"Ah yes," Rasad chuckled. "My forebears were a little paranoid, I think."

"About what?" Cody pressed. "I thought that Thorania hadn't seen war in centuries."

Lucy shot him a look. It had been Lady Yasmin who had told them that.

"That's true," said Rasad comfortably. "King Abner's foreign policy is not new. He follows a long tradition from his predecessors."

"What policy is that?" Matheus asked curiously.

"Thorania prefers to isolate itself from the affairs of other kingdoms," Rasad said, his voice smooth.

The thought sparked Lucy's memory, bringing to mind the comment in Haydn's journal about Thorania's determination to remain isolated from the issue of Balenol's slave trade.

"We have not traditionally involved ourselves in any disputes or relations between our neighbors," Rasad was continuing. "Either here in the South Lands or further afield."

"You're talking about the conflict between Balenol and Kyona," said Cody flatly, his thoughts clearly going in a similar direction to Lucy's. "How Thorania never took a side on the slave issue."

Rasad regarded the Kyonan man steadily. If he felt any discomfort over discussing the topic with a former slave, he showed no hint of it. "Among other things, certainly. But the policy of isolation has had many applications." He returned his attention to his food. "Still, just because that's the way it has been, doesn't mean it must always continue that way. I have hopes that change is coming to Thorania."

"What kind of change?" Lucy asked slowly. "It's a little late for Thorania to get involved in the slavery debate, don't you think?"

Rasad chuckled. "As always, Luciana, you are absolutely right." He inclined his head toward Cody. "We can all be happy that issue is no longer a problem."

"It doesn't sound like it was ever much of a problem for Thorania," said Cody dryly.

There was an edge to Rasad's smile. Lucy thought it almost had a hint of satisfaction. He didn't respond directly to Cody's comment, steering the conversation into less personal territory.

The meal passed quickly. The visitors had learned before now that Rasad wasn't one to linger over his food. He was the first to rise, inclining his head to his guests before leaving the room.

"Don't let me rush you." As always, his eyes found Lucy. "My steward is waiting for me now, Luciana, but once my business is complete, there is something I would like to show you."

"Sounds fascinating," Cody cut in, before Lucy could answer. "We'd love to have a look."

Rasad met the other man's eyes for a pregnant moment, a faint hint of amusement on his face. But again he gave no direct response, simply bowing himself from the room. Cody frowned after him for several long seconds before turning to Lucy.

"What was he up to this morning? On your ride?"

Lucy gave Cody a chastising look, raising her eyebrows toward the servants who were industriously clearing their master's place. Only once they had all left the room did she reply.

"More of the same. What did his steward want with you two?"

"To keep us distracted," said Cody.

Matheus grimaced. "Might have been more effective if he'd chosen a more interesting activity. Most boring tour of all time."

"I don't know about that," said Cody grimly. "I learned a lot. More than he intended me to, I think."

"Like the armory?" Lucy prodded curiously.

Cody shook his head. "No that was intentional, I'm sure. He probably hoped to intimidate us."

"Did it work?" Lucy asked, dipping some of the flat bread into a spiced paste. The food was just as unfamiliar as what they'd eaten in Balenol, but she liked Thoranian fare better.

"Not really." Cody shot her a quick grin, but his expression instantly became serious. "I'm sure his comment about change coming to Thorania was no accident, either." He drummed his fingers on the table. "What did he mean by that?"

Lucy frowned. "It was strange, wasn't it? But I suppose it's no surprise that he wants to increase diplomatic relations between the kingdoms. This whole visit was his idea, after all. He convinced King Abner to contact the Kyonan crown and request that someone come here to look into the situation of Kyonan descendants living in Thorania."

"What?" Cody asked, startled. "How do you know it was his idea?"

"He told me," said Lucy. She frowned at the look on Cody's face. "What is it?"

"I don't like this." Cody sounded more uneasy than she had ever heard him, and it made Lucy's own heartbeat pick up. "I didn't realize he'd orchestrated the whole thing." His tone turned dark. "Although perhaps I should have guessed it. He seems to pull most of the strings around here."

Lucy glanced at the door before replying, making sure it was still closed and they were still alone. "That sounds like Lady Yasmin talking."

"When Lady Yasmin talks," Cody retorted, "I know what she's trying to say, because she says it straight out." He frowned at the door. "That's more than I can say for our host." He returned his gaze to Lucy. "Don't be fooled by his smooth words, Lucy. Whatever his reasons for drawing the royals out here, he wasn't thinking of the good of Kyona."

"No," Lucy agreed slowly. "I suppose he was thinking of Thorania. But—"

"Do you remember what Lady Yasmin said in your suite?" Cody cut her off. "About how her family is dedicated to Thorania's interests, but not at the cost of everything else?"

Lucy nodded slowly.

"She meant it," Cody continued. "She told me that her family spoke out about the slaves. They wanted the crown to intervene."

Lucy exchanged a glance with Matheus. "Are you sure she wasn't just telling you what you want to hear, Cody? She knows your history, after all."

Cody flicked off her words with an impatient hand. "I know who I can trust, Lucy. And so do you, if you would stop doubting your instincts. Lady Yasmin was only a child at the time, but her father was well known for pushing for Thorania to become involved. His father had been the same. Like many Thoranians, they have Kyonan blood mixed into their ancestry."

"Lady Yasmin does?" Lucy asked, surprised.

Cody nodded. "And Balenan, apparently. I know back home it feels like your family is completely unique. But if your mother was able to overcome the prejudice and see us Kyonans as humans, of course there were other Balenans like her. Your parents are hardly the first Balenan and Kyonan to fall in love with each other."

Lucy stared at him in astonishment. "You saw other couples like my parents when you lived in Balenol?"

Cody shook his head, helping himself to more of the flat bread. "No. But from what Lady Yasmin says, it did happen occasionally. Of course, there was no future in Balenol for such couples, not with the slave trade happening. And they couldn't cross the sea to Kyona because of the curse. So either they were caught and the Kyonan was executed—like your grandfather tried to execute your father when he found out your mother was in love with him—or they fled to Thorania, and settled here. Lady Yasmin's mother has one such couple in her ancestry, apparently. That's part of why her father was always in favor of intervening more on the Kyonans' behalf."

Cody looked up from his food, seeing the surprise on both Lucy's and Matheus's faces. He shrugged. "So it's not like Thorania has ever been unaware of the plight of the slaves. The crown may have chosen isolation, but the issue was the subject of real debate in Thirl for generations."

"I'm glad to hear that someone cared," said Lucy. "But what does this have to do with Rasad?"

"It was one of the reasons for the tension between their families," Cody said. "Rasad's family were always outspoken on the other side. They didn't want to help the Kyonans, and they didn't want to help the Balenans. They wanted to stay neutral. And they got their way."

"But..." Lucy rubbed her forehead, trying to make sense of it all. "Rasad just said that he doesn't want to remain neutral. He wants Thorania to change, and get more involved."

"He didn't say what he wants," Cody corrected grimly. "All we know is he has plans of his own for Thorania's future. And I doubt they're plans designed to help anyone outside Thorania. His family's influence has been built on arguing for the opposite."

Lucy remained silent, thinking it over.

"And don't forget what Lady Yasmin said about convenient coincidences," Cody added. "I think we would be smart to be suspicious of every circumstance, until we know for sure what Rasad is planning."

Still Lucy didn't answer. She had also thought often of Lady Yasmin's words, not least her comment about the military muster coinciding with the royal visit from the North Lands. She had been surprised, and a little discomfited, when they left Thirl to see that there was another military encampment on the northern side of the city. If anything, it was larger than the one she had seen upon their arrival.

A servant entered and began to clear empty plates, which they all took as a prompt to leave. Lucy had intended to wander toward the impressive training yard Rasad had shown her, to practice her archery. But she was pulled from her abstraction by the realization that Cody was slipping down a corridor in the opposite direction from his room. It was his casual movements that caught her attention—she knew all Cody's tricks for being inconspicuous.

"Where are you going, Cody?" she hissed, detaining the older man with a hand on his arm. "What are you up to?"

"I'm just stretching my legs," said Cody unconvincingly. Seeing her expression, he dropped his voice, his tone becoming more serious. "If Rasad has plans, there must be evidence of them somewhere."

"Cody..." Lucy started, anxiety curling in her stomach.

"I'll be fine, Lucy," said the older man impatiently. "I'm just going to have a look around."

Lucy opened her mouth to protest, but a passing servant was shooting them a curious look, and she let go of Cody's arm. He slipped away without another word.

"He knows what he's doing, Lucy," said Matheus reassuringly, his voice low. "He's good at getting out of trouble."

"I'd rather he didn't get into trouble in the first place," Lucy muttered. But before she could say anything more, Rasad strode into view.

"There you are, Luciana, Matheus." He smiled at them. "Do you have time to see my treasure now?" He glanced around, pressing on before they could respond. "But where is your companion?"

"Oh, he, uh..." Lucy could have cursed her stumbling tongue. "I think he went for a walk."

Rasad waited, but when neither sibling added to the explanation, his smile took on a hint of amusement. "Such a shame. I thought he was eager to join us. Ah well, perhaps another time."

"Yes," Lucy managed. She didn't dare meet Matheus's eye, and before she knew it, the two of them were being shepherded by Rasad down a corridor she hadn't visited before.

CHAPTER TWENTY-SIX

At first Lucy was too distracted by what would happen if Cody was caught snooping to pay attention to her surroundings. But as they went deeper into the building, it gradually dawned on her that Rasad was taking them to his private wing. She wished Cody was there, but it was a great relief to at least have Matheus with her.

Rasad led them into what was clearly his own suite. The receiving room was large and richly furnished, but not overly luxurious. Lucy looked around surreptitiously, noting the subtle signs of wealth, but also the lack of pretentious display. Rasad led them across the room. At first she thought he intended to take them through a door set at the far end of the space, but he stopped before reaching it.

"And here," Rasad said, opening a beautifully carved writing desk placed near the closed door, "is the treasure I wanted to show you."

He pulled out a leather journal, and Lucy gave a small start of surprise. For a moment she thought he had been into her own room and found Haydn's book. But as she drew closer, she realized that the journal, although similar, was not identical.

"Do you remember, Luciana, that I told you that I have Kyonan blood in my ancestry?"

She nodded, noting Matheus's raised eyebrow. She had obviously forgotten to mention that detail to her brother.

"It's far enough back that in the normal course of events I probably wouldn't even know about it. My family hasn't recorded our lineage as meticulously as noble families tend to do." He flicked through the journal. "But my Kyonan forebear kept a journal, and it has been preserved in the muniment room here. It was during her time that the Bastion was built, actually."

"Her?" Lucy repeated.

"Yes, my Kyonan ancestor was a woman," Rasad confirmed. "She escaped slavery in Balenol, and made her way to Thorania. She wasn't the only one. But she was more successful than many back then at carving out her place in our kingdom. Our family didn't yet own this land, but they were wealthy, and well respected. In marrying my forefather, she gained not only a comfortable life, but the opportunity to have influence in the future of Thorania. Would you like to take a look?"

"Of course," said Lucy mechanically.

She thought Rasad would hand her the journal, but instead he laid it back on the desk, holding it open and inviting her to approach with a gesture. There was a slight ringing in her ears as she complied. It was too unlikely a coincidence to be true, surely. She leaned over the page, her eyes scanning the short entry quickly.

*I*T HAS BEEN *three months since the wedding, and everything is all I hoped it would be. After the indignity of the slave barracks, and the hardships of life in the jungle with the rebels, my new home in Thirl feels like luxury. My husband has showered me with gifts, but they are not the true prize. Already we have been to court, and met with* *the king himself. Perhaps my noble blood has helped to open doors there.*

My husband is as supportive of my desires as I knew he would be. I have no doubt that together we will achieve a great deal. It is only the beginning.

Already, my time with the rebels feels like a dream. My imprisonment I will never forget, and I would not want to. It is the fuel that will keep me moving forward. But it's strange to remember when I first escaped, how eager I was to return to Kyona. It was all we thought of or planned for.

I laugh at that former version of myself. I would not return now even if I could. Kyona will never be my home again. My future is in Thorania.

Isidore

LUCY DIDN'T NEED the signature at the end to know that her suspicions were correct. She could hardly believe Haydn's lost love was Rasad's ancestor. What strange chance had brought her to Haydn's journal, undiscovered in the rebel base for decades, then here to Rasad's Bastion, where its counterpart could be found?

A memory flitted through her mind, something Jocelyn had said about Elddreki, her dragon friend. He had said that chance is just what humans call any purpose they don't understand. Well, Lucy certainly didn't understand what purpose was at work here.

"Amazing, isn't it?" Rasad asked, running a hand over the page. "To read the thoughts of those long gone." He looked up into Lucy's eyes. "So you see, Luciana. There is a long history of Kyonans falling in love with this land, of choosing to call Thorania home."

Lucy flushed at the implication, and Matheus cleared his

throat uncomfortably. She cast around for something to say, eager to turn the conversation from herself.

"The entry mentions noble blood," she said, glancing down at the page again. "I thought you said there was no nobility in your ancestry."

"Oh, well." Rasad gave a small chuckle. "Kyonan nobility. I wasn't counting that."

Lucy and Matheus exchanged a look, but neither commented. "Well, thank you for showing me," said Lucy after a moment. "It is very interesting, as you said."

Gesturing to Matheus with her head, she turned toward the door, but paused as a thought occurred to her.

"What is it, Luciana?" Rasad prompted, as she hesitated.

"I was just wondering...you said that when this Isidore married your ancestor, the family didn't yet own this land. But you also said that the Bastion was built during her life. Were she and her husband the ones who bought the land from Lady Yasmin and Lord Yosef's family?"

Rasad raised an eyebrow. "You have a good memory, my dear, and a sharp mind. You are correct."

Lucy nodded. "Well, thank you again for showing us the journal," she said, shepherding Matheus out of the room. To her relief, Rasad showed no sign of joining them, and within minutes the brother and sister were back in their own wing. Lucy ducked into her suite to quickly change out of her gown into training clothes, then the two of them made their way to the training yard.

"Why did you ask about Lady Yasmin and Lord Yosef's family?" Matheus asked as soon as they were properly alone. "I thought we didn't really want him to know we've taken an interest in them."

"I doubt I told him anything he doesn't know. I don't think

Rasad misses much," said Lucy with a frown. "I think he has a pretty good idea of where Cody stands, for example."

"What do you mean where Cody stands?" Matheus asked blankly.

Lucy just rolled her eyes as she selected a bow from the several available for general practice. "Speaking of Cody," she said. "Where do you think he's gotten to?"

"No idea," said Matheus, squinting at a target set up twenty yards away. "We didn't find him in Rasad's private suite, so I guess he's not snooping in there."

"Shh," Lucy hissed, glancing around to make sure no one had overheard the flippant remark.

Her brother clearly had unshakable faith in their mentor. But she was genuinely afraid that Cody's determination to find information for Lady Yasmin might lead him to push too hard on the wrong doors. And none of them knew how Rasad would respond.

As one hour turned into two, with still no sign of Cody, Lucy's fears grew. The older Kyonan had been trying—with limited success—to stick close to her since their arrival at Rasad's Bastion. She suspected that he had slipped away to do whatever he was doing because he thought Rasad would be tied up with his steward all afternoon. She had certainly been surprised at how quickly the Thoranian had finished his business. Whatever the reason, it was very unusual for Cody to be absent for so long.

After three hours, even Matheus started to be anxious.

They had long since lost interest in archery practice, and had retired to Lucy's suite. Thinking of the journal Rasad had shown them, Lucy found herself once again digging out Haydn's records.

"What's that?" Matheus asked. "You didn't swipe Rasad's journal, did you? You're even worse than Cody!"

"Of course not," said Lucy impatiently. She ran a hand over the cover. "It does look very similar, doesn't it? I think they were a pair."

"What do you mean?"

Lucy explained how she had come to have the journal, giving a brief summary of what she had so far read in its pages.

"You really think Rasad's ancestor is the woman this Haydn wrote about?" Matheus asked, astonishment clear in his voice.

"I'm sure of it," said Lucy. "Isidore's not exactly a common name, is it? And everything he said fits what I already knew perfectly. Did you notice that Rasad was pretty careful about which page of the journal he showed us?"

"Yes," said Matheus immediately. "It made me wonder what else was in there."

"It made me wonder the same thing," said Lucy. "And it occurs to me that we might be able to find out more without having to swipe Isidore's journal." She flicked the pages of the tome in front of her suggestively.

"Good idea!"

Lucy sank onto a settle, smiling over her brother's eagerness to investigate. Matheus joined her, and the two of them bent their heads together as Lucy flipped through the pages looking for any reference to Isidore.

She looked ahead from where she had last read, but Haydn was fully focused on Tara, and their life together once they were married. Lucy skipped over several pages describing the community's expansion to a second base. Haydn discussed their triumphs, their scares on the rare occasions when Balenan soldiers ventured deep enough into the jungle to threaten their exposure, the reluctance of most of the community to restart the resistance. Haydn didn't write often, it seemed. Only a few entries after the arrival of the newcomer from Thorania, he mentioned the birth of his first child, then a second followed.

Lucy sighed, sitting back. It seemed Haydn had moved beyond his past, and while that was surely a happy thing for him, it didn't help her to find out about Isidore.

Matheus leaned forward, turning the pages back to the start, clearly interested in the entries Lucy had already seen.

"Wow," he said. "He got a monkey right through the eye when he was learning to hunt." The fifteen-year-old got a faraway look in his eye. "Maybe I should be giving more time to archery and less time to swords."

"That doesn't help us," said Lucy impatiently.

"Hang on," Matheus said quickly. "He talks about Isidore here, look."

Lucy leaned forward again eagerly. Matheus had stopped at one of the entries that she had previously skimmed over, not interested in reading about jungle life. The name of Rasad's ancestor obviously hadn't caught her eye before, but now it jumped out, inserted between a story of a run in with a poisonous toad, and a description of which insects could be used for food.

I couldn't sleep last night. I was thinking about Isidore, even though I realize no good will come of brooding. I wish she was here. Her determination and intelligence would be a huge help to us. But she wouldn't want to help us, I suppose.

I still can't understand why she seemed to feel the failure of the resistance was a personal betrayal. It's not as though Alben, or any of us, knew what would happen. Doesn't she realize we would never have gotten on those ships if we'd known they would all sink? Alben paid with his life for the mistake, as well as so many others. I thought we were fortunate to survive, but I suppose she couldn't see it as good fortune.

And it was hard, agonizingly hard, to be so close to returning home, only to have it ripped away. I know she has so much more to return to in Kyona than most of us. I can understand the bitterness. But still, it was more heartbreaking than all the rest to watch the bitterness spread like poison through her. It's hard to write it, but...in the end, I think she even resented me.

Perhaps I never meant as much to her as she did to me. But how could I not be captivated by her? Her beauty, her sharp mind, her endless determination...it's no wonder her Thoranian admirer was drawn to her so quickly. But I wonder, sometimes, when I'm lying awake in the night...is he fool enough to believe she loves him? I think it would almost be easier to bear if I could believe she does. But I know that all she saw in him was opportunity. Opportunity to return to the life of ease she would have reclaimed if we'd made it back to Kyona.

But it must have been more than just the luxury of his wealth. She's too ambitious, too determined, to be satisfied with just comfort. I saw the way she watched him, the time she spent observing what she could of the court while we were trying to find a living in Thirl. I'm sure she saw in him a chance for influence.

I wish I understood what she wanted to do with that influence, but by that time, I could no longer read her. All I knew was that she had no interest in helping our fellow Kyonans, for reasons I still don't understand. We were well past the point where she would willingly tell me her thoughts.

She probably thought that I left because I was jealous of him. I was, of course, but that wasn't what drove me back to Balenol. I couldn't bear to watch the bitterness consume her. I didn't want to see what would happen if she let it continue to drive her. I wonder about her—I always will. But if I'm honest, I still don't want to know. I'd rather think of her as she once was.

"That's...ominous," said Matheus, after a long moment of silence.

"Certainly paints a different picture from the entry Rasad showed us, doesn't it?" Lucy agreed grimly.

"But...that was generations ago," said Matheus. "Whatever she was planning surely can't have anything to do with Rasad's plans."

"Yes," Lucy agreed slowly. "It is hard to believe that Rasad could still be carrying her same ambitions. I mean, we don't even know the names of any of our ancestors that far back, let alone feel any loyalty to their plans."

"Well," Matheus corrected dryly, "we know some of them were probably called Wrendal."

Lucy grimaced. "I'm not interested in any of their plans, though."

"Definitely not," Matheus agreed emphatically.

Lucy ran a hand down her face. Haydn's reflections hadn't given her much of use, but they had made her more uneasy than ever.

"I'm done waiting around for Cody," she said, tucking the journal into a pocket. "I think we should look for him."

"I agree," said Matheus, anxiety obvious in his voice.

As if in response to their decision, there was a knock at the door. Lucy ran eagerly to answer it, ready to upbraid Cody for making them worry with his prolonged absence. Her heart sank when she was greeted not by his familiar face, but by a young serving girl who had crossed Lucy's path a number of times since her arrival at Rasad's Bastion.

As the girl bobbed a quick curtsy, Lucy tried and failed to recall her name. The only reason she remembered the girl at all was that she had a thin scar running along her jawline. It wasn't particularly obvious, but Lucy had found plenty of opportunity to notice it when the girl was hovering nearby, ready to meet Lucy's needs.

In fact, now Lucy thought about it, she had been nearby a

lot. Perhaps it was less her physical appearance, and more her manner, that had made her stick in Lucy's mind. She hadn't put it into words before now, but the girl always gave Lucy the uncomfortable feeling of being watched. As though she was observing Lucy more closely that was really necessary. The thought crossed Lucy's mind that Rasad might have tasked this girl with spying on the visitors, and she made an extra effort to hide her anxiety over Cody as she addressed the serving girl.

"Do you have a message for me?"

"Yes, miss," said the girl. "The master asks if you would come to his study. You and your brother." Her eyes flicked to Matheus standing inside the suite, and it struck Lucy again that the sharpness of the girl's gaze didn't quite match her meek servant's posture.

Lucy exchanged a look with Matheus. The same apprehension she felt was clear in his eyes.

"Of course," she said to the servant, lifting her chin slightly. "We will come now."

The girl bobbed another curtsy before leading them out of their wing and into the main part of the Bastion. Rasad was waiting for them in his study. The girl ushered them in before melting away again.

"Luciana, Matheus." Rasad gestured them into seats before steepling his fingers. His expression was grave, and Lucy's apprehension increased. "Thank you for coming."

"You wanted to speak with us?" Lucy prompted, when the Thoranian didn't continue.

"Yes," said Rasad heavily. "I'm afraid I have nothing pleasant to say. I regret to tell you that there has been an...unfortunate altercation."

Lucy sat up straighter in her chair. She could feel Matheus's eyes on her, but she kept her gaze fixed on their host, trying to read his expression. "What does that mean?"

Rasad sighed, running a hand slowly down his jaw. "Your companion had a run in of sorts with some of my guards a short time ago."

"What's happened to Cody?" Matheus demanded, surprising Lucy with the ferocity of his tone.

Rasad looked faintly surprised. "Nothing's happened to him, Matheus. But it seems he was a little over eager to continue the tour from this morning. Some of my guards came across him in a part of the building where he shouldn't have been. All a misunderstanding, I'm sure, but as I said, the incident most regrettably led to a confrontation."

"So you've...what?" Lucy tried to keep her voice steady as dread pooled in her stomach. "Locked him up somewhere for wandering down the wrong corridor?"

"What?" Rasad sounded astonished. "Of course I haven't done anything of the kind. I wasn't even present. But it seems that he took offense at the conduct of my guards." He lowered his head. "It is possible they were too rough, misunderstanding his intentions perhaps. Whatever the cause, it seems that Cody didn't take kindly to being questioned. He has left."

CHAPTER TWENTY-SEVEN

"Left?" Lucy and Matheus repeated in unison.

"I'm afraid so."

The two Kyonans exchanged a look. "He can't have left," said Lucy firmly. "You must be mistaken."

"I'm not," said Rasad. His voice turned dry. "The missing horse from my stables confirms it." He sighed. "But I won't hold that against him. He was clearly extremely agitated."

"Rasad, this is nonsense." Lucy was on her feet, although she didn't remember standing up. "There's no way Cody would ever leave without speaking to us. If it comes to that, there's no way he would leave without taking us with him! Where is he?"

Rasad met her protest with a look of confusion that Lucy was sure Matheus found as unconvincing as she did.

"Well, you know him better than I do, Luciana. My guards seemed to be under the impression that he was riding for Thirl, that someone was waiting for him there."

Lucy opened her mouth, then shut it again. Rasad's mention of someone waiting for Cody made her pause. She definitely had the impression that Cody had spoken with Lady Yasmin without her, perhaps more than once. She could imagine him promising to tell the noblewoman if he found anything of interest. But he would never do so if it meant leaving his companions behind.

"Perhaps my guards misunderstood," Rasad was continuing. "Perhaps he just went for a ride to clear his head. I will send someone after him."

"No need, I'll go," said Lucy flatly, but Rasad had already nodded to a servant standing in the corner. The man ignored Lucy's protest, slipping out the door.

"It's no trouble," said Rasad soothingly. "I believe it isn't long since he left. I'll send someone in the direction of Thirl. If he's gone that way, they'll catch up to him. If I'm mistaken, and he's just out for a ride, he'll probably beat them back."

Lucy sat back down, trying to keep an impassive face as her thoughts swirled frantically. Something was clearly terribly wrong—she didn't know what was going on, but she did know with absolute certainty that Cody wouldn't take off on a horse in any direction without communicating with her and Matheus.

She took a deep breath, trying to hide her panic as she looked up at Rasad. There was no telling how much their host knew, and she didn't want to give him anything to work with.

"I don't know what to say," she said carefully. "I'm sure wherever Cody was wandering, he didn't mean any harm. I can't deny that I'm upset your guards overreacted."

"It's understandable that you're upset," said Rasad smoothly. "I'm very sorry this has happened, and I have already reprimanded the guards involved. Let's hope you're right, and Cody will return soon."

"Yes," Lucy agreed colorlessly. "In the meantime, I'd like to be alone."

"Of course." Rasad's manner was the perfect blend of politeness and regret as he dismissed them.

"Lucy!" said Matheus the moment they left Rasad's study.

"I know," Lucy muttered, her eyes on the serving girl who seemed to have been hovering nearby the whole time they were inside the room. "Wait until we're in my suite."

Matheus seemed barely able to contain his panic until Lucy's door was closed behind them, and the moment they were alone, he burst into speech.

"That was a pack of lies, Lucy, what are we going to do?"

"I don't know," said Lucy, her thoughts and her heart racing. "But I think we can safely assume that Cody is in trouble."

Matheus's face was whiter than Lucy had ever seen it. "Rasad wouldn't...hurt Cody, would he?"

Lucy knew what her brother was really asking, and she wished she had reassurance to give him. "I don't know," she said. "I don't know what he would do. But it's clear that Cody pushed too hard on the wrong door, like I was afraid he would."

"So do you think Rasad knows we're suspicious of him?" Matheus asked.

"I think he always knew that," said Lucy. "The question is what else he knows."

"Do you think there's any chance that Cody really did just go riding?" Lucy's heart wrenched at the hope in her little brother's voice.

"Maybe," she said. "Of course Rasad was hiding something from us, but the most convincing lies have a little truth in them. I don't think he mentioned about the missing horse for no reason. But if Cody really has left, it can't have been willingly."

"Maybe the missing horse was a message," said Matheus, painfully eager. "Maybe he wants us to sneak away, to follow him. Maybe that's why he let slip to the guards that he was heading for Thirl."

Lucy shook her head. "That doesn't sound like Cody. He's not one to speak in code. He would find us, and tell us what he wanted us to do."

"Not if he couldn't get away from the guards any other way!" argued Matheus, clearly taken with his theory. "Maybe he thought he could leave us clues."

"Or maybe Rasad made all of it up," said Lucy dryly. "Matheus, we don't know anything for sure." She frowned. "What we really need is more information." Her eyes fell on her brother, and she reached a sudden decision. "Give me some time to think, Matheus," she said. "I'll try to come up with a plan. If Cody isn't back by nightfall, we'll sneak out and steal some horses to follow him, like you said. For now we should play along with Rasad's story. Lie low in your suite, pretend you're upset about what's happened."

"I *am* upset about what's happened."

"You know what I mean," said Lucy impatiently.

Matheus frowned suspiciously. "And what will you be doing?"

"The same," said Lucy, not quite meeting his eye. "There's nothing more we can achieve by talking about it."

The younger boy hesitated for a moment, his eyes narrowed. Then he turned without another word, heading for the door.

Lucy waited only until she heard his door close across the corridor before slipping out herself. She didn't like to deceive Matheus, but there was no way she was letting him come with her. Cody's situation—whatever it was—was all the proof she needed that there was something to be found at the Bastion, something that Rasad didn't want his guests to discover. And she needed to know what it was before she figured out what to do about Cody.

Maybe everything Rasad had ever said to her had been nothing more than a strategy. But if there was a chance, any chance, that his admiration for her was real, it might protect her if Rasad caught her doing what she intended to do. It wouldn't protect Matheus, though. And with Cody missing, the last thing she wanted to do was lead her brother into danger.

Her heart raced erratically, but her steps didn't falter as she made her way through the same corridors Rasad had led them down earlier that afternoon. She passed a few servants, but no one paid her any particular attention. Perhaps news of the incident with Cody hadn't yet spread. To her relief, the building became more deserted as she neared Rasad's private wing. Maybe even his own servants were forbidden from coming here without specific instruction.

Lucy pushed the thought aside. The question of whether Rasad could be trusted was no longer abstract. Cody's life might depend on her finding out what the Thoranian was up to.

She had to hide behind a suit of armor to avoid a passing serving boy, but she managed to slip inside Rasad's suite without detection. After satisfying herself that she was alone, she hurried over to the writing desk where Rasad had placed Isidore's journal. It seemed like a good place to start.

At first she was surprised that the desk wasn't locked, but a quick search revealed that it contained nothing of interest beside the slim leather volume. If Rasad had written plans of a private nature, they were stored elsewhere.

She flicked through the pages of the journal rapidly, not sure how much time she had. Isidore barely mentioned Haydn, the early entries focusing mainly on her rapid courtship and marriage. Lucy felt slightly offended on the rebel's behalf, remembering how much Isidore had featured in Haydn's thoughts and writing.

Lucy skimmed over descriptions of Isidore's triumphs at court, not caring what methods the former slave had used to increase her influence in Thorania. She wanted to know why she had sought that influence with such determination, and whether her plans or opinions could provide any insight into those of her descendant. Certain passages jumped out at her across the pages, giving her no great liking for the long-dead Kyonan.

I'M PLEASED *to find the crown prince's opinions so poorly formed. He will make a very useful king one day—easy to encourage in whatever direction his advisors want. And I fully intend for my husband to be one of those advisors.*

...

We have identified the perfect plot for establishing ourselves, away up in the north where the air is clearer. I do not want to settle always in Thirl—I miss the ocean. The land is currently part of a noble estate, but I don't anticipate a problem. The current lord is a weak-minded man, and rumors say that he has too great a fondness for games of chance. With some patient encouragement in the right direc-tion, it shouldn't be difficult to help him reach a situation where he will be only too glad to sell some of his land for the kind of price we can pay.

...

The crown's preference for staying out of the affairs of other king-doms suits my purposes perfectly. There are those in the court who would have Thorania challenge Balenol for its continued exploitation of Kyonans. Not surprisingly, they thought at first that I would be an ally.

Fools.

What interest do I have in stopping the slave trade? Slavery was an indignity I was forced to suffer, but it is not who I am. I am the daughter of a Kyonan nobleman. The failure of the pathetic resistance has showed that I cannot return to my old home, but I can reach a position approaching what I deserve here in Thorania.

I have no desire to see this kingdom involve itself. I do not want to see Thorania come to the aid of either Kyona or Balenol. Does Balenol deserve support? They are barbarians and snakes. And is Kyona any better? They say that the Kyonan prince has stopped the trade, but where was the armada coming to rescue those of us stuck in Nohl? No one ever came.

Kyona has betrayed me as much as Balenol has, and I want nothing more than to see both kingdoms pay for what they have done. And as for those still in slavery...if they have been too stupid or too weak to free themselves, they deserve no help from Thorania either.

LUCY COULD FEEL her expression growing sour as she read. It was hard to believe someone as open-hearted as Haydn could ever have believed himself in love with this woman. Even as the thought occurred to her, the familiar name made one of its rare appearances, near the back of the book.

I WISH Haydn could see me now. Would he be impressed by all I have achieved, or would he still lecture me on the dangers of bitterness? All his talk about forgiving Kyona for failing to come for us still makes my blood boil. He was smart, and strong, so how could he be so blind in some ways? I think if given half the chance, he would even have argued that we should forgive Balenol.

And where did that get him?

I am weak enough to hope that he survived. But what kind of a life would it be, hiding in the jungle? He should have stayed. He could have had a part in our success here.

But he probably wouldn't even want that. He made his choices, and I made mine.

LUCY SHUT the journal with a snap. She had read more than enough. She replaced the book exactly where she'd found it, closing the desk as silently as possible. She certainly had a more accurate picture of Rasad's ancestor than he had given her with the selected entry. But she didn't see how it helped her figure out what Rasad might be up to now, or where Cody was.

She cast her eyes around the room. There were several doors leading off Rasad's receiving room, most of them standing open. Some doorways didn't even have doors, just colorful swaths of gauzy fabric hung over the opening. Lucy could see just such a doorway on the other side of the space, a glimpse of Rasad's bed visible beyond it. She turned her gaze away quickly, uncomfortable at the reminder of where she was.

Her attention was drawn to the door next to the writing desk. It was closed—in fact, it seemed to be the only door that was, except for the one leading back to the main corridor. Lucy tried the handle tentatively, and found that it was locked.

Her nerves and excitement mounted in equal measure. She examined the lock, then returned to the writing desk, searching through drawers for a suitable implement. She selected a carved letter opener, casting an anxious glance around the still-empty room before setting to work.

The absent Cody would be proud, she reflected, to know that his effort in teaching her to pick a lock hadn't been wasted. Of course, he'd probably also be annoyed that she was taking this risk, but he wouldn't exactly be one to talk.

After several minutes of focus, the lock gave way with a satisfying click. Lucy swung the door open, hesitating only a moment before slipping inside and closing it behind her.

CHAPTER TWENTY-EIGHT

She found herself in a small, airless room. The walls were polished stone, like the rest of Rasad's Bastion, and there was nothing to make the space remarkable except for the locked door.

There were no decorations in the room, and no windows. The only light came from a torch burning in a wall bracket. If Lucy didn't know that she was on the ground level, she would have thought she was on the way to a dungeon. There was even a small draft of cold air coming from the opposite direction from Rasad's suite.

Following it, she found a narrow opening on the far side of the room. The corridor beyond was only obvious once she reached the doorway, and she noticed that it sloped down after all.

Her heart pounded faster in hope. She had seen a dungeon in her initial tour of the place, but was it possible there was a second, secret one attached to Rasad's chambers? Would she find Cody imprisoned down there?

She hurried down the pathway, in and out of the small pools of light cast by the torches on the wall. She had become so convinced of her theory that her disappointment was sharp when she emerged into another room. There was nothing dungeon-like about the space, except for the lack of windows. In fact, if there had been some natural light, it would have been a very pleasant study.

It was certainly large for the purpose, but there was no doubt that it was Rasad's study. There was a desk in one corner, with a simple wooden chair behind it, and papers stacked neatly on the surface. There were also long benches around the walls, many of them littered with parchments as well. Lucy pushed her disappointment away. Whatever Rasad did here, it was clearly something he didn't want known, so she must be on the right track.

Glancing around, she noted that not all of the benches had papers on them. Some had other objects. Strange powders in brass scales sat next to potions in glass vials, and a small bowl of some kind of animal scales rested on a narrow bookshelf. A peculiar mixture of smells caught her attention as she approached the bookshelf. They were as unfamiliar—and as pungent—as the exotic scents of Thirl's markets, but nothing at all like those spices. When Lucy drew alongside the assortment of powders, the smell almost seemed to burn her nose.

She noticed that there was a squat cabinet next to the bookshelf, its doors closed but not locked. She pulled one carefully open, peering inside. A gasp burst from her at the sparkling light that suddenly leaped out into the room.

She was mesmerized by them, but she didn't dare to touch the crystals. There was a small row of the objects, half a dozen, on a shelf inside the cabinet. In shape they were uneven, jagged, although their sides were perfectly smooth. In spite of the golden hue of the light that danced out from their angles, the crystals themselves had a faint purplish color.

What were they? Lucy had never seen such objects before,

but she knew without needing to be told that they were special. Perhaps even—she hesitated to think the word—magical.

It wouldn't be the first time she'd heard of a magic object. All her life, her father had worn around his neck a rock from the Dragon Realm. It contained a powerful magic and gave him unnatural strength and energy, in the right circumstances. It had once had a counterpart, but she knew that had been destroyed long ago, and she had never heard mention of any other such talismans. Besides, her father hadn't said anything about seeing crystals when he entered the Dragon Realm in his youth.

She drew her eyes from the crystals, looking for clues elsewhere in the study. Scrunching up her nose, she approached one of the scales filled with the mystery powder. There was something metallic about the smell. Again she resisted the urge to touch it.

Instead she picked up a piece of loose parchment on the bench beside it. She frowned as she tried to decipher the writing. The hand was firm and neat, but the contents were unintelligible to her. Equations and calculations were scribbled across the page, with the occasional phrase like, "explosive ratio", and "finer powder". She puzzled over the words, "scales from jaw" for a moment, but could make no sense of it.

She hurried back over to the desk, acutely conscious of how long she had already been in Rasad's suite. A quick flip through the piles of parchment suggested that they would be much the same as the one from the bench. A large bound volume drew her eye, covered by a neat stack of papers.

She pulled it out, handling it carefully. It was clearly ancient, the leather binding cracking with age. The gilded letters on the front cover were barely visible: "Dragon Lore".

Lucy felt her eyebrows go up. Rasad had been studying dragon lore? Where had he found this tome? As far as Lucy was aware, no such volume existed anywhere in Kyona, and no other kingdom had as much history with the creatures. She opened the cover tentatively, afraid the book would fall apart when touched. To her relief, the words on the first page were still readable.

THE DRAGON, *the mightiest beast of legend: is it myth, or history? There is no definite answer. But it is worth noting that while dragons are believed by most to be nothing more than legend, still the legends persist, generation upon generation.*

Do they have a basis in truth? Perhaps we will never know.

I have attempted to here collect all the information I have come across in my search that seemed to me credible. Some of it has no doubt grown in the telling. But for myself, I have no question that there is truth in these pages.

THE UNEASE in Lucy's stomach grew. Whatever Rasad's interest in dragons might be, she had a feeling it was nothing good. She opened the book at random, and the pages parted easily to a chapter about halfway through. She squinted at the title, her stomach flipping uncomfortably as she made out the words: "Dragon Alchemy: The use of draconic objects in magical experimentation".

Lucy's eyes scanned quickly down the page, the contents of Rasad's secret study taking on more sinister meaning as certain phrases jumped out at her. "Although almost impossible to harvest, dragon scales are said to retain their magic even after separation from the host...most potent when reduced to powder...can be mixed with other substances...items dragons have touched, even the very land their feet have walked on..."

She shut the book with a shudder. She had never been comfortable with the idea even of her best friend possessing some kind of mysterious magic. The idea of Rasad harnessing such power was nothing short of horrifying. Lucy replaced the book under the papers, trying to make it look untouched.

Her hand stilled on the parchment on top of the pile. It wasn't notes on experiments, like many of the other papers. It was an undated letter, short and to the point.

RASAD

Have followed rumors to their source, I believe. I am heading for a town called Arinton, in the east. Will update further in due course.

Scanlon

LUCY GASPED, her eyes widening at the familiar name. Her mind reeled as she tried to understand how Rasad had come to be corresponding with the uncle she had killed, and what possible interest the Thoranian could have in the movements of the older Balenan man. She rifled frantically through the other papers in the pile, but no more letters from her uncle appeared.

She turned her back on the desk, her heart beating wildly as she once again surveyed the room. If she had still needed convincing, the information that Rasad had been working with Scanlon was proof enough that his intentions were not good. Her eyes fell on the bowl of scales resting on the bookshelf, and she ran a shaking hand over her face. She had assumed the scales to be from a fish, or perhaps some kind of lizard found in the jungles of the South Lands. But it seemed clear that they were something much more rare.

"Almost impossible to harvest," the book had called dragon scales. And supposedly no one in the South Lands had ever even seen a dragon. So how had Rasad gotten his hands on a whole collection of scales from such a creature, even if he was working with Scanlon?

A shiver ran through Lucy, and it took her a moment to realize that she wasn't just unnerved. She was actually cold. The sensation was so rare in the South Lands that it distracted her. The corridor leading to this study had sloped downward, but not far enough for her to be properly underground. She looked around for the source of the draft, and realized that there was a wall hanging behind the bookshelf. Its design was faded and unremarkable, but it was conspicuous as the only decoration in the room.

She hurried toward it, ripping it back without hesitation. As she had suspected, it concealed another opening, and it was immediately clear that this one led to a deeper level. With one glance backward at the well-lit study, and a reassuring touch to the hilt of her weapon, she plunged into the darkness of the narrow tunnel.

She tried to hurry, but it was dark, and she had to keep her hand on the wall in order to keep her balance. The floor was uneven, and the walls were not polished like the rest of the Bastion. Whether this place was dug out later, or simply never intended for public view, she didn't know.

After a few minutes of blind groping, she began to discern a dim glow ahead of her. She hurried toward it, trying to shake off the feeling of suffocation that increased with her descent. The only sound other than the scuffle of her feet was a quiet dripping from ahead, strengthening the impression of a subterranean cave. It was hard to believe that such a short distance behind her was Rasad's well-appointed, luxurious receiving room.

The tunnel ended suddenly, and Lucy stumbled out into a cavern five times the size of the study above. Blinking off the blackness of the tunnel, she raised her eyes to the sight before her.

What she saw was so horrifying that for a moment she was paralyzed, unable to move, unable to think. Her gaze was riveted to the form before her, such a contortion of the creature she had seen in her dream-vision.

It was a dragon, no question. But it had none of the majestic presence of Qadir, who had been so overpowering even in dream form. It wasn't just that this dragon wasn't nearly as large as Qadir had been. It was something much more than that. In death, this mighty beast had been robbed of its glory, and the empty shell of the creature was more disturbing than Lucy would have imagined possible.

Unlike Qadir, this dragon's scales were not black, but a shimmering blue, with shots of orange appearing at random. Lucy could picture that it would have been beautiful in life. Here, in Rasad's hidden underground chamber, it was tragic, pathetic. Unwilling to dwell on the question of how Rasad had felled such a powerful beast, Lucy instead tried to figure out when the dragon had died. She knew that Rasad had been in Thirl, and before that in Nohl, for some time. But the carcass in front of her didn't look at all decomposed.

She realized with amazement that the glow that lit the space came from the dragon itself. Even in death, some of its magic lingered. She frowned as she noticed some dimmer spots on its hide. Leaning closer, she saw with a rush of cold horror that there were multiple patches where the scales had been removed, displaying grayish skin beneath.

Said to retain their magic...most potent when reduced to powder.

Lucy stumbled back a step. The small bowl of scales she had seen in the study above didn't account for a fraction of what had been stripped from this poor creature's hide. What use had

Rasad found for the other scales? What might he still be planning?

She turned, unable to bear the sight of the degraded beast for another moment. She raced blindly back up the tunnel, with no aim but to get out of this place of horrors, and reach the relative safety of her own room.

She emerged back into the study, panting slightly as she paused to catch her breath. Everything was as she had left it, but the stillness was suddenly broken by the sound of footsteps approaching up the corridor leading to Rasad's main suite.

Lucy looked around frantically, her blood pounding in her ears, but there was no time to hide. A moment later Rasad strode into the study, his brow furrowed and his steps confident.

CHAPTER TWENTY-NINE

Rasad glanced up casually as he entered the room, his face freezing when he caught sight of Lucy, still breathing hard as she stood next to the bookcase.

"Luciana." His voice was mild. "This is a surprise."

Lucy didn't answer, her mind blank and her feet frozen to the ground. Her hand, however, reached instinctively for her weapon.

The Thoranian's eyes traveled from Lucy's face to the wall hanging behind her, and understanding lit his features.

"Ah. It seems you've found your way to every corner of my private rooms."

It was the familiar hint of amusement in his voice that snapped Lucy out of her stupor, spurring her into speech.

"I have," she said boldly, making no attempt to hide the blade now clutched in her hand. "And I found some things that I think you'd better explain."

"I am willing to do so," said Rasad, eyeing her dagger with a raised eyebrow. "But shall we talk in my receiving room? It's much more comfortable, after all."

Lucy hesitated. She had half expected him to murder her on

the spot and throw her into the cave with the dead dragon, so his receiving room was a pretty good offer. But still she didn't move. What was his game?

"I don't trust you."

Rasad sighed. "I was afraid that was the case, and I'm sorry for it." He glanced around. "I didn't intend for you to see my experiments quite so soon, but I hope I can still change your mind about me."

Lucy frowned, confusion battling with suspicion. "I saw what's down there," she said, gesturing toward the wall hanging. "So I'm not sure how you think you can convince me that you're not mixed up in something you shouldn't be."

"I didn't kill the poor creature, if that's what you're implying," said Rasad, sounding shocked. He gave a small chuckle. "You can't know much about dragons if you imagined that I did. They're basically impossible to kill. Certainly no human could ever do it."

"And yet," said Lucy, a bite in her voice, "there's a dead dragon in your secret hidden dungeon."

"Yes," said Rasad, the amusement back on his face. "And there's an explanation for that. But first, please humor me, and return to my receiving room."

Lucy hesitated for another moment, but all things considered, she decided she'd rather confront whatever was coming back in the daylight than down in this sinister place.

Rasad seemed to realize that she didn't want to turn her back to him, so he preceded her out of the room. She followed at a distance, breathing a sigh of relief when she emerged back into the main part of Rasad's suite. But she didn't waste any time in rounding on her host.

"Where's Cody?"

Rasad looked at her blankly. "I already told you, Luciana. I don't know where he is. All I know is that he left, and he took a horse with him."

Lucy frowned, wondering how far to push it. She decided that there were more immediate matters. She jerked her head toward the door into Rasad's secret study. "What are you up to down there?"

"Luciana, you're distressed." Rasad's voice was patient, and infuriatingly calm. "Sit down. Let me order some refreshments."

"I don't want refreshments," Lucy snapped. "I didn't drop by your suite for a social visit." Her gaze flicked toward the opening into Rasad's bedchamber, and a new flicker of unease curled through her stomach. "So don't get any ideas."

Rasad chuckled. "Surely you must know better than to think I have any designs on your virtue, Luciana. Would I do anything to harm the reputation of the woman I'm hoping will be my wife?"

Lucy's hot retort died on her lips. For several long seconds she was silent, stunned into immobility by the unexpected declaration.

Rasad's eyebrows were once again raised. "My intentions can't come as a surprise, can they? Have I been so subtle? I wasn't trying to be."

"I...you..." Lucy stammered. "You're trying to distract me, but I—"

"Not at all," Rasad interrupted smoothly. He turned away from her, crossing the room and bending over a small chest in one corner.

Lucy ran a hand across her brow, trying to gather her scattered thoughts.

"In case you doubt me," said Rasad, straightening up, "I have proof that I have been hoping for some time to win you over."

Lucy blinked stupidly at the jewelry Rasad was holding out

to her. It took her a moment to recognize it as the amethyst set that Rasad had tried to buy her in the market in Thirl.

"You went back for it," she said blankly.

"Of course." Rasad's smile was indulgent. "It was appropriate for you to decline, but I could tell that you liked it."

He approached Lucy with a measured step. Her instincts told her to run, but she felt frozen to the spot, unable to master the avalanche of emotions racing through her. Before she fully knew what he was doing, Rasad had attached the necklace around her throat. He didn't linger, but his hands felt strange and sensitive on her skin.

"It suits you."

The satisfaction in Rasad's voice unlocked Lucy's legs. She stumbled back a step, raising her hand to the necklace. It felt like a shackle.

"I don't want to marry you," she said clumsily.

Rasad sighed, but he didn't look especially discouraged. "I know I'm being too abrupt. I intended to be much more charming."

"You don't want to marry me either," Lucy said, her thoughts sluggish. "You're just trying to make me forget what I saw."

"I'm perfectly serious, I assure you," Rasad said. His expression warmed as his eyes rested on her face. He smiled at her—the open, genuine smile Lucy had once found attractive. Now it made her feel like she'd drunk sour milk. "And I don't want you to think it's just that you're beautiful, Luciana. You are, of course, although I expect you're sick of hearing it. But there's much more to admire in you. You're sharp, but you're young, and have so much to learn. I believe I could help you become even sharper."

"I don't want to be sharp," Lucy said. Tears were stinging her eyes, and she wiped them away angrily, feeling foolish.

Rasad's smile became indulgent. "I know you tell yourself

that, but we both know it isn't true." He took a step forward, his voice turning eager. "I have so much to offer you, Luciana. With me you can be everything you were born to be. I know you've never really belonged in Kyona, any more than you belonged in Balenol. But in Thorania you can become so much more than you imagine."

Lucy shook her head, hating the tiny part of herself that still found the picture enticing. The image of the dragon in the cave below reared up in front of her eyes, and she banished the traitorous thoughts with a flick of her head.

"If you wanted to marry me," she said icily, "you wouldn't be trying to conceal from me what you're up to."

"I'm not trying to conceal anything," said Rasad calmly. "As I said, I didn't intend to show you my experiments so soon, but I always meant to tell you everything, once you were ready."

"Experiments?" Lucy repeated. "What does that mean?"

"It's incredible, Luciana," said Rasad, once again eager. He took another step forward.

Lucy fell back, a warning in her eyes. If Rasad noticed, he gave no sign.

"The endless possibilities, explored by so few before me," he continued. "It's more than I ever imagined. When I first heard the rumors that came out of Balenol when I was a small boy, of dragons, and magic, I hardly dared to believe there could be any truth to it. But I was captured all the same. I began to study, to search everywhere I could for any hint of information. My family has always been wealthy. When I was young, I had more opportunity than most to travel, to follow the scent."

He shook his head, his eyes fixed on the distance as he spoke. "So few others ever bothered to question the rumors. I only ever found one person who saw a glimmer of the potential behind them."

Lucy's sharp intake of breath brought Rasad's eyes back to her.

"Scanlon."

Rasad nodded, holding her gaze. "I know you had no love for your uncle," he said bluntly. "And truth be told, neither did I. We had a partnership, built on mutual interest in the possibilities behind dragon magic, nothing more."

"So I suppose you had no idea that he planned to cause a civil war within Kyona," said Lucy sarcastically. "That he wanted to punish the kingdom for Balenol's decline. That he was determined to kill my whole family for personal revenge."

Rasad shrugged. "I knew he wanted to access dragon magic. I didn't ask what for. He had his plans, and I had mine." His eyes again softened. "Certainly had I known you then, I would have done all in my power to protect you from his intentions."

Lucy scoffed. "I was probably still a child when Scanlon was making his plans."

"True," mused Rasad. He chuckled. "Probably swooning over that foolish prince of yours." He gave her a searching look. "Is it the age difference that makes you reluctant to accept my offer?"

Lucy drew a shuddering breath, unreasonably infuriated by Rasad's scornful dismissal of Eamon. "No, it's you," she said bitingly. "And I'm not reluctant, I'm adamant."

Rasad was silent for a moment, regarding her steadily. "There's no need for a hasty answer."

"You said you had your own plans," said Lucy, ignoring the comment. "What were they? What are you doing with all that?" She waved a hand toward the closed door.

"I'm discovering," said Rasad simply. "Inventing, even." He made a scornful noise. "Scanlon was short sighted. And he didn't have the patience I have. I had been conducting my research ever since I heard the rumors of your father's magic artifact." He leaned forward. "Have you ever held it? Is it really as powerful as the stories say?"

Lucy recoiled from his eagerness. "What does my father's rock have to do with any of this?"

"Everything," said Rasad. "It was the first evidence in centuries of the possibility that dragon artifacts could hold a magic of their own. A magic that could be manipulated and used by humans."

"So those crystals," Lucy asked slowly. "They're dragon artifacts of some kind?"

"Ah, you saw those, did you?" Rasad asked enthusiastically. "Aren't they beautiful? Yes, they come from the Dragon Realm. The poor creature below brought them to me."

"Brought them to you?" Lucy asked, stunned. "Willingly?"

Rasad chuckled. "I already told you, Luciana. The dragon was not my victim. He got from our bargain exactly what he wanted."

"What, death?" Lucy challenged.

Rasad nodded solemnly. "Precisely."

Lucy opened her mouth to protest, then shut it again as she remembered the details of Jocelyn's adventures. "That's the dragon who forfeited his power to Scanlon on purpose. The one who wished he hadn't chosen immortality, and wanted to die. He knew that by giving up his magic, he would waste away. The crystals aren't from the Dragon Realm in Kyona's mountains, where my father's rock comes from. They're from the Dragon Realm off the coast of Valoria. The one Joss and Kincaid entered."

"That's right," said Rasad, seeming pleased to find her so well informed. "Scanlon was immediately captured by the possibility of receiving the beast's magic into his own body, impetuous fool that he was. I am more cautious. And as usual, I was the only one to see the true breadth of the potential.

Through my experiments, I can make use of many kinds of magic, without warping my own being."

"But...how?" The instinct to run was still there, nagging at Lucy's mind, but Rasad's revelations held her in thrall.

"It's incredible," Rasad said enthusiastically. "There are so many things to try, with the scales particularly. It's been months, and there has been no breakdown at all. I could probably spend years experimenting. But it's the crystals that really hold the magic." He shook his head. "Such power, when applied correctly. Such a shame that I have so few."

"How do you have *any*?" Lucy pressed. "Why would the dragon bring you crystals? If Scanlon gave him what he wanted by taking his magic away, why would he bring you gifts?"

Rasad gave a grim smile. "Scanlon did have his uses. He was wily, and very persuasive. I financed most of his activities, and he had his end of the bargain to fulfill. He didn't agree lightly to the exchange with the dragon. He convinced the creature that more was required of it. Retrieving the crystals was one part of that deal. What you saw below was the other part. You see, dragons usually return to their own realm when they approach their end. But this one," Rasad's teeth flashed in a grin, "came here."

Cold ripples of horror passed over Lucy at the enthusiasm with which Rasad spoke of the death of the dragon, and the way he and Scanlon had swindled the poor, foolish creature. He didn't even seem to realize that he had lost her, too caught up in his satisfaction to take in her expression.

A knock at the door interrupted the flow of words. Lucy turned, tensing as she once again raised her weapon.

"Enter," Rasad said, his voice as calm as ever.

Lucy started forward with a gasp at the trio who entered. Matheus looked pale and afraid, but he didn't appear to be injured. The observation did little to soften the sight of her younger brother being restrained by two burly, armed men.

"What's going on?" Rasad asked his guards, his faint surprise almost more maddening than the situation itself.

"We caught him following the other one," said one of the guards gruffly. "He stole a horse as well."

Lucy scowled at her brother. So much for protecting him by keeping him out of it. She should have predicted this after he gave in so easily.

"You were trying to follow Cody?" Rasad asked, still unruffled. "It wasn't necessary for you to do that, Matheus. I told you that I sent people after him. And if you did want to join the search, you didn't need to be clandestine about it. I could have provided you with a horse if you'd just asked."

Matheus didn't respond, and the blankness of his expression sent a tendril of fear curling up Lucy's spine.

"Did you catch up to him?" she pressed. Matheus was an excellent rider, better than Cody. Perhaps, if Cody really had only just left...

"Almost." Her brother's voice was so quiet she had to lean forward to hear him.

"What do you mean almost? Matheus, where's Cody?"

Matheus met her eyes at last, and she could see the intensity of the emotion he was trying not to show.

"He's dead."

CHAPTER THIRTY

Lucy took an involuntary step back, her senses swimming.

"No." She shook her head stupidly, refusing to consider the possibility. "Matheus, that might be what they want you to think, but Cody can't be—"

"I saw, Lucy." Matheus's voice was anguished. "No one told me anything. You know I'm a better rider than Cody. I thought I could catch him, and I was right. I was in front, with the others not far behind me. I almost had him, Lucy. I'd almost caught up when I saw..." He trailed off, swallowing hard.

"Saw what?" Lucy demanded impatiently. If she focused on her irritation, she wouldn't have to acknowledge the terror beneath it.

"Saw his horse carry him straight over the edge into the ravine."

Lucy felt frozen to the spot, unable to make sense of the words. She could only stare blankly at her brother, searching his face for some sign that he was making this up, that it was some kind of trick to fool Rasad.

"So he *was* heading for Thirl," said Rasad quietly. He turned to Lucy. "Luciana, I'm so very sorry. It's treacherous terrain, and my people had reported that the horse he took was a new stallion, not fully broken in. He must have—"

"Stop." Lucy held up a hand, not even willing to look at Rasad. "I don't want to hear any more of your lies." Her eyes met Matheus's, pleading with him. "Maybe he survived. Did you go to the edge, did you...?"

Matheus was shaking his head, bitterness in his expression. "They caught up to me and restrained me. They dragged me back here."

"Luciana," said Rasad gently. "There's no way he could survive that fall."

For the briefest moment Lucy felt grief welling up inside her, threatening to burst out with terrifying violence. But her eyes were still locked on her brother's, and she could see the devastation behind his pale face. She drew a deep breath, forcing everything else down. Matheus was only fifteen. And if Cody was really gone, there was no one but her to protect him. She couldn't fall apart.

She turned to Rasad. "Let us go. Let us both leave, and return to Thirl."

Rasad raised an eyebrow. "You speak as though you're prisoners."

Lucy looked pointedly at the two guards still restraining her brother. Rasad sighed, but made no order for Matheus's release.

"I understand that this is a crushing blow for you both, truly I do. But I would so much prefer you to stay."

"How kind," said Lucy sarcastically. "But we would like to leave."

"Yes, well." Rasad sounded politely regretful. "The difficulty is, you've been a little too hasty in exploring my personal belongings. If you'd wished to leave yesterday, there would have been no issue. But now..." He shrugged. "I'm afraid I'm reluctant to part ways without some kind of assurance that you're not my enemy."

"What does that mean?" Lucy spat.

"Well..." Rasad looked back toward the closed door into his secret study. "The things you observed could be misunderstood by some, and I would hate for—"

"What do you want from me?" Lucy cut him off.

Rasad took a step forward, reaching out to touch a hand to the necklace she still wore. "I thought I'd already made that clear," he said softly.

Lucy recoiled, unable even for the sake of her brother to contemplate the idea. "That's not going to happen."

"But Luciana, you've only seen a glimpse of what I can offer," said Rasad. His voice was once again eager and his face alight, no sign of regret over Cody's fate remaining. "If you knew the scale of my plans, how much you would gain from allying yourself with me—"

"Over my dead body," interjected Matheus unexpectedly, his voice fierce.

"You took the words out of my mouth," said Lucy grimly, retreating another step away from Rasad.

He sighed. "I wish you would reconsider," he said, a hint of pleading in his tone. "I would so much prefer to work together. You could be of such assistance if you were only willing."

"I'm not assisting you with anything," said Lucy, her voice trembling. "I don't know what you're up to, but I've seen more than enough to know that I want nothing to do with it." She drew a shuddering breath. They were past pretense. "And you killed Cody. I don't know how you did it, but I know you're behind it."

Rasad regarded her silently for a moment. Then he waved a hand lazily to his guards. For one hopeful moment, Lucy thought that they were going to release Matheus. But only one guard relinquished his hold on the boy, moving instantly toward Lucy. She raised her blade, backing away, but Rasad's voice drew her up short.

"I have the highest respect for your fighting abilities, Luciana, but I don't think we need a display at this moment. Given your position, Matheus is of little use to me. If you resist, he will be disposed of." He gave a curt whistle, and two more guards appeared in the doorway, joining the one who still held Matheus.

Lucy froze, fury battling with fear within her. It went against every instinct to relinquish her weapon without a fight, but the blade now being held to Matheus's throat made it clear that she had little choice.

She threw her dagger down with a clatter, glaring death at Rasad. "If you're just going to kill us, why prolong it?"

"I'm not going to kill you," said Rasad, amused. At a sign from him, two of the guards seized Lucy's arms. "I would have preferred your cooperation, but even without it, you're extremely useful to me."

Lucy glared back at her suitor-turned-captor, but underneath the brave front, her blood was running cold. She didn't know what use the advisor planned to make of her, but she had no desire to find out.

"You won't get away with this," she spat. "Do you think we won't be missed in Thirl? Our friends will—"

"I'm so pleased you brought up your royal friends," interrupted Rasad with a smile that made Lucy's skin crawl. "I'm very much hoping that you're right, and that they will take an interest in your...situation." His eyes lingered on her in mocking amusement. "One of them in particular."

Lucy felt her face burning at what she had no doubt was a reference to Eamon. The last thing she wanted to do was to involve him in the consequences of her foolishness.

"Your own king will ask questions if we disappear," she tried again. "He invited us to stay in his palace."

"*I* invited you to stay in his palace, my dear girl," Rasad reminded her indulgently. "And I will decide what becomes of you. He will accept whatever version of events I choose to give him."

"He's your puppet, is he?" Lucy asked scornfully. "Do you expect us to believe that you're above all consequences? King Abner didn't listen to you when you wanted to use me to destroy Lord Yosef."

Rasad frowned, looking genuinely displeased for the first time. "Of course King Abner isn't my puppet. I am his advisor, and I have earned his trust, but that doesn't make him weak minded. I take offense at such a suggestion."

"Really?" Lucy spoke flatly. "Of everything, that's what offends you?"

"I have devoted my life to the service of His Majesty and our great kingdom," said Rasad. He was still frowning, and he spoke as though he was admonishing a child. "Thorania is the strongest and most prosperous kingdom in either the North or the South Lands, and when my plans are fulfilled, it will be even stronger."

He gave a scornful snort. "Certainly stronger than a flimsy little fiefdom like Kyona, which passes its crown from bloodline to bloodline like children sharing a ball. Kyona was too weak to protect its citizens from exploitation by Balenol, and Balenol was too weak to prevent the ruin brought on its people by Kyona's retribution." He stood a little straighter. "Such a thing could never be said of Thorania. And I would never have devoted myself to serving a king who wasn't worthy of the role, like that indolent fool who ruled Balenol at the time of the slave revolt."

Lucy remained silent. From all she had heard of King

Siloam, the uncle of Balenol's new King Giles, Rasad's description was accurate. The slight against Kyona was less just, but she was too stunned by Rasad's sudden outburst to think of an adequate response.

Rasad was watching her, and his features suddenly relaxed into a smile. "You're right that I didn't get the outcome I was hoping for out of Lord Yosef's attack, but I'm glad King Abner didn't blindly follow my advice. He wouldn't be worthy of my respect or my service if he did. He has a strong mind, and he will make the greatest ruler Thorania has ever seen." He frowned again briefly, staring into the distance as he added, "I do at times wish he was a little less short sighted regarding our isolation from—" He cut himself off, shaking his head. "No matter. Every problem has a solution, after all."

Rasad looked between Lucy and Matheus, a small chuckle breaking out at their expressions. "You think I care only for my own interests, don't you? You misjudge me. My plans are all to benefit Thorania. He turned to Lucy, a hint of eagerness back in his voice. "It's not too late to change your mind, and work with me. The kingdoms of your parents are both unworthy of your service, but Thorania is not like them. It's a magnificent kingdom, and you could help me make it even greater."

Lucy met his gaze steadily. "From everything I've seen of Thorania, it is a magnificent kingdom," she agreed, her eyes narrowing. "And from everything I've seen of you, the best thing for Thorania's future would be if you have no hand in it."

Rasad's face darkened. "That was not polite, Luciana." He regarded her for a moment in silence. "It seems your mind is made up." He transferred his gaze to the four guards. "Bind them. Securely. I will need to think further about how best to proceed."

Lucy and Matheus struggled, but they were unarmed and outmatched in strength. Within minutes, the guards had them both bound at the hands and feet, gags shoved into their mouths. At a sign from Rasad, the guards all left the room, no doubt stationing themselves outside the door in case the prisoners tried to escape.

For a moment there was silence, Lucy trying vainly to think of a way out while Rasad stared thoughtfully at the closed door to his study, his expression focused, and his fingers steepled.

"There are many options," he mused aloud. "None of them perfect, of course, but still serviceable." He returned his eyes to his silent audience, watching furiously from the floor where their captors had dumped them. One of Rasad's eyebrows went up as he took in their state. "That was unnecessary," he said, crossing the room with smooth strides and removing Lucy's gag. "I didn't mean for them to silence you, my dear. Has anyone ever told you what a musical voice you have?"

"Has anyone ever told you that you're a snake?" Lucy spat, over the top of Matheus's muffled growls.

Rasad chuckled as he also removed the younger boy's gag. "You sound like Lady Yasmin, Luciana. I would love to know what she said to you during your little training session at the palace. Was it then that you stopped trusting me?"

"I never trusted you," Lucy snapped. "And I didn't need Lady Yasmin's warnings to know you were up to something."

"Really?" Again that maddening eyebrow went up. "I was under the impression that you weren't quite sure what to make of me. That you found me...how shall I put it? Magnetic."

Lucy flushed in mingled embarrassment and fury at how easily he had read her. She had thought of him in just such terms more than once.

"I find you despicable," she said angrily. "And if I needed any proof that you're mixed up in something evil, the dead dragon hidden below your bedchamber is more than enough."

"Dead—what?" Matheus spluttered, his eyes growing wide.

"He was in league with our dear old uncle," said Lucy grimly. "He's got the body of the poor beast who gave its magic to Scanlon, and he's been experimenting with how to use it to manufacture magic for himself."

"Such a crude explanation," said Rasad, pained.

"He's got magic?" Matheus asked, clearly horrified.

Lucy shook her head. "Not in him, like Scanlon did. He just uses objects, like Father's rock."

"So you admit that your uncle had magic, do you?" asked Rasad casually. "I thought it was all a load of nonsense, made up by your weak minded prince to excuse his bad decisions."

Again Lucy flushed. "How do you know about—?"

"My dear child," Rasad interjected indulgently. "There's very little I don't know about you, or any of your companions. Do you think I invited you to my kingdom, to my *home*, without doing my research?"

He chuckled. "Not that much research was needed. Your little prince made it so delightfully easy to read the whole story on his face every time you were around. I have him to thank for making it clear from the very beginning just how useful you could be to me." He smiled fondly as his gaze lingered on Lucy, and she had never longed for her weapon more. "But as I got to know you, I warmed to you for your own sake, of course."

"You used me from the start," said Lucy, her chest heaving. Her mind ran rapidly over every interaction between her, Eamon, and Rasad. It was so clear in hindsight how he had manipulated every word, every look, to play on Eamon's jealousy, bringing out the prince's least mature side, and making himself look wise and measured by comparison. "You used both of us."

"Used is an ugly word," complained Rasad. "I've already told you that my plans are not for my own selfish gain. If I could bring you into them, why shouldn't I do so?"

Lucy opened her mouth to repeat that she wanted no part in Rasad's plans, but she froze mid-word as a thought occurred to her. "You used me," she repeated slowly. Her face hardened in accusation as she again remembered the magnetic appeal that Rasad had held from the moment she met him. "You used magic on me," she said. "You...I don't know, bewitched me or something!"

"Bewitched you?" Rasad actually threw back his head, laughing more heartily than she had ever seen him do before. "I'll take that as a compliment."

"I meant," said Lucy, gritting her teeth, "you used some kind of magic to make me trust you, to turn me against Eamon."

Even as she said the words, she heard the irony in them. She had refused to acknowledge that Eamon had been induced by magic to trust Scanlon, to turn on those he cared about. Was this how it had felt for him? It was more horrible than she'd imagined. And the revelation of Rasad's dabbling in magic hadn't really changed her mind about Eamon's story. It had only forced her to confront the reality that, if she was honest, she had always known Eamon was telling the truth.

However bad Lucy felt, Rasad's next words made her feel even worse.

"My dear, dear Luciana." The hateful man was still chuckling. "No magic was necessary. My artifacts are powerful and limited in number. I don't use them lightly, and certainly not if I can achieve my means easily without them. Almost as soon as I met you, it was perfectly clear to me that you could be brought to my point of view with very little persuasion."

"I don't share your point of view on anything," Lucy growled.

"Don't you?" Rasad smiled. "Well it certainly didn't need my help to turn you against your prince. And I think you do share my views on the inferiority of both Kyona and Balenol." He shook his head. "I was so hopeful that you would willingly join my plans. You have as much cause as anyone to wish to see both kingdoms fall. Both have rejected you, haven't they? I didn't have to plant the seed of bitterness in you. It was already strong and healthy."

"Kyona hasn't rejected me," said Lucy. Her eyes were stinging as Rasad casually pressed on her deepest insecurities, but as she spoke the words she knew they were true. "And neither has Balenol."

Rasad's smile was infuriating. "Really? My own observations suggest otherwise."

Lucy glared back at him, again seeing all her conversations with Rasad in a new light. It was galling to realize how skillfully he had played on her humiliation every time someone in Balenol spoke spitefully of her, how subtly he had encouraged her bitterness. The advisor had outmaneuvered her in every way, and she had never felt more foolish. Or more angry.

"A few narrow-minded or jealous courtiers don't represent the kingdom," she retorted. "Balenol's royals welcomed us like family. Which we are! And Kyona is my home. I have a family there, a community where people care about me. Our family may not be noble, but the king and queen themselves host me in Kynton any time I go. I mean, the princess is my best friend!" Lucy could hardly believe her own stupidity as her words came faster and faster. Why had she ever let herself believe she was an outsider? "And the prince is—"

Her throat was suddenly thick, and she couldn't continue. But Rasad was only too ready to finish for her.

"In love with you, the poor soul." The advisor's eyes raked over her form, bound as she was. "He little knows what a tease you are."

"Don't talk about my sister like that!" Matheus struggled against his bonds, but it was clear from his wince that his wrists were tied as tightly as Lucy's.

"He's not even worth your indignation, Matheus," said Lucy scornfully. She drew a deep breath as she looked back at Rasad. "And unlike you, Eamon has every reason to complain that I led him on. But he's never done it." She narrowed her eyes. "But never mind that. I can see now that you tried to manipulate me into wanting to punish both Kyona and Balenol. But why? I thought you only cared about Thorania's interests."

"I do," said Rasad comfortably.

"Then why have you been trying to turn Lucy against our own kingdom?" Matheus challenged. He was still pale, but his expression was fierce as he continued to struggle against the rope around his wrists.

Lucy's gaze had been drawn to the writing desk in the corner, but she returned it to Rasad. "I read Isidore's journal," she said abruptly. "I know all she cared about was punishing the kingdom that had abandoned her, and the one that had exploited her. But what do you care about that? You really expect us to believe you've carried her grudge for generations? And you say Lady Yasmin and her brother are foolish to dislike you because of an old land dispute."

"Of course I'm not carrying a grudge," said Rasad, sounding astonished. "I have my faults, Luciana, but pettiness isn't one of them." His mouth twisted, a hint of scorn showing through his calm. "My Kyonan ancestor certainly succeeded in teaching her descendants to resent the other kingdoms. I was raised myself in the belief that Thorania shouldn't concern itself with anything beyond our borders." He paused. "Our current borders, I should say. But my forebears were painfully short sighted. Who cares about some supposed insult from ancient history?"

"What do you mean 'current' borders?" Matheus asked ominously. "Are you saying King Abner plans to invade Balenol? I don't believe it."

"Neither do I," said Lucy. But even as she said it, she remembered the huge military force camped right outside Thirl at that very moment, and it was all she could do to keep her face impassive.

"Always thinking so small," Rasad mused. "Is there no one who shares my vision?" He sighed. "King Abner doesn't always share my vision either. But he'll come through at the crucial moment. You'll see."

"I thought he wasn't a puppet on your string," said Lucy acidly, trying to hide the fear bubbling in her stomach.

For a moment Rasad looked genuinely regretful. "I do wish I could convince him without needing to—" He sighed. "But I'm wise enough not to fight a losing battle. It's worth just one little push to turn him into the emperor he was born to be."

Lucy and Matheus exchanged a look, but neither of them spoke.

"But why am I troubling you with matters that are already settled?" Rasad said politely. "The question we need to answer is what to do with you."

CHAPTER THIRTY-ONE

"If you're going to kill us," said Matheus belligerently, "why not get it over with?"

"Whoa, whoa," Lucy interjected. For all her oldest brother was usually more level headed than the younger two, every now and then their father's impetuousness came through. But whatever plans Rasad had to make use of her, she had no intention of letting Matheus throw his life away.

"I quite agree, Luciana," said Rasad humorously. "I see no need to be so hasty." He looked her over thoughtfully. "Yes, I think Prince Eamon is a good place to start. I'm sorry that we can't be partners, Luciana. Truly sorry. But it is fortunate that your lack of vision won't significantly hinder my plans." His gaze passed from her to her brother. "I hate to inconvenience you, but would you mind waiting here while I get myself organized?"

The siblings just glared at him, unwilling to enter into his charade. Rasad slipped through the door to his study, not even bothering to threaten them with capture or punishment if they tried to escape. They were in his power, and they knew it as well as he did.

"Are you all right, Matheus?" Lucy asked as soon as they were alone.

Her brother met her eyes for a long moment, the anguish of Cody's loss and their own perilous situation swirling unspoken between them. Then he rolled his shoulders with a sigh.

"Yes. You?"

Lucy nodded absently, trying again to think of a way out.

"Well, this isn't good," said Matheus.

Lucy shot him a look. "Not great, no. What happened to waiting in your room?"

"I can see that's what you did," said Matheus, and Lucy let it drop with a grimace. "What are we going to do?" Matheus pressed on.

Lucy shook her head slowly. "I don't see what we can do." She wriggled her wrists behind her, but it was clear that she wasn't going to be escaping her bonds anytime soon.

"We could try calling for help," said Matheus doubtfully. "There are a lot of people who work here. Maybe someone would be willing to intervene."

Lucy barely held back a snort. "This is Rasad's world, Matheus. His empire. No one is going to stand up to him on our behalf."

"All that talk about King Abner being born to be an emperor," said Matheus uneasily. "What did that mean?"

"Nothing good." Lucy's voice was grim. "Did you hear him talking about Thorania's 'current borders'? And saying that we were thinking small when we talked about Thorania invading Balenol?"

"Yes," said Matheus. "But surely he wasn't talking about Kyona. Thorania couldn't hope to extend its territory into the North Lands, could it?"

"I don't think King Abner has any such hope," said Lucy. "Just Rasad."

"But surely it's not possible," protested Matheus.

Lucy stretched uncomfortably in her bindings. "I don't know what's possible," she admitted. "I don't know what kind of magic he's harnessed. He clearly plans to use magic on King Abner, to convince him to march on Balenol."

"Yes," said Matheus slowly. "That's what I heard, too. He said that King Abner would change his mind at the crucial moment. But when is that moment?"

"I have a bad feeling that it's soon," said Lucy. She met her brother's eyes, wishing she could protect him, knowing she couldn't. "Matheus, I'm so sorry. This is all my fault."

"Of course it's not your fault!" Matheus said firmly.

There was no time to argue about it, because at that moment the door to the study opened again. Rasad emerged, carrying a small tray with several objects, which he placed carefully on the writing desk.

"Now," he said briskly. "Sorry to keep you waiting. Luciana, I would like you to write a letter for me, please. There are some things I would like to communicate to your prince."

"I'm not doing anything for you," Lucy hissed. "And Eamon has nothing to do with any of this."

"He may not have any place in your plans, my dear, but he has quite a significant place in mine. And the first step is your letter." Rasad took in the look on Lucy's face. "Oh, it won't require too much effort on your part," he reassured her. "None at all, really. I can do the actual writing."

"Eamon knows my handwriting," said Lucy belligerently. "And he'll know it's not from me."

Rasad chuckled. "I'm counting on him knowing your handwriting." He smiled genially at his captives. "I think you'll appreciate this little trick. It's quite a clever one, if I say so myself. Have you heard of the Balenan chameleon?" Lucy and Matheus remained silent, glaring at him. "No?" Rasad went on, unperturbed. "It's a species of lizard that lives in the jungle. It has the peculiar property of being able to change its coloring depending on its environment. For camouflage, you know."

"You're into studying the local wildlife, are you?" Lucy asked sarcastically.

"I'm interested in anything that can further my research," said Rasad calmly. "And I discovered, after a great deal of experimentation, that there are many uses for combining chameleon scales with dragon matter. When applied correctly, it can allow one person to take on the properties of another, so to speak."

"What does that mean?" Matheus demanded.

"Many things," said Rasad. "But in this case, it means that I can save your sister the effort of writing anything herself." He smiled at Lucy. "It would be challenging with your hands tied, after all. But knowing your skills as I do, I'm not eager to release you. So this is a neat solution, don't you think?"

Lucy said nothing, trying not to show her apprehension.

"Now," said Rasad, his tone turning businesslike. "I think your hair will be enough."

Lucy pulled away as he leaned forward, but she was unable to prevent him from plucking a hair from her head. He turned his back on them, blocking his activities with his body as he did something with the items on his tray. The silence stretched out, and Lucy could feel her brother's eyes on her. She tried to keep her own expression impassive, not wanting to add to his panic.

A strange smell filled the air as Rasad turned back around. "I'm not being a very entertaining host," he said apologetically. "Alchemy is a delicate business, you know. It requires my full focus. But I think we're ready now."

He reached into the writing desk and pulled out a piece of parchment. "How shall we begin?" He stared into the distance for a moment, then nodded as he drew a quill from an ink pot sitting on the desk. "Dear Eamon," he said, writing fluidly. "I know you may not want to hear from me, but I don't know who else to turn to."

He grinned provocatively at Lucy as he held up the parchment. "That opening should be enough to bring him running no matter what else I write, don't you think? But I'm confident I can do still better."

Lucy opened her mouth, a furious protest on her lips, but her gaze fell on the words scratched onto the parchment, and she froze. The words might be Rasad's, but the writing was undeniably her own, as familiar as her face in a mirror.

"That's not possible," she whispered.

"It's not, is it?" Rasad agreed, enthusiasm in his voice. "And yet, it's happening right in front of your eyes!" He turned back to the writing desk. "But this is no time to get distracted. How's this? 'Rasad has asked me to marry him, and I'm not sure what I want. He's coming back to Thirl, but I don't want to be seen in the city with him until I've made up my mind. Will you meet me at—'" Rasad stopped reading aloud for a moment, although he continued to scratch something out onto the parchment, presumably directions for where Lucy supposedly wanted Eamon to meet her.

"I don't want anyone else to know," Rasad added after a moment's thought, again dictating as he wrote. "So please come alone." He made a great show of underlining the last sentence before signing off and looking up at Lucy and Matheus. "I didn't think there was any need to bore you with the details of the rendezvous, but you get the idea."

Lucy felt heat and ice rushing over her body in quick succession. She could imagine Eamon's reaction to receiving such a letter from her, and the thought was terrifying. Rasad clearly believed he had found a foolproof way to lure Eamon out to whatever location he had chosen. And the most horrifying part was that he was right.

"Leave Eamon out of this," she said, her voice trembling. "There's no need to involve him."

"I hate to contradict you, Luciana," said Rasad briskly, sealing up the envelope. "But there's every need. I assure you, it's not personal. I have nothing against him," he inclined his head toward her in mock deference, "other than our rivalry for your affections, of course. But he's rather in the way."

"What are you going to do to him?" Lucy demanded.

Rasad continued as if she hadn't spoken, packing the letter into a leather satchel as he did. "If he was a child, like King Giles's heir, perhaps he could be allowed to live. The Balenan crown prince is only twelve, and I can't imagine his presence will do much to counteract how deeply Balenol will be weakened once the new king tragically dies."

The sharp intake of breath from both listeners was audible, but Rasad kept speaking, his tone dispassionate.

"But Kyona is stronger than Balenol, and sadly King Calinnae is not currently in my reach. However, I think disposing of his heir will be enough of a blow to the kingdom to serve my purposes well enough."

"You won't get away with this!" shouted Lucy, struggling furiously. Her wrists were rubbed raw by the ferocity of her attempt to escape, but she barely noticed it. Her mind was clear, but her vision swam, as if she was blinded by her rage over her own powerlessness.

"Actually," said Rasad, again ignoring Lucy's words, "speaking of King Giles's approaching death reminds me of another count against Prince Eamon. His irritating intervention set my plans back most unhelpfully."

Lucy gasped. "You *were* behind the attack on King Giles." For a moment she felt a hint of confusion among the fear and fury, as she pictured the face of Eamon's guard as the Kyonan threw the knife at King Giles. He had certainly seemed to be acting of his own will. "You used magic on him somehow," she said slowly. "On the guard."

Rasad sighed. "I did, and I very much resent Prince Eamon causing me to waste one of my precious crystals. It takes powerful magic to have that kind of impact on someone's mind and intentions. It would have helped me out if the guard had been weaker minded, of course. But the crystal was strong enough—and it worked so perfectly on him, it was maddening for it all to come to nothing. Even a failed attempt by a Kyonan guard to kill the Balenan king should have at least succeeded in destroying any idea of an alliance between the two kingdoms." He frowned. "But thanks to Prince Eamon being the one to save the day, it didn't even achieve that."

"How devastating for you," said Lucy, her voice trembling with suppressed anger.

Rasad shrugged. "Oh, I wouldn't say devastating. The idea of having Kyona be behind the assassination was only one of many possible courses. If I remove the Kyonan heir, it should be enough. It's not like any alliance has been formalized. I'll just have to act quickly enough that there's no time for Balenol to go running to the North Lands for help."

"Eamon won't let himself be killed by a pathetic weasel like you," Matheus spat. His voice dripped with scorn, but it wasn't enough to hide his fear.

"Oh, I won't personally touch a hair on his head," said Rasad calmly. "I'll leave that part in more capable hands."

Lucy stopped struggling for a moment, hanging her head. Matheus might think Eamon was unbeatable, the valiant fighter seen by girls like Sonia and Vanessa, back in the Kyonan court. But she knew him better. He was strong, and he was a good fighter, but he wasn't invincible. He could be overpowered by superior numbers just like anyone else.

He was human, with failings and vulnerabilities, the same as the next man. He was as overconfident as he was kind hearted. As impatient as he was good humored. He saw so much more than she had given him credit for, but he frequently missed things that should have been obvious to him. Generally even tempered, he was hot headed to the point of stupidity on the rare occasions when he let himself be provoked. He was charming, and handsome, and infuriating, and wonderful. He was both much less and so much more than the perfect image of him that Lucy had carried as a girl.

And the worst thing was, Rasad knew all this. He had taken the time to learn how best to manipulate Eamon, just as he had done with Lucy. The advisor was going to ensure that Eamon wasn't at his best, because he was going to draw the prince out by pressing on his greatest vulnerability—her.

Lucy barely held back a sob. She had no doubt that if Rasad succeeded in luring Eamon into a trap, the prince would fall, and fall hard. And the knowledge that she herself was being used to do it was more bitter than anything that had come before. She had given Eamon little reason to want to humor her in her supposed request for his help, but she didn't doubt for a moment that he would drop everything to come to her. He would move the moon in the sky for her if he could, despite the way she had treated him the last few months.

And what would he think when he realized he had been tricked? Would he die believing she had willingly played a part in Rasad's treachery? The thought was unbearable.

"Don't do this," she said, her voice strangled and quiet. "Please. I'll do anything."

She could see Matheus's shock out of the corner of her eye. She knew that hearing her beg would scare her brother more than the rest, but for the moment she had no strength left to fight.

"Anything?" Rasad repeated, studying her thoughtfully as he paused in his preparations. "Even marry me?"

Lucy recoiled, unable to hide her horror, but a moment later the advisor was chuckling.

"That's not a flattering reaction, but I won't take offense, since it has become very clear that you don't share my capacity for vision. There's no need to look so disgusted, my dear. I was only joking. I wanted you as a willing partner in my endeavors—I'm not interested in a wife who had to be coerced into the role. If you have no interest in my plans, it's really much simpler for me to make use of you in more direct ways."

Lucy glared at him, trying to steady her breathing. She wanted to do whatever it took to save Eamon, but selfishly she was glad she wasn't being asked to make such a choice. There must be another way.

"You can't win, you know," said Matheus. His words were furious, but unless Lucy was mistaken, there was a hint of relief in his voice as well. "Even if you could kill Eamon, Jocelyn would just become heir."

"Don't let it worry you," said Rasad calmly. "My plans for Princess Jocelyn are already underway."

Lucy hadn't thought it was possible, but her horror increased. The idea of something happening to Eamon was awful enough, but the thought of her best friend in danger as well made her feel like she was being suffocated. It had seemed over the top before, but she was suddenly grateful that Jocelyn's new husband was rattled enough by the attack in Balenol that he didn't like to let his wife out of his sight.

"Kincaid won't let you hurt her," she said without thinking.

Rasad just smiled as he strode for the door. He seemed to have finished with his immediate preparations, and a moment later he had called his guards back in.

"I wouldn't be so sure," he said to Lucy, his expression alarmingly smug.

Lucy's fear mounted. Kincaid was besotted. Rasad couldn't use his magic to turn the Valorian against his own wife. Could he?

"Escort our guests to their new sleeping quarters," Rasad was telling his guards coolly. "I will leave for Thirl first thing in the morning, and they will accompany me."

He watched dispassionately as the guards immediately seized the two Kyonans. Seeing Lucy glaring at him, he gave her a charming smile. "I look forward to your company on the journey, my dear."

Lucy turned her face away, unwilling to play his game. Had it really been only that morning that she had gone riding with him by the ocean, and a small, guilty part of her had been tempted by the luxurious life he could offer her? How could she ever have doubted he was a deceitful, murderous villain?

The guards obviously had no difficulty understanding Rasad's vague instructions, because they dragged Lucy and Matheus straight to the Bastion's more official dungeons. It was surreal to be hauled like criminals through the corridors they had been wandering as honored guests for the past week. Servants shot curious looks at them, but no one showed any inclination to intervene or ask questions. In fact, no one even looked especially surprised. It all just added to Lucy's fury with herself for ever doubting the nature of Rasad's intentions.

The siblings were thrown into adjoining cells, and mercifully their bindings were removed once they were secured inside. Any hope of escape quickly died. The guards knew what they were doing, and they gave their prisoners no opening. The dungeons were solid, the bars unyielding. The only benefit was that Rasad apparently felt no need to set someone to watch the cells. Once they had deposited their captives, the guards withdrew, leaving Lucy and Matheus free to talk.

"What are we going to do?" Matheus asked at once.

"I don't know," Lucy admitted.

"We have to stop him!" Matheus insisted.

"I know," said Lucy, rubbing her eyes wearily. "We can't let him kill Eamon and Jocelyn. Or King Giles."

"Or let him invade Balenol, then move on to Kyona," added Matheus dryly.

Lucy groaned. "Valoria too, I'm pretty sure. He wants Thorania to be an empire, remember? He wants control of both continents."

Matheus shuddered. "But he basically admitted that King Abner has no interest in expanding Thorania's borders. Do you really think he can use magic to persuade the king to give the order? It's a pretty big thing to change his mind about."

"I really do," said Lucy grimly. "Rasad has been planning this for a long time. You can be sure he wouldn't move unless everything was in place. And if he can bring King Abner on board, the rest will be easy. You saw how many troops are camped outside the capital for this military muster! They're provisioned, and trained, and their presence so close to the border won't even make the Balenans suspicious, since the muster happens every year. The army will obey the king's orders, and it will be too late to stop it."

Matheus groaned. "Lady Yasmin was right—it's no coincidence that the military muster is happening right now, while the royals are in Thirl." He was silent for a moment, thinking. "But first Rasad has to kill King Giles. He won't move against Balenol unless he's sure the kingdom is weak. We have to warn King Giles somehow."

"Yes," Lucy agreed. "But first we have to make sure that letter never makes it to Eamon." When she remembered what the letter said, all the fight suddenly went out of her. "Listen to us," she groaned. "Full of great plans about stopping this disaster." She gestured around hopelessly. "We're locked in a dungeon, completely in his power. We can't do anything."

She felt uselessly for her weapon, knowing perfectly well that she had surrendered it in Rasad's suite. "You don't have an extra blade hidden on you, do you?" she asked hopefully.

Matheus shook his head. "They took it from me when they seized me. I should have fought harder, but I'd just seen Cody go over the edge, and I was..." His voice trailed off, and he swallowed hard. "I can't believe he's gone, Lucy," he whispered. "I know it's a long way down, but I can't help hoping he survived."

"We can't dwell on it," said Lucy firmly, blinking back the tears that stung her own eyes. Cody had always been strong, and she couldn't help the sliver of hope inside her either. But she didn't say so, not wanting to give her brother false hope. "We can't think about it now. Not yet. Cody would tell us to stay focused on the bigger problem."

She squeezed her eyes shut. Regardless of what she said, she couldn't keep her eyes on the bigger problem when she thought about the way Rasad intended to lure Eamon out.

"This is all my fault," she whispered. "I'm as bad as Isidore."

"Of course it's not your fault," said Matheus, sounding irritated.

"It is." Lucy's voice was hollow. "Cody told me that I knew who to trust if I would just listen to my instincts, but I let myself be blinded by my bitterness, and I let Rasad manipulate me." She ground her teeth. "He played on my insecurities, and I did everything he wanted me to do."

"Not everything," said Matheus meaningfully.

Lucy shuddered at the reference to Rasad's twisted marriage proposal, but brushed the thought aside. "Even you warned me. You said I was wrong not to tell Eamon everything, about Lady

Yasmin's warnings, and our reasons for accepting Rasad's invitation. But I was too stubborn. If I'd been honest with Eamon and told him my suspicions about Rasad, he wouldn't be fooled into thinking I was considering a marriage proposal from him. If I'd told Eamon that Lady Yasmin had reason to think that Rasad was behind the attack on King Giles, and that we were coming to the Bastion to investigate, Eamon would know better than to obey a cryptic letter telling him to come alone to an obscure meeting place."

"When you put it like that," said Matheus fairly, "he should know better without being told all that."

Lucy groaned. "He should, but he won't. He loses his head when I'm concerned, and Rasad knows it." She covered her face with one hand, her voice barely audible. "I'm never going to get the chance to tell him."

Matheus didn't ask what she wished she could tell Eamon. But Lucy had a feeling her brother knew she didn't mean warning Eamon about Rasad's plans.

CHAPTER THIRTY-TWO

"What have you done to Jocelyn?"

Rasad looked down at his captive in surprise. "Did you speak to me, Luciana? I thought you were preserving a dignified silence."

Lucy just glared at him, unwilling to give him the satisfaction of a reply. It was true that she had refused to respond to every attempt to draw her out on the first part of their journey. But after a long and brutal day of rapid travel—the worst part of which was definitely crossing the ravine, when Lucy had been unable to stop herself from picturing Cody's fall—even she realized that her silence had become less dignified, and more of a sulk.

And now, as the morning sun of a second day beat down on her unprotected face, she decided that she was wasting potentially precious time to get more information from her captor. At the rate they were moving, they would reach Thirl by nightfall. So when Rasad's horse drew alongside the cart, she seized her opportunity.

"I said," she snapped, "what have you done to Jocelyn?"

Matheus shifted beside her, still dozing fitfully. Lucy had no idea how he'd managed to fall asleep at all, but she wished she could do the same. At least the hours would pass more quickly for him.

"I haven't done anything to the princess," said Rasad placidly. "As you know, I've been in the north for over a week."

Lucy gritted her teeth. The sight of her captor sitting comfortably on his horse somehow seemed to increase the screaming protest of her own limbs. Every bit of her ached from being jostled around in the back of a cart, with bound hands and feet, for a day and a half. She had begun to wonder if she'd even be able to walk once they were eventually let off the wagon.

"You said you had plans for her. Plans that are already underway."

"Well, something had to be done about her," said Rasad, his tone matter-of-fact. "She is probably the biggest thorn in my side, if truth be told."

"What did Joss ever do to you?" Lucy demanded.

"Oh, it's not her fault," said Rasad. "I blame your uncle for the whole fiasco." He sighed. "Scanlon's failure was maddening enough as it was—he was supposed to create enough conflict within Kyona to weaken the kingdom to the point where our army would be able to walk right in. And using the crown prince to do it was the perfect way to ensure the wounds went deep. But somehow he bungled the whole thing completely. He doesn't even seem to have made good use of the incredible power both the prince and the princess carry inside them." Rasad shook his head. "A fascinating phenomenon, and from what I can tell, Scanlon made no real attempt to study it."

"I thought you didn't know or care what Scanlon's plans were," said Lucy bitingly. It wasn't a surprise to discover that Rasad had lied to her, of course. She spoke mainly to cover her alarm that Rasad knew about Eamon and Jocelyn's magic.

Rasad just gave her an amused smile, clearly not perturbed

at being called out. "Fortunately Prince Eamon's presence here in Thorania has provided a perfectly acceptable alternative for how to weaken Kyona," he continued, as if she hadn't spoken.

He shook his head. "But Princess Jocelyn's situation is more complicated. It is probably Scanlon's greatest failure. Well," he amended, "as far as my own plans are concerned. Your fool of an uncle would probably care more about his failure to eliminate your family and punish the kingdom. But he was as petty and short sighted as my own ancestors."

"I don't understand," said Lucy stiffly, resenting the fact that Rasad had her hanging off his every word, as he clearly intended. "What does Jocelyn have to do with your plans?"

"Nothing at all, prior to the invitation she received to visit Valoria with a view to marrying their crown prince," said Rasad fairly. He sighed. "Perhaps I should share some small part of the blame after all. When news reached me of that arrangement, I pushed Scanlon to act before he was fully ready. The last thing I wanted was an alliance between Kyona and Valoria."

He frowned. "But not only did Kyona remain as strong as it was before—which isn't saying much—Princess Jocelyn ended up making a marriage of alliance after all." Rasad tilted his head to the side, his expression confused. "Even if she wasn't considered worthy of the heir. I did hope at first that passing her off to the younger prince might indicate that Valoria's interest in an alliance was only half hearted. But," he sighed again, "from what I can find out, that doesn't seem to be the case."

"Of course it's not the case," said Lucy, offended on behalf of both her friend and her kingdom. "Jocelyn is more than worthy of Valoria's crown prince. But she didn't want him. She married Kincaid instead because they fell in love." She narrowed her eyes. "Something I wouldn't expect you to understand."

"I don't understand it," Rasad admitted readily. "I see nothing logical or admirable in letting emotion interfere with one's best interests. But it's no concern of mine, after all. In fact, I should be grateful. If Princess Jocelyn had married the heir, she and her husband would likely have been too important to be sent on this trip."

His lip curled slightly. Lucy suspected that his overdeveloped pride in his kingdom had made him resent that Valoria had sent its younger prince rather than its heir. A moment later, Rasad met Lucy's eyes, his expression smoothing out again.

"So here I am, through no fault of my own, needing to find a way not only to remove Princess Jocelyn to destroy Kyona's succession, but to do it in a way that breaks the unfortunate alliance that her marriage represents." He smiled. "For a lesser man, that might have proven difficult."

"If you think you can come between Jocelyn and Kincaid, you're mad," said Lucy automatically. "It will never work."

"Won't it?" Rasad smiled infuriatingly.

"No, it won't," said Lucy firmly. "And the alliance is secure."

"Oh, Luciana." Rasad's chuckle made Lucy long to have her blade in her hand. "Your innocence is so refreshing. You clearly haven't spent enough time in court if you think anything is secure. A humiliating betrayal on the part of the Valorian prince's new bride should be enough to make Valoria think twice about whether it's really obligated to risk its own borders to race to Kyona's assistance."

"Jocelyn would never betray Kincaid," said Lucy. "No matter what magic you threw at her."

"Ah, but wouldn't you have said the same about your own dear prince before Scanlon got to him?"

Lucy opened her mouth furiously, but no words came to her. She felt a cold rush pass over her in spite of the noonday sun. Once again Rasad was right, and once again the despicable man knew it. And, to make Lucy feel even more wretched, once again he was forcing her to admit to herself that she had always known that Eamon's actions weren't entirely his own. He would never have turned on the freedmen without magical interference.

"Eamon didn't betray me personally," she said quietly. "At least, he didn't mean to. Scanlon's...unnatural influence may have confused him about what was really best, but it's not the same. There's no magic that can make Jocelyn forget she's in love with Kincaid and think she's in love with someone else."

"Isn't there?" Rasad pressed, smoothing one hand along the satchel he had kept on his person since they left the Bastion. She knew the fake letter was in there, and she had looked in vain for an opportunity to get her hands on it ever since they started their journey.

Lucy tried to hide her alarm, but all she could see was the dancing light of the crystals in Rasad's study, and the curious powders next to the bowl of dragon scales. Who knew what power Rasad had harnessed in his experiments?

"Even if you could manipulate her emotions," she said evenly, "she won't act on them. You underestimate her."

"I very much hope you're wrong, my dear," said Rasad. "I think you underestimate the power of dragon magic. With the right technique, my artifacts can do astonishing things." That light of excitement came into his eyes as he continued. "Powdered dragon scales, when combined with the venom of a particular type of toad from our western jungles can make the weak minded extremely susceptible to suggestion. Scales from the jaw of a dragon, when mixed with certain minerals from our own Jeweled Peaks, can create dragon fire, would you believe! Incredibly destructive."

"Wait," said Lucy slowly, something flickering in her memory. "Dragon fire?"

But Rasad was no longer paying attention to his listener. "Slow acting potions, with no antidote. There are many, less complicated means of creating poisons, of course, but this one is completely undetectable."

Lucy's eyes grew wide. "King Rupert's illness," she whispered. "The dowager queen said it was sudden. You didn't just take the opportunity to attack King Giles at his coronation. You created the opportunity by assassinating the previous king."

"Imagine the blow to Balenol," said Rasad enthusiastically. "Losing two strong kings in a row to illness and accident, leaving only a child to lead."

"But King Giles's death wouldn't have looked like an accident," Lucy started, then broke off as the pieces came together. "Dragon fire," she breathed. "The flame I saw—the impossible flame that somehow made stone crumble. The balcony collapse was you as well."

"For what it's worth," said Rasad conversationally, "I didn't bear you any ill will for ruining that plan, even though it cost me valuable resources. I was frustrated at first, I'll admit. But I had come prepared for contingencies, and I quickly realized that it would suit my plans even better to have the visiting Kyonans be behind King Giles's death."

"You're a monster," whispered Lucy.

Rasad looked her over coldly. "The insult of an inferior mind, unable to accept that it has been bested. I'm disappointed, Luciana. I really thought you were capable of sharing my vision."

Lucy turned her face away, unmoved by the insult. "You were wrong."

"Evidently," said Rasad disapprovingly, spurring his horse forward.

Lucy closed her eyes, longing desperately for the oblivion of sleep. But there was no relief, either from the beating sun, or the constant images flashing through her mind—Cody falling endlessly, Eamon tricked and surrounded, Jocelyn bewitched into betraying Kincaid, Matheus discarded as soon as he was no longer useful to Rasad, King Giles murdered in his sleep, or while he ate, or as he walked in the castle gardens...

She drew a shuddering breath. She had been plagued by dreams both bitter and sweet for months now, but this was much worse than any of them. There was no escape from this nightmare.

Matheus stirred, and Lucy forced her roiling emotions down. It was easier to be strong for her brother than for herself. As the hours dragged on, Rasad entered her line of sight only occasionally. But even so, she could see the change in his demeanor as they drew closer to Thirl. His casual cheerfulness had enraged her before, but the serious focus now descending on him was more alarming.

Rasad might have claimed to be no soldier, but he was undoubtedly preparing for war.

THE SUN HAD long set by the time they reached the outskirts of Thirl. The Jeweled Peaks lay dark and solid behind them, no longer taunting Lucy with their beauty as they had all afternoon.

The group came to a stop before they were in hailing distance of the military encampment. Under cover of the darkness, Lucy and Matheus were pulled unceremoniously from the back of the cart and dumped into a small tent.

"We'll have to part ways here, at least for a short while," said Rasad pleasantly, joining them in the tent. His eyes lingered on their bindings. "If I took you into the palace with me, your presence would raise all kinds of inconvenient questions. I'm sure you understand."

He nodded to one of his henchmen, who began tying gags around the captives' mouths. "I would leave you in the encampment, but I wouldn't want to disrupt the soldiers. Tomorrow is going to be a big day for them, and they need their rest." His gaze rested on Lucy. "As do you, actually. You have a dawn meeting out toward the peaks, after all. I suggest you get some beauty sleep—you wouldn't want to look haggard for your prince, when he's going to such effort to meet you. Do give him my regards. And I'll check on the princess for you, shall I?"

Lucy glared at the advisor as she struggled furiously against her bonds. They were as unyielding as ever.

Rasad ignored her efforts, turning to the guards who had stationed themselves at the tent's only entrance.

"Our herald has gone on ahead to Nohl, and I anticipate that King Abner will give the order for the army to march by noon. Take these two to the meeting point. Keep them out of sight, but somewhere they can witness your work." He glanced carelessly back at the siblings. "I think it will do them both good to see that I mean what I say. But once you've disposed of the prince, follow me to Nohl, and bring them with you. I anticipate a number of possible uses for them there."

The guards gave curt nods, and without a backward glance, Rasad exited the tent.

It had been hours since the prisoners had been fed, and Lucy's stomach gave an audible rumble. One of the guards glanced back at her, smirking. She returned his look with a glare, trying to conceal the tremors running over her. It was terrifying to see how far advanced Rasad's plans were. They were on the edge of disaster, moments from plunging off the cliff, and she still had no way of saving Eamon or warning King Giles. Let alone helping to extricate Jocelyn from whatever mess she was embroiled in.

She fretted the hours away, unable to sleep, even once Matheus fell into an uneasy doze beside her. Every now and then, the fear would overwhelm her, and tears would fill her eyes. But she refused to let them fall—this was no time to indulge in grief. She knew she should be forming some kind of plan, but she had no ideas, and all she could think of was Eamon. Had he received her false note yet? Had he left for the meeting point? He would have to give the rest of the group the slip in order to obey her supposed request, because Lord Rodanthe would never let him leave unaccompanied. That was probably why Rasad had chosen such an early hour, to improve Eamon's chances of slipping away in the darkness.

And what must Eamon be thinking of such a request? If only he was as petty as she had been—if only he would ignore her invitation, just to punish her for how cold she had been toward him.

But she knew he was incapable of such vindictiveness. As far as he was aware, she was asking for his help, and his chivalry as much as his heart would drive him to come to her aid.

It was still a few hours before dawn when the guards entered the tent and hauled their prisoners to their feet. They couldn't walk with their legs still bound, and had to be carried back to the cart. Lucy rotated her wrists as much as she could, ignoring the way the ropes chafed on her raw skin, trying to wriggle her fingers to retain some feeling. Her whole hands had started to feel alarmingly numb.

She had hoped someone from the military encampment might see their plight and come to investigate, but the cart gave the tent city a wide berth as it trundled back toward the east, in the direction of the Jeweled Peaks. Two mounted guards led the procession, guiding their horses at a walk so as to allow the rest of the party to keep up. With a sinking heart, Lucy counted another ten guards, armed and alert, walking behind the cart. Eamon had no hope against such a number, not alone. The journey felt endless, but Lucy wished it would last forever rather than bring them to the destination Rasad had planned for them.

The first hints of dawn had begun to lighten the eastern sky when the cart started to climb up a slope, and Lucy realized that they were in the foothills of the colorful mountain range. It was still too dim to make out the mesmerizing colors in the sand, but she had no heart for beauty anyway.

The two were pulled from the cart and dragged the rest of the way up a short incline. A thickset guard tied them to a large boulder, close enough to the edge of the hill to see a broad plateau below them.

"Pay attention now," he said quietly, twisted humor in his voice.

Lucy ignored him. She had no indignation to spare on this pawn. She knew who her real enemy was, and she felt a surge of vicious satisfaction that Rasad had ordered for her to rejoin him. She would make him pay, whatever it took.

A moment later all thought of Rasad fled as a lone figure rode into view from the direction of the capital. Lucy's horror at the sight of Eamon, alone and vulnerable, quickly eclipsed the illogical rush of joy she had felt at the appearance of his familiar form. She and Matheus both struggled, trying to shout a warning through their gags, but all it earned them was a sharp blow to the head from the guards on either side of them. The rider didn't even glance up. He was looking carefully around the area, clearly expecting Lucy to appear.

Lucy's head spun, both from the blow and from the nightmare of it all. A guard stayed on each side of the captives, but the rest melted away into the sandy hills, drawing their weapons silently as they went. Lucy's fear and anger became a silent scream inside her head, but she was powerless to stop the trap from being laid.

"Lucy?"

Eamon's clear voice made her strain forward even harder, the familiar sound quiet, but nevertheless carrying across the still dawn. The prince hesitated, resting his hand on the hilt of his sword as the silence stretched out. Lucy was glad to see he was on his guard, but she knew it would make little difference.

She watched in horror as the two mounted guards suddenly burst from behind a mound of sand, rushing on the prince. Eamon's sword was in his hand before she could blink, his steel meeting the weapon of the first attacker in a practiced parry. For a moment she thought he would hold them off, but the horse of the second guard suddenly reared. Eamon's horse screamed in alarm, rearing as well as it tried to avoid the flailing hooves. Eamon held on skillfully, but in his distraction, he missed the menacing figures creeping toward him on foot. A moment later, two of the guards had seized his legs and hauled him from the saddle.

CHAPTER THIRTY-THREE

For one heart stopping second, Lucy thought it was all over, but miraculously Eamon recovered himself. His horse had shied away, and he had no hope of remounting, but he managed to make it to his feet, his sword in front of him, before any of the guards could take him down.

Even in the midst of her anguish, Lucy felt a fierce stab of pride at the sight of her childhood friend, standing tall and strong, bravely facing down an unbeatable enemy without a tremor. When had the boy she had played with become this capable, powerful man? He looked every inch the unbeatable prince that Sonia and Vanessa had fawned over before his departure from Kyona.

But Lucy's pride quickly gave way to despair as Eamon's attackers closed in. She remembered the words of the admiring noble girl—that Prince Eamon could fight off anybody—but there were just too many.

At first the Thoranians approached the prince cautiously. Even from where she was tied up, Lucy could see the grim determination written in every line of Eamon's body. The attackers were clearly confident of their victory, but none of them were eager to be the ones Eamon took down before being bested himself.

One of the guards lunged forward, and Eamon parried quickly, managing to disengage his blade in time to deliver a sharp slash to the man's arm. The guard drew back, cursing, but another one instantly took his place. In spite of everything, a critical part of Lucy's mind admired Eamon's excellent form as he dueled fiercely with the guards. He had always been a good swordsman, but clearly she wasn't the only one to have trained relentlessly in the time since they had sparred together as teenagers.

One of the guards circled around behind the prince, and Lucy's cry of warning was swallowed in her gag. But Eamon had seen the man, not that it did him much good. He was already holding off two men, the clang of metal seeming deafening in the still morning air. His feet shifted in the sand as he pivoted, trying to keep both attacking groups in sight. The Thoranians were probably used to fighting in this terrain, but the unsteady ground seemed to slow Eamon's movements, putting him at an even greater disadvantage.

Lucy was so intent on the battle below, she was taken completely by surprise at the quickly stifled cry of the guard beside her. She turned her head to see him crumple to the ground. For a moment she stared in bewilderment, struggling to make sense of the arrow protruding from his chest.

Then the clang of steel drew her eyes to the other guard. Lucy watched in amazement as the man, wielding his sword frantically, failed to defend himself against his opponent. He fell, and Lucy found herself blinking into the calm face of Lady Yasmin.

Without a word, the older woman strode forward and ripped the gags from their faces.

"Eamon's in trouble down there!" Lucy gasped the moment

her mouth was free. She jerked her head toward the plateau as Lady Yasmin efficiently cut the bindings from her bruised and chafed wrists. "He needs help!"

"I know," said the Thoranian grimly. "Why do you think I'm freeing your hands?" Within moments, she had both Kyonans free. They staggered to their feet, stumbling against each other as their aching limbs protested.

Matheus took only a moment to roll his wrists, wincing, before seizing the sword from one of the downed guards. Lucy reached for the other man's weapon, but Lady Yasmin stopped her with a hand on her arm.

"Take this," she said, thrusting her curved blade into Lucy's hand and seizing the guard's larger weapon instead.

Lucy didn't pause to thank her rescuer, or ask any questions. She rushed forward, hoping desperately that he hadn't succumbed to his attackers during her distraction. Her feet slipped in the sand as she slid down the incline toward Eamon.

When she made it to level ground, she saw with confusion that he was no longer standing alone. He was back to back with another fighter, and her mouth dropped open in astonishment. Matheus's sharp gasp told her that he had also seen, but she gripped his arm to stop him from calling out. They were still heavily outnumbered, and any element of surprise they could retain would help.

Even as she watched, though, one of the attackers went down to a lightning-quick thrust from Cody's blade, and another to a skillful attack of Eamon's. The two men fighting in tandem were a sight to behold, equally matched in skill and determination, their feet scuffling in the sand and their arms flashing out and back as their blades danced around those of their opponents.

But there was no time to admire their fighting. Brandishing her own weapon, Lucy threw herself into the fight, slashing at the nearest attacker from behind before he realized she was there. The man went down without even a yell, but his closest companion raised a shout, and everyone's attention turned to the latest additions to the fight.

Lucy locked eyes with Eamon for the briefest moment, a multitude of emotions flashing across his face. Then her focus was claimed by one of Rasad's guards, who advanced on her with deadly purpose. She raised her weapon to meet his with a metallic clash, forgetting all else in the grip of the fight. She pushed forward relentlessly, seeing with satisfaction the moment when the man changed from attack to defense, shock in his eyes to discover such a fierce opponent in the slim girl.

She was no longer distracted by fear for Eamon, even though he and Cody were each fighting two challengers at once. She did know a moment of concern for her fifteen-year-old brother—she could feel him fighting furiously beside her—but she forced herself to keep her attention on her own fight. There were only seven guards to their five defenders now, and the arrival of the unexpected reinforcements had turned the tide unmistakably.

Still, the outcome wasn't sure. Sweat rolled down her face as the sun's rays began to reach them over the top of the hills. The sand sparkled in the growing light, the colorful sediment that flew in puffs from beneath their feet creating a beautiful display that was wasted on the fighters, each battling for his or her life.

Lucy didn't relish the idea of being once again forced to choose between killing, or letting someone she loved die. But she knew their only hope of not just surviving, but averting the coming disaster, was if none of Rasad's guards escaped alive to warn their master of the failure of his plan. So she fought with an extra edge of desperation, letting her training take over in the familiar rhythm of deflect and attack.

Then, suddenly, a cry of pain from her brother ripped her thoughts away from her own duel. He was still standing, but he was now bleeding heavily from one arm. Lucy lunged sideways, throwing herself and her blade in between him and the guard who was clearly ready to press his advantage. Fear threatened to bloom inside her, but she forced it back ruthlessly, knowing she needed every bit of energy and focus to hold off the two guards now facing her.

Her breath was coming in gasps—the light, curved blade moving more quickly than she could have achieved with a normal sword. She was just wondering how long she could hold out, when Lady Yasmin suddenly appeared beside her, clearly having felled her own opponent. Lucy didn't allow herself the indulgence of relief as she shifted position to better synchronize her defense with the Thoranian noblewoman.

The two guards paused, drawing back. After eyeing the two determined women and exchanging a glance, they suddenly pulled away, turning in unison to join the attack on Eamon. Apparently they had remembered their original mission.

Lucy drew in a sharp breath as she realized Eamon and Cody had become separated in the fighting, and the Kyonan prince was now standing alone, facing off two guards. Even as she watched, he executed a flawless lunge, bringing one of them down. But the prince had no opportunity to celebrate his victory, as the two new attackers instantly appeared to take the place of their fallen comrade.

A quick glance showed that while Cody had also managed to take out one of his opponents, the other was fighting ferociously. The older Kyonan was hard pressed to hold him off, and would not be racing to the prince's rescue any time soon.

Lucy took a step forward before remembering her brother. She turned quickly toward him, but Matheus waved her off with his good arm. His face was pale, but his voice was strong as he prompted her.

"I'm fine—help Eamon!"

Lucy needed no further encouragement. With Cody's opponent fully occupied, and the remaining three determined to eliminate Eamon, there were no further threats to her brother.

She could see Eamon's exhaustion as she ran toward the fight. As much as she told herself to stay focused, she still stumbled slightly as she saw Eamon finally take a hit, one of his opponent's blades breaking through his defenses. The prince raised his sword desperately, deflecting the blow aimed for his heart so it instead pierced his shoulder. But Lucy felt no relief, just an overpowering surge of fear and anger.

She threw herself into the group, Lady Yasmin close behind her. For a moment even Lucy was startled by the ferocity of the battle cry that burst from her as she fell upon the guard who had succeeded in injuring Eamon. She was dimly aware of Cody running to join them, having bested his opponent at last, and of Lady Yasmin's blade dancing dangerously beside her as she forced one of the guards to turn his attention away from the prince.

None of that mattered. All that mattered was reaching Eamon. The guard fell back before Lucy, clearly shocked and alarmed by her unexpected skill and intensity. Lucy pursued her advantage grimly, some part of her mind recognizing from the sudden stillness around them that their duel was the only one still going. She felt Eamon's presence—as captivating and unmistakable as ever, even amidst the chaos of battle—as he appeared alongside her. All at once, the guard dropped his weapon, holding his hands up in surrender.

For the briefest second Lucy battled with her frustration. She could still see the man's blade plunging into Eamon's shoulder, and she realized she didn't want him to ask for mercy—she wanted to finish him.

The brutality of her thoughts alarmed her, and she lowered her weapon, breathing hard as clarity returned. Of course she couldn't run a man through who had surrendered. After a moment's reflection, she raised the curved blade again, her hand steady as she held it to the man's throat. The immediate danger might be over, but fear still swirled within her at the thought of what Rasad had set in motion. She only hoped it wasn't too late as she remembered the advisor's comment that a "herald" had already left for Nohl.

"What's Rasad's plan for King Giles?" she asked without preamble.

"I don't know," the guard gulped, his hands still raised and his eyes on her sword.

"Yes you do," said Lucy, unimpressed. She lifted the blade slightly, so he had to tilt his head back. "It will have to be quick if the army marches today, but I know he wants it to look like an accident, so the Balenans won't be on their guard against attack. So what's his plan? I won't ask you again."

"His horse will throw him," the man spat, still extending his neck unnaturally to avoid her blade. "Rasad will make the creature lose its mind somehow. I don't know the details."

Lucy frowned. "That might look like an accident, but I don't see how he can guarantee it will be fatal."

The man hesitated for only a moment. "He'll lure the king out to the logging camp. Then the horse will throw him into the river."

Cody's sharp intake of breath convinced Lucy the plan must be more carefully crafted than it sounded. She lowered her blade, stepping back slightly as she looked over at her mentor with a frown.

But her question was never formed. A cry of warning from Matheus snapped her focus back to the newly released guard. He had produced a dagger from somewhere and was lunging for Eamon, clearly determined to complete his task, regardless of what followed.

Eamon hadn't even seen the movement, his eyes on Lucy, and his sword hanging loosely at his side.

Lucy didn't hesitate, propelling herself forward to intercept the attack, blade raised. The man didn't divert from his target, but he had underestimated her speed. It cost him his life, Lucy's blade felling him once and for all before his dagger so much as nicked the prince.

For a moment Lucy stared down at the man's unmoving body, her mind too full of emotions to identify any particular one. Then she looked up and straight into Eamon's eyes. The anxiety she saw there as his eyes searched her figure for signs of injury seemed to unlock her own mind, as she relived again the intense fear of thinking time after time that he was on the point of death. The blood blooming from his injured shoulder was a vivid reminder of how close she had come to losing him forever.

Her breath came in a shuddering gasp, the tears she'd been holding back starting to gather at last. His eyes locked with hers, his movements tentative as he reached a hand toward her.

"Lucy."

The one word was more than enough. Lucy threw herself onto his chest, abandoning all effort to hold in her emotions as she clung to him. His uninjured arm closed instantly around her, and he buried his face in her hair, murmuring unintelligibly into the dark, unruly tangle.

"I'm so sorry, Eamon," she sobbed, her words tumbling out in a barely coherent rush. "I thought you were going to die, and it would be my fault, and I would never get to tell you that I didn't mean any of it."

Eamon's arm tightened around her, his injury apparently no hindrance as he put his other arm around her too, locking her securely against his chest. "Lucy, none of this is your fault," he whispered, his lips so close that his breath stirred the hair falling over her ear. In spite of the fear still pumping through her, a delicious shiver went down her spine. But she shook her head against his tunic, her words coming out muffled.

"It is my fault. You don't know everything that's happened. I couldn't bear the thought that he used me to lure you into a trap. I thought you were going to die not even knowing that I never for a moment wanted to be with Rasad, or anyone but you."

Eamon's whole frame went suddenly still, his arms vise-like as they held her close.

"Lucy," he whispered, his breath warm against her ear. "Do you mean that?"

She pulled back enough to look him in the eye. "Of course I do. I've been a bigger fool than you ever were, Eamon, but I didn't really stop loving you, not even for a minute."

Eamon's eyes bored into hers, aflame with the intensity she'd only ever seen him direct toward her. Then, heedless of their audience, he pulled her against him again, lifting her feet from the sand with the strength of his embrace as he crushed his lips down onto hers.

Lucy responded immediately, extricating her arms and attempting to avoid his shoulder as she wound them up around his neck to pull herself even further into him. Her feet were inches from the ground now, their faces level as Eamon continued to hold her up. Her lips moved eagerly against his, her exhaustion forgotten as new energy coursed through her.

This was nothing like the sweet kiss he'd given her in the forest. She'd thought she loved him then, but she hadn't known him—or herself—like she did now. She'd told herself that his actions during the recent crisis had showed the true weakness of his character, but in reality, his behavior since had offered constant evidence of its strength. She couldn't help but be attracted by his confidence, but he'd proven himself capable of humility as well. And while Rasad's maneuvering had skillfully illustrated Eamon's youth and inexperience, the duplicity and ruthlessness of the older man's true self only served to highlight the honor that had always defined Eamon.

Without breaking their embrace, Lucy's hand crept from Eamon's neck around to his cheek, her fingers trailing over the roughness that told her he hadn't paused to shave before riding out to keep their dawn tryst. He had come to her aid without question, just as she had known he would.

Eamon's own arm moved in response, his grip on her loosening as he tangled one hand in her hair. This wasn't the kiss of childhood sweethearts playing at being grown up. Lucy knew down to her very bones that Eamon was the man she wanted to spend her life with, that she could trust him with her future.

But thoughts of the future made her pull back, suddenly recalled to the danger still to be overcome. Eamon let her go regretfully, his eyes holding hers for a moment longer once his arms had released her.

"Well," Matheus's voice sounded faintly nauseated, "that was hard to watch."

"It was a little," Cody agreed, his tone as unemotional as usual.

Lucy ignored them both, too overwhelmed with her relief, and fear, and joy, to have room for embarrassment. She glanced around at the grim scene, the bodies of Rasad's guards strewn across the sand, which was now sparkling in a multitude of colors under the morning sun. It was an awful sight, but there was no time to dwell on it. She looked up at Eamon.

"This isn't over. Killing you was only the beginning of Rasad's plan."

CHAPTER THIRTY-FOUR

"Yes, I gathered that," Eamon said, frowning. "You said he means to kill King Giles?"

"That's right," Lucy confirmed. "He wants to weaken Balenol ready for annexation. He poisoned King Rupert, and he was the one who bewitched your guard to attack King Giles. He was even behind the balcony collapse—it was dragon fire, that's the flame I saw before it crumbled."

"The flame?" Eamon asked, clearly struggling to put all the pieces together.

"Never mind that," said Lucy impatiently. "Just one of the many things I should have told you at the time but didn't."

"So he is using dragon magic," Lady Yasmin breathed, her eyes wide. "We'd wondered, but it seemed too far-fetched..." She narrowed her eyes. "The guard said Rasad would bewitch King Giles's horse to throw him off. Can he really do that?"

"Yes," said Cody shortly. "I can tell you from personal experience that Rasad can bewitch a horse."

"That's how you ended up riding off from the Bastion, and how your horse ran straight into the ravine!" said Lucy, suddenly understanding. She turned to the older man, her mind catching up with her words. "Cody! You're alive!"

"Noticed my presence, have you?" he asked dryly, a glint of humor in his eyes.

She gave a shaky laugh, closing the distance between them and throwing her arms around him. He gave her a perfunctory squeeze.

"I thought your horse looked half-crazed when it plunged over the edge," said Matheus. His voice was weak, reminding Lucy of his injury. She was glad to see that Lady Yasmin was binding it, her movements confident and efficient. Even as Lucy watched, the older woman cut a large wad of fabric from the tunic of one of the fallen guards, tossing it to Eamon for use on his own wound. "Why didn't you throw yourself off its back long before you reached the ravine?"

"I was tied to the saddle," said Cody curtly. "I uh...happened to be in the right place at the right time to overhear Rasad having a very informative conversation with one of his guards, and unfortunately he caught me eavesdropping. He had me tied onto a horse, did something strange to it, and sent us out the gate without further ado." His eyes narrowed. "Very apologetic about the whole thing, he was. He said something about it not being personal, but he'd known from the start I was going to be problematic and would have to be disposed of sooner or later."

"That sounds like him," said Lucy grimly. "How did you survive the fall?"

"I didn't fall," said Cody. "At least not far. It took me the whole ride to get myself free of the ropes, and it was only just in the nick of time to throw myself from the horse's back as we went over the edge. I managed to land on a ledge not far down. The poor creature wasn't so lucky."

Lucy shuddered as she pictured the huge drop of the ravine, and the raging river at its bottom.

"You're lucky to be alive," said Matheus, his voice hollow. "I hoped you'd survived somehow, but I didn't really believe it was possible until I saw you fighting beside Eamon."

"We're all lucky you're alive," said Lucy fervently. "We would have been lost without you." Her gaze encompassed Lady Yasmin as well. "Both of you."

"I'm just glad we were in time," said Lady Yasmin grimly. "We almost weren't."

"How did you know we were in trouble?" Lucy asked.

"It wasn't hard to figure out that you must be, once Cody arrived," said Lady Yasmin, and everyone turned to look at the Kyonan.

His eyes lingered on the Thoranian woman as he spoke. "After I managed to pull myself back up from the ravine, my first thought was to go straight back to the Bastion, to try to get you two out. But then I thought better of it. I knew I was on the land of Lady Yasmin's family, and she'd told me before we left Thirl that if we ran into any trouble while with Rasad, we would find help there."

Eamon turned to Lady Yasmin with a frown. "But you've been in Thirl the whole time they were away. I saw you just yesterday."

She gave a grim smile. "Yes, I have. But I sent Yosef home in disgrace after his exhibition in the markets. And I asked him to keep an ear out for trouble at Rasad's Bastion while he was there." She sent Lucy an apologetic look. "He's more capable than he seemed, you know."

Lucy just shrugged. She bore the hotheaded young nobleman no ill will for his failed attempt to abduct her.

"I told Cody that Yosef would be there," Lady Yasmin continued, "and I'm just glad he took up the offer of help."

"So am I," said Cody. "It took me hours to reach the family home on foot. It was well after dark by then, and it wasn't until the next morning Yosef was able to discover that Rasad had left suddenly for Thirl. We set off immediately, but we had to stay far enough behind you not to be seen on the road. We reached the capital some hours after you did last night."

"Where they came straight to me," Lady Yasmin took up the tale. "Of course we didn't know the specifics of what Rasad was planning, but we went straight to Prince Eamon."

Lucy glanced at Eamon, and saw that he looked startled.

"Unfortunately you'd already left," said Cody. "It's a good thing you left this behind." He pulled out a folded parchment and waved it idly in the air. "I knew at once that it was a trick of Rasad's to draw you out."

"Can we please burn that hideous letter?" shuddered Lucy. "It makes me sick to think of it."

Eamon stopped pressing the wad of material against his shoulder in order to put his good arm around her in a reassuring gesture. But his expression was confused as he looked down at her.

"So you didn't write it, then? I would have sworn it was your handwriting."

"It was my handwriting, but I didn't write it." Lucy shook her head as his bewilderment grew. "Rasad has been dabbling in all kinds of strange dragon magic, but there's no time to get into that now."

"I'm just glad it wasn't true," said Eamon darkly.

"Some of it was," admitted Lucy. "Rasad did propose to me," she scowled, "but I didn't need help from you or anyone to know what answer to give."

"I should think not," interjected Matheus with a shudder. "It was the most warped proposal in the world."

"Well," said Eamon, trying and not quite managing to speak lightly, "the fact that he proposed in front of your brother is already a failure." He locked eyes with Lucy.

She felt her cheeks heat, the tingle passing all the way to her toes at the promise in his eyes, of further, more private, conversations to come.

"But we're wasting time here," she said quickly, pulling her thoughts back to the present with an effort. She turned to Lady Yasmin, anxiety on her face. "I'm eternally grateful to you for coming to our rescue, but I'm afraid we've drawn you away from Thirl at a terrible moment. Even now Rasad is probably with King Abner, convincing him to march against Balenol immediately. You were right that the timing of the annual muster was no coincidence."

Lady Yasmin looked startled, but she shook her head firmly. "King Abner won't agree to that, there's no way. Thorania hasn't seen war for centuries, and His Majesty is very committed to keeping it that way. Rasad's influence isn't that strong."

"He's not relying on his normal influence," said Lucy impatiently. "He has crystals that come from the Dragon Realm off the coast of Valoria. They have powerful magic in them, and he's going to use one to convince King Abner to give the order to invade. This isn't opportunistic, like when he tried to use Eamon's guard to assassinate King Giles. He's been planning this for a long time, and I have no doubt all the pieces are in place."

Lady Yasmin looked horrified. "But the whole court will protest. No one wants to annex Balenol. I've never heard such a thing suggested, even when the kingdom was crippled by the exodus of the slaves."

"It won't matter who protests if the king gives the order," said Lucy. "And Balenol is just the beginning. Rasad wants to see Thorania become an empire, with mastery of the North and South Lands. He lured Eamon here, and Jocelyn and Kincaid, with the intention of weakening Kyona and Valoria in preparation."

"Now I know why he didn't care about leaving Thirl and

missing the negotiations," said Eamon furiously. "And they've been going so well. But he never intended for Thorania to honor any of the promises of peace and trade that the other advisors have been making."

"Remember he doesn't speak for the kingdom, Your Highness," said Lady Yasmin quickly. "Those promises were made in good faith."

"I'm not blaming your king for any of this," said Eamon, waving a hand impatiently. "But Lucy's right—if Rasad has harnessed dragon magic, it doesn't matter what King Abner really wants. Rasad will get his way if we don't intervene."

Lady Yasmin still looked unsure, and Lucy was glad she had such faith in her monarch. But she didn't know what they were dealing with.

"Don't underestimate what dragon magic can do to people's minds," she said seriously. "My uncle was an evil man, and he almost destroyed Kyona from within when he used dragon magic to manipulate Eamon into doing things completely against his character." She glanced up at Eamon. "Rasad was in league with Scanlon, by the way."

He'd been staring down at her, his heart in his eyes at this first admission that she believed he hadn't acted of his own free will. But surprise overtook the other emotions at her last comment.

"Never mind that," Lucy hurried on, seeing a hundred questions rising to his lips. "We need to get moving." She looked at his shoulder with concern. "Will you be all right to ride?"

"Of course I will," scoffed Eamon. "It's not as deep as it looks, and it's not my fighting arm."

"Which means it's the same arm that's already been injured," Lucy reminded him, but Eamon shrugged it off.

"I'll be fine."

Lucy frowned, not entirely satisfied, but she didn't press the point. The wound seemed to have stopped bleeding, at least. She glanced around. "Where did your horse get to?"

Eamon squinted in the morning sun, turning as he scoured the area. Following his gaze, Lucy appreciated for the first time just how beautiful their surroundings were. The red, purple, and yellow of the sandy slopes was even more breathtaking when amongst it than it had been riding along the edge of the range. It was a shame there was no time to enjoy it.

"There," said Eamon, catching sight of his mount beyond a small rise of sand. He turned back to Lucy. "You can ride double with me, it's too far to the capital for you to walk."

"I'm sure that would be very romantic," interjected Cody dryly, "but not efficient. Two of Rasad's guards were mounted. Lucy and Matheus can take their horses."

"What about you and Lady Yasmin?" Eamon asked, looking slightly put out.

"We rode here on steeds of our own, of course," answered Lady Yasmin. She glanced around the group. "Let's get going, if everyone's well enough to ride."

"I can understand you're anxious to get back to Thirl and find out what Rasad is doing," said Lucy quickly. "But I don't think I can afford to go back to the capital. It may be too late to stop King Abner from giving the order, and I need to get to Nohl, and warn King Giles about what's coming."

Lady Yasmin frowned, tapping her fingers on the hilt of her blade. "I understand," she said at last. "Your loyalty is to Balenol before Thorania."

"Yes," said Lucy softly. "I am, and always will be, Kyonan. But the Balenans are my people too. Especially the royal family."

The words felt right as they came out. She felt a belated surge of anger about the way Rasad's manipulation of her insecurities had sabotaged her attempt to connect with the kingdom that was responsible for half of who she was. She glanced at

Eamon, and saw pride in his eyes. She had almost forgotten his fears that she wanted to stay in Thorania.

"Of course," Lady Yasmin responded. "But you must realize the same isn't true for me. I would like to help King Giles if I can, but I must go to Thirl without delay, and do what I can to stop Rasad's plan at this end."

"I'll go with Lucy to Nohl," said Eamon. He met her eyes ruefully. "We all know that if I go back to Thirl, Lord Rodanthe won't let me out of his sight again. He certainly won't let me go to Nohl. And I want to see this thing through."

Cody frowned at Eamon thoughtfully, perhaps seeing the justice of Lord Rodanthe's likely objections as much as Lucy could. But Cody must have realized the futility of trying to change Eamon's mind, because he kept his peace.

"I'll go too," Matheus cut in quickly, but Lucy shook her head.

"You can't, Matheus. Your injury is worse than Eamon's. You need to have it looked at, and someone needs to warn Joss and Kincaid what's happening." She winced. "And Lord and Lady Rodanthe, I suppose."

"I'll go with you, Matheus," said Cody. Lucy raised an eyebrow, surprised he wasn't refusing to let her go without him.

He sighed in acknowledgment. "I don't like splitting up," he said. "But this is bigger than us, and your parents would understand that." His eyes rested on her face, their expression serious. "Plus I know you can take care of yourself, if you don't hold back."

"I won't," Lucy promised sincerely. The time for downplaying her capabilities for the sake of appearances was long past.

"I won't let anything happen to her," said Eamon firmly.

Cody just grunted. Lucy knew he wasn't one to be impressed by lover-like posturing. She was glad to know her mentor was putting his faith in her own skills, not in Eamon's ability to protect her.

"Bypass the city to the north," advised Lady Yasmin. "There's a ford where you can cross the river. It's your best bet if you want to get to Nohl quickly and undetected."

"How will we find the ford?" Lucy asked doubtfully.

"I'll send Yosef after you as soon as I reach Thirl," Lady Yasmin promised. "He'll show you."

"We're going to be riding hard," objected Eamon. "We can't afford to wait around for him."

Lady Yasmin smiled indulgently. "He'll catch up, don't worry." She turned to Cody. "Will you and Matheus be all right to follow at your own pace if I go ahead to Thirl?"

Cody nodded curtly, clearly seeing her impatience to reach her king. "Go."

Without another word, Lady Yasmin turned away from the group. She put her fingers in her mouth and gave a shrill whistle. It wasn't especially loud, but its melodic quaver carried across the still morning air.

For a moment after the note ended, there was silence. Then the sound of galloping hooves made them all turn their heads. A beautiful palomino stallion was thundering toward them, its coat seemingly made from the sand across which it pounded. Its focus was on Lady Yasmin, and as it approached, she strode forward, breaking into a run as the horse turned, slowing its pace but not stopping.

In front of her astonished audience, the noblewoman intercepted the horse, swinging herself onto its back in one fluid motion. The horse wore no saddle, and Lucy couldn't for the life of her figure out what Lady Yasmin had grabbed in order to hoist herself up. It had been too quick. They all stared after the pair in silence as the horse resumed its gallop within moments, the two of them disappearing rapidly westward, toward Thirl.

"Wow," breathed Matheus, after a prolonged moment.

"Yes," Cody agreed, looking almost as dazed as his young companion. "Wow."

Lucy tore her eyes from Lady Yasmin's retreating form to look at her mentor. She didn't know whether to laugh or stare at Cody's starstruck expression as he watched the noblewoman ride away.

She remembered Cody's description of the kind of woman who might make him take notice. Someone "more interested in adventure than in the cut of her dress", if she recalled correctly. She had a feeling Cody had been "caught" at last.

"Well," she said briskly, breaking the moment. "I can see why she doesn't think her brother will have any trouble catching up with us. We need to go, Eamon." The prince nodded, and she turned her attention to the other two. "Are you sure you'll be all right?"

Matheus rolled his eyes. "There's no time to waste on fussing, Lucy."

"Go straight to Jocelyn and Kincaid," she said, disregarding his words. "I don't know for sure who else we can trust. Tell them everything, and whatever you do, stay together." She frowned. "We're going to be scattered enough as it is." She met Cody's eye. "Lord Rodanthe isn't going to be happy."

"You let me worry about that," Cody said firmly. Lucy nodded gratefully, understanding his silent message that he would shield Matheus, and take whatever anger might be directed toward them for bearing their news.

Lucy drew a breath, remembering Kincaid's easy acceptance of his wife's magical power. "You never know, Joss might be able to intervene, even if no one else can. Maybe she can use her power to change King Abner's mind."

She glanced over at Eamon, and was surprised by the discomfort suddenly obvious on his face. "What is it?"

"Nothing," he said quickly. She raised an eyebrow, and he sighed. "Things have been a little...weird for Joss and Kincaid while you've been away, that's all. I just hope they won't be too distracted to do whatever needs to be done."

"Weird how?" Lucy asked ominously.

"Well..." Eamon looked more uncomfortable than ever at being asked to comment on his sister's relationship with her husband. "Maybe it's normal after the first few months of marriage, I don't know. But there's been a tension between them the last few days that I've never noticed before. I don't know what the cause of it is, but Jocelyn's been keeping to their rooms a lot, and..."

He trailed off, and Lucy pulled in a long breath. She had momentarily forgotten Rasad's veiled comments about Kyona's princess, but now a thrill of fear went through her. It sounded like Jocelyn was trying to fight whatever manipulation of her emotions Rasad was attempting, if she was hiding herself away most of the time.

But still, Eamon said there was tension. Were the advisor's plans to drive a wedge between Kincaid and Jocelyn—and by extension Valoria and Kyona—advanced enough for him to move to the next step? The one where he arranged for Jocelyn's death in order to wipe out Kyona's succession altogether?

"Jocelyn's in danger," she said suddenly. She glanced at Eamon. "And I don't think whatever tension you've witnessed is normal. Rasad's behind it."

Eamon still looked uncomfortable. "I don't think it was Rasad," he said awkwardly. "There's this man—I don't think he's a member of the court, but he seems to be wealthy, at least. He started paying her a lot of attention about a week ago, and—I'm not saying she encouraged him, exactly," he added hastily, seeing the look on Lucy's face. "But she didn't rebuff him quite as strongly as I would have expected, and—"

"Trust me, Rasad's behind it," Lucy cut him off grimly. She turned to Matheus, realizing he'd been asleep when Rasad told her about his plot against the newly married couple. As concisely as she could, she recounted the little she knew. She could feel Eamon's growing fury beside her, but she was fully focused on the problem now, no space in her mind for anger about the advisor's villainy.

"Tell Joss all of that," she finished. Matheus looked slightly ill at the suggestion that he raise the topic of Jocelyn's marriage with the princess, and Lucy's eyes flicked to Cody. He gave a curt nod, and she was satisfied. Cody wouldn't dodge the delicate conversation.

Eamon nodded too, his eyes fixed unseeingly on the sandy peaks before him. "It won't have occurred to her to look for magic," he mused. "But I have a feeling that once it's named, it will lift the veil from her eyes. She'll be much more able to fight it when she sees it for what it is."

"Let's hope so," Lucy said shortly. She gripped her brother's good arm. "Be careful, Matheus. Don't get yourself killed." She glanced up at Cody. "You either."

"Likewise," he said, with his usual lack of emotion. "If I can, I'll follow you to Nohl. It just depends what we find in Thirl."

Lucy nodded, already turning away. If only Cody was likely to be the only one chasing them toward Nohl. She would like to think Lady Yasmin would be successful in influencing her sovereign, but she had a feeling King Abner's troops would be at the border by nightfall.

CHAPTER THIRTY-FIVE

"I think I hear the river ahead."

Lucy nodded, the anxiety within her mirroring that in Eamon's voice. They had ridden hard for hours, stopping only briefly to make use of the water skins and basic rations conveniently stashed in the saddlebags of their borrowed horses.

The growing moisture in the air alerted her to their progress as much as the changing landscape. They would be at the border soon, and they still hadn't seen any sign of Lord Yosef. Lady Yasmin hadn't even attempted to describe the location of the ford to them, and they had no hope of finding it without the Thoranian nobleman's help.

"I'm trying not to think about what might have delayed him," she said grimly, her thoughts on their own people still in Thirl. But before Eamon could answer, Lucy's ears pricked up at the sound they'd been listening for. Hoof beats, approaching from the south.

"Sounds like more than one horse," said Eamon. "We should take cover, just in case."

They'd been riding through slowly thickening jungle for

some time, and they retreated hastily deeper into the trees. The foliage wasn't yet dense, like the jungle surrounding Nohl, but they still couldn't see the riders until they were almost alongside them. When they came into sight at last, Lucy started forward with a cry.

"Cody!"

The two horsemen pulled up sharply, and Lucy and Eamon urged their mounts forward.

"What are you doing here?"

"I said I would try to follow you," said Cody with a shrug.

"I didn't think you meant so soon!"

Cody exchanged a glance with his companion. "Neither did I, but when I reached Thirl to find that Yosef still hadn't left, I changed plan."

"Where's Matheus?" asked Lucy.

"With Princess Jocelyn and Prince Kincaid."

Lucy raised an eyebrow, and Cody grimaced. "They're all being more or less held captive by Lord and Lady Rodanthe. You were right that they weren't happy when they heard what was happening. I had to...be creative about getting away to join Yosef."

"What delayed you?" Eamon asked the Thoranian.

Lord Yosef grimaced. "It wasn't easy to get out of the capital and across the main highway unobserved. Not with the troops marching out."

It was exactly what she'd expected, but Lucy's heart seemed to drop into her stomach nonetheless. "So King Abner gave the order?"

The young nobleman nodded. "When we left, my sister was still determined to talk him down, but I don't think there's much hope. His mind is set. I still can hardly understand it. He's not angry, and he doesn't seem unreasonable, until you hear what he's saying. I think he genuinely believes he's making a wise decision, although his reasons make no sense. It's like he's still himself, but his opinions have been…"

"Commandeered," said Eamon grimly. He and Lucy exchanged a glance.

"We've seen it before," she said. "And no amount of reasonable argument is going to change his mind. How long until the army reaches the border?"

"They'll be there before dark," said Lord Yosef.

Lucy steeled herself, hoping desperately that the man Rasad had sent on ahead hadn't already done anything permanent.

"Then there's no time to waste."

Lucy stared up at the walls of Nohl, relief warring with exhaustion inside her. She only hoped they weren't already too late. She still wished they could have ridden through the night, but it was simply not possible in such thick jungle. It was a good thing Cody was with them, as even Lord Yosef didn't have any experience with spending a night in the open in that kind of terrain.

The few hours of uneasy sleep hadn't done much to make the day of hard travel easier, and the time had felt endless as they pushed through the jungle. They emerged back onto the main road only when they were confident they were well ahead of the scouts Rasad would surely have sent in advance of his force.

But they were here at last, and Lucy could barely restrain her impatience as the guard on duty grilled Eamon suspiciously about their unexpected return. She made no attempt to intervene, well aware that in spite of her connection to the Balenan royal family, her status in Nohl was questionable. As a foreign prince, Eamon at least had some credibility.

It probably helped that he was dressed in costly clothes that he'd only been wearing for a couple of days. Lucy was still in the training gear she'd donned when she and Matheus went to practice their archery at Rasad's Bastion, a lifetime ago.

Finally the man let them through, and they crossed the city within minutes, pushing their weary horses for one final stretch.

Lucy didn't wait for an invitation, falling from the saddle the moment they reached the castle courtyard and racing through the entryway. She ignored the scandalized looks she received as she ran toward the royal family's private wing, the others close behind her.

"Halt!"

She drew up in frustration as she was hailed by one of the guards outside the dowager queen's private suite.

"I need to see Her Majesty," Lucy demanded. "Urgently."

"That's not going to happen," the guard said flatly.

Lucy opened her mouth to argue, but she was interrupted by an astonished voice.

"Luciana?"

She turned with relief to see the dowager queen approaching down the corridor, a lady-in-waiting at her side.

"Heavens, child!" Lucy's great aunt looked from one disheveled traveler to the other, her eyes wide. "Are you all right? How did you come to be back in Nohl?"

"Aunt Mariska," said Lucy, hurrying forward. "We've come to warn King Giles of a plot against him, and there's no time to waste. Where is he?"

"A plot against my son?" the older woman repeated, a sharp edge replacing her bewilderment. "Another one?"

Lucy barely restrained a grimace at the way the dowager queen's eyes flicked to Eamon as she spoke. She had forgotten when bringing Eamon on this mission that it had been his guard who had almost taken King Giles's life last time.

"Not exactly," she said, conscious of the listening guards, and the lady-in-waiting. "It's part of the same one, and I can explain it all, but we can't afford to delay."

To her relief, her great aunt nodded briskly, gesturing for the travelers to follow her as she turned away from her rooms. She led them swiftly through the corridors, not saying a word until they reached an elaborately carved wooden door. She paused outside it, frowning at the two guards standing sentry.

"I thought he was here, meeting with some of his advisors, but there aren't enough guards." She directed her question to one of the men flanking the doorway. "Is the king still inside?"

"No, Your Majesty," said the guard, standing to attention. "King Giles left a short time ago."

Lucy's heart picked up speed, some sense warning her that the guard didn't mean King Giles was simply elsewhere in the castle.

"Where is he?" she demanded. "Did he ride out into the jungle?"

The guard gave her a disapproving look, but didn't dare ignore her question altogether, not with the dowager queen looking at him expectantly.

"I don't know where he went, Your Majesty," he said, directing his answer to the older woman. "But the advisors are still inside."

"We will ask them," said Lucy's great aunt, and the guards hastened to open the doors for her.

"I don't like this," muttered Eamon into Lucy's ear. She gave a tight nod, but didn't respond, hurrying to follow Aunt Mariska into the room.

They were greeted by the sight of half a dozen men, grouped around a polished table. They hastened to their feet at the sight of the visitors, bowing to the dowager queen.

"Your Majesty," one of them exclaimed, his eyes traveling to Eamon. "Your Highness." The man's expression turned from bewildered to scandalized as it passed to Lucy, attired in her training gear. He clearly recognized both her and Cody from their previous visit, but apparently they didn't merit a personal greeting. Lord Yosef he regarded with evident confusion before turning back to the dowager queen. "Is anything amiss, Your Majesty? Can we be of assistance?"

"My Lords." Lucy's great aunt nodded to everyone present. "We need to speak with the king urgently. Where is my son?"

"He left the castle a short time ago," said the spokesman. "He was called away by urgent business."

"What business?" Lucy demanded, exchanging a look of alarm with Eamon.

The nobleman remained silent, his expression slightly sour. Looking between him and her great niece, the dowager queen interjected impatiently.

"You can speak freely in front of our guests. Where has my son gone?"

"To the logging camp. A messenger came, reporting a disturbance."

Cody let out an audible breath. "We're too late, then," he said grimly.

But Lucy wasn't giving up so easily. "Maybe not." She turned to the local nobleman. "How long ago did he leave?" The man simply raised an eyebrow, and she made an impatient noise in her throat. "There isn't a moment to waste—King Giles's life is in danger!"

"I hardly think you're qualified to make such a judgment," said the man disdainfully, his gaze traveling up and down her person. "However much you might imagine yourself to be some kind of guard."

Eamon shook his head in disbelief. "This woman has come to you at her own peril to warn you of a plot against your king, and all you can think about is her attire?"

"I mean no offense to the customs considered acceptable in your kingdom, Your Highness," said the nobleman, in a tone that nevertheless managed to be offensive. "Of course any *credible* report of danger to our king would be taken seriously by every man in this room. In any event, His Majesty has his royal guards with him."

"I don't have the time or patience for this," interrupted the dowager queen. "I have lost my husband—I will not take any risk, however small, of also losing my son. Everyone in this room is aware that an attempt was recently made on the king's life."

"By *his* guard," cut in another nobleman, tilting his head toward Eamon. "If we seem unconcerned, Your Majesty, it's because the most likely threats to the king are currently contained within this room."

The Balenan nobleman may only have mentioned Eamon's guard, but it was clear as his eyes flicked between Lucy—daughter of the treasonous resistance leader—and Cody—potentially embittered former slave—that the prince wasn't the only one the advisors mistrusted.

Lucy tried to remind herself that after her mother's secrets, the men had some reason to treat her with suspicion. "I tell you, we're no threat to King Giles," she said earnestly. "We've come to warn him," she cast her eyes around the room, "and all of you, of an impending attack. There's a plot to assassinate King Giles, to weaken the country for invasion. Even now Thoranian troops are massing at your border, waiting only for confirmation of the king's death to march across. Someone needs to go after the king immediately, and in his absence, you need to give the order to close the city and prepare for attack."

The advisors exchanged looks of amusement, and Lucy ground her teeth in frustration. She knew she was moving much too quickly, but there wasn't time for diplomacy.

"She's telling the truth," said Eamon firmly, and the Balenans stilled, their expressions becoming more serious as they listened. "You're all in danger, and there's no time to waste."

The men exchanged uneasy glances, and Lucy felt an equal mixture of relief and irritation. Eamon's words rang with authority, and she felt the call to urgent action herself. But it was annoying that they had ignored her and listened to Eamon. Why was it so much more convincing when he said it, even to her own ears?

All of a sudden, she realized why, and she wanted to kick herself. Of course Eamon should use his power to convince them. Why hadn't she thought of it before?

"I understand that in Kyona things work differently, Your Highness," said the first nobleman, speaking more cautiously now. "But here, in order to give such drastic instructions in the king's absence, we require more substantial evidence than accusations by some girl, who in addition to having no rank or formal role in your delegation, has shown by her behavior that she is not fit to—"

"Be careful how you finish that sentence," interrupted Eamon, a dangerous edge to his voice. "If your king seeks friendly relations with Kyona, he won't thank you for damaging any chance of an alliance by speaking disrespectfully of our kingdom's future queen."

Eamon's words were met with a prolonged moment of silence as everyone, Lucy included, blinked in surprise. Lucy felt her cheeks heating, but a glance at Eamon soon brought her back to reality. He was glaring at the nobleman, distracted from the point when they had no time for distractions.

"I know our claim seems sudden and extreme," she said quickly, returning to the original topic. "But this plot has been planned for a long time. The balcony collapse, the attack by the guard—"

"The attack by a *Kyonan* guard," interrupted another advisor.

"You say your claim is extreme? It's preposterous. Balenol has been at peace with Thorania for centuries, and we have no reason to doubt King Abner. If anyone is plotting to weaken Balenol, it would be Kyona!"

"That's right," chimed in another man. "Your attempt to turn us against our neighbors is transparent and embarrassing. You really expect us to believe Thorania seeks war with us?"

"No," interjected Lord Yosef quickly, speaking up for the first time. "My Lords," he gave a quick bow, "I am Lord Yosef, of Thorania. My king does not wish for war with Balenol."

"There," said one of the local nobles, gesturing toward Lord Yosef and speaking as though he had himself made an irrefutable point. "You see?"

"But these Kyonans are telling the truth," Lord Yosef hastened to add, at a glare from Lucy. "King Abner has never had any intention of aggression toward you, but there are treasonous forces at work in Thorania. The king has been manipulated by magic."

There was another painful moment of silence after this declaration. "That's even more absurd than the girl's claim," said a new nobleman gruffly. "Talk of magic does nothing to make your tale more credible. And even if there were some kind of magic at work, it would only further implicate the Kyonans. Dragons—if such creatures do exist—belong to Kyona, do they not? Not that I believe any such talk, of course." He leveled his gaze at Eamon, a challenge in his eyes. "If there was truth to these tales that your royal house has access to dragon magic, Your Highness, would we not have seen some evidence of it in the alliance negotiations you commenced during your recent visit?"

"Quite right," approved the first nobleman curtly. "We're not interested in any trouble you may be looking to stir up." He spoke to Lucy, but his gaze passed between Eamon and Lord

Yosef, a hint of contempt in his eyes. "You may have your ways of convincing Kyona's rulers—and the younger, more foolish members of Thorania's court—of your wild claims. But you will not find us so persuadable."

Eamon stiffened, but personal insults were the least of Lucy's concerns. It was clear that even with Eamon's power in play, convincing these men would not be the work of a moment. And they simply didn't have the time.

She was surprised to hear one of these serious noblemen echo the rumor she had overheard one of the girls at the gala discussing, that Kyona, through its dragon allies, intended to offer magical protection to Balenol as a gesture of peace. It tickled something in her mind, but whatever it was, she didn't have time for that either.

She looked at Eamon, but he was still glaring at the most recent speaker. Lucy turned to Cody, knowing he wouldn't be distracted by his emotions. "We're wasting time here," she muttered. "We need to go after King Giles ourselves."

Cody gave a curt nod, not sparing another glance for the nobles as he turned from the room. Lucy and Lord Yosef followed him. It took Eamon a moment to realize they'd left, but he soon caught up with them in the corridor.

"Luciana!"

Lucy turned in surprise—she hadn't realized her great aunt had also followed them out of the room. The older woman looked between the four travelers, her expression grim.

"I don't know what to think about this talk of magic," she said frankly, her eyes resting on Lucy. "But I trust your intentions, and I don't want to take any chances, not if you think Giles is in danger."

"He is," said Lucy earnestly. "I just hope we're not already too late."

"What can I do?" asked the dowager queen, her face pale.

"We need fresh horses," interjected Cody curtly. "Immediately."

She nodded, turning away, but Lucy stopped her with a hand on her arm. "And an army really is marching for Nohl, Aunt Mariska," she said earnestly. "I don't know if it's in your power, but do whatever you can to prepare the city."

The older woman looked anxious, but she nodded again. "The horses will be brought to the castle courtyard immediately. And I'll send a page ahead of you to the river gate, to make sure they let you through."

She was as good as her word, and within minutes, the four of them were once again swinging themselves into the saddle.

"Do you think we have any hope of catching him before it's too late?" Lucy asked Cody anxiously as they urged their horses through the streets.

"Some hope," said Cody unemotionally. "They may have said he was called away urgently, but a king traveling with a squadron of his royal guard won't move as quickly as we will. It helps that we know exactly where we're going."

"Why would Rasad want the king to go to the logging camp?" Lucy asked. "Why is it so much worse for his horse to throw him there than anywhere else along the river?"

"Rapids," Cody grunted, and Lucy drew in a sharp breath, belatedly remembering some of her parents' stories.

"Could he survive them? If he's a strong swimmer?"

Cody shrugged. "No one ever has, as far as I know."

Lucy asked no more questions, setting her face southward as she steered her mount through the cobbled streets.

As quickly as they traveled, the dowager queen's page had reached the gate ahead of them, and they passed through without hindrance. Once out of the city, they gave their horses their heads, galloping along the broad road with total disregard for the protests of the various pedestrians making their way to or from Nohl's southern gate.

Cody led them along the road for some time before he drew his horse up. They were a fair way from the city now, and there wasn't much foot traffic to be seen.

"What is it?" Lucy asked urgently. "Why have we stopped?"

"I think we should cut through the jungle from here," he said, casting his eyes over the group. "Prince Eamon, Lord Yosef —which of you wants to stay with the horses?"

Lord Yosef looked taken aback, but Eamon just shot Lucy a rueful look, apparently not offended that, in Cody's eyes, the competition for least useful was between him and the Thoranian nobleman.

Of course, offended or not, he wasn't going accept Cody's assessment. "There's no way I'm staying with the horses, Cody."

"Neither am I," said Lord Yosef quickly.

Cody gave the two of them a measuring look, but Lucy jumped in. "There's no time to argue about it, Cody. We'll tie them loosely to that tree right there. If we're unable to come back for them, someone from King Giles's group will surely recognize them as royal horses and take them back to Nohl."

Cody didn't look impressed, but he didn't push the point. As she tied her horse up, Lucy heard Lord Yosef mutter to Eamon, "I don't see why no one suggested Luciana could stay behind."

Eamon's cheerful answer wasn't nearly as quiet. "I imagine Cody didn't think he could do without her. I mean, she did best you in a fight, didn't she?"

Lucy ruthlessly suppressed a smile as she turned away, pretending not to see the flush rising up Lord Yosef's neck.

She was once again glad not to be in a gown as they dove into the jungle. Cody gave no reprieve—his proficiency in the terrain apparently not dulled by the years that had passed since it had been his home—and just keeping up took all of Lucy's focus. She was still aching from her time in Rasad's cart, but she pushed herself mercilessly, knowing they couldn't afford to slow down. To be fair to Lord Yosef, the Thoranian nobleman didn't seem to struggle. He must be more experienced in the jungle than either Lucy or Eamon, after all.

Even with Cody's rapid pace, the time still felt far too long to Lucy. As the afternoon shadows lengthened, she kept picturing King Giles, sucked under the thrashing torrent of the rapids, unable to escape. War between the South Lands kingdoms would be inevitable if he died, and with how unprepared Balenol was, she had no doubt Rasad would be one step closer to his empire within a week.

And while she was alarmed by the threat that would pose to Kyona—even without Eamon removed from the picture—it was more than that. For all its past crimes, she didn't want to see Balenol fall. King Giles was a good man, as well as being her kin, and she had no doubt that under his leadership the kingdom had a real chance of coming out from under the cloud that had darkened it for so long. A people who produced her mother couldn't be all bad.

Distracted by her thoughts, Lucy barely noticed the growing sound of rushing water, or the steady rise in the ground. But suddenly, Cody came to a stop, holding up a hand in a silent command for the others to do the same. The four of them crept forward, and suddenly they were looking down from a ridge.

The thick foliage of the jungle thinned out in front of them. The trees here were younger, more sparse, and moss-covered stumps protruded here and there as testimony that the space had once been fully cleared. Even in the dim light of early evening, Lucy could clearly see the river racing past at the bottom of the slope, and squinting across it, she could make out what must be the logging camp. A series of huts was scattered throughout a large cleared area, and the river's edge was lined with piles of enormous lengths of cut timber, ready to be transported by water to the city.

"Huh." Cody's voice was dry. "I guess they don't need to fence it in, now the workers aren't prisoners."

Lucy raised a questioning eyebrow, but Cody just shrugged. She could only guess that the former slave camp looked a little different from how it was when he'd last seen it.

"Look!" Eamon's sharp voice brought Lucy's attention back to the reason they had come. Following the direction of his gaze, she saw a group of mounted men, their horses fidgeting in place in the center of the camp.

"It must be the king's guards!" she said, hurrying forward. The others followed, picking their way between saplings. They paused near the water, still partially concealed by the young trees. Lucy strained her eyes, relief coursing through her as she made out the commanding figure at the front of the group. "We're not too late!"

"We might be," Lord Yosef said uneasily. "What's his horse doing?"

Looking again, Lucy drew in a breath. The creature was stamping its feet, its movements quickly escalating beyond the normal shuffling of the other horses in the group. She cast an eye across the group of guards. Was one of them a traitor, perhaps Rasad's "herald"? She had no idea how Rasad had managed to coordinate the timing of the enchantment, but it didn't matter.

As Lucy wondered how to intervene, the horse began to rear. King Giles was clearly a good horseman, holding his seat as he tried to calm the creature. But the horse's panic was too strong. Before their horrified eyes, the pair broke from the rest of the group, the horse plunging and kicking as it lurched toward the river.

"What do we do?" Lucy cried, as the king's guards also began to shout. Some of them attempted to bring their mounts along-side their sovereign's, but the horse's flailing legs kept them out of reach. She turned to Cody and saw that he was watching the scene with slightly narrowed eyes, his expression calculating rather than alarmed.

"It's going to throw him in," he said matter-of-factly. "I don't think we can stop it."

"But—"

He pushed on, cutting off Lucy's protest. "I'm going into the river. You three stay behind the tree line, and meet me downstream."

"You can't," said Lucy sharply. "You said no one can survive the rapids."

"I won't have to," said Cody, kicking off his shoes and handing them to her. "Take these."

"But what are you going to—"

"There's no time to explain." Cody's voice was as calm as ever, but his movements were efficient. "Meet me on the other side of that rocky mound." He gestured with his head. "And stay out of sight, just in case."

Lucy had no opportunity to argue further. A collective shout from across the river drew her attention back toward the king's predicament, and with a thrill of horror she saw the moment they had been trying to prevent. King Giles's horse broke free of all attempts to restrain him, plunging wildly as it ran straight into the surging river.

CHAPTER THIRTY-SIX

Lucy heard Eamon's sharp intake of breath beside her, but her throat seemed to have closed over. She looked to Cody, and suddenly realized he was gone. Her eyes searched the water frantically, straining in the dying light. She could just make him out, striking out from the near bank, toward the center of the river, and the powerful current.

The members of the royal guard didn't seem to have noticed Cody, many of them throwing themselves from the saddle and racing toward the water's edge. But they seemed to be having as much trouble as Lucy locating the king in the torrent. She saw the horse's head emerge for a moment, its hooves still flailing, and knew a moment of pity for the poor creature. But her eyes quickly moved on, scanning the foaming mass for any sign of either King Giles or Cody.

It was useless. The light was too low now, and they were too far away. She turned to Eamon, anxiety written all over her face. After getting Cody miraculously back from the dead once, it would be all the more devastating to lose him now.

"Do you see either of them?"

Eamon shook his head, his expression tight. "No, but I think we need to trust him. Let's get downstream."

Lucy swallowed, hating being powerless but knowing that plunging into the water after her mentor would achieve nothing.

The three of them picked their way carefully through the undergrowth, keeping out of sight as Cody had instructed. Not that anyone seemed to be looking for threats on the far side of the bank. Everything was still pandemonium, the guards searching frantically for their king, and the bystanders from the logging camp milling around uselessly.

Cody's directions about where to meet had been vague, but they stopped on the other side of the mound, preparing to wait. As time passed, the light faded further, then disappeared altogether. Lucy's anxiety mounted with each passing minute, cold chills running over her in spite of the humid air.

"Hey." Eamon's soft voice made her jump. She hadn't realized he'd approached so close in the darkness, but he had to in order to be heard over the sound of the nearby rapids. He took her hand, and she returned his grip tightly, glad of the solidarity. "It's going to be all right. Cody knows what he's doing."

"But where are they?" she whispered back, her voice strained. "If they'd avoided the rapids, wouldn't they have been out of the water by now?"

"And how long do we wait?" Lord Yosef asked grimly. Lucy was surprised he'd even been able to hear their conversation over the water's roar. "If the king is dead, we need to get back to Nohl if we have any hope of preventing war."

"If the king is dead," Eamon replied heavily, "I don't think anything we do will prevent war. Besides," he glanced around, "what can we do but wait? Without Cody, I don't see us finding our way back to Nohl through the jungle."

"Maybe we can find a way across the river," said Lord Yosef doubtfully. "Then we can take the road back to the city."

Lucy glanced across the river. She could barely see in the darkness, and the rushing water made it hard to hear much either. But it seemed the commotion had died down, and most if not all of the guards seemed to have left. Perhaps they had ridden for the city to call for help, or—she suddenly realized—more likely they were searching for a body downstream from the rapids. She shuddered at the thought of not only King Giles, but Cody being found.

A soft whistle made her whip her head around, her eyes searching the darkness hopefully. She knew that call.

"Cody?"

"Yes." The familiar voice, calm as ever, had never sounded sweeter. Cody's form rose up from the riverbank, dripping and solid and alive. "We're here."

"We?" she said eagerly. "You were able to stop King Giles from being pulled into the rapids?"

"He was," came another voice, not sounding quite so calm. "For which I am eternally grateful."

"Your Majesty!" Lucy gasped, as the king appeared behind Cody, unmistakable even in the moonlight. "You're all right!" She bobbed a curtsy, but King Giles waved an impatient hand.

"Let's not worry about formalities. What in the kingdom is going on?" His eyes passed over the group, his forehead creasing in confusion as he recognized Eamon, and presumably didn't recognize Lord Yosef. He turned to Cody. "Gratitude aside, you owe me an explanation. Why did you keep me in that cave?"

"What cave?" Eamon asked, confused, but Lucy was suddenly remembering another of her parents' tales.

"There's a hidden cave behind a breakwater," she exclaimed. "If you know where to aim for, you can swim under the rock shelf and escape the current."

"That's right," said Cody. "It was used as a resistance hideout a number of times."

King Giles shook his head slowly, water dripping from his hair. "It's quite a phenomenon. I certainly had no idea of its existence." He gave Cody a rueful look. "If you'll excuse me for saying so, when you started pulling me under the water, I thought you were trying to drown me."

"I don't blame you, Your Majesty," said Cody, with a smile. "But if I'd wanted you to drown, I could have just let the rapids do their work. I hope you'll take my intervention as evidence that we really are friends to Balenol."

The king frowned, his gaze passing thoughtfully to Lucy. "I would certainly like to believe that. But if you mean me and the kingdom no harm, why did you prevent me from coming back out of the cave immediately?"

"I thought it would be best to wait until your guards had given up searching for you," said Cody cheerfully, taking his shoes from Lucy and putting them back on.

The king looked at him suspiciously. "And why would you want me not to rejoin my guards?"

Cody shrugged. "I think it will do your court a great deal of good to believe that you've died in a sudden, suspicious accident Your Majesty."

Lucy caught Cody's gaze, a confused question in her eyes. He raised his eyebrows meaningfully.

"We tried telling them directly, and it did no good whatsoever. Maybe showing them will be more effective."

For a moment Lucy blinked, then understanding hit her. "When those advisors get word that the king died in a tragic accident at the logging camp, as we predicted—"

"And when they then discover that it's not Kyona, but Thorania, who has an army conveniently ready to attack the moment the king is gone..." Eamon cut in.

Lucy nodded. "They'll see we were telling the truth. They'll have to see."

"What?" King Giles asked sharply. "Thorania? Attack? What are you talking about?"

Lucy took a step toward him. "Your Majesty, that wasn't an accident, what happened with your horse."

The king's forehead creased as he met her look. "It must have been an accident. I will admit, I've never been more astonished...that horse has been one of my favorite mounts for years, and I've never once..." He trailed off, glancing between them. "But how could it have been an intentional attack? Even if it were possible, you expect me to believe that Thorania, after centuries of peace, is suddenly seeking to attack us?"

"No, Your Majesty," jumped in Lord Yosef hastily, but Lucy forestalled him.

"Not exactly," she said, directing her words to King Giles. "Your Majesty, Cody spoke the truth when he said we're friends to your kingdom. You're my kin. And although Kyona will always be my home, I have no wish to deny the claim Balenol also has on me. I want to see your kingdom thrive. I want to save it from the disaster that's hanging over it." She took a deep breath. "I can explain everything. It's going to sound unbelievable, but I swear I will tell you only what I know to be true." She held the king's gaze steadily. "Do you trust me?"

For a long moment he stared silently back at her, his expression difficult to read. "Yes," he said at last. "I trust you."

Lucy nodded, a weight lifting from her shoulders. "Good. We have a lot to tell you. It's going to take time, and this isn't the place." She turned to Cody. "What's your plan? Where are we going?"

Cody shot her a grin. "Where else? Back to the base tree."

LUCY WOKE FEELING anything but rested. The trip through the jungle in the black of night had been tortuous and exhausting, and hadn't left nearly enough time for sleep. King Giles's astonishment at the discovery of the secret hideout located so close to his city had been entertaining to watch. But all too soon his thoughts had returned to the present matter, and Lucy had been called upon to give the promised explanation.

That had proved even more exhausting, and she still wasn't sure the king believed half of what the group had told him. She suspected that if he had been confident of finding his way, he wouldn't have gone along with their plan to keep him out of sight until the morning. But she couldn't blame him for his impatience. She felt guilty herself at the thought of what the dowager queen, and all the rest of the king's family, must be feeling.

But if they prevented a crushing invasion through the deception, it would be worth it. And it was clear that King Giles, as much as his court, needed to see for himself that Thorania was ready and waiting to attack the moment the king was gone in order to believe that the neighboring kingdom was behind the accident.

The trouble was, Lucy wasn't sure King Giles's survival would be enough. Even with their king at their head, Balenol's forces were woefully unprepared for the attack that was imminent. Lucy just wished she knew of some way to even the odds.

"You look like you slept as poorly as I did."

Lucy turned at the sound of the king's voice. She was standing just outside the entrance to the base tree, looking out at the jungle through the haze created by a light but constant drizzle of rain. She couldn't help but wonder how he managed to look so regal, even in his disheveled state.

She glanced at Eamon, deep in conversation with Cody nearby. As attuned to her as ever, he met her eyes, and a smile softened her face in spite of everything. She might have to ask King Giles for tips, now that she was going to have a place among Kyona's royals after all. Provided they survived all of this, of course.

"I slept very little, Your Majesty," she said, returning her attention to him.

"Perhaps no sleep is better than troubled sleep," he said darkly, his eyes scanning the jungle. "And my dreams were very troubled indeed."

Lucy froze, staring at him with her mouth slightly open. The king looked over and caught her expression, raising one eyebrow.

"What is it?"

"Dreams," Lucy whispered. The thought that had been tickling her mind since their confrontation with the court the day before had finally taken shape. Was it total madness to think that it might work?

King Giles frowned, looking bewildered and a little alarmed. "What?"

"Nothing." Lucy shook her head, not wanting to give him any assurances she might not be able to fulfill. She hurried over to the other Kyonans, interrupting their conversation.

"What's the plan, Cody?"

Cody frowned in the general direction of the city. "Honestly, I'm not sure. I assume Rasad's agent has brought word by now that the assassination was successful."

Eamon nodded. "If I was Rasad, I would have given the order for the army to cross the border at first light." He looked troubled. "But the court," he lowered his voice, "and the king, probably won't believe that until they see it for themselves."

"Which might not be until they're approaching the city, if Rasad has managed to incapacitate any scouts or sentries," said Lucy grimly.

Eamon nodded. "Exactly. And at that point, they might believe our story, but it won't help much. The Thoranian army will still find Balenol unprepared and ripe for annexation. We can't offer any practical help, beyond restoring the king."

"Actually," said Lucy, "I might have an idea about that."

"What?" asked Cody, frowning.

Lucy shook her head. "It might not work, but I might be able to get some...help."

Eamon looked as confused as Cody, but he didn't have the chance to ask questions. King Giles was approaching, clearly done with waiting.

"Your Majesty," Eamon greeted him with a half-bow. "I know you must be eager to get back to Nohl—"

"No." The king cut him off. "I want to see this army you claim is marching against my kingdom now that I'm supposedly dead."

Cody gave the king a considering look. "If we had mounts, we could probably reach a good vantage point to see their approach and still have time to comfortably return to the city ahead of Rasad. But not on foot."

"Somehow I doubt our horses would still be tied up where we left them," said Lucy dryly.

"For their sakes, I hope not," said Lord Yosef, appearing alongside the king.

Cody gave a light chuckle. "If I go back to Nohl, I don't think I'll have any trouble acquiring us some horses. But I might have difficulty getting five steeds out through the gate unnoticed."

"*Acquiring* horses?" King Giles repeated dryly, but Cody just grinned.

"Being good at acquiring things was a necessary part of life in the resistance."

"I'm sure," muttered the king, but he didn't press the point. "I'd better go. I can retrieve horses, and warn my general to mount what defense he can, just in case."

"Your Majesty," said Lucy, alarmed. "I know you're not

entirely convinced of all this, but if you show yourself in Nohl, Rasad *will* find out, and we'll lose any benefit we've gained by letting him think he succeeded in killing you."

King Giles frowned. "I understand that, Luciana, but I don't see how else I can check the truth of your claim for myself." He glanced at Cody. "I think you overestimate your ability to even get back into the city undetected. If I'm believed to be dead, Nohl will be on high alert. I wouldn't be surprised if the gates were closed to pedestrians."

"Oh, I won't use the gates," said Cody cheerfully. "I'll just go through the tunnel."

"There's a hidden tunnel into my city?" King Giles demanded, clearly shaken.

"Of course," said Cody. "Not far from here in fact. How do you think your cousin nipped from the Overseer's manor to this base almost every night?"

King Giles ran a hand over his face. "One of these days, Scarlett and I are going to have a conversation about all the things she neglected to mention last time she was here."

Lucy chuckled in spite of herself. "So it's decided, then. Cody will go."

King Giles didn't look entirely satisfied, but he didn't argue further. "Is there parchment down there in that base of yours? I want to write a message for you to take to my mother. She knows you came after me, and she'll believe you when you tell her I'm alive. She'll have some influence with my general. And she can certainly supply you with five horses."

Cody nodded, ducking back into the base tree to retrieve the parchment.

"She'll only need to get four horses," Lucy said to King Giles. "I'm staying behind."

"What?" Eamon protested.

"I need to explore that idea I told you about," said Lucy,

lowering her voice. "I can meet you all in the city when you come back. Aunt Mariska will look after me."

"There's no way we're leaving you alone in the jungle," said Eamon flatly. "I'll stay with you."

Lucy hesitated for only a moment before nodding. She had made the mistake of not trusting Eamon with her secrets before. She wasn't going to do it again.

As soon as King Giles had written his note, Cody led the group carefully through the trees. They were all soaked through within minutes, and the mud made progress painful, but it was still easier than the nighttime trek to get to the base tree.

It wasn't far to the entrance to the tunnel. The city walls were in sight, but still a stone's throw away when Cody bent down to clear some bracken. An opening was revealed, and King Giles peered inside in fascination.

"It looks like it's been recently disturbed," he said, sounding alarmed.

"Yes, I took Matheus through here when we were in Nohl a few weeks ago," said Cody cheerfully. "He was impressed."

Lucy thought King Giles looked torn between being impressed himself, and being irritated by the further evidence of deception on the part of his guests. All things considered, it wasn't entirely surprising he wanted to see the truth of their story about the Thoranian army with his own eyes before taking action.

Cody wasted no time in entering the tunnel, and Lord Yosef and King Giles began preparations for their trek east through the jungle toward the road, where Cody would meet them with the horses.

"Safe travels, Your Majesty," said Lucy, as the two pairs said farewell. "Don't fall afoul of anything deadly out here."

King Giles gave a rueful smile. "You know, I've never admitted it, but part of me was a little jealous of your mother, after I found out about her double life. I thought it must have been quite an adventure to be a jungle rebel." He glanced up at the canopy above, dripping constantly with rain. "The folly of youth, I suppose."

Lucy smiled. She had indulged in similar envy herself. "I don't know what's going to happen, Sire," she said. "But I swear to do all in my power to prevent the destruction Rasad is trying to bring on Balenol."

King Giles nodded curtly, his expression instantly becoming serious again at the reminder of the threat to his kingdom. He and Lord Yosef disappeared into the foliage without further conversation, and Lucy and Eamon found themselves alone.

For a moment they just stared at each other. They hadn't had a moment to stop since Lucy's declaration back at the Jeweled Peaks. There was so much between them, so much they still hadn't said, so much that would still have to wait.

"So what do we do now?" Eamon asked at last.

Lucy drew a deep breath. "Now, we hope this works." She took Eamon's hand suddenly, and although he was startled by the gesture, he returned her grip firmly. She closed her eyes, turning her face toward the sky.

"Qadir! Can you hear me?"

CHAPTER THIRTY-SEVEN

It was barely a moment of suspense. Almost as soon as the words left her mouth, Lucy's senses began to swim and spin strangely. She opened her eyes and jumped back with a gasp.

Qadir was standing in front of her, his huge form impossibly folded into the confined space of the jungle.

"You came," she gasped. She could hardly believe it had worked. And now that she had the dragon's attention, she was more nervous than ever as to the wisdom of her mad idea about what to do with it.

"You called, young Kyonan," the dragon replied expressionlessly. "I had not yet checked in on you in the short time since I told you I would keep an eye on you, but surely you didn't think I would fail to hear my own name."

"No...that is...how did you get here so quickly?"

"I am not with you in flesh. I am projecting my image into your mind, as I did at our last meeting."

"But I'm not asleep," Lucy protested.

Qadir's mouth stretched strangely in a reptilian smile. "It's true, your mind is less susceptible to manipulation when awake. But only marginally. It is no challenge for me."

Lucy turned to Eamon, and was startled by the way he was looking at her.

"What?"

"Who are you talking to?" he asked uneasily.

Lucy looked between the prince and the dragon in astonishment.

"He cannot see me," said Qadir patiently. "As I said, I am visible in your mind." He gave Eamon a considering look, and the prince suddenly gasped. "But I have no objection to including you in our communication, son of kings. We are old friends, are we not?"

Eamon, clearly able to see the dragon now, recovered himself quickly. He bowed deeply, looking every inch the prince as he addressed the creature.

"I am honored to continue the friendship of my fathers."

Qadir inclined his head in acknowledgment before turning back to Lucy. "I must assume you called me for a reason, young slayer. What was it?"

Lucy shook off any discomfort at the form of address, getting straight to the point.

"The South Lands are in trouble. Thorania is going to invade Balenol, and we need help desperately if there's any hope of preventing a takeover."

Qadir flicked his tail slightly, the movement creating no effect on the undergrowth around him. "What is your purpose in telling me such information? We do not involve ourselves in disputes between kingdoms."

Afraid he was about to disappear again, Lucy cut in quickly, trying to speak with more boldness than she felt. "But you said I had done a service to dragonkind. You said you were in my debt."

Qadir leveled a long look at her, and she gulped, wondering if she'd stepped over a line. The creature was alarmingly huge, and knowing that he was only a vision did nothing to reduce the impressiveness of his monstrous form.

"I did say that, but that does not equate to an offer for my colony to fight a war for a kingdom with which we have no connection."

"But there is a connection," Lucy interjected hastily. "Rasad, the man behind the invasion, is using dragon magic to manipulate Thorania's king, much like Scanlon manipulated Eamon."

Qadir went still, his interest clearly captured. His gaze was uncomfortably intense as he fixed his orb-like eyes on her, but Lucy met his scrutiny steadily.

"You mean to tell me this man also received forfeited dragon magic, from the same dragon who gave his power to your uncle?"

"Not exactly," Lucy clarified. "He didn't receive magic into himself, like Scanlon. But he convinced the dragon to bring him crystals from the Dragon Realm off the coast of Valoria before it passed away. And..." she swallowed, nervous about describing what she'd found in Rasad's secret dungeon, "he also convinced the dragon to go to Thorania to die. He has the creature's body still. I've seen it, at his fortress in Thorania's north."

She could feel Eamon's astonishment—she hadn't yet told him that detail—but she didn't allow herself to get distracted. "Rasad has been experimenting with the crystals, and scales and such from the dragon's body. He's been using dragon magic to control people, animals, and now whole kingdoms. He wants to create an empire that will swallow the South and North Lands."

Qadir's already enormous form had seemed to swell as she spoke, and Lucy could tell that it wasn't Rasad's political ambitions that had ignited the beast's fury. Because fury was the only way to describe the deadly glint growing in the dragon's eyes.

"You tell me this man dares to collect pieces of the Dragon Realm as though they are his possessions? He has the effrontery to use our brethren's body like his personal apothecary? He has desecrated the remains of one of our kind in order to dabble in magic he has no business even knowing about?"

Lucy flinched at the dragon's tone, but she nodded earnestly. Maybe there was hope of Qadir intervening to stop Rasad after all.

Without warning, the dragon opened his mouth wide, and spewed out a jet of startlingly orange flame. Eamon's cry of horror reached Lucy a moment before she felt his arm go protectively around her. She knew a brief second of terror, sure that Eamon would be killed as he tried to throw himself between her and the dragon fire.

But of course there was no heat, no agonizing death by burning. The flames were a vision as surely as the dragon was, the real fire being released into the air somewhere across the sea, presumably in Kyona's mountains.

Eamon drew back, his expression showing the same mixture of relief and embarrassment that Lucy felt. But Qadir didn't seem to have even noticed the reaction of the humans. His initial rage had cooled, but he was no less determined.

"We will certainly become involved," he said. "No dragon can be left to rot in the hands of a human. We will investigate, and destroy these crystals and experiments you speak of. No trace will be left."

"And..." Lucy hesitated. "What about the invasion? Can you break Rasad's hold on King Abner? Or at least, stop the army before it reaches Nohl?"

"I already told you," said Qadir patiently, "we do not involve ourselves in disputes between kingdoms." He inclined his head. "We will, of course, endeavor to be swift in destroying the human who has dared to desecrate one of our kind, and any who march with him. Whether we do so before they reach their destination I cannot say for certain."

"What?" cried Lucy, aghast. "You can't destroy the whole army! The Thoranians are innocent in this, other than the few who are knowingly working with Rasad. They're just following the order of their king, and he's not in control of his own decisions!"

Qadir gave a rippling, reptilian shrug. "That is not my affair."

"Please," Lucy said earnestly, horrified by the results of her intervention. "Please don't kill them all."

"What did you expect me to do, young human?" Qadir asked, lowering his head to look more closely at her. "You sought my intervention, but now you do not wish for it?"

"I thought you would stop the army without slaughtering them all!" said Lucy.

Qadir frowned at her. "I do not intend to take chances with the kind of evil you have described. This Rasad must be destroyed."

"I don't dispute your right to take action against Rasad for what he's done," said Lucy hastily. "But surely you don't need to kill everyone else as well!"

The dragon inclined his head. "It is the surest way to be certain he has not escaped. And did you not wish to prevent the invasion of Balenol? It seems to me that you should welcome my intended action, since it would have that effect."

Lucy put a hand to her head, her mind reeling at the unexpected direction of the conversation. Was she going to have to choose between the total annihilation of either Thorania's or Balenol's forces? Neither outcome was one she could live with.

"What if we can separate Rasad from the rest of the army?" asked Eamon quickly. "We'll draw him out somehow. We can identify him after all, and then you'd be sure you had the right person."

Qadir fixed the prince with his snake-like stare. "That is an acceptable alternative," he said calmly. "But be warned. If you do not succeed in separating this Rasad from his army, and doing so efficiently, we will destroy the entire force, to ensure the threat has been fully contained." His gaze passed between the two humans. "I take my leave of you."

Lucy opened her mouth and closed it again. If anything, they were now further from a solution, but she was afraid of the outcome if she made further requests of the dragon-ruler.

"Wait," said Eamon unexpectedly. "You spoke of the friendship that exists between my fathers and yourself, and I am honored to be included in that history. But I also have a... connection with another dragon. I believe Elddreki lives in the other Dragon Realm now, in Valoria. But am I right in assuming you can communicate with him, even from a distance?"

"You are," said Qadir, inclining his head.

Lucy looked at Eamon questioningly. She had no idea what he was getting at.

"Would...would you be willing to take a message to Elddreki on our behalf?" the prince continued. He swallowed. "I don't mean to be disrespectful with such a paltry request, but since you said you were in Lucy's debt..."

Qadir paused, his gaze passing from the prince to Lucy. "Do you wish me to render you that service?"

"Yes," said Lucy quickly. "I would be grateful if you would tell him what I've told you, about Rasad's use of dragon magic, and his plans to invade first Balenol, and then Kyona."

She'd never met the younger dragon, and she didn't know if Eamon was right that telling Elddreki would achieve anything more than telling Qadir had. But it was worth a try. Jocelyn seemed to have a deep fondness for the creature.

"And," she added hastily, chasing that thought, "please tell him that Jocelyn and Kincaid are in trouble. Rasad has used dragon magic on them in order to cause them mischief, and he intends to kill Jocelyn before this is over. They're in the Thoranian capital now, and I don't know whether or not they're safe."

Qadir gave her a long look. "It is not the custom of dragons to be messengers for humans," he said at last, and Lucy held her breath. "But," the dragon added, "I did say that I was grateful for your service. I will do as you have requested."

Lucy let out a long and grateful breath. "Thank you."

The dragon inclined his head one last time. "Do not forget what you have agreed to do," he said, the warning directed at both of them.

Forgetting for a moment that the dragon wasn't actually present, Lucy was expecting him to take flight. But instead, he simply disappeared, leaving her blinking in the drizzling rain. She turned to Eamon, to find him watching her with an inscrutable expression.

"So I take it that wasn't your first meeting with the dragon-ruler?" he said dryly.

Lucy shook out her shoulders, feeling like she was emerging from deep water. "What gave you that impression?" She sighed. "He visited me in a dream the night we were on the road, on our way from Nohl to Thirl."

"What was the service you rendered him?" Eamon asked.

"Killing my uncle," said Lucy shortly.

Again, Eamon's expression was hard to read, but he didn't pursue the point. "Well, it seems we'd better get moving," he said instead. "We can figure out how we're going to separate Rasad from the rest of the army as we go."

"I'm so sorry, Eamon," said Lucy, anguished, and he looked at her in surprise.

"Sorry? What for?"

"For making it worse!" Lucy exclaimed. "Qadir said he'd

keep an eye on me. I knew he wasn't watching closely—I mean, he would already know about the dead dragon in Rasad's dungeon if he had been—but I thought there was a chance he'd hear if I called him. I had this foolish idea that the dragons might help hold off the army. I thought that in addition to saving a lot of lives, it would convince the Balenans once and for all that Kyona is a formidable enemy and a desirable ally. But now we just have another impossible task, with the lives of two armies' worth of men in the balance."

"Hey," said Eamon, stepping forward and putting a hand on her cheek. She closed her eyes briefly, indulging for a moment in the comfort of his touch. "You didn't make it worse. The dragons might not be interested in intervening, but if they show up, I have a feeling it will stop the fighting, whether they intend that or not."

"That's small comfort," said Lucy bitterly, "if the way they stop the fighting is by killing everyone present. Which is what will happen if we can't draw Rasad out."

"We'll draw him out," said Eamon, his voice grim. "I just make no promises about leaving him for the dragons to deal with." His face lifted as he met her eyes again. "Plus, Qadir is going to tell Elddreki. He might still help us."

"Maybe," said Lucy heavily. She glanced up at the city wall, just visible through the trees and the drizzling rain. "I don't think there's much point going after the others. We won't catch up without mounts, and I for one don't need further evidence in order to be convinced that Rasad's army is already marching for Nohl."

"I guess we head into the city then," agreed Eamon, following her gaze. "I suppose we could follow the wall all the way to the gate, like the king and Lord Yosef are doing. I don't think the guards would bar our entry."

In spite of her anxiety, Lucy couldn't help but smile at the wistful note in Eamon's voice. "You're dying to try this tunnel as much as I am, aren't you?" she accused, and Eamon grinned.

"It's a secret rebel tunnel into the city, that not even the king knew about!" He gave her a provocative look. "It would be a shame for Matheus to be the only one who got to actually go through it."

Lucy shook her head, still smiling. "You don't have to convince me, Eamon. I'm not at all sure the guards would let us through without argument anyway."

That was enough for the prince, and in moments the two of them were crawling into the fissure. Lucy let Eamon go first, doing her best to cover the opening again behind her, in case of unfriendly eyes. The tunnel was small, and crisscrossed with spiderwebs, despite Cody's recent passage. They had to crawl on their hands and knees, and for perhaps the hundredth time, Lucy was grateful she was wearing her training gear, not an impractical gown. She followed Eamon closely enough to keep his mud-encrusted boots in sight, but it wasn't long before even the dim light from the opening behind them faded away, leaving them in blackness.

The steady scuffling sound from in front of her told her that Eamon was still moving, but otherwise there was nothing to tell either eyes or ears what was coming. At first the ground sloped down fairly steeply, the air feeling close and even more moist in the enclosed tunnel, but then it leveled out. After what felt like an eternity of blindness, Eamon's shuffling stopped.

"What is it?" she asked, annoyed by how breathless her voice came out.

Eamon's words were muffled. "The tunnel just stops. There's wall on all sides."

Some part of Lucy's mind wanted to panic at the thought of being stuck in the confined space, but she mastered the instinctive response quickly. "Try upward."

Eamon shifted around, then she heard him grunt. A moment later, there was a grating sound, and a thin shaft of sunlight penetrated the blackness around them. She shuffled forward, squeezing up next to Eamon to help him push the stone slab to one side. It was heavy, and she was impressed Cody had managed to move it alone. After much pushing and the dull scrape of rock sliding across dirt, an opening was revealed. Lucy lowered her gaze from the hole above her to the prince beside her.

"I guess we made it into the city."

Eamon didn't answer, and Lucy's grin faded into something else. Her breath was suddenly more constricted, and it wasn't because of the confined air of the tunnel. In order to help with the slab, it had been necessary to press herself right up against Eamon in the small space. She hadn't thought about it while moving the covering, but suddenly his proximity was all she could think about.

"Lucy." Eamon's voice was unusually husky.

"Yes?" She was embarrassingly breathless again.

"We should probably climb out."

"Yes," Lucy repeated quickly, giving her head a little shake before scrambling up through the hole. Eamon followed swiftly, looking as dazed as she felt. But he was right that it was no time for such distractions.

Looking around, Lucy saw that they had emerged into a dilapidated old building. It was clearly unoccupied, and had been for some time, judging by the thick layer of dust and the broken items of furniture strewn around. Her eyes were drawn to the clear trail through the dust left by the last person to use this passage.

"Do you think Cody is gone from the city by now?" Eamon asked, following her gaze.

"Probably," said Lucy. "He won't have wasted any time."

"So what do we do now?"

Lucy sighed, looking up at Eamon. "It's too late to stop Rasad from marching with the army. We'll have to try to separate Rasad from the rest of the force once they get close to Nohl. Until then, what else can we do but wait?" Her voice turned grim. "And hope Qadir doesn't reach them before they're within our reach."

CHAPTER THIRTY-EIGHT

The hours felt interminable, but Lucy did her best not to show her restlessness. At first she wanted to try to sneak into the castle, to find Aunt Mariska and see what, if anything, had been done to prepare the city for attack.

But it didn't take much discussion to realize that after their bold declaration of a plot against King Giles the day before, followed by their disappearance and the king's tragic accident, their arrival might be greeted with suspicion. And the combination of Lucy's scandalous attire and Eamon's Kyonan features made it unlikely they could pass through the city unnoticed.

So they waited.

They talked in circles, speculating about how long it would take Qadir to pass on the message to Elddreki, and what the younger dragon would do in response. They debated endlessly about how they might draw Rasad out, knowing they couldn't make plans until they saw what they were facing, hoping they wouldn't be too late to prevent the slaughter of all the Thoranian troops.

Eventually there was nothing more to be said about the looming crisis, and they subsided into silence for several long minutes. But there were too many things Lucy still needed to say, and it was too good an opportunity.

"I'm sorry about the letter, Eamon. You must have been... horrified when you read it."

"I was," said Eamon candidly. "But you know," his voice turned pensive, "a tiny part of me was actually relieved."

Lucy looked at him, startled. "You were relieved I was supposedly considering marrying Rasad?"

"No," said Eamon quickly. "Of course not." He shuddered. "But it made me realize...I'd been trying for months to please you, to figure out how to get you to forgive me. And when I read that letter, when I thought you were so far from where we used to be that you were genuinely considering marrying another man, a near stranger more than a decade older than you..."

He shrugged. "I realized no amount of apologizing and saying what I thought you wanted to hear was going to bring you back to me. It was strangely relieving. Don't get me wrong," he added hastily, "I wasn't about to give up on winning you back. Quite apart from my own feelings, I knew you'd regret it if you married Rasad, even before knowing what he was plotting. It seemed like for some reason you couldn't see that, and I could. I was done doubting myself, and I was determined to convince you not to do it. I rode out that morning intending to say what I really thought, no matter how angry it made you. But," he flashed her the smile that had always made her heart flutter, "it turned out you didn't really need convincing."

"Of course I didn't," said Lucy, not displeased by the return of Eamon's usual self-assurance. "I was dazzled by Rasad's atten-tion, I can't deny it. But I still knew better than to trust him blindly. I accepted his invitation mainly to see what I could find out, at Lady Yasmin's request." She grimaced. "I was just too proud and too stubborn to tell you that. I'm ashamed to admit I was still punishing you, and I can't tell you how I regret it. If I hadn't let you think Rasad was sweeping me off my feet, it wouldn't have been so easy for him to lure you into his trap."

Eamon shrugged, a small smile on his face. "No harm done."

Lucy's eyes were drawn to the wound still visible on his shoulder, but she didn't correct him. There was something else on her mind. "When you say you were determined to convince me," she said slowly. "Do you mean...were you planning to use your power to persuade me not to marry Rasad?"

"What?" Eamon had gone still, his tone difficult to read.

Lucy kept her gaze on his shoulder, not quite able to meet his eyes as she continued. "Obviously it's not news to me that you've been trying to win me over for months. I've wondered, a lot of times, why you didn't...I mean, you could have convinced me that you were telling the truth, persuaded me to forgive you and trust you again whether or not I wanted to, couldn't you? From what Jocelyn's told me, all it would take would be a few well-chosen—"

"Lucy." The sharpness of Eamon's voice startled her as much as his sudden movement in grasping one of her hands between both his own. His larger fingers encased hers completely, the hold firm and warm. "I would never have done that, not ever. I would lose you forever before I abused your trust in such a way."

The earnestness in his voice compelled her to look up, and his eyes searched hers seriously. "I know you're not comfortable with my power. And I wish you didn't dislike it so much, because I think it's a gift. But it's also a huge responsibility. Jocelyn's right—with a well-placed word I can have an enormous impact. Do you think I take that lightly? Do you think I use it on a whim, whenever I feel like it? Using my power to convince King Giles I was telling the truth when I said Kyona wasn't behind the attack on him, or trying to persuade the nobles that Thorania's army is on the way...that I would do again in a heartbeat. But using magic to tamper with your emotions and opinions on something as deep and personal and crucial as matters of the heart? Lucy..." he squeezed her hand, his expression pained, "I would prefer never to use my power again."

There was no doubting the genuineness of his words, and Lucy felt tears starting to her eyes.

"What is it?" Eamon asked anxiously. "I swear I'm telling the truth."

She shook her head, smiling a little weakly. "I know you are. Believe me, I know. Because I know you. I've been so sour about everything, telling myself that I didn't know who to trust anymore. As if what happened on that one awful day at Raldon could erase seventeen years of friendship. I know you as well as I know anyone, and I know I can trust you. I'm ashamed of what a fool I've been."

"So you really can forgive me?" Eamon asked, a shadow of the old anguish in his eyes.

"Of course I can," said Lucy. "I should have forgiven you the first time you asked, like everyone else did. I'm the one who should be asking for forgiveness. Scanlon used magic to manipulate your mind—you weren't even fully in control of yourself. Rasad never used magic on me, and I still let myself be manipulated. He almost succeeded in using me as a pawn in his plan to kill you and invade three kingdoms."

Eamon looked like he was about to argue the point of who was more to blame, but Lucy wasn't interested in more words. She leaned toward him, and she could see from the sudden glint in his eye that he was more than ready to abandon conversation.

But before he could do more than raise his hand to her cheek, they were startled by a shuffling sound coming from the direction of the tunnel. Lucy hurried over to the hole, which they had left exposed, in time to see Cody's familiar head emerge.

"Oh good," he said approvingly. "You two are here. We won't have to waste time hunting you down."

"What did you find?" Lucy demanded, as the older Kyonan climbed out of the hole much more gracefully than she'd done. "What's happening?"

"What's happening," King Giles emerged right behind Cody, his voice grim, "is that there's an army a few bare hours' march from my city, and not a single scout seems to have reported that fact to anyone in Nohl."

"Well, we did tell you," said Eamon.

Lucy shot him a quelling look, suspecting he was more annoyed by the timing of the interruption than by the king's lack of trust in their report. She turned her attention back to the new arrivals, as Lord Yosef climbed out of the hole as well.

"Did you explore your idea, whatever it was?" Cody asked Lucy.

She exchanged a glance with Eamon. "Ye-es. But we still don't really know if it will help." *Or lead to even more mass slaughter.* She didn't add the last thought aloud.

"Lord Yosef," said King Giles, his thoughts clearly not on their conversation. "Can I borrow your traveling cloak?"

"Of course, Your Majesty," said the nobleman, surprised. He pulled off the expensive garment, and within moments King Giles was drawing the hood over his distinctive head.

"It's time for me to resume control of my city," the sovereign said grimly. "But I'm not sure I want everyone to know I'm alive just yet. If this Rasad has managed to prevent word of his army's approach from spreading through any of the normal channels, he clearly has people inside." He scowled. "I just wish I knew how deep inside."

"I don't think we'll be much help to you at the castle," said Cody. "We'll head for the southern gate, do what we can to secure it."

"Yes," King Giles agreed distractedly. "That's certainly where the army will attack. I'll send someone to reinforce your efforts as soon as I can." His expression was still very dark. "Someone I trust."

"I think perhaps I should go with you, Your Majesty," said Eamon unexpectedly. "It's a...a virtue of my bloodline that I can sense magic, to an extent. When my guard attacked you, I felt a surge of power a moment before he acted, for example. I might be able to help identify whether any of your advisors or military commanders have been influenced by Rasad's magic."

King Giles regarded the prince in silence for a moment. "It seems I still have much to learn about Kyona," he said at last. "I would be grateful for your help."

He spoke mildly, but Lucy could see the surprise, almost discomfort, in his eyes at this discovery of Eamon's innate ability. She smiled grimly. She could only imagine the king's reaction if he knew the full extent of Eamon's magic.

"Good," said Cody curtly, his gaze passing over Lucy and Lord Yosef. "We'll see what we can do at the gate."

Eamon cast a regretful glance at Lucy before following King Giles out of the building. She gave him an encouraging smile. She knew he didn't like splitting up, but they both knew this crisis was more important than either of them. And a thought was forming in her mind about how to put their separation to good use.

The two royals had already left, and Lord Yosef was striding through the doorway. Lucy started to follow him, but Cody stopped her with a quiet word. She turned inquiringly to him and barely held in a startled cry at his sudden movement. She whipped her blade out without conscious thought, only just intercepting his sword in time.

"Cody!" she hissed. "What are you doing?"

"Making sure you're sharp," Cody responded calmly, continuing to advance. She deflected his attack impatiently.

"This is no time for fooling around," she snapped, her tight words almost drowned out by the clash of metal on metal.

"I'm glad to hear you say that," said Cody unemotionally. His blade moved swiftly, pressing her hard enough to require her full focus as she retreated across the room.

A flash of anger raced through Lucy, and she lunged forward, swapping to the offensive and forcing Cody back a step. "I mean it, Cody," she panted, "what are you doing? We're on the edge of war, and you think this is a good moment for a training session?"

"This is the only moment," said Cody grimly.

With a neat flick of his blade, he sent hers flying across the small space. For a moment Lucy stood there, breathing hard as she glared at him. But his unusually earnest expression melted her anger.

"Like you said, Lucy," Cody said seriously, "we're on the edge of war. Like it or not, we're about to be plunged into a battle, and I need to know you're ready for it. I can't have you going into an armed conflict distracted and mooning over your prince."

"I'm not *mooning* over anyone," Lucy spluttered indignantly. Her eyes flicked to the doorway, where Lord Yosef was framed, his astonishment evident as he took in the scene before him.

Cody followed her gaze, but instead of acknowledging the Thoranian nobleman, he pinned Lucy with a meaningful look. "And I can't have your hands tied behind your back because you're embarrassed for people to see you fight."

Lucy retrieved her weapon. "I understand, Cody. My hands aren't tied behind my back."

"Do you understand?" Cody pressed. "People will die today, and if you don't want to be one of them, you need to be ready.

The training isn't enough." He stepped forward unexpectedly, tapping two fingers to her temple. "Half the battle is up here. And there's no time to fight that part once the actual battle begins."

Lucy met his eyes, trying to show she was taking him seriously. "I understand, Cody."

"I hope so," he said, sheathing his blade.

The three of them made their way through the streets, the rain still falling lightly, but steadily enough to drench them within minutes. The mood of the city was subdued, as Lucy would expect from a people whose king was missing and presumed dead, but not panicked as they surely would be if they knew an army was hours away from their walls. The southern gate was still standing wide, the river flowing beneath the open doors.

Whatever King Giles had found in the castle, he obviously hadn't found someone he trusted to send to the gate, at least not quickly. After an hour of fruitless argument with the guard on duty, the portal was still wide open, and Lucy could stand the inactivity no longer.

She pulled Cody aside. "There's something I need to do, Cody, and I think in order to do it, I have to be on the other side of that gate."

Cody frowned at her. "What is it you need to do?"

"I have to draw Rasad out, separate him from his army."

Cody's frown only deepened. "That sounds dangerous and unnecessary. Is this about revenge?"

"Of course not," said Lucy quickly. "It's not personal." She took a deep breath. "Eamon and I spoke with the dragon-ruler when you were gone. Never mind how we did it, but that's the help I was hoping to get."

Cody stared at her, and she pushed on hastily. "It didn't go quite as I hoped. The dragons want to stop Rasad, all right, but they don't care about preventing war. They're going to slaughter not only him but everyone who's marching with him unless I can draw him away from the army."

"Was Eamon part of this plan?" Cody asked shrewdly, and Lucy sighed.

"It was his idea. And no, he won't be happy about me doing it alone. But I'm not going to pick a fight with Rasad. I just want to find out where he is, and keep him in sight. As far as we know, Rasad still thinks Eamon is dead, and I don't think we should give up that advantage. And let's not forget why Rasad wanted to kill Eamon in the first place. Kyona could barely survive such a blow. It's much safer if Eamon doesn't come with me."

"All of which is true, but none of which is why you don't want him to come," said Cody dryly. "You just can't stand the idea of anything happening to him."

Lucy made no attempt to deny it. "I know you don't understand that, but—"

"Actually," Cody cut in unexpectedly, his eyes on the distance, "I'm starting to." He brought his gaze back to her. "Let's go then."

Lucy shook her head. "You're more use here, Cody. You need to do what you can to defend this gate. Lord Yosef won't get anywhere on his own, and when they realize the Thoranians are attacking, he may need your protection."

Cody looked toward the nobleman, who was still arguing with the guard, and his creased forehead told Lucy he knew she was right.

"You're not going to pick a fight with Rasad?" he probed. "Just find out where he is?"

Lucy nodded. "I'm not really asking your permission, Cody," she added dryly. "I know you feel it's your job to protect me. But you said it yourself—my parents would understand this is bigger than us. You're needed here, and I'm needed," she jerked her head toward the open gate, "out there."

Her resolve was harder to hang onto an hour later, when she was perched up a tree, wet to her skin, and still hadn't seen any sign of the army. She was just starting to doubt she was needed out there or anywhere when she finally saw the sign she'd been looking for.

The scout was moving stealthily through the trees, conveniently on the same side of the road where she had chosen to conceal herself. He caught her eye at once—it had been some time since she'd seen so much as a pedestrian on the road, and she had no doubt Rasad had somehow blocked all traffic.

Lucy moved as silently as she could, counting on the dripping rain to mask the shifting of the branches as she climbed further down the tree. Like she had done, the scout had chosen to stay close to the road, just far enough into the tree line to not be seen. She stilled as he passed beneath her hiding place, waiting for the exact right moment before dropping like a stone on top of him.

The man's startled oath was cut short as he was knocked to the ground. She had taken him completely by surprise, and after a short struggle he stilled, her blade against his throat.

"Make a sound," she said calmly, "and it will be your last."

The man stared at her, his eyes wide and his breathing heavy. He was young, Lucy suddenly realized.

"Are you a scout for the Thoranian army?" she asked, her voice quiet.

The man hesitated only a moment before nodding. Lucy felt sympathy, mixed in with her calculating satisfaction that it was clearly not going to be difficult to get him to talk. She could see no resolution in his eyes, just fear. He likely had no idea why he was suddenly marching in war on his kingdom's long-term friends and allies. Probably the rest of the army was equally confused.

"How far away is the force now?" she asked.

He swallowed visibly before answering. "Less than an hour. Maybe as little as half an hour."

Lucy kept her face impassive with an effort. "Is King Abner with the army?"

The scout shook his head. "His Majesty stayed in Thirl, to deal with the renegades."

"Renegades?" Lucy asked sharply. "What do you mean?"

The man looked nervous at her tone. "All I know is that one of the noblewomen was arrested for trying to counter the king's order to march."

Lady Yasmin. It had to be. "What happened to her?" Lucy demanded.

"She was thrown into the dungeon, along with the Valorian prince and princess and the half-Kyonan, half-Balenan boy. Apparently they were helping her."

Lucy let out a breath. The man hadn't said anything about Lord and Lady Rodanthe. She wondered if they were in the dungeon as well, or outside it, trying to negotiate for the release of the royals. Well, it could be worse. At least she knew Rasad hadn't yet tried to kill Jocelyn off. The thought returned her mind to the more pressing situation.

"What about the king's primary advisor? Rasad. Is he with the army?"

The man nodded.

"Leading the charge?" Lucy guessed dryly, but the scout shook his head.

"He's giving the orders, on the king's behalf. But he's not at the front. He's following up the vanguard, with the second battalion."

Lucy frowned thoughtfully. Of course. It wasn't Rasad's style to put himself at the front. He preferred to stand just behind the leader, pulling the strings. She wasn't sure whether that would make it harder or easier to draw him away from the main force.

"Thanks for your help," she said tartly. Then, before the man could blink, she flipped her blade around, bringing the hilt down on his head. The scout crumpled into the undergrowth, unconscious.

After reassuring herself his pulse was steady—after all, he wasn't to blame for the looming disaster—Lucy left him where he lay, picking her way south again. If the force was only half an hour away, she was out of time to intercept them before they reached Nohl. But she might be able to set eyes on the advisor before the fighting began in earnest.

CHAPTER THIRTY-NINE

The scout hadn't erred in his estimation—it was an alarmingly short time later that Lucy spied the first of the troops. She'd passed a couple more scouts, but had opted to evade them. She had enough information for her task. She scaled a tree once again, watching with narrowed eyes as the armed cavalcade advanced down the road toward the city. Her eyes scanned the ranks, looking for the unpleasantly familiar head of her former admirer. As the scout had said, he wasn't leading the force.

The first battalion passed, all on foot. The second, mounted soldiers moving at a slow walk, followed immediately behind. Lucy could see no sign of Rasad among the horsemen, and she hesitated, unsure what to do. Should she keep waiting, in case the scout had been wrong or dishonest, and Rasad was actually further back? Or had she missed him?

There was no time to wait around. If Rasad was still ensconced within the ranks of the army when Qadir arrived, the Thoranians would be massacred. Lucy slipped silently from her tree, picking her way further back into the jungle before winding as quickly as she could through the undergrowth, back north toward Nohl.

She had little opportunity to observe the army as she traveled, needing to stay far enough away not to be seen. But all too soon, the soldiers nearest her came to a stop, those preceding them presumably having reached the walls of the Balenan capital. The road ran alongside the river now, meaning there was no more jungle on the far side of the thoroughfare. Lucy was glad she'd chosen this side of the road to hide on, because it would certainly be impossible now to cross over unseen.

She took the risk of moving closer to the road as she continued northward, scanning the ranks of the second battalion once again. Where was he? The group, horses and riders alike, were so spattered with mud that it was no wonder she could hardly tell one individual from the next.

She crept forward until the walls were in sight, scaling a tree yet again to get a good vantage point. To her relief, the city's gates were closed, whether at Cody's instruction or King Giles's, she had no idea.

A lone horseman stood between the army and the gate, a Thoranian official. She didn't recognize him, but judging by the military decorations on his uniform, he must be someone senior.

"Why do you come against us in force?" the Balenan guard on duty called out, his voice barely audible through the patter of the rain, and the stamp of the shifting horses' hooves.

"In the name of King Abner, we demand entry to the city," the Thoranian replied. "He seeks to bring order and stability to your tumultuous kingdom."

Lucy winced as Rasad's crimes were laid at his sovereign's door. Even if they averted battle, it was hard to imagine the former friendly relationship between the two kingdoms being restored in a hurry.

"We do not recognize the authority of King Abner here," the guard said in a hard voice.

"Then let your own king come forward," the Thoranian retorted. "Let him look me in the eye if he is so fit to lead you."

Lucy narrowed her eyes. She suspected that Rasad, not his mouthpiece, had chosen those words. The advisor was presumably referring to King Giles's son, believing the crown to now sit on the head of a terrified and unprepared twelve-year-old. She wondered if the spokesman even knew that the Balenan king was supposedly dead.

The small pedestrian entrance alongside the river gate suddenly swung open. Lucy caught her breath as King Giles rode out, his horse champing at the bit, picking up his rider's pent up energy. Only half a dozen guards flanked him.

"Certainly I will look you in the eye," the king said, his voice ringing with authority as he threw back the hood of his borrowed cloak. Lucy had never felt more proud of the relationship. "Although I would prefer to treat with the master, not the puppet." He scanned the ranks. "Where is this Rasad?"

The king was looking at the men right at the front as he made his bold pronouncement. But Lucy's eyes moved frantically over the mounted men in the second battalion, looking for anyone with a visible reaction to King Giles's appearance.

She leaned forward eagerly as she spotted the telltale sign of activity throughout the battalion. Following the ripple to its source, she saw Rasad at last, issuing instructions to the ring of soldiers closest to him, his eyes fixed on the Balenan king. He looked more calculating than alarmed. Lucy should have known it would take more than this surprise to discompose him.

It was clear he wasn't going to openly respond to the king's challenge, or claim responsibility for the attack. Doing so would hardly further his goal of casting King Abner as a conquering emperor.

But it didn't matter. Lucy had located him, and that was enough. She heard a rushing sound, and looked up in alarm. It was just a gust of wind moving the rain-drenched canopy above her, but it reminded her that wrathful dragons could descend at any second. She needed to move now.

She dropped out of the tree, her boots squelching in the mud as she picked her way along the edge of the jungle, away from the wall and toward where the Thoranian advisor was watching events unfold.

She heard startled cries as a few of the soldiers spotted her, but no one stopped her. The Thoranians and Balenans were probably equally confused as to her identity and purpose.

It was too much to hope that Rasad's own guards would be so dismissive. One of them detached from the advisor's side, moving into the trees himself to intercept her before she reached his master's position. She lost sight of him for a moment, then he suddenly appeared between the trunks, blade raised as he rushed on her.

She ducked instinctively as she drew her own weapon, slashing at his knees before she straightened. She knew her best hope was to maximize on his inevitable underestimation of her skill, and she lunged forward aggressively. The guard parried her attack, but didn't anticipate the swiftness of her follow through. She caught him in the side, and he fell to his knees with a grunt of pain, dropping his weapon.

She didn't wait to see the extent of the injury, racing forward through the trees again, her eyes on the glimpses of cavalry she could see between moss-covered trunks. She'd lost track of what was happening at the front, and she didn't realize until she burst out of the jungle again that King Giles had retreated back inside the walls.

No one was paying her any attention, all focused on the walls before them. Even as her searching eyes found Rasad, she heard him give the order to advance. She glanced back toward the gates, and was reassured by how strong and solid they were. Archers had appeared at the top of the walls, and the first few Thoranian soldiers to come within range fell quickly to their arrows. Lucy's heart wrenched at the unnecessary loss of life, but she pushed the thought aside. She couldn't afford to let emotions distract her.

She looked between the advisor and the advancing troops. Rasad must know that sending infantry against a fortified gate was pointless. So what was his plan?

Even as she wondered, she saw a row of Thoranian archers moving into position behind the front of the army. At a shouted command, they released a volley of arrows, providing some small measure of cover for their advancing comrades.

In the temporary lull as the archers on the wall repositioned themselves to be more difficult targets, a Thoranian archer at the front of the ranks caught Lucy's eye. He was nocking an arrow to his string, but there was something strange about it. Where the arrowhead should be, the projectile had a small leather bundle attached to the shaft.

Lucy glanced uneasily at Rasad and saw that he was watching the archer with rapt attention. She wanted to cry a warning to the defenders on the wall, but she hardly knew what, and there was no time to do anything. The archer released his missile. Time seemed to slow, then speed up, as Lucy watched it whizz through the air toward the broad wooden gates.

She knew from so far away she wouldn't be able to hear anything, but she could already imagine the thud of the leather bundle hitting the wood. What she didn't expect was for the impact to create a deafening explosion that splintered the wood as it struck. The noise was so loud that for several long seconds afterward, Lucy couldn't hear a thing.

But she could still see the chaos unleashed by the unnatural arrow. The Balenans who were visible ran frantically across the top of the wall, as incredibly—impossibly—a furiously potent flame leaped into existence at the point where the arrow had hit the drenched wood of the gates. It licked at the timber, turning solid beams into blackened splinters within moments.

The Thoranians closest to the gate had been thrown from their feet, but the archers in the ranks were ready. Seeing the success of the first one, several more soldiers pulled out similar missiles. They looked shocked at the dramatic effect of their attack, but their aim was true as they sent more of the magic arrows toward the gate. Each one created an explosion as thunderous as the first, and Lucy watched in horror as the flames spread with impossible speed. Soon the whole portal was engulfed in what she realized was dragon fire.

She turned away from the inferno, her determination rising as she once again picked out Rasad. He was issuing orders to a soldier, who spurred his own horse forward. Lucy noticed for the first time that a group of soldiers further back were overseeing teams of horses as they hauled an enormous wooden platform along the river. If they succeeded in securing it in the gaping hole that would soon be left by the disintegrating gates, the rushing river would become a clear pathway for the Thoranian troops to enter the city.

Her alarm grew. No doubt the advisor intended to advance on the city the moment the gateway was clear. She steeled herself as she strode forward, away from the shelter of the trees. She wished she'd been able to think of a clever way to draw Rasad away from the army, but there was no more time for that. Only boldness was left.

"Rasad!" she shouted, raising her blade in front of her as she paced toward him.

In spite of the roar from the nearby flames, Rasad's head

snapped around at the sound of her voice. He looked surprised, and—to Lucy's irritation—admiring, as he looked her over from head to toe.

The men closest to him—whom Lucy recognized as some of his personal guards—started toward her, swords raised threateningly. But Rasad stopped them with a lazy hand. Lucy stalked forward heedlessly, but even when she was mere feet from him, he showed no hint of alarm from his elevated position on the back of his mount.

"Luciana," he called, an eager glint in his eye. "I'm glad you're here. When my guards failed to bring you to me as instructed, I was afraid you might have been killed in some kind of scuffle. But here you are, not only alive, but ready for battle."

His eyes passed from her furious expression to her curved sword. "I seem to have succeeded after all in bringing out your full potential. I see you're no longer holding back, and if you will allow me to say so, my dear, you are nothing short of resplendent."

Lucy spat on the ground, her eyes narrowing as she searched his form for any opening. If only she still had the dagger he'd taken from her back in his rooms. She was a good shot with a throwing dagger. Even when she was at war with herself, she'd shown Scanlon just how good a shot. And this time she would know no hesitation. But all she had was her sword, and she wasn't close enough to use it.

"Stop this madness, Rasad," she said. "Either way, I promise you will die today. There's no need to take all these others with you."

Rasad just chuckled. "I can't find it in me to be sorry you're here, though I assume I have you to thank for the Balenan king's unfortunate survival. How is it you're more enchanting when threatening me than you were when trying to impress me? This is your natural state, Luciana. Don't fight it. You were born to be a conqueror, like me." He leaned forward in his saddle, and his guards shifted nervously in their semi-circle around him. "It's not too late, you know. I can't help but notice you're out here with my army rather than inside the walls with your Balenan kin."

Lucy ignored his words, well able to recognize now that he was trying to manipulate her. She didn't care what he thought. Let him imagine her aptitude for fighting indicated a heart as black as his. All that mattered was drawing him away from the army before Qadir arrived.

"If you really want to convince me I have a place with you, come down from your horse and let's talk on the same level," she said evenly. She jerked her head toward the nearby jungle. "Away from your henchmen."

Rasad chuckled. "Just because I find you delightful doesn't mean I'm blind to the murder in your eyes, Luciana. I don't have any desire to pit my combat skills against yours. I bring an army with me for such things."

He nodded, and one of his guards moved forward. Lucy kept her eyes on Rasad until the man was within reach, then flashed out in a movement so swift he didn't parry in time. He fell back, clutching his injured arm with a curse, and Rasad chuckled again.

"She might look delicate, but don't underestimate her," he chided. "It might be your last mistake with this one."

Lucy raised her sword in front of her as three more guards advanced, more cautiously this time.

"Detain her, but don't harm her unnecessarily," Rasad instructed lazily.

Lucy felt no such need for restraint, but she knew it wasn't enough of an advantage. And it was hard to keep her focus on her own fight when she heard Rasad raise his voice, giving the order for the army to advance. The gates must be completely destroyed.

Her blade flashed furiously in front of her, holding one attacker at bay and inflicting a superficial injury on another. But with three of them, she was quickly surrounded, and it was only a matter of minutes before one managed to pin her from behind. Her weapon fell to the ground, and the guard kicked it out of reach as his strong arms restrained her.

"Take her into the jungle a little way," said Rasad, his eyes not on the pair. "Keep her out of the way for now. She will undoubtedly be useful later."

Lucy wanted to scream in frustration as the guard started to drag her toward the trees. It was Rasad who needed to be removed from the area, not her. She followed the advisor's gaze, and her heart sank at the sight of Thoranian troops pouring through the ruined gates. The wooden platform had been secured in place. It was even longer than Lucy had realized, and although not as convenient as an ordinary road, it formed enough of a pathway to allow the Thoranians to pass through more quickly than the few Balenan defenders could handle.

Battle was well and truly joined now, and Lucy's small conflict was surrounded by the clash of metal and the shouts of men.

Just as the guard reached the tree line, Lucy felt the man's arms suddenly fall away from her. She turned quickly, raising her fists since she was now unarmed. Her hands dropped to her sides at the sight of her rescuer, standing over the body of her captor.

"Eamon! What are you doing out here?"

"What am *I* doing?" Eamon protested, his expression grim. "What were you thinking going after Rasad alone, Lucy?"

"There's no time to argue about it," she said impatiently. "The army has breached the walls, in case you hadn't noticed."

"I had actually," said Eamon dryly. "They were a little in the way when I was trying to get out here to reach you."

"We can't let Rasad get into the city," Lucy hurried on. "If he's inside Nohl when Qadir arrives, the dragons will probably burn the whole city to the ground, just to be safe."

Eamon peered through the trees, his expression scornful as he took in the advisor, still seated calmly on his horse. "I don't think he's planning to enter the city himself, somehow. At least not until the fighting is over."

Lucy followed his gaze, her expression hardening at the unmistakable satisfaction on Rasad's face as he watched the battle intensify before him. "Of course he's not. He prefers someone else to do the dirty work." She glanced at Eamon hopefully. "I don't suppose you brought a bow and arrow with you?"

Eamon shook his head regretfully. "I should have armed myself with one, but I didn't even think of it. King Giles had his hands full back at the castle. At least one of his senior advisors, and a couple of mid-level military strategists, were under the influence of Rasad's magic, to some extent."

Lucy raised her eyebrows. "Where are they now?"

"In the dungeons," said Eamon curtly. "Along with my guard."

Lucy nodded, her eyes drawn to the fighting she could glimpse through the ravaged river gate. King Giles couldn't have had much time to rally troops, and the awkwardness of the Thoranians' entry point was probably the only reason the defenders weren't already overwhelmed. She just hoped Cody was managing to stay alive in the midst of it. She knew without doubt he'd be in the thick of the fight. It was where she was itching to be herself.

But she had another job to do, and she turned resolutely away from the chaotic scene. "So how do we draw Rasad away? Even if he doesn't go into the city, there are still way too many troops around him, with no idea of the fiery death about to rain down on them."

Eamon frowned. "I could try to use my power to persuade him. I know Jocelyn has figured out how to use hers in its purest form, but it still comes most naturally to me through my words. That's the way we discovered it, and the only way we knew how to use it, before Elddreki started training Joss."

"So we need to get you close enough to speak to Rasad," said Lucy grimly. Her eyes were on the Thoranian advisor, still securely ringed by his guards. "It won't be easy, but I don't have any other ideas."

She started toward the edge of the trees, then paused, looking up at Eamon. For all she knew one or both of them might be about to die. There was surely something she was supposed to say right now, but her mind was too full of the fight to figure out what it was.

"Eamon..."

He reached out quickly, cupping one of his strong hands around the back of her neck in a gesture that was somehow both fortifying and intimate. "I know. Let's not say it now."

Lucy gave a curt nod, relieved there was no need to explain anything. Cody hadn't been wrong that she couldn't afford to moon over her prince at such a moment, and Eamon clearly knew it.

Without another word, she dashed out of the cover of the trees, scooping up her blade from where it had fallen. The drizzling rain had finally stopped, but everything was still wet, and she wiped the mud from her hilt as she ran.

Rasad glanced over, his attention drawn by their movement, and Lucy saw annoyance flash across his face at last. He and his entourage stood apart from the main force. Most of the troops were focused on their advance toward the city walls, but his guards were alert to his directions. At a flick of his hand, they advanced on the Kyonan pair.

As the first guard reached them, Lucy and Eamon took up a position back to back, blades extended and expressions grim. The guards circled them slowly, no one in a hurry to be the first to run forward.

"It seems you've been more of a hindrance to my plans than I'd realized, my dear Luciana," Rasad called out.

He tried to speak evenly, and his voice curled more caressingly than ever around her name, but to Lucy's ears he sounded put out. Apparently Eamon's survival irritated him more than King Giles's. She smiled grimly. It seemed the calculating advisor wasn't entirely above the petty emotions awoken by his rivalry with the prince, after all.

Unfortunately, neither was Eamon. She heard him growl at the familiarity of Rasad's words, and she could sense his focus slipping. One of the guards saw it, too, lunging forward to attack the prince at last. Eamon held him off skillfully, but the clash seemed to be the signal for the rest of them. Within moments they were both battling for their lives.

"It is a delight to see you in action, my dear," Rasad said, his words addressed to Lucy, but his eyes on her companion. "It really would be a dreadful waste for you to perish alongside this stripling."

To Lucy's relief, Eamon gave no outward reaction this time. Whether it was because he realized Rasad was trying to bait him, or because he was too hard pressed by his fight, she wasn't sure.

"If we're close enough for him to taunt us," she said quietly, her voice coming out in a pant, "then we're close enough for him to hear you."

Eamon gave a curt nod, even as he lunged suddenly forward. The guard dueling with him went down hard, and didn't rise.

Others were waiting to take his place, but they hesitated as the prince called out.

"Rasad! Is your whole strategy built on tricks and counterfeit? Or do you have anything real behind the facade?"

The Thoranian chuckled. "My tricks, as you call them, have proven fairly successful, don't you think?" He gestured around to the battle.

"But there's no substance behind them," Eamon argued, his eyes on the closest of the guards, who was inching toward him again. "You couldn't even get our delegation to Thorania without subterfuge. Your messenger claimed there were Kyonan descendants wanting our help, but no such people ever emerged."

"The success of that trick lies entirely at your door," said Rasad, watching Lucy's ongoing struggle with a casual air. "I wanted you to come, and I knew I could count on your arrogance to do the rest." He scoffed. "As though any Thoranian, regardless of ancient Kyonan descent, would ever wish to relocate to your inferior kingdom. But I knew all I had to do was plant the idea, and your royal house would be conceited enough to race to the rescue, as if only the great Kyonans know what we barbaric South Landers need."

He nodded, and one of the guards engaged Eamon again, the clash of steel momentarily silencing their conversation.

"Poisonous words, Rasad," Eamon grunted, his tone clipped as he held the guard off. "But still just words."

Rasad's voice turned indulgent. "Do you think you can shame me into fighting you, little prince? I have nothing to prove to you."

"Not to me, to yourself and your king," panted Eamon.

Rasad's smirk became a frown. To Lucy's amazement, he waved a hand, calling off the attack. The guards dropped back a step, maintaining a loose ring around Lucy and Eamon. Lucy wiped her forehead with the back of her hand, trying to catch her breath before the unexpected respite inevitably ended.

"I am proving my worth and my loyalty to my king as we speak," said Rasad, a bite in his voice.

"But are you?" Eamon pressed. "Can his empire last if you build it through deception and paltry tricks? King Giles is not dead, as you've seen. Why not come down from your horse, and treat with him man to man? Negotiate the outcome you want, with everything in the open, and then no one will be able to take it away from you."

Rasad's frown deepened, and Lucy could see that the contrast drawn between this forthright approach and his own underhanded tactics had rattled him. She was impressed—she would have had no idea how to use the power of stability to try to destroy rather than build confidence.

Almost as if he didn't realize he was doing it, Rasad dismounted, striding up to the Kyonan prince. "Listen here, boy. The Thoranian Empire will be the most secure in history."

"Nothing stolen can ever be securely held," Eamon contradicted, and Lucy realized to her surprise that she was nodding in agreement. She shook her head to clear it. She might not be able to sense magic, but clearly she was still affected by it.

But apparently Eamon had pushed his power too far. Rasad's expression suddenly sharpened, and he took a step back.

"You're using it now, aren't you?" he breathed. "I can sense it. My word, you must be skilled at holding it back for me not to have felt it before now. It's powerful."

Lucy's heart sank. Evidently Rasad's dabbling in magic had given him some kind of sensitivity to it. Quite apart from her alarm at the unmistakable greed in Rasad's eyes, she knew from what Eamon had told her that when someone was aware of the power, they were less likely to be manipulated by it.

They needed a new plan, and quickly. But they were surrounded and outnumbered, and Lucy could think of nothing.

A sudden rushing sound made them all look up, and Lucy's heart seemed to jump into her throat at the vision of menace now filling the sky.

It was too late. They were all going to die.

CHAPTER FORTY

But although several reptilian shapes were grower larger by the second, none of the creatures looked like the dragon-ruler who had promised to return with swift vengeance.

They were all dragons, certainly. And there was no denying they made a terrifying picture, talons, scales, and razor-sharp teeth all glistening in the weak afternoon light as they descended from above.

But there was something strange about their shape. Lucy ignored the screams rising from every side, focusing on the dragon in front as she tried to identify what it was. The dragon was almost upon them before she realized the anomaly wasn't part of the beast, but a burden it carried.

The creature, whose scales were a mixture of blue, green, and purple, landed in the space in front of the gate, supremely unconcerned by the seething mass of men who had filled that place moments before. Of course, the ground was clear by the time the dragon's talons alighted in the mud, all the fighters scrambling in their haste to get out of its path. It uncurled its front claws from its load, and Lucy started forward with a cry.

"Jocelyn!"

The princess's head whipped around, and she stumbled toward them, looking windswept but determined. Lucy hadn't even realized that Rasad's guards had all retreated at the appearance of the dragons, but no one hindered her as she ran to meet her friend.

"Are you all right?" Jocelyn asked, gripping Lucy's shoulder. Her eyes passed to her brother behind, and Lucy saw the relief on her friend's face as she confirmed they were both alive and unharmed.

"We're fine," said Lucy quickly, scanning the other dragons who were landing beside the first. She let out a long breath at the sight of her brother being placed on the ground by another dragon, this one a smaller beast with dull red scales. Kincaid landed soon after, carried by a yellow dragon, and Lady Yasmin was the last of the strange burdens to be released.

Matheus and Kincaid hastened to join the little group gathered in the mud, but the Thoranian noblewoman gave them only a cursory glance. Turning, she sprinted toward the ruined gates, drawing a blade as she went. Whether her priority was stopping the battle or finding her brother—or perhaps Cody— Lucy didn't know.

Not that there was much battle to stop at that moment. Everywhere Lucy looked, men had paused their clashes, staring with wide and terrified eyes at the group of dragons perched outside the gateway.

"What's happening, Lucy?" Jocelyn asked urgently. "Is King Giles—?"

"He's alive," said Lucy. "Or at least, he was when the battle started."

"And Cody?" Matheus's sharp question brought Lucy's attention to him, and she gripped his uninjured arm briefly.

"Same. He's fighting with the king, in there somewhere." She jerked her head toward the city.

"We have to stop the fighting," said Eamon tersely, joining Lucy. "These men don't have any idea why they're even here. They don't deserve to die any more than the Balenans."

His words jolted Lucy's thoughts back to their task. In the tumult of the dragons' arrival, she had momentarily forgotten about Rasad. Glancing around, she saw to her dismay that he had disappeared along with his guards. She gritted her teeth. They'd wasted their opportunity.

"Ah, you are Prince Eamon." The dragon's voice made all the humans start, looking up at the creature now towering above them. "I have wanted to meet you." He leaned down, extending his mighty neck until his bearded face was inches from Eamon's. He took a deep breath through his nostrils, then made a strange guttural sound that made Lucy step back involuntarily. "You smell like me as well. How fascinating."

Eamon exchanged a dazed look with Jocelyn before bowing low. "You must be Elddreki," he said formally. "I'm honored to meet you."

"And I you, young prince," said Elddreki, inclining his head. "You are much like your fathers."

"Yes, yes, but surely you can do all this later, Elddreki," Kincaid cut in impatiently.

Lucy blinked, trying to imagine being so casual with this mighty and fearsome beast.

"Isn't there a war going on here?" the Valorian prince was continuing. He wasn't wrong—while no one in their immediate vicinity was fighting, the sounds of distant conflict were still drifting from the city.

"And that's not even the biggest of our concerns," Lucy said quickly, recovering herself.

"What do you mean?" Jocelyn asked sharply. "What is?"

"The dragons," said Lucy. She looked uncertainly at Elddreki, bobbing an awkward half-curtsy before adding, "I mean the other dragons."

"Ah," said Elddreki, nodding wisely. "You mean the group from Vasilisa." He glanced at the yellow dragon, who had moved forward to stand alongside him. The others remained where they had landed, looking with interest at the grisly chaos around them, left by the interrupted battle.

"We come from Wyvern Islands," the yellow dragon explained, "the Dragon Realm situated off the coast of Valoria. But another group has come to the South Lands, from Vasilisa, the Dragon Realm in Kyona's mountains."

"Yes, Qadir's group will be here soon," Elddreki agreed.

Lucy stepped forward, her nerves forgotten. "Do you know that for sure?"

Elddreki's eyes focused on her, and he looked faintly surprised at the question. "Certainly. We dragons have our own way of communicating with one another, even across great distances."

His face seemed to harden, and his gaze shifted to the sky. "Although I took my group straight to Thirl, to check on Jocelyn and Kincaid, Qadir shared with me from afar the desecrations the others discovered at the stronghold in the north."

"They've been to Rasad's Bastion?" Lucy asked quickly. "They found the body of the dragon, and Rasad's experiments?"

"They certainly did," Elddreki said grimly. He twisted his vast reptilian head back and forth. "Where is the culprit?"

"I don't know," said Lucy, frustrated.

"We had him," Eamon said through clenched teeth, following her gaze. "And we let him get away."

"Well," Lucy grimaced, "if we're honest, he had us. We were trying to draw him away from the army, and above all to make sure he didn't get into the city." She saw the confusion in Jocelyn's eyes, and quickly explained the nature of their deal with Qadir. The color drained from the princess's already pale face, and she exchanged a look with her husband.

"Can you stop it, Elddreki?" Kincaid asked the dragon quickly. "Can you change Qadir's mind?"

Elddreki considered the matter dispassionately. "Unlikely," he said at last. "Qadir is not easily influenced, and his wrath is great after what he found at the stronghold."

"What happened when the dragons went to Rasad's Bastion?" Lucy asked uneasily.

"They destroyed it," Elddreki said simply.

"Rasad's experiments, you mean?" Lucy asked cautiously.

"All of it," Elddreki clarified. He shook his head slowly. "I witnessed it through Qadir's sight. It was a total annihilation. There is no risk of any of his experiments surviving." He saw the look on Lucy's face and explained kindly, "Dragon fire is extremely destructive, you know. I doubt one stone of the fortress is left standing."

"But..." Lucy exchanged a glance with her brother. He looked as alarmed as she felt. "What about all the people? Rasad's servants and such. Did they get out safely first?"

A strange rippling motion passed over Elddreki's frame, from his shoulders to the tip of his tail. It took Lucy a moment to realize it was a shrug.

"I do not know."

"You mean," Matheus's voice sounded faint as he addressed the dragon for the first time. "You mean they might have all died?"

Elddreki did his rippling shrug again. "It is possible, I suppose. As I said, I do not know. Weren't they in league with the desecrator? What is your concern?"

Matheus swallowed visibly, looking to Lucy. She gave a slight shake of her head. She got the sense it would be futile to try to explain their reaction to the dragon.

"Well, the Thoranian soldiers aren't in league with Rasad," she said quickly. "At least, not most of them. We don't want Qadir and the other dragons to kill them all, or the Balenan defenders."

"Please," Jocelyn chimed in, her expression earnest as she met Elddreki's eye. "Isn't there anything you can do? To stop the fighting, and to hold Qadir off until we can find Rasad?"

The dragon regarded her silently for a long moment. "If you wish it, I will try," he said at last. He crouched, clearly preparing to take off, but Jocelyn suddenly started forward, laying a hand on his scaled hide.

"Wait! Take me with you. We'll go where the fighting is fiercest. I might be able to help stop the battle, if I can change people's minds about whether they need to be fighting."

"Jocelyn," said Kincaid, a warning in his voice. "You need to be careful."

"I will be," she promised, grasping his hand and giving it a quick squeeze before turning to Elddreki. The dragon gripped her shoulders with his talons, and a second later the pair was gone, a rush of wind blowing Lucy's hair back from her face.

"Come on," said the yellow dragon to Kincaid, a hint of humor in her voice. "You don't need to tell me—you want to keep an eye on her."

"Thanks, Raqisa," said Kincaid gratefully, stepping toward the dragon. He hesitated as he reached her though, looking at the other dragons. "Oh, do you think your companions would be willing to return to Thirl for Lord and Lady Rodanthe? If they're willing to travel this way, that is." He grimaced at Lucy and Eamon. "We didn't exactly stop to say goodbye to them before we left. They've been trying to get us released from the dungeons, but something tells me they won't have been thrilled at our method of getting out."

Raqisa nodded to the other two dragons, and they took off without delay, disappearing toward the south east. Kincaid nodded his thanks to Raqisa. Before Lucy could blink, the two of them were in the air as well, leaving Lucy, Eamon, and Matheus alone in the midst of a muddy and deserted battlefield.

Lucy turned to her brother. "Matheus. Are you really all right?"

"I got carried by a dragon," the fifteen-year-old answered, looking dazed. "We flew all the way from Thirl, but it hardly took any time at all! It was..." he shook his head, "...there are no words."

"That's good," said Eamon curtly, "because no offense, but we don't have time for words." He met Lucy's eyes. "We need to find Rasad."

Before Lucy could respond, she heard a rushing, even louder than the one that had heralded the approach of Elddreki's group. Looking up, she felt dread settle over her at the sight she had feared—a second group of dragons, this one unmistakably led by the dragon-ruler, his dark form absolutely monstrous as it blocked out the sky.

"Yes, we do," she said grimly. "Right now."

But none of them made any move to search for the advisor, all held in thrall by the sight before them. Unlike the first group of dragons, Qadir and his companions didn't come looking for Lucy and Eamon. Whether it was because the dragon-ruler was too enraged by what he'd seen at Rasad's Bastion to show restraint, or because he considered their time to be up, Lucy couldn't guess.

Regardless of the reason, the dragons converged on the city of Nohl, where the fighting was still going on. There were more of them this time, perhaps as many as ten. Lucy drew in a sharp breath as the creatures began to swoop. Flames curled from their nostrils, but mercifully none of them were actually breathing fire onto the buildings or their inhabitants. At least not yet.

"What are they doing?" Matheus breathed.

"I think they're trying to sniff Rasad out," said Eamon grimly. "Smell his magic, so to speak."

"Does that mean they're not going to kill everyone else?" Matheus asked hopefully. "That they're just going to target him?"

"Maybe," said Lucy flatly. "Or maybe they just want to make sure that he's actually here before they set everything on fire."

As she spoke, Lucy saw Elddreki launch himself from the roof of a building, intercepting Qadir mid-air. The two dragons circled around each other slowly, communicating mid-flight. It was a curious and impressive sight, but Lucy knew she'd been distracted long enough. They couldn't afford to waste whatever time Elddreki might buy them.

She turned her gaze from the city, scanning the area. The immediate vicinity was still mostly deserted, but a movement just behind the tree line drew her eye.

"There!" she cried, amazed at the unexpected windfall. She'd been afraid Rasad was long gone, but there he stood, hardly seeming aware of the Kyonans' presence as he stared at the sky in fascination.

"Rasad," she shouted, and his eyes flicked briefly to her, their expression unfocused.

"They're even more magnificent than I imagined," he breathed. "Do you see the power in their every movement? Can you feel the magic dripping off them?" His gaze returned to the sky. "Endless potential."

Lucy felt disgust well up inside her. Rasad sounded almost mad, talking of the dragons like they were resources for him to experiment with. She supposed she should be grateful his obsession had kept him from fully fleeing, as most of the soldiers had shown the sense to do. But she felt no satisfaction as she watched Rasad drool over the beasts' magic, as though the lives of hundreds of men didn't hang in the balance.

Screams suddenly rent the air, and turning around, Lucy saw with dismay that flames were springing up from some of the buildings. The dragons appeared to be done with restraint.

She started forward, not stopping to think about it as she brandished her weapon at the mastermind of all this needless suffering. A cry of challenge burst from her unconsciously, and Rasad gave her his full attention at last. He looked surprised by her bold attack, but he managed to bring a weapon up in front of himself in time to intercept her blade.

She heard Eamon's shout behind her, and was dimly aware that he and Matheus were both rushing to join her. Three of Rasad's guards materialized from the trees at that moment, racing to meet the two boys, apparently seeing them as the greater threat to their master.

Lucy ignored all this. She would have to trust both Eamon and Matheus to defend themselves, because Rasad was the only way to end the carnage going on behind her. She disengaged her blade from his with a flick and pressed forward instantly, immersing herself in the familiar sound of steel against steel, the heady weight of the weapon in her hand, the exhilaration of the fight. In that moment, nothing else mattered.

Rasad had said he wasn't a soldier, but he clearly had some weapons training. He met her challenge without hesitation, his movements slower than hers, but his form good as he deflected attack after attack. Lucy fought with everything she had, pushing herself until her breath came in pants. He was bigger, and stronger, but she was more skilled, and she was determined to break through his guard.

"Was it you who called the dragons?" Rasad panted, holding his sword horizontally as he deflected a blow. "It seems you held out on me." There was a manic gleam in his eye. "Tell me how you induced them to leave their own realm. I must know!"

Lucy's lip curled. "It—wasn't—hard," she spat out between blows. "I told them about your experiments. They've come to kill you, and thwart your invasion attempt."

A flicker of alarm passed across Rasad's features. Lucy pressed forward mercilessly, but he quickly recovered his poise.

"They will not interfere in my plans. From all I know, dragons are uninterested in human politics."

Despite his bold words, he cast an uneasy look at the dragons still swooping on the city of Nohl. This time, Lucy didn't waste his distraction. She lunged forward with all her strength, her blade passing through Rasad's guard and piercing his shoulder.

He gave a cry, dropping his weapon as he sank to his knees. Lucy moved unhesitatingly, kicking his sword out of the way as she laid her own against his throat. Rasad's expression was calm, but his eyes gave him away. They gleamed as he looked up at her.

"Well, if nothing else, it's satisfying to see you embrace your identity as a killer, Luciana."

Lucy just shook her head. "You have no power, magic or otherwise, to manipulate me. I know who I am."

She stepped back slightly. "And although I don't enjoy killing, and I'm not careless with others' lives like you are, I would be willing to kill you if that was what needed to be done."

Rasad was still clutching his shoulder, but he smirked slightly as he looked up at her, clearly sensing she didn't intend to finish him. The rain had started to fall once again, this time increasing quickly from a light mist to a heavy downpour. The drops ran down Rasad's face, looking like tears—a mockery of the remorse he should feel, but seemed incapable of.

"But I won't kill you," she said. "Because believe it or not, someone else has a bigger grudge against you." She raised her face to the sky, closing her eyes as the rain instantly drenched her cheeks.

"QADIR! He's here!"

She wasn't sure whether the dragon's ears were good enough to hear her through the downpour and across the distance, or whether he was still attuned to her with his other sight. Either way, it was only seconds before he materialized, his vast form blocking out what little light there was.

"This is him?" the dragon demanded. "This is the one who desecrated our kin with his experiments?"

"Yes," said Lucy, trying not to sound breathless. Qadir's demeanor was very different from the last time they had spoken. Even though she knew it wasn't directed at her, his fury was terrible to behold, and she could no more prevent the instinctive rush of fear than she could fly.

"Your Mightiness," Rasad gasped. Incredulously, Lucy saw that in spite of his obvious fear, there was still a small gleam of calculation in the Thoranian's eyes as he gazed in awe at this most impressive example of the creatures of his obsession. "Allow me to—"

"A dragon does not have speech with a worm," Qadir cut the human off, his voice deep and awful. Without warning, he seized Rasad around the middle, shooting up into the air with lightning speed.

The three Kyonans stared into the sky, too startled to speak as Qadir went higher and higher. And as little love as she had for the man, Lucy couldn't help the sharp gasp that broke from her at the sight of Rasad's tiny form being released from the dragon's talons at a terrifying height.

The advisor plummeted to the ground, and Lucy winced involuntarily at the sickening thud with which he landed, no more than ten yards away from where she still stood. For a moment there was silence, the three of them staring at Rasad's body, too shocked by the suddenness of his death to speak.

Qadir landed beside his victim, reaching one taloned limb toward him. Lucy winced again, afraid she was about to see the dragon rip Rasad's body to shreds. But instead, the dragon-ruler slashed at the advisor's clothes. With surprising dexterity for such a large creature, he searched the motionless form, uncovering two crystals and a series of leather pouches. He tossed them all into the air, releasing a jet of bright orange flame that engulfed and destroyed them instantly.

Then Qadir let out an unearthly shriek, wheeling back toward the city without a further glance at the humans. The dragons who had come with him rose up to meet him, some of them roaring for good measure as they launched themselves into the air. They fell into some kind of formation, their faces pointed northward. Within moments, they were lost to sight, winging their way toward the ocean.

CHAPTER FORTY-ONE

A deadly hush descended on the whole scene, and for several long seconds Lucy could only stare stupidly into the sky. Eventually she brought her gaze back down to the city before her. She drew a long rattling breath as she realized with relief that the flames were not as advanced as she'd thought. Only a few buildings still smoldered, and the steadily pelting rain was having its effect.

She turned to Eamon, hardly knowing what to think or how to feel.

"It's over," she said shakily.

He nodded, reaching a hand toward her. She fell into his arms, resting her head against his chest for a moment, listening as the frantic rhythm of his heart slowed to a more normal pace.

"Please don't kiss again," Matheus said, sounding nauseated. "I don't think I can take it on top of everything else."

Lucy pulled free of Eamon's arms with a shaky laugh, punching her brother lightly on his uninjured shoulder. "Don't be ridiculous."

She looked at Eamon, and saw that he was watching Rasad's body, a strange expression on his face. "I'm sorry I never got the chance to fight him myself. I wanted to make him pay for what he did to you."

"What, proposing?" Lucy asked lightly.

Eamon almost smiled. "No, manipulating you, tying you up, almost certainly planning to kill you eventually." He paused. "But yes, if I'm honest, also the proposing thing."

Lucy chuckled, running a shaking hand down her face.

"I need to find Joss," said Eamon tightly, and Lucy's desire to joke fled completely.

"And Cody," she said, with a terse nod.

The three of them squelched their way toward the splintered gate. The hush of the battlefield outside the city was mirrored within its walls, which Lucy took to be a good sign. She couldn't hear the clang of metal anywhere, and the flames seemed to have been extinguished by the downpour.

Somehow, without talking about it, they found themselves heading toward the castle. The steady increase in people seemed to support their guess as to where the action had been centered. Everywhere Lucy looked, she saw dazed Thoranian soldiers, wandering idly or huddled in groups. From what she could see, they still outnumbered the Balenan troops significantly, but there was no more sign of fighting, and they were clearly unsure what to do next.

The castle courtyard was a bustle of activity, with people buzzing around in spite of the rain, tending to the wounded and patching up the damage caused by the dragons. It didn't seem as though the castle itself had sustained any serious attack, for which Lucy was glad. The Balenan monarchy didn't need any more impediments.

"Joss!" At Eamon's cry of relief, Lucy's head whipped around, her eyes picking out her friend in the chaos. Eamon raced forward, and Lucy and Matheus followed close behind.

Lucy realized when she reached Jocelyn just how exhausted

the princess looked. She was pale, and she swayed slightly on her feet as she stepped forward to meet her brother. Kincaid had an arm around her waist, supporting his wife with a slightly anxious look on his face.

"Are you all right?" Lucy asked, alarmed at Jocelyn's weakness.

The other girl smiled at her. "Of course I am. I've just tired myself out, that's all. I'll be fine once I've had a good rest."

"It was incredible," said a new voice, and Lucy turned to see Lord Yosef at her elbow. Other than a long scratch along his jaw, he seemed to be uninjured. "I've never seen anything like it. That colorful dragon flew low over the fighters, carrying her like some kind of standard, and it was like there was an invisible ripple following them. Everyone got confused, and most of the soldiers stopped fighting altogether. I think they're still trying to figure out what hit them."

Lucy glanced back at the former combatants, Balenan and Thoranian alike, who were still milling around looking lost. She shook her head slowly. No wonder Jocelyn was exhausted, if she'd used her magic on that many people all at once. It was still a little unnerving just how powerful her best friend could be.

Eamon was gripping Jocelyn's shoulder now, seeking further reassurance that she was unharmed. Lucy turned away from them, scanning the crowd anxiously.

"They're over there," Lord Yosef said helpfully, an understanding smile in his voice.

A huge burden lifted from Lucy's shoulders as she followed the direction of his pointing finger and saw Cody, standing on the other side of the courtyard with Lady Yasmin. The two of them were deep in conversation with King Giles, all three clearly having escaped any serious injury.

Lucy and Matheus hurried across the drenched flagstones,

reaching the group in time to hear King Giles say, "I will allow your men to tend to their wounded, but the army must cross the border before nightfall tomorrow. I intend to close our border to all other traffic until this mess is straightened out."

"I understand, Your Majesty," said Lady Yasmin quickly. "I will convey your message to King Abner, and I fully expect that he will offer reparations for this regrettable incident."

The Balenan king gave the noblewoman a long hard look before responding. "I will not hesitate to respond strongly to any further hint of aggression from Thorania," he said at last. "But," his face softened slightly, "you may tell your king that I have no more desire for war than I did before all this began." He ran a hand through his hair, glancing around and noticing the newcomers for the first time. "I've seen enough this last day to be willing to consider the possibility that a power beyond King Abner's authority was responsible for the attack on my kingdom."

"You are most gracious, Your Majesty," said Lady Yasmin, inclining her head deeply. "And I can only beg you once again to believe me when I say that neither my king nor the majority of my countrymen were party to Rasad's schemes."

"I'm pretty sure his guards were," Lucy chimed in.

Cody turned quickly at the sound of her voice, his body losing some of its stiffness as his eyes passed over the two siblings. He gave Lucy a weary smile, which she returned. There was no need for words.

"I got a good look at most of Rasad's guards," Lucy continued. "If they can be rounded up, I can help identify them. I imagine King Abner will want to detain them, at the very least."

"He may have to borrow your dungeons though, Your Majesty," cut in Kincaid's cheerful voice.

King Giles turned to the Valorian prince, who along with the

Kyonan royal siblings, had just joined the group. The king raised a questioning eyebrow, and Jocelyn's face twisted into an expression that was half grin, half grimace.

"Elddreki was a little...overenthusiastic in breaking us out of the dungeons at the Thoranian palace. It will be a little while before King Abner can lock anyone else up there, I'm afraid."

Lucy shook her head. "It must have been quite the excitement for the people of Thirl, having dragons descend out of nowhere."

Kincaid and Jocelyn exchanged a look. "It was pretty eventful, yes," the prince agreed.

"So what now?" Lucy asked, sensing rather than seeing that Eamon had drawn up alongside her. Too weary to worry about appearances, she leaned into him gratefully, letting his shoulder take her weight.

"Now, there's a great deal of cleaning up to do," said King Giles grimly. His eyes softened as they passed over the group. "But I owe all of you a great debt of thanks. It seems Kyona is an ally worth having, and I don't think anyone in my court will dispute that now we've seen your dragon allies for ourselves."

"We can thank Lucy for their intervention," said Eamon, giving her shoulder a squeeze. "She's getting a head start on the duties of a crown princess, showing the other kingdoms how strong we are."

Jocelyn raised an eyebrow, looking pointedly between her brother and her best friend. Lucy felt her face heating, but she couldn't quite restrain a grin as she met her friend's eye. Jocelyn's weariness seemed to be forgotten as her whole face glowed. She gave Lucy a piercing look that promised a full inquisition at a later opportunity.

King Giles's attention was quickly claimed by someone else. Lady Yasmin and Lord Yosef bent their heads together, clearly discussing the logistics of returning the army to Thorania. Cody's attention seemed to be fixed on the noblewoman, but when Lucy started to move away, he stopped her with a hand on her arm.

"You all right?" he asked softly.

She nodded, smiling wearily up at him. "You?"

"Of course," he said dismissively. His eyes searched her face. "Rasad is dead, yes?"

Lucy nodded.

"Your doing?"

She shook her head. "The dragons, actually. But I handed him to them."

Cody nodded, his gaze shrewd. "You didn't hold back, Lucy. I'm proud of you."

Lucy smiled. "You should be. You taught me everything I know."

Cody shook his head, the tiniest of smiles on his face as his eyes drifted back toward the Thoranian siblings. "Not everything. You taught me a couple of things."

"What are you going to do?" Lucy asked quietly.

Cody brought his gaze back to her, making no pretense of not understanding her meaning. "I don't know. We'll all have to see how things unfold here in the next days and weeks. But when you all sail back to Kyona, I think I'll return to Thorania, at least for a while." He gave a rueful smile. "If she'll let me, that is."

Lucy tried to hide her dismay at the thought of losing Cody, but she wasn't able to entirely mask her surprise. He shook his head. "I'm not going anywhere just yet, so don't think you can get out of training for the rest of the trip."

Lucy rolled her eyes. "I don't want to get out of training. If you're going to abandon us for Thorania, I need to get every ounce of knowledge I possibly can out of you before you disappear."

Cody chuckled. "Abandoning you, am I?" His expression softened as he searched her face. "I won't leave until you're actually on the ship, I promise. You won't need me during the voyage." His gaze passed to something over her shoulder. "You'll have plenty to occupy you, I'm sure."

Lucy glanced behind her to see Eamon hovering patiently. The others seemed to have wandered into the castle, probably hoping for a meal and somewhere to rest.

Lucy smiled up at the prince. His answering smile was more intimate than words. In spite of all the tension and drama of the last few days, that smile still made her heart jump as erratically as it had when she was fourteen.

"You waited for me."

"Of course," Eamon said. "Always, as long as it takes."

Lucy stepped forward, not caring in the least about the curious looks of passersby as she placed her hands on Eamon's chest.

"We will have to wait a while, you know," she said, her tone turning serious. "They're going to say eighteen is too young for a crown prince to get married. And," she grimaced, "I'm not even quite eighteen yet. I'm pretty sure my father at least is going to insist we wait until I am before anything is formalized." She gave a dry chuckle. "He's going to be less than impressed that I'm coming back engaged after all, when his parting words to me were to forbid anything of the kind."

"Firstly," said Eamon, his eyes dancing with humor as they looked down into hers, "we've been friends since before you could walk. Do you really think I don't know when your birthday is, and exactly how old you are? Secondly, I'm pretty sure I can bring your father around, since I want you to live in Kynton with me, not on the other side of an ocean. And lastly," his expression warmed, "I already told you, I'll wait as long as it takes."

Lucy smiled up at him, but there was still a hint of anxiety in her voice. "It's not going to be easy, though, is it? A lot of the court won't like it."

Eamon scoffed. "You think I care about the complaints of a bunch of hen-witted noble girls who are just jealous they're not half as beautiful, intelligent, or capable as you are?"

Lucy couldn't help smirking a little as she thought of Sonia and Vanessa. Let them try swooning over Eamon now, see how that turned out. But she shook her head. "I didn't mean that, although of course all the girls our age won't like it." She sobered as she met his eyes. "I meant the people with real influence in the court. It's not going to win anyone's favor that I'm half-Balenan. Or that I'm, you know..." She gestured down at herself, in her mud-splattered, form-fitting training gear, lethal blade hanging at her side.

"Perfect?" Eamon suggested. She shot him a look, and he became serious again. "I know what you mean, and it won't be altogether easy. But," he looked around pointedly, "we've handled worse, haven't we? I have no doubt we can face whatever gets thrown at us, as long as we face it together." He tangled one of his hands through her hair. "I would fight much more formidable enemies than stuffy courtiers in order to be with you, Lucy."

"Yes." Lucy ducked her head to hide her smile. "You've proved that, I think."

"And I'll keep proving it," said Eamon, touching her chin gently so she looked back up at him. "Don't worry about the influence of the critics, Lucy. No one has more influence in the Kyonan court than my parents, and I know they'll be completely behind us, so we're sure to win in the end. Besides," he grinned roguishly, "I'm not above using my power to win over the more fastidious if necessary."

Lucy laughed, her heart feeling lighter than it had in a long time. "Then I don't see how we can lose."

It was some time before Lucy found herself alone in a guest suite. She'd finally eaten a solid meal, and she was more than ready for sleep. But she was still so filthy, she couldn't rest without washing first. It was as she began to undress that she discovered Haydn's journal. She'd forgotten all about it, but she vaguely remembered putting it in her pocket before answering the door to the overly observant serving girl, back in her suite at Rasad's Bastion.

She clutched the slim book for a moment, surprised by the rush of emotion it brought on. None of her other belongings had made it back to Balenol with her, but it seemed fitting that this journal had returned to its origin, somehow.

She didn't intend to read through it, she just flicked the pages idly as she went to put it down. But a short paragraph caught her eye, alone toward the back of the journal, several blank pages separating it from what she had believed to be the last entry. She peered at the page in confusion, sure the handwriting looked different from the rest of the records.

This is the journal of my ancestor, handed down in my family as a precious treasure.

His history is my history, not least because it's thanks to him that even after generations, everyone in our nomad community learns from childhood how to read and write.

It comforts me to know that, as hard as this life is, even as nomads we build our successes on the backs of those who came before. We are his legacy, and I hope he would be proud.

- Raldo

. . .

Lucy's breath caught in her throat at the name, so familiar to her although she had never met the owner in person. Haydn was Raldo's ancestor? It made sense—why else would the journal have been in Raldo's section of the base tree?

She pressed the book to her heart, doubly glad it had survived. It would be precious to her mother, she knew, as well as to many others in Raldon.

She read again what the former rebel had said about his ancestor's legacy. Thinking of Isidore's choices—the way she'd abandoned herself to her bitterness where Haydn had chosen to move forward—she could only grieve for the legacy the noblewoman had left. The evil in Rasad's heart had grown from seeds planted a long time ago, and innocent lives had been lost today as a result.

Surely Haydn would have been proud of a descendant like Raldo. Lucy hoped Raldo himself would be proud of his own legacy, the strong and vibrant community that now bore his name.

Lucy could only be more grateful than ever that she hadn't gone any further down Isidore's path herself. Her own lapse in judgment in her dealings with Eamon was more than worth it, because it had showed her the hypocrisy of her bitterness toward him.

Haydn had forgiven much worse crimes than Lucy had ever suffered, and she vowed to let his example keep her accountable. Like her, he was a product of both Kyona and Balenol, their good and their bad.

Lucy looked out the window at the rain still falling steadily on the harsh gray stone of the city. She'd helped to save this kingdom from annihilation today, and she was glad. It was part of who she was, brutal history and all, and she no longer had any desire to disown it.

After all, knowing who she was, and embracing it, was something she couldn't put a price on. It was something the exalted position she was about to assume could neither give her nor take away from her.

And she would never let herself forget it.

EPILOGUE

Lucy took a deep breath, running her hands over her skirts one last time.

"You do know your dress is just as perfectly smooth as it was when you did that two minutes ago, don't you?" Eamon asked humorously.

"As a matter of fact," she said wryly, "I do."

He grinned. "Are you ready?"

Lucy drew another deep breath. "Absolutely, and not at all."

Eamon chuckled, leaning close. Lucy's hair was elaborately styled, but she couldn't bring herself to remind him of that as he laid his head against hers. "You're perfect, Lucy, and you're more than ready for this."

She raised her face to his. Glancing quickly around to make sure they were still alone in the antechamber—except for his ever-present guards, of course—Eamon pressed a quick kiss to her lips.

"You don't seem nervous," Lucy said ruefully, and Eamon chuckled again.

"Why would I be nervous? I finally get to formalize my

betrothal to the woman of my dreams. I can stop worrying someone else is going to cut me out."

Lucy rolled her eyes. "Because you've been so nervous about that."

Eamon smiled down at her. "Not nervous, exactly," he admitted. "But it has been the longest six months of my life." He cocked his head to the side. "Actually, the months before it, when you hated me, felt pretty long."

"I never hated you!" Lucy protested. Eamon gave her a long-suffering look, and she grinned. "But I guess I wanted you to think I did, so I won't quibble."

Eamon's retort was lost as they heard the herald in the adjoining ballroom announce them. It all felt surreal. Lucy knew it was Kyonan custom to confer the title of lady on a woman betrothed to the king or his heir, but it was still strange to hear herself referred to as Lady Luciana. It was going to be even stranger to be Princess Luciana in a matter of months.

Every eye was on them as they entered the ballroom. But Lucy was determined not to be disconcerted, either by the resentment in the eyes of some of the disappointed noble girls, or the admiration in the eyes of some of the men.

She was admittedly a little uncomfortable under the expressionless scrutiny of Lord and Lady Rodanthe, standing with some of the other senior nobles of King Calinnae's court. They had been polite in their congratulations on her betrothal to Prince Eamon, but she had a feeling it would take a lot of time and effort to reach any kind of warmth with them. They hadn't said it, of course, but she had the sense they largely blamed her for the series of disasters that the delegation to the South Lands had turned into. And perhaps they had reason, she acknowledged to herself.

But she drew strength from the warmth of King Calinnae's and Queen Elnora's smiles as they greeted her, and formally welcomed her to her new role. Eamon was right. If the sovereigns approved the prince's choice, no one else was in any position to oppose it.

She remembered how dazzled she'd been when she'd entered this room for her first ever ball. She bit back a grin as she glanced up at Eamon, his stride stately and regal as he escorted her down the long dining table. Even then, this had been what she had most dreamed of. And now it was real, and a hundred times more raw, and complicated, and beautiful, than she had imagined.

Lucy had thought there might be some tradition that would require her to sit with her parents, or even some of the senior courtiers. So she was delighted to instead be seated between Eamon and Jocelyn.

"I'm so glad you were able to come for this," she said to Jocelyn during the soup course, for perhaps the tenth time. "It feels like years since I've seen you, rather than months."

Jocelyn beamed at her. "We wouldn't miss it for anything."

"Having said that," Kincaid amended, leaning around his wife to address Lucy and Eamon, "don't let them drag their heels too long planning the wedding, or we might have no choice but to miss that." He considered. "Unless you wait another year or so."

"Absolutely not," said Eamon flatly, and Kincaid grinned.

"Nonsense, Kincaid," Jocelyn scolded her husband. "There's no need for them to wait until afterward. The wedding will be in a few months' time, and I'll be here," her expression turned grimly determined, "if I have to travel by dragon."

"Something tells me the Valorian royal physician won't recommend that," Lucy said dryly, giving a significant glance toward Jocelyn's hand.

The princess laughed self-consciously, returning her hand to the table. Her stomach had only just begun to stretch, but Lucy had noticed she frequently rested a hand protectively over the little bump, the gesture apparently unconscious.

"Ah, our physician is a stuffy old creature," chipped in Princess Lavinia cheerfully, from her seat on Kincaid's other side. "If he tries to stop you traveling here for the wedding, by dragon or otherwise, I'll help you escape, Joss, don't worry."

"Why does that make me more worried?" Kincaid asked darkly, but Jocelyn just laughed.

Eamon chuckled too, and Lucy shook her head with a smile. Princess Lavinia's presence had certainly enlivened Jocelyn and Kincaid's visit. She wasn't quite sixteen yet, and this was her first state visit, but she didn't suffer from any lack of confidence.

Lucy had been a little wary of the younger girl at first, remembering how she had flirted with Eamon at Jocelyn and Kincaid's wedding. But when Eamon had discovered the reason for her sudden reserve, he'd thrown back his head and laughed. After reassuring her that he wasn't in any danger of succumbing to the charms of a precocious child, he confided in her that the princess's behavior at the wedding really had nothing to do with Eamon, and everything to do with a certain Lord Henrik, Kincaid's dashing best friend.

He wasn't laughing quite so hard when Lucy commented that she remembered Lord Henrik well, and that it was a shame he couldn't have joined the delegation too. But remembering how shamelessly she'd flirted with Henrik at the wedding—for reasons uncomfortably similar to Princess Lavinia's schemes—Lucy couldn't really blame him. And she could only admire Lavinia's open friendliness toward her. Clearly the young princess was less prone to holding a grudge than Lucy.

"It's strange not to have Cody here," said Lucy wistfully, glancing over at her family and some of their closest friends, seated nearby. Unlike her, Matheus looked relieved to be placed with the others from Raldon rather than the royals. He was close in age to Princess Lavinia, but nowhere near as eager to be the center of attention.

"It was a nice letter he sent for the occasion," Eamon said, squeezing her hand sympathetically.

Lucy rolled her eyes. "You mean Yasmin sent. Cody would definitely never have thought of such a thing. I'm still sad we missed their wedding."

It still rankled a little that the older couple hadn't had to wait so long, and it had been too soon to justify another voyage for either Lucy or Matheus.

"Mother and Father said it was beautiful," Lucy continued. "They were both very taken with Thorania." She considered for a moment. "Although in Father's case, I think he was just happy to spend some of their trip in a kingdom where he wasn't worried someone was going to chop his head off at any minute."

"I thought he said it was a pleasant visit," Eamon said, surprised.

Lucy shook her head indulgently. "Oh, he wouldn't complain about it. He likes to tease her, but he'd do anything for Mother, and he knew how excited she was to visit her homeland again after all these years."

"Well, at least Cody and Yasmin plan to be here for our wedding," Eamon said.

"That will be nice," said Lucy, more cheerfully.

"I didn't know you'd had a recent letter from them," Kincaid interjected with interest. "How are they? Is it true King Abner gave them Rasad's lands?"

"That's right," Eamon confirmed. "Apparently there really was nothing at all left from Rasad's Bastion. But I think they prefer to start fresh, anyway."

"I should think so," Lucy agreed, shuddering at the thought of Cody living in the luxurious but tainted fortress of the deceased advisor. "They're building their new home right by the ocean, apparently. Lady Yasmin's family are thrilled to have the land back in the family, even if it's remaining a separate estate."

Kincaid shook his head. "It's hard to imagine Cody settling down as a married man, isn't it?"

Lucy chuckled. "Married or not, I doubt there's going to be much settling down going on. They're probably racing horses bareback across the moonlit desert at this moment." The thought made her smile. She missed Cody—everyone at Raldon did—but she couldn't really regret his decision to stay in Thorania. She was sure he would thrive there.

The evening passed in a blur. Of course Eamon was required to dance with a number of important people—and to Lucy's surprise, she now had similar duties to perform—but as it was their betrothal fest, they were at least allowed to open the dancing together. And Eamon told her he didn't care about politeness tonight, and any dance he wasn't strictly obligated to give to someone else would belong to Lucy.

To her vindictive delight, neither Vanessa nor Sonia were senior enough to qualify as a requirement. She had a petty desire to chuckle at the memory of Sonia saying that Eamon could fight off anyone. The girl had been more right than she knew, although Lucy suspected Sonia hadn't intended to include herself in that declaration.

Midnight had long since passed when Lucy found herself hovering near a refreshment table, alone for a rare moment. Eamon was across the room, saying goodnight to Jocelyn and Kincaid. The crowd had begun to thin, but the Valorian prince and princess were the first of the young people to retire. Jocelyn had done well to last so long—she looked like she could barely keep her eyes open.

"Well, Cal, here we are."

Lucy didn't need to turn her head to know who was speaking nearby, and not just because the voice was so familiar. No one but her father would be audacious enough to call the king by his nickname at a public event.

"They're well suited, I think," the king's voice returned, full of satisfaction. "They'll be very happy together. And she'll make a capable queen one day." Clearly the pair hadn't noticed her proximity, and Lucy flushed with pleasure at the compliment.

"Of course they're suited," her father replied cheerfully. He gave a contented sigh. "Well, it took a long time to get my own back. You stole the crown from me when we were teenagers, Cal, but at last I've managed to get my line on the throne."

Lucy whipped her head around, horrified at her father's flippant joke. She already had enough of an uphill battle to win the court over. The last thing she needed was for him to start a rumor that he had planted her in Eamon's life with treasonous intentions.

But no one else was in earshot, and Uncle Cal's deep chuckle reassured her he hadn't taken offense.

"It took a long time indeed," he agreed. "I certainly wouldn't have guessed when we were searching the beach for crabs as children that either your children or mine would ever wear a crown." He paused. "Or that we would have the same grandchildren one day, for that matter."

"Neither would I," said Lucy's father, sounding taken aback at the idea of becoming a grandfather. There was a moment of silence. "Kind of a nice thought, though, isn't it?"

"Yes." Lucy could hear the smile in the king's voice. "It is, actually."

Her heart swelled with satisfaction as she watched Eamon make his way back across the room toward her. Nice was an understatement, really.

The future was brighter than she could ever have imagined.

NOTE FROM THE AUTHOR

Thank you for reading *Downfall of the Curse*. I hope you enjoyed Lucy's journey, and the chance to explore the last of the four kingdoms on the map of Kyona and Beyond. I would be so grateful if you would consider leaving a review on Amazon—it would really make a difference!

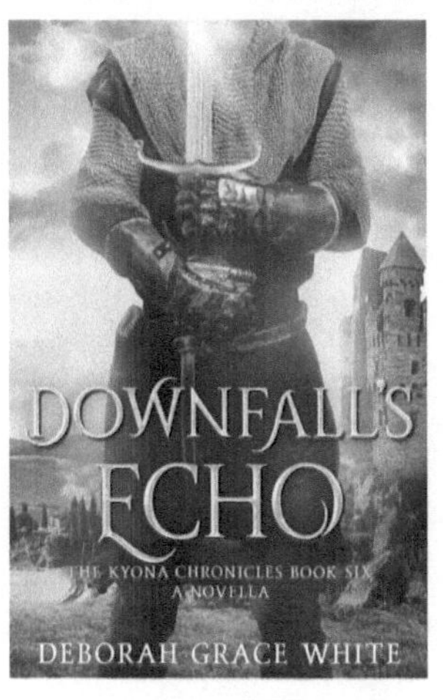

If you're wondering about the fallout of Rasad's defeat, or what becomes of the dashing Lord Henrik and the spirited Princess Lavinia, check out *Downfall's Echo*, the sixth and final installment of the Kyona Chronicles, where more adventure, fantasy, mystery, and romance await.

Join up to my mailing list at deborahgracewhite.com to be kept up to date on new releases, specials, and giveaways, such as bonus chapters. You will also receive *Dragon's Sight*, an 8,000 word prequel to the series, told from Elddreki's perspective.

Again, thanks for entering the world of the Kyona Chronicles! I hope to see you back again.

ACKNOWLEDGMENTS

Having told the story of Cal and Elnora's daughter in *Legacy of the Curse*, it was especially satisfying to spend some time with Jo and Scarlett's daughter. Not to mention Thorania needed to be explored!

This installment only happened because of the support of some wonderful people. Firstly, my husband Ray, thanks for cheering me on. Your enthusiasm for the story is worth more than gold, and your suggestions always make it better.

Thank you so much to my beta readers, Adrian, Tamara, Andrew, Dad, Mum, Cherilyn, and Ali. You guys are amazing, and I'm so grateful for your ongoing interest. As always, double thanks to Dad for your developmental and copy editing and all your practical work for release, and to Mum for your line editing.

The cover is another masterpiece by Karri—I absolutely love it. And Rebecca, I'm so pleased that every corner of your incredibly beautiful map has now been explored!

To you, the reader, thank you for giving me the privilege of being an author.

And above all, to God. It's thanks to You I know who I am. Thank You for giving me an identity that can never be taken away from me.

ABOUT THE AUTHOR

I've been a reader since I can remember, growing up on a wide range of books, from classic literature to light-hearted romps. The love of reading has traveled with me unchanged across multiple continents, and carried me from my own childhood all the way to having children of my own.

But if reading is like looking through a window into a magical and beautiful world, beginning to write my own stories was like discovering that I could open that window and climb right out into fantasyland.

I cannot believe how privileged I am to actually be living that childhood dream and publishing my own novels. I do so from my hometown of Adelaide, Australia, where I live with my husband and our two, soon to be three, little munchkins.

I've never outgrown my love of young adult stories, and my first series, The Kyona Chronicles, is a young adult fantasy series of six installments.

Feel free to email me at deborah@deborahgracewhite.com

and introduce yourself! Or subscribe to my mailing list at deborahgracewhite.com for free giveaways, sales, and updates.

www.ingramcontent.com/pod-product-compliance
Lightning Source LLC
Chambersburg PA
CBHW030656190726
48286CB00001B/46